BACCHANAL

BACCHANAL

VERONICA G. HENRY

47NORTH

Text copyright © 2021 by Veronica Henry
All rights reserved.

Published by 47North, Seattle

www.apub.com

Amazon, the Amazon logo, and 47North are trademarks of Amazon.com, Inc., or its affiliates.

ISBN-13: 9781542027816 (hardcover)
ISBN-10: 1542027810 (hardcover)

ISBN-13: 9781542027755 (paperback)
ISBN-10: 1542027756 (paperback)

Cover design by Faceout Studio, Molly von Borstel

Cover illustration by Christina Chung

Printed in the United States of America

First edition

For Hosea and Ressie,
who taught me the meaning of sacrifice
and endured my childhood eccentricities

Harlem, New York, February 1930

There are those in this country who arrogantly suggest the old religion's dead. As if any amount of torture and erasing could sever those blood-deep ties. *What do they think kept their chattel alive?* Stephanie St. Clair's chuckle is as bitter as a centuries-old grudge.

Even those lost lambs who don't recognize it practice it all the same. She calls it Yoruba. Other children of Africa label it Santeria, candomblé, even voodoo. Name doesn't matter, though; they're all follicles from the same nappy head.

Like every religion—old and new—there's a good side and a bad side. Which one you call on depends on your particular situation.

Stephanie's situation is what you'd consider the bad side. A city girl through and through, she isn't keen on being anybody's wife or mother and would sooner sail back across the Atlantic on an old tire than be somebody's maid again. Good with figures, she's carved out a little business for herself. Running numbers never hurt anybody. Well . . . not much of anybody.

And now that cagey swindler Obeah has been threatening to steal her business. He *is* practiced in the old ways and isn't afraid to use them to further his cause either. Stephanie needs to call on some help of her own. She has a nephew to think about now, especially since it doesn't look like her sister is going to be long for this world.

Her throat is dry, hands sweaty. She knows the words but can't spit them out; it's like the letters are running away from each other, crashing around in her head.

She recalls how Obeah marched up to her in the bar and, loud enough for everybody to hear him, announced that Stephanie was done. Rage and shame, they unlock the words.

Mo pe awon dudu emi.

A raindrop appears, suspended in midair. It ripples and warps. Wobbles and grows until it rips open, flooding the room with the salty tang of the ocean and something her eyes can't quite discern. Stephanie drops to her knees and plants her forehead on the floor.

The demon's voice crashes against her like a storm wave. "Face me."

Stephanie doesn't try to hide the trembling, but she does shield her eyes. The demon doesn't have a human form. All smoke and dizzying fire. It writhes with something akin to amusement.

The demon calls herself Ahiku. After some coaxing, Stephanie lays out Obeah's plan to muscle in on her business. How his arrogant declaration of war may see her dead because she'll sooner die than hand over what she's built. "Obeah is a powerful witch doctor. Seems to me, the son of one so powerful might be of interest to you."

It works: the demon positively sizzles. The weight of what she's suggested wedges itself in a corner of Stephanie's stomach and festers.

"There is another child," Ahiku hisses. "One that has your strong chin."

Stephanie's face hardens. "I don't have the right to, but I ask that my nephew's soul be spared. If not, I send you back home."

"A hunter with only one arrow does not shoot carelessly," Ahiku says. "You offer me passage, knowing what it will mean to this country's children, yet you think only of yourself and yours. Unwise but bold. I deem you worthy. I will spare your nephew, but he will work for me in this realm."

Stephanie swallows; what choice does she have? Better this than her nephew being consumed. The demon glides around the room, exploring. "Even the lowly village elder understands this—an enemy must be destroyed. Dispense with that guilt you are nursing; you're fouling the place with it. I will cripple this Obeah's spirit when I consume his son, but you must deal with his physical form. And when that is done, make your own people dependent—do not teach them all that you know. Keep a little something to yourself."

"I recognize wise words when I hear them."

"As long as I have passage here, you will rule. I will hunt down and destroy those that can stop me." She pauses. "And one last thing."

Stephanie struggles to keep her breath. Even though the demon has no eyes, it feels like her deepest secrets lie exposed under her gaze.

"Never oppose me."

The new Queen of Harlem heartily agrees.

CHAPTER ONE

FLEDGLING

Louisiana Swampland, February 1935

Eliza liked to delude herself by fancying the crude contraption as humane, merciful, but no matter how carefully she'd ground down the iron teeth and wrapped cloth about the sharper points, it was still a trap.

A captured possum writhed in agony before her, its beady eyes pleading. Cocooned within the wet thickness of the swamp, Eliza sat cross-legged atop a woven mat laid on the perpetually moist Louisiana earth. Her pygmy marmoset, Mico—a furry six-inch ball of silent angst, and her constant companion—sat perched on her right shoulder.

Little light penetrated the dense canopy of tangled cypress trees and brush. Crickets and swamp things caterwauled their ceaseless nocturnal games of predator and prey. The sodden brew of centuries-old wood and wet soil, more muddy than solid, coated the air as thickly as a sloppy layer of tar spread over a dirt road.

It was perfect for her test. She released the possum.

Eliza's oval face was bowed, tormented by scads of failures past. She'd loosened her hair, and thick braids now fell to either side of her face, inky black against skin the color of exquisitely aged dark walnut.

The possum's heartbeat thumped rapidly, the leg bloodied but not broken. Eliza closed her eyes. In her mind, she conjured an image of a gentle stream, of herself and the possum—uninjured—sitting on a grassy knoll. Mico dug his nails into her shoulder. Her breath quickened, her heartbeat matching the possum's as their connection grew deeper. Her blue cotton dress, already soaked with sweat, clung to her body.

Their combined energy bubbled up from her stomach, cold, as if a block of ice were lodged in her belly. But it didn't erupt, didn't arc out of her like it had so many times before. She was controlling it.

She inhaled a deep breath and conjured up another image: a grassy hillside plump with savory worms and slugs. She settled the picture around the possum, pushing it across the mental connection that bound the animal as surely as its physical trap had—and waited.

The possum jerked once and tensed. Its racing heartbeat slowed to normal. Emboldened, Eliza quickly formed another image. She wanted to convey the relationship that she shared with Mico, who shifted to her left shoulder, wrapping tiny fingers around her earlobe in a gesture of support. Her heart filled. Though she'd had a tenuous relationship with other animals, Mico had simply found her one day, and their connection had been an easy one. She figured someone, somewhere, still wondered where their pet had gone off to.

Clumsily, Eliza formed more images of her time with Mico—there was so much to choose from—and sent them to the possum in a tangled clump. They were too much. Before she could snatch them back, the animal on the ground lurched. Its shriek silenced the surrounding swamp. With a rattling exhale, it died.

She snapped her eyes open with a fluttering of long lashes. Cursing under her breath, she picked up the empty trap and hurled it off into the shadows. The weight of her shame and guilt, dizzying. The thin leather cord around her neck tingled, and she pulled the amulet from beneath the bodice of her dress, fingering the three discs: the elephant, the raven, and the badger. She imagined each stared back at her in mute admonition. What did they mean? Why had her mother demanded she keep the amulet—no explanation—before disappearing?

Almost a woman, full grown now, she still didn't know.

Her father had had two opinions of his abnormal daughter: first, that she was a handsome girl but would never be considered a beautiful woman; and second, overheard as it carried on a lethargic breeze one sleepless night, that she was a monster.

Looking down at the dead possum, it seemed a fair call.

~

1939

"How long does it take one silly girl to clean a toilet?" Mrs. Shippen hovered in the doorway of the sole boardinghouse bathroom with her bony arms folded. The woman had the look of an orange a week past its prime, left out in the sun to bake. Pockmarked skin covered a too-round head, set atop legs thin enough that a good wind might topple her over.

On her knees scrubbing, Liza ignored the barbs. She didn't have much choice but to take what Mrs. Shippen doled out, as she had nowhere else to go. Her family had abandoned her. Her previous employer, Mrs. Margaret, had treated her well. She'd been fed and taught manners and reading. In exchange, she cooked and did the housework, though her benefactor was such a tidy woman that it never amounted to much. Mainly, she acted as a companion, especially after Mrs. Margaret's husband died, her only other family in England—a place that, for reasons she never said, she would never return to.

But when Mrs. Margaret died, Liza found herself truly on her own.

She had considered herself lucky when she'd ambled down Reddy Street; deliverance was a sign outside Mrs. Shippen's boardinghouse that said HOUSE GIRL WANTED. She would have only to clean in exchange for room and board. But as she soon learned, Mrs. Shippen had obviously never had a happy day in her life and was determined to exact revenge for that fact on her boarder. Liza's other wishes had all died unanswered, so now she tirelessly guarded the one where the old biddy got what was coming to her.

Still bent over the toilet, her back to her landlady and employer, Liza made a face and rolled her eyes but covered it with an impassive gaze when she turned around. "If the good, God-fearing people that you righteously call your *tenants* didn't go out and get drunk every night and throw up all over the place, I expect I could be done a lot sooner."

Mrs. Shippen parted her lips, but finding no adequate retort, she clamped them into a thin line. She swam her hands over her hair, settling on the ever-present bun at the nape of her goose neck. "Take a lot of nerve for a child whose own family didn't want her to make comment on how my tenants spend their time. Best you come to terms with who you are, your station in this life. You finish up here and come on downstairs. Albert's got a problem with his calf. He's hoping you can take a look. He'll give us two months of milk in exchange." Mrs. Shippen spun on her heels, her simple cotton housedress swirling about her legs, and marched down the stairs.

"The monster has turned into the tender to wayward animals and livestock," Liza said under her breath. She dropped her brush and rag in the cleaning bucket. "The things we do for free milk."

She stepped out on the porch. But Albert wasn't waiting out front. He was clustered with a group of other men down the road. Curious, she paced softly down to see what the fuss was about. Strangers. Two of them, one Negro dressed better than most, the other one white.

The men fell silent as the Negro peeled himself away from his white companion and approached. He was no more than a boy really, near her age or a bit older. His eyes drank her in as he passed, appraising her like a piece of livestock. "Boorish," an elegant word from an otherwise unremarkable novel, came to mind. What could the strangers want? Baton Rouge wasn't a place that people came to for fun, 'cause there wasn't much fun to be had; that's what New Orleans was for. Anybody traveled this far north usually had a specific reason.

"Afternoon," the boy said to the group in an unmistakable Louisiana accent. "Name's Jamey. Jamey Blotter." The men's suspicion seemed to fade, replaced with tentative smiles and kind nods. He was one of theirs. Liza listened as he told them he was a prospector for a traveling carnival. *Traveling!* What if she could get out of this godforsaken town?

He asked about the alligator-wrestler show, said his goodbyes, and headed back over to the white man. As the pair turned to walk away, Liza followed. There was opportunity here. She could feel it like the bubbling of a toe blister.

The boy was handsome enough. Lean but not too skinny. Nice brown skin a bump or two darker than hers. His back was straight; he didn't hunch over or wrestle his hat between his hands like some old runaway slave. Most men in Baton Rouge were afraid of her, but this stranger had met her eyes like he owned the place.

She trailed the men at a distance, Mico in her shirt pocket, chittering. "Hush now," she chided the little monkey.

Shortly, the younger man—Jamey, if memory served—walked into a five-and-dime. His companion continued on along Main and lingered outside the sheriff's office a moment before joining him.

There was little more on the main drag, because everything else had closed up. Many, many times before, Liza had watched the store owners pack up and head out in their trucks and wagons—she dreamed of going with them, slipping beneath a blanket, remaining quiet till they got wherever they were going. It didn't matter where, as long as it was away from here.

Maybe she'd happen across her parents and track down her little sister, Twiggy. She wanted more than anything else to be back with the people who had discarded her. Not because she still held on to any fancy feelings of love—and she did, even if she didn't want to admit it—but because her father was probably the only person who could help her learn to control her most unusual *gift*. He had worked with her before he'd walked away, and in all her time looking and wondering, she had never found another person with it—but her father had to know how to control it, didn't he? And she missed Twiggy so much some days she didn't even want to get out of bed. That was the most unforgivable thing: they hadn't given her a choice in leaving her behind.

The people in Baton Rouge tolerated her. When they needed help with an animal, they couldn't get to her fast enough—but accidentally kill one or two trying to help, and she became a she-devil. Never you mind the fact that they killed and ate almost anything that moved without batting an eye. Only because she cleaned the rooms and worked around the house did Mrs. Shippen give her a roof over her head and a stingy bowl of gumbo every day. Sometimes it was only rice. Liza was determined to get out of this town, but she hadn't worked out all the particulars yet.

She'd see what these strangers were up to—and if they could somehow be her ticket out. Then she'd tend to Albert's calf. And she prayed she wouldn't hurt it in the process.

~

Liza plastered her back against the wall outside the store and willed her heart to calm itself down. She'd already drawn a few stares. A quick peek confirmed the strangers were still inside sipping coffee. Should she barge in or wait? Indecision kept her sweaty hand clutched at her side instead of on the screen-door handle.

"Almost didn't see you there," the Negro boy said as he swung the door open. He'd have caught her toe if she hadn't jumped back.

Instead of moving aside, Liza lingered awkwardly, blocking the stranger's path. They exchanged a curious glance.

"I . . . ," Liza began and then swallowed hard. "I was hoping there might be some work for me in your carnival. I can cook, clean, do whatever needs doing." She left out the part about the animals—of that, she wasn't quite so confident.

"Afraid we don't need any domestic help," the redheaded man answered as he appeared at his companion's side. "But I do invite you to come check out our show. We'll be setting up just outside of town."

They parted around Liza like a stream moving around a boulder and moseyed on down the street. She watched them go, all other pleas unspoken.

CHAPTER TWO

WHAT TREASURES LIE BEHIND
THE SECOND CURTAIN

Clay removed his hat and swiped the back of his arm across his fore-head, clearing a spattering of sweat that returned almost as soon as he'd wiped it off. Always some hopeless strays with stars in their eyes, want-ing to run off with the carnival. That girl'd be better off staying put. At his side, Jamey tilted his head up, drinking in the sun. "You Yankees sure can't handle a little bit of heat."

"I was born in Chicago—that don't exactly make me no Yankee. 'Sides, hard as I try, I can't see why anybody would want to live in a swamp."

"Shoot, Chicago still Yankee territory last I checked. And I was born right here," Jamey said. "Folks gone now, but it was all we knew. Read all about snow. That didn't truck with me much neither."

"Guess ya got a point," Clay said. Clay had a thin, muscular build from years of backbreaking work as a carnie. First as a roadie, a game runner, a caller. The drudgery had ended when Geneva offered him . . . well, some secrets you took to the grave. Shocking orange-red waves of hair were slicked back over his head. Try as he did to keep his hair in place with pomade, a strand or two always managed to fall forward to frame his face. Dark-brown eyes complemented his ruddy, leather-worn complexion. He wore a T-shirt and slacks held up by striped suspenders he'd nabbed from a drunk mark he'd had to drag out of the cooch tent back in Pensacola.

They walked a ways and paused in the center of Baton Rouge, as it were, the midafternoon sun painting a wet pallor over everything. People lazed about in storefronts or dragged themselves from shade puddle to shade puddle. Even though it was closing time, no one moved quickly; there was no rush. Jamey turned around in a circle. "A lot of change since I been back last. I don't recognize nothin'."

"Would have been nice to tell me that before. What do you think I brought you out here for?" Clay said. "Guess you wanted to get out for a spell on my dime, huh?"

"The wrestler sets up shop at the edge of town," Jamey said, ignoring the barb. "They say the show usually starts on time. He charges a nickel, wrestles one or two gators, dependin'. Boasts for the crowd a bit—he get a little extra moola that way. He wraps up real quick-like and disappears somewhere in the swamp where he live. Don't know much more 'bout him." This time, Jamey paused to wipe the sweat from his brow. "You think we gone be able to finish up here and get back 'fore dark? Maybe we ought to stay in town for the night."

"Naw. We need to get back," Clay said. "Let's see if we can grab some grub before the show. This here is your town. What's good?"

Jamey fingered his chin. "Well, now. Old Mr. Huff's place is empty most days but still hangin' on a few doors down. The boys say the food is as good as it ever was."

"You go on ahead—I'll be there lickety-split," Clay said. "I'll have a chat with the local brass first."

At the end of the main drag stood a little structure made of weathered wooden slats. The mayor's office was a shotgun building, propped up on blocks. Two front windows looked out on the street, one half-open and the other closed—as if the building had a lazy eye. An old wooden sign over the door read SHERIFF'S OFFICE.

"Come in," called a voice at Clay's knock.

When he stepped inside, he found that the sheriff shared the oblong open space with the mayor. The mayor's "office" was to his right, official books stacked on his desk, a state flag sagging against the wall. The sheriff, a lean outlaw type with shifty eyes, occupied the left side of the room. He wore a gun at his waist, and the case behind him held two shotguns. At the rear of the room was a lone jail cell, partially covered by a curtain.

Two payoffs. Wonderful.

"What can I do for you?" the sheriff said.

"I'm Clay Kennel, owner and proprietor of the G. B. Bacchanal Carnival." Clay stuck out his hand. "I'm here to see if we can set up a show for a few days to entertain the good folk of Baton Rouge."

The sheriff appraised Clay's outstretched hand, and the mayor stepped up behind him.

"You'll need to talk to me." He stuck out his own hand, more of a bear mitt. "Mayor Wade Hampton Bynum. Good mayor to this here fine city of ours for the last ten years."

"Fine town you got here," Clay said.

"It's a dump," the sheriff said, spitting something brown and slimy into a tin cup.

Clay ignored him and turned to the mayor, who at least wanted to feign some type of propriety. "Here on business but taking in the people of your town got me to thinking. What do ya say about us pulling a wildcat? You know, do something on short notice. Wouldn't take much for us to get set up."

Clay's research had revealed the mayor was up for reelection. That meant it couldn't hurt to bring a little fun into the city. Make people forget about the jobs he'd likely promised but, according to all the closed shops, hadn't delivered on.

The mayor and sheriff were probably salivating at their good fortune.

"Well, there's a license to operate," the mayor said, looking up in the air and calculating with his fingers. "'Course you got your inspection and associated fees. Cleanup and swamp-preservation charges . . ."

"Let's say we start off with one date. Ten-dollar flat fee." Clay looked from the mayor to the sheriff. "For the both of you. No inspection, no license. If we take a liking to the area, maybe we do a few more dates and negotiate that part later."

"And you own this here carnival?" the sheriff asked, a little brown spittle on his chin.

"Down to every last fork and spoon." The practiced lie rolled off his tongue with the ease of a pitchman's rhetoric. There was no way a woman, let alone a Negro woman, would be allowed to handle these negotiations. Geneva had found Clay and entrusted him, and he'd never let her down. For being the much-needed white male face of the carnival, she paid him better than he'd ever made before, gave him responsibility and authority. Hell, he may as well own the carnival, since he ran everything.

The mayor and sheriff exchanged a conspiratorial glance. "A regular P. T. Barnum," the mayor said.

"Barnum ran a circus." A correction Clay had made countless times before. "I run a carnival. Two different animals." Bacchanal did well, better than most, and Geneva provided everything they needed. But circuses were known to pull in more money—the mayor was angling for a bigger payday.

The mayor pressed his palms onto the marred wood tabletop. "Guess they are."

Silence hung in the air. Clay steeled himself. As far as negotiations went, these hillbillies were pushovers, but they didn't have to know his thinking on the matter.

"Twenty-five dollars apiece," the mayor said, tentative. "And, uh, you got any cooch dancers in your outfit? Might need to . . . inspect them for violations of local decency laws. Could probably get the fees down to an even twenty if you could swing in a special show for us."

Got 'em.

"I'm afraid you've got us mixed up with some of the bigger outfits." Clay painted a look of dejection on his face. "That much I flat out can't afford. Thank you, gentlemen. We'll be moving on. I hear tell Lake Charles has a need for some entertainment such as my outfit offers."

He sauntered out the door and was down the steps and well on his way when the mayor and sheriff rushed out behind him. Red faced, the mayor said, "Ten dollars apiece seems a fair offer to me. As long as we still get a go at our . . . inspections."

Clay turned and stared them down. "Five dollars apiece. That is, if you ask me real nice."

～

After Clay and Jamey had eaten, they went to see the alligator show, which started promptly. The pit was crudely constructed, clear water rising little more than ankle-deep. The fence around the pit was only three feet high; the gator inside was eight feet of rough hide, menacing eyes, and barbed teeth. The gator snapped at the sizable jeering crowd. Clay turned up his nose at the foul mishmash of smells, where sweat met unwiped butts and mixed with fetid swamp water and smoking meat.

A tall, well-muscled man circled the crowd, collecting money and admonishing them not to throw things at the gator or get too close. "We won't be held responsible for any loss of limb, folks!" he called out to the anxious crowd.

The alligator wrestler was a large, barrel-chested man wearing a one-piece bathing suit. He swung his arms wide, pounded his chest, and gestured. He flexed his muscles in a deep bend reminiscent of the carnival's strongman, Bombardier. The crowd, lowly, dusty, and dead eyed, came to life, cheering him wildly. Clay recognized the same thing in his customers. Folks who were down and out had only a few options: booze, sex, entertainment. None of them filled an empty belly, but they *could* take the edge off.

Clay dropped a dime into the hat for him, and Jamey folded his arms, skeptical. They often did this type of scouting for Geneva, and more often than not, they ended up finding fakes or charlatans who couldn't do half what they claimed. Geneva had a strange set of requirements—it wasn't only about the act. She had to get a sense of the person, as if there were something more she was looking for.

After the wrestler had dispensed with the gesturing and prancing, he leaped into the pit. He and the animal tussled something fierce. He antagonized the gator, grabbing at its tail and giving it a good yank. Mud and water splashed the crowd, but if anything bothered them, they didn't show it. Some even cheered on the gator. Despite themselves, Clay and Jamey perked up. They exchanged an excited glance, and before long, they were joining in the cheering and jeering.

The wrestler scrambled onto the animal's back and tucked an arm under its mouth, putting it in a headlock. He gestured to the crowd—grinning a smile devoid of his two front teeth.

"He's a good one, sure 'nuf!" Jamey said.

"Yeah," Clay said. "I think we got one. Folks are going to love—"

The gator's tail lashed out, projecting its body forward and toppling the wrestler, who fell with a gigantic splash. The gator's massive jaws hinged open and clamped down on the man's midsection. The crowd gasped and screamed with the wrestler.

But a girl, the same one who had waylaid them in town, shoved her way forward. Agitated shouts quieted, and the crowd cleared a path as she stepped through the gate.

Jamey started, looked to Clay. The girl focused her gaze on the gator, her concentration as steady as his convictions had been before he'd met Geneva.

"What the hell is this?" Clay said, looking at Jamey. "Part of the act?"

"No, I sure don't think it is," Jamey said.

The alligator stopped its thrashing and released the man. Blood painted the water an obnoxious red like the gash in the man's side. The crowd remained parted around the girl, while the gator lumbered to the front of the pool—its eyes almost ashamed. Clay and Jamey, along with the rest of the crowd, were transfixed. If Clay hadn't taken leave of his good sense, something the girl did had actually saved the man. Suddenly the alligator wrestler was forgotten, replaced by someone wholly unexpected.

The man who had been collecting the money finally snapped out of it. "Well, shake a leg, help me get him out!"

CHAPTER THREE

A CHANGE OF FORTUNE

Liza almost fainted with relief. She'd done it. She'd saved the alligator but now struggled to understand what she'd done differently. She had simply sent the gator an image she hoped would calm it: a group of alligators sunning themselves on a sandy riverbank. Murky green waters with tasty hidden treasures awaiting nearby. The animal spun away from its target as it sent Liza images of its own, the long life it had lived. The swamp animals and people it had harassed. The eggs grown to life and those lost. It had opened its maw, let out a gasp of swamp-tainted breath, and waddled into a corner like a chastised puppy.

The alligator wrestler had been dragged bleeding and semiconscious from the pool, and the crowd had dissipated with only a spattering of taunts and barbs. And the two strangers from earlier—the handsome one and his redheaded friend—had seen the whole thing.

She'd steeled herself for more when the redheaded man removed his hat, stepped forward, and offered his hand. He introduced himself as Clay Kennel and his companion as Jamey Blotter. His words lingered in her head like a treasured passage from one of her pulp magazines. *That's some trick you got there. Should've said something about it before. If you're ready to blow this swamp trap, we'd like to make you an offer to join the G. B. Bacchanal Carnival.*

It didn't take Liza long to clear her things from the old boardinghouse. She grabbed her satchel and stuffed in a couple items of threadbare clothing and underpants, serials scavenged from the trash, the family photograph her father had given her, and the amulet—the only thing her silent, detached mother had ever given her.

She was leaving Baton Rouge for good. And just as Mrs. Margaret had taught her, she hadn't appeared overly eager at the offer. She'd even managed to negotiate her pay.

Mrs. Shippen was skeptical. She'd sneered, "If living by yourself here ain't bad enough, now you go running off to some carnival? A woman! You'll be back, and don't think your room will be sitting here waiting for you."

Liza smiled at the sad little woman bent from the years, face hardened into the same ugly expression she'd had since her husband ran off with that prostitute from New Orleans. "One thing for sure, Mrs. Shippen. Bet you'll still be here, now won't you?"

She left the woman standing in her room—her old room—as she hightailed it downstairs and stepped outside to see her escape in the form of Clay and Jamey standing beside a truck, right in her grasp. She raced down the steps, ignoring the small crowd that had gathered around them.

"Eliza Meeks, you'll need to come with me." The sheriff stepped out from the crowd, alongside the bandaged alligator wrestler, supported by two other men. The boardinghouse door opened, and Mrs. Shippen stepped outside. She smiled at Liza and tossed a small pouch to the sheriff.

Liza froze. Questions swirled in her head, but when she opened her mouth, all that escaped was a groan.

"What's going on here?" Clay said as he and Jamey elbowed their way forward.

"The freak's a goddang thief," the alligator wrestler spat.

"Lies from the mouth of a no-'count drunk," Liza shot back with a sharpness she didn't really feel.

The sheriff took her by the arm. Mico screeched before she quieted him with an image of her hand over his tiny mouth. "She stole the wrestler's take after the accident. Got a witness to the fact. Bet she caused the gator to go feral, too, but unfortunately can't prove that. Our good Mrs. Shippen found this here pouch in the girl's room. Don't need much more proof than that."

"Menace!" someone in the small crowd hissed.

"Highfalutin thief!" shouted another.

Murmurs rose as the sheriff led Liza down the street toward the jail. She finally got her voice. "I did no such thing, and you know it!"

"Tell that to that pouch full of coins," the wrestler said, wincing in pain.

The walk to the jail was all too short. She knew these people had been waiting for the right chance to punish her, and they had no trouble with lying to ruin her. Her heart sank.

And when the jail door closed and locked behind her, she fumbled onto the bunk and wondered whether she should ask them to set Mico free. She watched with some satisfaction as the wrestler hurled curses at the sheriff when he told him he'd have to keep his money as evidence.

As the wrestler exited in a huff, the redheaded man from the carnival stepped inside.

"Looks like we got ourselves what they call a quandary." Clay strolled over confidently to the sheriff.

"How's that?" the sheriff asked.

Clay counted off the issues one finger at a time. "You got my potential new act locked up back there. We got a show to put on, one I paid you for already, and don't expect I'd be obliged to do it without what I come for. We've agreed to accommodate your request for a special inspection of the cooch show. And the good people of Baton Rouge are already expecting some entertainment. Your alligator show is done for. Seem to me, you need me more than you know."

The sheriff glanced back at Liza, and she averted her gaze. She dared not hope.

"Let's take a walk," the sheriff said.

As soon as the door shut, a rat scurried into her cell. Liza yelped and backed into a corner but in the next instant set aside her foolishness and settled her thoughts around the rodent. The image: the keys the sheriff had tossed onto his desk next to her satchel. The rat, however, was not quick to agree. It sent a message of its own: a raw, painful hunger. It wanted . . . Mico!

That wouldn't do, so she promised it something else to eat. She didn't exactly like rats, with all their scurrying and leaping, but when this one sailed through the air, landed on the desk, and snatched up the keys, she didn't even flinch.

CHAPTER FOUR

A Tough Act to Follow

Liza and Jamey saw each other as she was sneaking away, and he caught up with her down the road and hustled her into the truck bed. She bristled when he swung around to go back and get Clay but kept her mouth shut and her head down as Jamey parked around the corner from the jail.

Soon enough, he called out that he'd spotted Clay and waved him over. They rushed into the truck and sped away, keeping it moving for long enough for Liza to guess the town was out of sight. Jamey then skidded to a stop.

"She's gone," she heard Clay say. "When me and the sheriff got back to the jail, all we found in that cell was a dead rat clutching a key. I slip out while the sheriff is flinging curses and orders like a madman, and what do I find? You and the truck gone."

The truck door creaked open, and Jamey said, "Follow me."

"You wanna tell me what's goin' on?" Clay asked as he slammed the truck door. Footsteps echoed as the two came around back to the bed. Liza poked her head out from beneath a blanket and hopped down. Clay grinned.

"It's not that I don't appreciate what you tried to do for me back there," Liza said, "but let's just say an opportunity to help myself arose, and I didn't turn it away."

Clay smacked Jamey on the back, more a fatherly gesture than she would have expected. He whistled his appreciation. "Whatever you did, best we get on back."

Liza waved off Clay's open door and climbed back into the bed of the truck. She sank onto a bale of hay beneath the open back window.

Being in that cell, even for that short time, had made it difficult to breathe. She needed air. And she refused to answer when Clay asked how she'd managed to get herself free.

They rode in silence for a spell. Baton Rouge was behind her now. She would work hard in this carnival to earn her keep, and that would be that.

"You born and raised here?" Clay asked, glancing over through the window.

Liza shifted and looked at him from the corner of her eye. She hated the inevitable questions that came along with meeting new people. They only wanted to know where you were from to fit you into whatever little box they wanted to. "Born in Florida, around Pensacola."

Jamey jumped in as he drove. "What you doing all the way in Louisiana by yourself?"

"Would you feel better if I was married or something?" Liza said.

"No, only meant, you know, a woman—"

"Maybe with three or four babies?"

"Now, that ain't what I said—"

"And another one on the way? Maybe I shouldn't even own a pair of shoes or slacks, huh?"

Jamey worked his mouth, but the poor boy's words must have been crowding and fumbling all over his tongue, because he couldn't get out another peep.

Clay grinned at Jamey's squirming and changed the subject. "We got a couple animals we keep with the carnival, but maybe now with you, we can pick up some more. Question is, Can you control that, uh, gift of yours? Heard a lot of mutterings from them town folk. But the small-minded can puff up a story till it's got no kinship whatsoever to the truth."

What could she tell this man? He wanted to pay her a wage and see that she was fed. She couldn't admit that she was still learning how to use her gift, that sometimes—no, oftentimes—the animals died. She couldn't jeopardize her freedom that way.

"I won't kill the acts," she said and then rolled her eyes at the back of Jamey's skull.

They trekked through bleak countryside, the truck rattling and shaking with every rut and gaping hole in the pockmarked road. They passed a family walking along the side of the road—a ragtag bunch draped in shabby clothes, miles of dust turned to muddy streaks on their too-thin bodies. A young child held on to his older sister's hand, the parents walking ahead of them. The boy looked up at the passing truck and locked eyes with Liza. There was nothing of a child left in that empty gaze.

The road was filled with more of the same, some loners, some groups. All helpless to the crushing heartbreak they had endured for the better part of the decade.

The swamp fell away on both sides and the sun was beginning to set, a gigantic searing orange mass, determined to suck the life out of everything in its path. There were few cars on the road, but when they did pass one, the driver gave an obligatory wave. Southern hospitality at its best.

In what seemed like hours but was actually only ten minutes, the chaos that was the carnival started to emerge on the horizon: tents, people, trailers, and stray dogs that seemed right at home. As they pulled up and parked the truck, Liza's eyes grew wide. For all the nomadic traveling her family had done, she'd never seen anything close to this. Even without everything all set up, the carnival was the biggest rolling playground she'd ever seen. The collage of colors, the smell of meats she hadn't had in years—why, this may as well have been New York City.

Jamey stalked off, and Clay guided her past the gawkers.

"How do you decide?" Liza asked as they walked. Color and activity exploded behind her eyes whenever she closed them. "You know, where you set up the carnival?"

A youngish, muscular man ran past them dragging a set of poles. There were about four of them, and he struggled mightily. "Dang it, Lou," Clay said. "You gonna splinter the wood. Get somebody to help you."

Liza stifled a smirk.

"Boy don't got the good sense his mama gave him." Clay made sure the boy set down his bundle before he continued. "Anyway, I track out for a few days and do some scouting. If the local law and the townsfolk seem ripe, that's where we go."

"My family traveled a lot." If she could be of use helping guide the carnival, that would help earn her keep, and maybe he'd be more forgiving if she made a mistake on the other front. "My mama sold baskets. African baskets she learned to make when we stayed with the Gullahs in South Carolina. I been most everyplace south, from Florida over to New Mexico. I read and write. I bet I could help you plot the course."

Clay's expression brightened in what Liza hoped was admiration. "Might well save me some travel time. And money. You might prove yourself useful yet."

After a short time, they came into view of a bright-red trailer, set aside from most of the others.

Clay turned to Liza and stopped her. "Now, there's a bunch a rules that we'll go over later, but the first one is this. I'm taking you to the red trailer, the management trailer. I handle carnival business there. Nobody goes in that trailer but me. Got it?"

Liza shrugged. All white men had their weird quirks. Probably kept all his money squirreled away in there. Mrs. Shippen once had a boarder like that, never wanted Liza to clean his room. Figured out later that he'd been cutting out pictures from nudie magazines and plastering the walls with them. Mrs. Shippen had been apoplectic.

"You got a problem with that, you can turn tail, and I'll get Jamey to drive you back."

Liza chewed her lip. Food and money and freedom in return for keeping her nose out of his business. Wasn't a hard choice. "I understand."

Clay hustled her about ten paces away from the trailer and held up a hand. "Stand right here."

Two of the most striking women she'd ever seen stood at the trailer's entrance. They wore plain clothes but were decorated with bands of beads on their arms, around their hips, and on their right ankles. The women stared at her but didn't open their mouths to say a polite hello.

Were . . . were those knives at their waists? Were they some type of guards?

"That there's Zinsa on the right and Efe on the left. They make sure nobody goes in there but me. Straight from your dark continent— Dahomey soldiers, they were. Fight better than most men I served with," Clay said. His expression told Liza he wasn't exactly comfortable, and she wondered why he would choose guards he was scared of.

He left her standing alone to enter the trailer. Liza endured the women's appraisal.

Staring was impolite . . . but they were mirror images in stature: strong and lean, with fine skin of burnished tar. High cheekbones and chiseled features. They wore their pride as easily as some folks slip on a pair of trousers. What kind of outfit was Clay running here?

Clay had a foot on the first step when the soldier on the left spoke, loud enough for Liza to hear.

"The white man with the taste for dark ladies," Efe said. Maybe they'd done some courting, although Liza doubted even the fire-headed Clay could handle a woman like that. Efe brushed a finger across the beads at her waist. "What mischief you bring now?"

Power radiated off the warriors.

Clay muttered a response that Liza couldn't hear.

The other soldier, Zinsa, piped in. "Where else do you think she would be, out scouting? No, that is your job, which I might add you do poorly."

"As poorly as your band of Amazons did against the French?"

The smiles faded from their faces, eyes narrowed. Zinsa hissed something that made Clay visibly swallow. He pushed past the women and knocked once before disappearing inside.

Liza wondered who this *she* was. Was Clay married? Did his wife live inside the trailer, and was he keeping her prisoner in there? Despite her promise, she wanted to take a peek inside. The Dahomey women settled their fierce gazes back on her, and she decided it was better to let it go.

CHAPTER FIVE

AHIKU COMMUNES WITH THE BONES

"That girl doesn't look anything like an alligator wrestler," Ahiku said as soon as Clay closed the door.

"Well, Geneva, that's because she ain't." Ahiku was known to these Americans as Geneva Broussard now—only a few at the carnival knew her by her true name. Clay shifted from foot to foot, and she knew her front man hated himself for betraying his discomfort. "The gator man got bit something awful, but guess who saved him? That little lady out there, that's who. Stopped that giant lizard right in its tracks without lifting a finger. Don't know how she did it, but she talked to the damn thing and it listened. Got it to back off the wrestler while he got out of there. Folks in town say that's her talent. They give her a wide berth but use her to, uh, parley with their animals when they need to. Figured we could put her in some fancy getup and use her as an animal tamer. The marks would love it." Clay clamped his mouth shut; he'd been rambling. The hard sell never worked on Ahiku.

Ahiku sighed. "I'll see about her. Have a seat."

Clay eased back into the corner near the door but stayed on his feet, his eyes fixed on her.

Ahiku arranged the bones on the table and sprinkled out a series of plants and herbs. She recited a few words, and a tendril, invisible to all but her, snaked beneath the curtain along the wood-plank floor and through the cracks of the door.

The girl waited impatiently with some type of little monkey perched on her shoulder. The tendril eased over the earth, a wisp of evil. Before the tendril reached the girl, the unmistakable sound of an elephant's trumpeting echoed. Ahiku frowned; there were no elephants in her carnival. But her spirit friends could be mischievous. The girl looked startled, as if she, too, had heard it, but it was clear that Zinsa and Efe hadn't noticed a thing.

The tendril curled about the girl's body, probing. Tense minutes passed before it uncoiled, slithered back to the ground, and returned to its lair. As the tendril settled on the bones, they rearranged themselves in the "no" position. Ahiku opened her eyes, disappointed. How many years had she been steering the carnival around the country, searching for Oya's daughter? Just as she'd promised the wannabe queen, she'd hunted down her potential enemies one by one. She had traveled year after year in this godforsaken carnival, seeking every oddity she could find, destroying a few who actually had dangerous power. But recently she'd been coming up empty-handed time and again. Surely the last person who could defeat her, end her, was close. She could taste the trail Oya's daughter had left as she ran from her.

This girl with the strange talent was harmless. The bones had never been wrong. This time they had, however, revealed a chance for amusement. The girl's thoughts were full of a certain landlady with a vile enough nature to earn her sway in the underworld.

"She may stay, Clay. Good job."

Clay had a hand on the door handle almost before she'd finished. "Thanks, Geneva. I'll be going to get her settled."

"You do that," Ahiku said and then dissolved into a putrid black smoke as she escaped back to the underworld.

She knew Clay hated that part.

CHAPTER SIX

The Beginning of a Beautiful Friendship

Liza and Clay navigated the carnival grounds with the last scraps of sunlight warming their backs and a flimsy breeze providing little relief from the heat. Though the boardinghouse was only a ten-minute ride away, it was another world. Her senses were accustomed to a much slower pace, and she struggled to dissect the bustling activity.

When they'd arrived, Clay had told a few of the workers—"carnies," they were called—to start getting ready for a weeklong date in Baton Rouge. That's when things came to life. Tents were raised, some striped with reds and blues and greens, some with intricate colorful prints, a few needing repair. Orders were shouted. Grunts of physical exertion echoed. And the people were mostly like her. She'd never seen so many Negro folks working in one place, outside of a farm.

Her stomach growled at the lingering smell of a dinner full of delicacies she could only dream about. The pitiful plate of rice she'd had before the gator show had been insufficient moments after consumption, a bitter memory now.

"And this is the cook tent," Clay said, seemingly in answer to her secret prayers. He pointed to a largish tent with row after row of remarkably neat wooden picnic tables covered in checkered cloth. Along the back edge was a long buffet holding a spattering of metal food containers that were being carted off one by one. From the looks of it, she'd missed dinner. *One more night, and me and hunger can part ways amicably.*

She grinned inwardly, always pleased when she could use one of the big words Mrs. Margaret had drilled into her head. Sometimes it was as if she spoke three languages: a heap of southern colored, seasoned with half a pinch of an African language she couldn't name and tossed up with a sprinkle of the King's English.

"You get three squares," Clay said. "And Mabel's a damn fine cook. Don't bug her when she's cooking, though, or she'll bite your head clean off."

"When do I get paid?" Liza was overwhelmed at the prospect of the three squares, but she'd need money if she truly hoped to be able to take care of herself and, one day, hopefully Twiggy. Her heart squeezed, as it always did, as she wondered if her little sister was okay.

"When you put together an act that's worth a damn, we can talk." Clay went on to explain that right now the animals were presented as an exotic zoo exhibit. They didn't do much but sit in a cage, and people paid a full nickel to get a look at them.

"From the sound of it, anything I do will be a step up."

Clay stopped and turned. "Gettin' ahead of yourself, don't cha think?"

Liza hunched. She tried to put on a face of calm. Confidence. But inside she was as scared as that time she spotted a bear in the Pensacola woods. There was still a chance she could hurt, or kill, one of the animals. "You asked me to come here. I wouldn't dare to call your good judgment into question, Mr. Kennel."

"You got the mouth," Clay said. "That much I can see."

They moved behind the cook tent to the trailers where the carnies and performers slept. Most were lined up like a long trail of marching fire ants. Two others sat apart—namely, that red trailer that Clay was all closemouthed about and another, plainer trailer.

Liza thrust her chin at the plainer one. "Supposing that red trailer is yours, who sleeps in the other one?"

"That one *is* mine."

"Your wife's got her own trailer, then?" If Clay kept his wife holed up like a prisoner, best Liza know now that was the way women were treated around here.

Clay's expression oozed a warning. "My wife is none a your concern. She ain't here noways. And you'll get one reminder." He held up an oil-stained index finger. "Not another word about the trailer."

She nodded meekly. Why couldn't she just have kept her mouth shut?

The stare-down lasted a moment longer, perhaps to drive home his point, and then the carnival owner moved on as if the exchange hadn't happened.

"Here is where you'll be bunking up. Ain't a palace or nothin', but you get a bunk to yourself, and there's only two to a car for the performers. Hope here's our fortune-teller—you won't be bunking with her, but she'll help you get settled."

The woman, who had been walking up, looked startled. "Well, a good evening to you, too, Mr. Kennel," she called at Clay's back as he took his leave. He waved a hand behind him.

She smiled at Liza. "I'm Hope," she said. "Hope Child."

She has good bones. Mrs. Margaret's words came to Liza's head unbidden. A crop of dense curls brushed her shoulders and framed a perfectly heart-shaped dark-brown face. Doe-like eyes sat above chiseled cheekbones. A full nose and mouth that accented but didn't dominate. Her smile was marred only by a chipped side tooth. For the first time, Mico stuck his head out of Liza's right pocket.

Hope's eyes slid down to the oddity. Most backed away at the sight of the creature, but this woman held firm. She gave Liza's hand a quick shake. As their fingers brushed, the fortune-teller shivered. There was something unreadable in her eyes—in a good way, though.

33

"You okay?" Liza asked.

For a moment Hope only blinked. "Yeah, I'm fine." She turned her attention back to Mico and grinned even wider and bent down to take a closer look. "Who do we have here?"

"His name is Mico."

"And what, where—" Hope stuck out a tentative finger to try and pat the fuzz coating the pygmy marmoset's head. And to Liza's surprise, instead of Mico taking a good chunk out of the finger, he let it rest, briefly, on his head before he shook it off.

"He found me," Liza said. "I don't know how. I woke up one day and he was there. That was four years ago."

Hope straightened, her long crystal earrings glittering. Judging from the way they dragged her earlobes down, they were a bit too heavy. Liza fingered the plain silver bulbs in her own ears.

"And I'm Eliza, but folks call me Liza."

"If it please you, I like Eliza. My mama's name is Elizabeth, see. You got a last name, Eliza?"

"I do—does it matter to you?"

"It's polite to give your full name to somebody when you meet them."

"Polite ain't one of my strong suits. But the last name is Meeks, if it makes you happy to know it."

"Well, good to meet you, Eliza Meeks." Hope gestured at the trailer Clay had assigned Liza. "Shall we?"

Heart pounding, Liza shifted her bag to her other hand. Anything would be better than the moldy garret she'd been sleeping in. "I guess."

"It's tight but it's comfortable." Hope mounted the short flight of steps. The trailer was indeed small, but more cozy than claustrophobic. The scent of lavender hung in the air. Two bunks lined either side of a narrow floor. Faded white sheets and a thin blanket covered the made-up beds. One bed held a simple pillow in a white case; the other was piled high with colorful, beaded, tasseled pillows. Liza wondered what her roommate was like. Based on the beadwork, she had expensively tacky taste.

A lamp sat on a tiny round table against the back wall at the end of the path between the bunks. The last of the waning sunlight streaming in from the window above either bunk cast the small space in a most pleasant glow.

"You can put your things here." Hope gestured to two sets of drawers skillfully slotted beneath the bunk. A hook near the foot of the bunk held a clean towel, probably white at some point but now a faded gray. "You'll be bunking with Autumn. A little snooty, if you ask me. You'll see for yourself later."

"This looks fine to me," Liza said. The practiced cool expression she'd perfected covered her face like paint even as her emotions surged. The little slat of a window might provide her some reading light at night, if the moon cooperated. She hefted her bag onto the bunk. Inside, her only other pair of pants, another set of undergarments, magazines, Mico's toy, and a battered black-and-white photo of her family. Mico had scrambled out of her pocket and now made himself comfortable on the pillow.

"That your family?" Hope asked.

Liza sighed. "Not anymore." The trailer door had no visible lock. "I can leave my things here?"

Hope turned serious. "You don't have to worry about thieves in this carnival. Management . . ." She paused. "People who steal never do it more than once."

"Management?" Liza asked. "You mean Clay? And that weird red trailer that somehow is and isn't his?"

"Clay didn't give you the speech?"

"He did."

Hope tucked a curl behind her ear. "This carnival pays better than any of the other flea bags, and they ain't never been late. We get good food and are treated mostly pretty good. If people don't follow the rules, well, all I know is they disappear, gone. Look, I can tell this is your first time working a carnival, but some of the others are rough. We got some troupers here been working the circuit for a long time. Follow the rules: don't steal, do your job, and don't ask questions about matters that don't concern you."

Caution was Liza's constant companion, but her ever-curious mind weighed the thinly veiled warning. People sure were jumpy about that red trailer. Maybe Clay wasn't squirreling his wife away in there, after all, but he *was* hiding something, sure as the day was long.

Hope nestled a shoulder against the trailer's doorjamb and waited while the new girl arranged her things. There wasn't much to speak of. It all fit in one drawer, with a corner to spare. Eliza slid that drawer closed and was halfway out of her crouch but then kneeled again, took out her magazines, and carefully smoothed and stacked them in the other drawer by themselves.

Hope had accumulated what her husband called an unreasonable amount of clothes and flashy jewelry over the last couple of years, but she'd first come to Bacchanal with just the clothes on her back. She recognized the signs of a hasty escape.

The girl was polite, pleasant even, only she hadn't smiled. Not once. What had her all wound up? And that odd jolt from when their hands touched. Nothing she could pin down good or bad; it was too quick. Probably something to do with whatever Clay had seen in the girl. Every performer who joined the carnival seemed to drag in two sets of baggage: one you could see, and the other, trickier variety, all tussled up on the inside.

With the little monkey settled on the bunk, the girl stood and nodded. Well, it *would* be nice to have someone new to talk to. Hope wasn't much of a bookworm, but she did fancy having a new mystery to unravel.

"Tell me again," Hope said. "You can talk to animals?"

"Not out loud, like." Eliza held her hands open, as if searching for the right words. "We can communicate, but it's not like the way I talk to people. Know what I mean?"

"No, I sure don't." Hope chuckled. "But it must be pretty special. Clay only takes folks that got real talent. It took some time and what I guess was a whole lotta money to get the few animals we keep. 'The carnival's ace in the hole,' Clay calls them."

"Can you take me to the animals?"

Hope sighed. The day had been a long one. She'd never gotten used to the whole traveling part of being in a traveling carnival. A fact that her husband never ceased to tease her about. Come to think of it, he'd probably be looking for her soon.

"It's late," Hope said. But the pitiful girl deflated so, and she relented. "Oh, all right."

"I didn't see any signs in town. How are we going to do a show if nobody knows about it?" Liza asked as they strolled back outside.

"Oh, believe you me, Clay probably put somebody on it as soon as he got back," Hope said. "That one don't miss a thing. He swung by to look for some gator wrestler before heading on to Lake Charles. But they came back with you instead, and guess now we got a show to do."

"And how is it you can tell people's fortunes?" Liza asked. "Several people I met when my family traveled claimed to have the gift, but most of them were putting everyone on."

"Another nonbeliever? Don't you know nothing about your African roots?"

"My mother wasn't a talker." It was quick, but Hope registered Eliza's grimace and felt awful.

"And I couldn't shut my mother up," Hope said. A well-placed joke at one's own expense was a cure for all ills. "My people are Yoruba. The

37

gift was dragged 'cross the Atlantic in the belly of them ships right along with us. It may skip a generation or two, but it is always there. I only use them cards because that's what folks want to see. But if they give me permission, I get a vision. I guess I can't explain it no more than you can tell me how you talk to animals. I can see some things—not all of it—and sometimes it don't even make sense."

"But a person has to give you permission first?"

Hope hesitated. Eliza seemed earnest enough. Still, she wasn't sure how much she should share. "Yes, ma'am. Otherwise, they as blank to me as a tree."

They rounded a bend and stopped in front of the animal tent. "Here we are," said Hope. Eliza positively beamed. "Nice, isn't it? Not even sure who came up with the look of it. It's been this way since—"

Eliza's eyes went wide. "There's a man creeping up behind you, and I swear he's the biggest man I've ever seen."

Hope took in her new friend's slack-jawed expression. "Oh." She turned, then grinned. "Meet my husband, Bombardier."

Just like the first time they'd met, when he smiled, the sun, the moon, and the stars burned with envy.

～

By the time Hope and Bombardier brought Liza back to her trailer, the clamor of activity had abated. Carnies lazed outside their trailers or chatted and laughed in groups like old friends.

The woman inside was asleep. Careful to make as little noise as possible, Liza settled onto her bunk. The night air of a Louisiana summer limped in through the window and settled down on her like a prickly wool blanket.

The animal tent had been an unexpected surprise. The tapestry matched the intricate stitching from some of her mother's baskets: red, gold, green, blue, orange. Colors woven in alternating square patterns.

Mama had called the pattern "kente." A kente weave in the middle of an American carnival was unsettling. Clay seemed to have an obsession with African things.

All Liza had wanted was a peek. Inside the tent were two cages. A man wearing overalls and the weariness of a full day of hard labor had refilled a water bowl and slid it into a cage. One animal looked like a strange dog; the other—and she blinked to make sure—looked like nothing more than a big turtle. This was the "ace in the hole" exhibit?

After seeing the animals, Liza felt less sure than before. How was she supposed to create a show out of those poor creatures? They looked well cared for, but an unmistakable sadness hung in the air around them; that much she could tell without conjuring a single image. Hope had given her an idea, though. She'd never thought to ask the animals' permission. Would an animal even understand the concept?

She'd only sat with them this first time, letting them get used to her presence.

If Mico had picked up anything from the animals, he hadn't let on. He'd only watched, curious, like her. Why folks would pay a nickel to gawk at a dog and a turtle was beyond her. Life in a carnival was strange indeed.

Liza shifted on her bunk, her stomach lurching. These animals must be something special. If Clay found out she couldn't fully control her power, not only would she be out on her butt with no money, but the way he seemed to have these people scared to even talk, there was no telling what this man could have in store for her. She would have to find a small creature to test on again. She didn't want to do it, but she couldn't afford to practice on the carnival animals.

After a time, she drifted into a loose and disquieted slumber, her dreams rising and falling to the carnival's collective heartbeat.

CHAPTER SEVEN

INSATIABLE

Toby watched as the closed-up storefront was plastered over with a banner line of painted canvas squares showing the wonders of the carnival. Some of them were giant black and white, some colored, each plugging a different part of the show. There was a big man in a muscle-bulging pose, a lady in a dress so short his ma near about fainted. He didn't know the word scrawled at the top in fancy lettering, *Bur-les-que*, which he sounded out under his breath. The next one showed another lady in a long dark robe, a scary-looking third eye sitting smack-dab in the middle of her forehead, with rays of light shooting out around her head as she looked up at the sky.

Ma said some hooligans were plastering up the whole town. "It's so's everybody will know the carnival's opening tomorrow night."

Toby wriggled out of the vise grip Ma had on his hand and barreled a few doors down to gawk at the men slapping up another poster. He stopped short, and one of the men beamed down at him. As if he knew Toby couldn't read it, the man did it for him: *"Come one, come all, to the G. B. Bacchanal Carnival. Oddities, freaks, feats of skill and wonder. Try your hand at games of chance. Bring the family to the rides. Good eats! Don't miss it!"*

Toby grinned in wide-eyed wonder until Ma's rough fingers clamped down on his shoulder. Pa moseyed up alongside her and shot him the look, the one where he cocked his head forward and narrowed his right eye. *Run off again, and I'll tan your hide and good,* the look said.

But Pa's sour look couldn't put a damper on Toby's delight. Here he was, one night away from his all-time biggest wish ever. *A carnival.* The picture of a candy apple called to him so strongly that it may as well have had his name carved right there on the side. The Ferris wheel—why, he'd have to ride that one, sure enough.

A girl, one he recognized from the only day he spent at school last year, was walking down the road with her folks, headed straight for him.

He tugged at his ma's hand; he didn't want the girl to see him. His knickers were a couple of inches too short, and just yesterday he'd had to wallop another boy for snickering about them. Ma ignored him, and luckily the girl turned down another path.

If Ma and Pa had offered him the choice of a full supper or the carnival, he wouldn't have given his answer a second thought, even though they'd had only watery soup with a half-rotten potato all day, and his stomach rumbled painfully. He'd told his parents that there was sure to be a booth loaded up with french fries, cotton candy, and those shiny red apples, but Pa told him there wouldn't be money for treats tomorrow any more than there was today.

He was real sore at Pa and was about to tell him so when a man with the reddest hair he ever saw came up to them.

"Bet that boy of yours would like to try his hand at the balloon and darts game tomorrow night," he said, plucking at his suspenders. "Toy truck to the winner."

"I'm much obliged, stranger," Pa said. "But I reckon that carnival will cost me a pretty penny, one I ain't got to spare."

That meant he wouldn't get a shot at winning the toy truck.

The redhead winked at the boy. "You're in luck, friend. This here token will buy you one free game."

Toby pleaded with his eyes and fidgeted in that quiet space before, sure enough, Pa shook his head and turned away.

The boy and his parents strolled home, their spirits low. When they reached their one-room shack, Toby begged to stay outside for just a little while longer. With a warning to stay close, Ma and Pa went on in.

As soon as the door closed, he got an idea. The stranger had said the carnival was setting up just outside town, and boy, would it be fun to get a peek at it. With one glance at the house's only small, dim window, he darted off into the growing shadows.

He stood at the end of the road, suddenly afraid. He couldn't see anything; maybe he'd heard it wrong. Just then a truck rolled past, and the red-haired man waved to him from inside. "Can't wait till tomorrow, I see. Hop in—I'll give you the tour."

Pa had passed a few words with the man, so he must be all right. Toby climbed into the cab and slammed the door. The man asked him all kinds of questions about his folks. But the boy started to feel uneasy. Ma would worry.

"If it's all the same to you, mister, I need to go back home now."

But when Toby clambered out of the truck, he caught a glimpse of the lights. Then the sounds caught up to him, too, bell dings and music and laughter. *The carnival.* He sought cover behind a tree. He was crouched there, straining to see, when a lady appeared at his elbow.

"My guess is that you have your eye on winning a magnificent toy truck." She pointed toward the carnival. He could just picture a bright-red one sitting on a shelf loaded up with other toys.

Toby glanced over his shoulder and eyed the road home.

Ma had warned him about strangers and such. But she was such a pretty lady. That had to be real gold around her wrist, and her dress was as colorful as the quilt on his bed. Why, she looked like a black rainbow. Pretty ladies were supposed to be nice.

He squirmed, picking at the tree's rough bark, and gave the lady a sideways glance. "That's what I want, all right, and I'm gonna win it tomorrow."

The lady smiled. It was a real friendly smile. "Well, who says you have to wait until tomorrow? There's a special attraction tonight. And there'll be loads of tasty treats for all the children."

Toby wanted a toy truck more than anything, and he figured he could pocket a few treats for Ma and Pa too. So when the lady offered him a special invite, of course he followed.

～

The boy's colorless face was slack, lips partially opened. A sliver of drool fell from the left corner of his mouth. It was as if, at ten years old, he had suffered a terrible seizure. He sat in a simple wooden chair, his feet dangling several inches from the floor. One shoe remained on his right foot; the other, badly in need of a new sole, lay where it had been kicked across the room. The child was dressed in the rough navy-blue slacks and dingy white shirt of a poor farmer's son.

His green eyes were wide in semi-permanent fright, pupils dilated to the size of the marbles still in his pants pocket. While he couldn't move his head, his gaze roamed over the inside of the trailer. Dim light filled the space, which was still and close; the shadows seemed to climb atop one another, struggling for room to stretch out. Countless masks covered the pale-yellow walls that had maybe once been white. The wooden masks wore scowls, had long pointed chins, strange carvings. Others looked like they were made of plaster, painted in bright colors, freckled sparkles, blank holes for eyes.

Ahiku swayed to the thrum of spirited African drums. There may as well have been a man pounding out the rhythm right there behind her and her prey. The boy probably wondered where the music came from. There was certainly no man, and no phonograph either.

He looked longingly at the windows on either side of the trailer, and Ahiku could imagine him picturing a daring escape. No matter, though; he was hers. There was a thick curtain at the back of the trailer, behind which she disappeared. She hissed at the old woman bound in the corner—she'd deal with her after—and when she reemerged, she was wearing her smile. The boy had a panicked stink about him: something sweet trying hard to cover the smell of a feral dog.

Ahiku had been told she had a natural iridescence like the coat of a most beautiful raven. Her dress, a cross between a gypsy's and an African queen's—all bright colors and flashy jewelry. Black skin with the sheen of a night sky, and she was near as tall as the boy's father.

A red scarf was tied around her head; several long kinky braids trailed down her back. She smiled, flashing a glimpse of perfect milk-white teeth.

She was visible only to her prey. The lure: a secret carnival attraction that only the most special kids could see, and there would be a treat—a toy truck—afterward. No—he shouldn't bother his parents; she'd have him back home before they even missed him.

He'd put his hand, with dirty fingers and rough skin, in hers and followed her. She imagined his mother came outside later and wondered aloud, "Where did Toby wander off to?"

As the door to the red trailer had closed and bolted behind him, he'd spun, pounded Ahiku with his little fists and clawed, but she easily lifted him, plopping him into a wooden chair in the middle of the trailer and binding him with a complicated hand gesture. Ahiku sang in her language, her voice like silk thread lining a rough sweater.

With more odd movements of her hands, she began to weave something into existence from the air. A shimmer that was there and then gone. The shimmer coalesced and took on the colors of the room. Ahiku blew a breath of cinnamon and spice, before her head, her neck, and the rest of her body dissolved into a trail of dark smoke, easing toward Toby.

Sweat rolled down Toby's frightened yet determined face as he struggled to move, to run. But Ahiku held him as if an invisible rope bound him to the chair. Her misty essence floated toward him and oozed into his nostrils. And his soul, escorted by Ahiku's deathly presence, rose up, out through his skull. His gaze lifted from where he sat in the chair to the wispy version of himself, and he twirled to look down on his own former body in horror. The wisp of Toby attempted to flee through a window, but Ahiku only raised an elegant hand toward his fleeing soul.

Toby's soul twisted and writhed until he tired, and soon he wedged himself in among the other small scared souls now existing only within her.

Ahiku looked at the small lifeless body, inhaled a satisfied gulp of cinnamon-spice air, and burped as if she had consumed the most sumptuous meal of her life.

Ahiku turned her attention to her second victim. Her right hand wove a pattern that lifted the old woman and dropped her into the center of the trailer. Though the woman was gray haired, her form bent, strength rippled from her. No match for a centuries-old demon, but her spirit was no ordinary one. And it may as well have provided a road map. As soon as they'd rolled into town, the witch's presence had pulsed, and Ahiku had hurried Zinsa and Efe off to capture her—their Dahomey countrywoman.

"Dear Yejide, it pains me to see you this way. Tell me what I need to know"—Ahiku flashed her smile—"and I will be generous. I am willing to limit your torture to a month. Where is my adversary, and how do you protect the children?"

The witch doctor was likely one of the last of her kind. Their ilk had shielded the continent's most precious children to such a degree that they'd driven Ahiku off to America in search of unprotected prey.

"I'm already dead, demon." Yejide looked up at her with disrespect-ful defiance in those clear eyes. "I will tell you nothing."

The woman had some meager defenses. Witch doctors of her line *had* their secrets. But the end came much sooner than Ahiku had hoped. And the meddling witch died without giving up a sliver of information or crying out even once.

As much as Ahiku wanted to banish the woman to the underworld for demon sport, she had to stand idly by, seething as the old woman's powerful ancestors claimed her soul.

~

Zinsa and Efe, stoic as thousand-year-old redwoods, graced either side of the stairs leading to the red trailer's door. They were dressed simply in white shirts and black slacks, with short, curved knives secured at their waists. Clay mumbled a greeting as he climbed the five short steps. The pair barely grunted in return.

He entered and averted his eyes from the lump on the floor. He looked at Geneva standing over the body, at her forehead, or her nose, anything but her eyes. He'd done it once, maybe five years ago now, and what he'd seen there still chilled his soul. Clay was tall, but Geneva had him by an inch or two.

What remained of Toby sat in a shapeless lump of gray, mottled flesh, bones sticking out at odd angles, the clothes he'd worn underneath. Clay remembered the child, the blond hair, the chin dimpled in the middle. He fought back the memory, but that was like constructing a dam over a great waterway of pent-up emotion. He couldn't quite do it.

"This boy had parents, Clay." Geneva bent down, moved aside the mass, and riffled through the clothing, then picked up the slacks. She was like a tigress, sniffing around the body of the lame young she'd had to kill. "You going sloppy on me?"

As much as he hated it, Clay took this part of his job seriously. He puffed up his chest at the perceived insult. "I know my job. Asked around. Parents poor, no home, no food, farm lost in the dust bowl." He counted off each point on his fingers. "Couldn't take care a themselves, let alone the boy. Did him a favor, is what I did."

Geneva sighed, a concession. "Treat him kindly. He deserves a good burial; he was a strong fighter." She turned the slacks over and over in her hands, ripped a small section of cloth free, and tossed the slacks back onto the pile. She held up the fabric, peering at it in the light, lifted the hem of her patchwork skirt, and pressed the patch against the cloth. Gold threading erupted from the skirt, grabbed hold of the new patch, and knitted it in with the others.

"I told ya . . . ," Clay started before coughing and beginning again. He and Geneva had an odd relationship. She didn't take adults for her little rituals, but she would sure as hell kill one if it suited her. Still, she relied on him. "If you could wait till I leave to do that."

"Do you still fear me, Clay?" Geneva admired the new patch on her skirt and sashayed over to the side of the trailer. She crossed her arms and leaned against the wall. "Have I not proven myself to be a dear friend to you?"

Clay looked up, focused on her right cheek, but he wasn't sure it fooled either one of them. "My ma always told me I was a cautious boy. Guess that didn't wear off none."

The corners of Geneva's perfect mouth turned down slightly. She'd let on that what little family she had had died with her friends over a century ago. Clay was the closest thing she had to a friend, even though he fancied her a monster. "By the time we reach Tulsa and make the circuit again, little Toby will be long forgotten. Have Zinsa and Efe leave something for the parents."

"You're the boss." No matter how many times he had done it, he still had to fight the nausea. He pulled a pair of gloves from his back pocket, slipped them on, and loaded what was left of Toby's body into a potato sack.

"Oh." Geneva waved an elegant hand beneath the window. "Take that also."

Clay narrowed his eyes. How had he missed the shriveled form of an old woman curled in on herself? He didn't dare ask about the body.

47

Outside, he passed along the message to Zinsa and Efe, who immediately strode off to do Geneva's bidding.

Clay dug a hole to bury both bodies. As he hefted the old woman, something fell to the ground. He lay her gently in the hole and picked it up: a longish leather cord, a round disk attached. He opened the little cover and, inside, flipped through three carved discs: an elephant, a raven, and a badger. He shrugged and tossed it into the open grave with the bodies.

With the deed done, Clay stole away to his trailer. There, he kneeled and crossed himself. Asked his God for forgiveness and protection from whatever demons or lesser gods Geneva had in her back pocket. He prayed that the children he'd chosen as sacrifices had died easily. He admitted that he was a coward; his only concern was that Geneva keep her promise, that she would never go after his son. Clay exhaled and, with his face once again under control, shuffled outside. He walked until the lights from the carnival were dim pinpricks and sat amid the brush and weeds.

Clay lit a match and watched the flame, transfixed. He cursed his cowardice, rolled his sleeve up above his bicep, and held the match to his arm, relishing in the deliciously torturous caress of the flame until he screamed.

CHAPTER EIGHT

Mischief Afoot

Liza slept fitfully until a stream of pale sunlight landed square on her face and she blinked her eyes open. Her trailer mate was beginning to stir.

A loud bang on the side of the trailer broke through the stillness. "Get up, you lazy carnies. We got a show to put on tonight. Up. Up!"

On the other bunk, the woman sat up and stretched: pretty, white but not too pale, with sparkling auburn hair and an age that one couldn't quite pin down. She had that fresh look that only a few could achieve first thing in the morning.

"You're the new girl, Liza, right?" The woman swung her legs out from beneath the sheet. When she yawned loudly, that fresh look was lost in the awful smell that wafted out. A night full of closed-up mouth and something else. Cigarettes? Stale coffee?

Liza sat up and fought the urge to wave away the scent. "That's what my mama named me."

"Welcome to hell." The woman wore a simple one-piece nightgown that clung to her formidable curves with a good night's sweat. "I'm Autumn. And let's get this out of the way now: I work the cooch show, and if you got a problem with that, you can keep it to yourself. And if you want, you can ask Clay to bunk somewhere else."

Living in Louisiana, Liza was no stranger to prostitutes or the attitudes men flung at them during the day while paying them good money at night. A prostitute had even lived in Mrs. Shippen's boardinghouse, but she paid a little extra on the rent. The payoff meant Mrs. Shippen only flapped her tongue about her to the other women.

"I'm in no position to look askance at anybody," Liza said. She grew overly proud at her word choice, sensing Autumn's surprise. "I'm a single woman who joined a carnival. What could I possibly have to say?"

"You'd be surprised." Autumn was rummaging through her things and emerged with a towel and a toothbrush. "Wanna follow me to the donnicker?"

Liza was dumbstruck. Autumn had thrown a fancy word of her own right back at her.

Autumn chuckled. "The bathroom. And the showers."

It hadn't occurred to her to ask where she'd clean up, use the bathroom, or anything. "Uh, yeah. Yes, please."

As Liza stood, Autumn slapped a hand to her chest, eyes wide, and pointed. "What is that?"

Had a snake somehow found its way into the trailer? No, there was only Mico, poking out from beneath her pillow, blinking his eyes wildly. Liza held out her hand, and he jumped into her palm.

"This is Mico," she said. "A pygmy marmoset."

"A pet?" Autumn took a tentative step forward.

"Guess you could say that."

Autumn held out her finger, and Mico took it. Her face brightened. "Well, aren't you the cutest little thing."

Mico chittered, his way of beaming at the perceived praise. Liza set him back down. "You wait here. I'll be back to get you after we clean up."

As they stepped out into the bright light of the morning, carnival workers ran to and fro with a quiet but frenzied efficiency. Already things had changed from the previous night.

"What happened to the last person who shared your trailer?" Liza asked.

Autumn looked startled but quickly masked it. "She moved on," she said. "Folks you see out here are the lower rung. They handle setup and takedown. Got it down to a science too. Sometimes it seems like we could be gone from a place in a matter of minutes and no trace of us having ever been there. We don't travel with that many roadies. We take on a few from among the locals if we need them. Other than that, we make do."

"What did you mean back there?" Liza ventured back into questionable territory. "When you said 'Welcome to hell.'"

A cloud covered Autumn's face for a moment, then cleared as though a high wind had sneaked up and blown it away. She plucked at her robe and fanned herself. "What else would you call a place this dang hot?"

Liza frowned.

"Oh," Autumn said with a snicker. "That's right. I guess you call it home."

More tents were going up. A carousel and Ferris wheel materialized alongside a few games. Liza stepped on a stuffed animal that squeaked in a child's voice. She picked it up and tossed it over the counter of one of the games into a man's outstretched hand and then paused, startled. She knew better but couldn't help staring. He was tall and well built, maybe close to six feet. The dingy overalls and wary, downcast eyes couldn't hide it—his face was like a rose, unaware of how beautifully it had bloomed. She held his gaze a moment more than was strictly lady-like. Her insides did a two-step when he tipped his hat, and she hurried to catch up with Autumn.

They came to an enclosed tent lined with shower stalls, a bucket of water beside each, probably drawn from the nearby tap. Across the path was a single row of four separate bathroom stalls. Hastily constructed wooden-panel affairs with a sheet stretched across the front.

Autumn tilted her head in that direction. "If you go early enough, you can avoid the worst of the smell, but still, we're in the south, and with this heat . . . it isn't the most pleasant experience. Do your business and get out as fast as you can."

Even when she'd lived with her parents, they'd gone to the bathroom in the woods, used things like leaves for wiping. But that was out in the open. Liza made quick use of the facilities—little more than holes in the ground—and moved to the crude shower, soaked her towel and soaped up, then washed and dumped the remaining water over her head.

Surprisingly clean, she changed into her other set of clothes—threadbare but skillfully mended trousers and a cotton button-up shirt—and was as well put-together as she could manage when Clay found her.

"Hope you got a good night's rest," he said. "Gonna need you to pitch in on some of the other acts until you get your own show up and running."

"I'll do whatever needs doing," Liza said. A small man walked past, and her breath caught in her throat. He wore no visible clothes, was about four feet tall, and was covered in what appeared to be a shaggy green coat of grassy hair from head to toe. He had striking hazel eyes, and his fingers ended in pointed claws. The little man turned and called out, "I cut quite the handsome picture, do I not?"

Clay followed her gaze. "Oh, that's Eloko, our little man from somewhere in Africa. Never said where. Been here as long as I have. Hear tell he came to America in a cage in the basement of a steamboat." When Liza cocked her head to the side, Clay added, "Not sure who bought his ticket."

"Humph" was all she could muster in response. If Clay owned the carnival, wouldn't he have been the one to recruit the little man?

"Ain't you never even *been* to a carnival?" he asked.

Liza blinked, looked down. "Well, I guess I haven't."

"Lordy, I sure did pick a green one." Clay wiped the sweat already streaming down his face. "Hope you're a fast learner."

"You don't have to worry about me," she said. "I learn fast. And remember, I'm good with writing and numbers too."

"You mentioned," Clay said. "I think we'll start you off with Autumn in the cooch show. Uh, the show, after the show."

Liza's mouth dropped open, and Clay grinned. She noticed that it was a half grin, as if it were hard for him to smile full on.

"Man, you *are* green," he said. "Listen, gonna need a word later on, get your thinkin' on where best to jump the show to next. For now, report to Mabel in the food tent. She can always use an extra hand. Later on, we'll work out what you can do with the animals, put together a little show of some kind. Right now, folks pay pretty good to come in and look at them. We can bump up a penny or two if you can get them to do something."

"I'll think on it," Liza said. Where to suggest they go next? Mama got most everything she needed from South Carolina: sweetgrass, bulrush, pine needles, sometimes palmetto palm. They sold them baskets all over the place. Some towns better off than others. Where would the carnival have the best run?

A little boy cut across their path, and Clay's expression went all anxious and angry. "What's that kid doing here?" he shouted.

Liza's gaze trailed Clay as he strode off yelling, chasing the boy away. You'd think the carnival boss would be pleased to see kids sneaking in early—they'd run home and get everybody else all fired up for the show.

The thought of children stirred the longing for her baby sister that lived just beneath the surface of her thoughts. With luck, this traveling carnival would steer Liza onto her sister's trail.

Liza let her nose and her rumbling stomach lead her to the food tent, its big red flag lolling in the nonexistent breeze.

Breakfast was in full swing with a long line stretched out the length of the cookhouse. Things were set up buffet-style. Dented metal plates on one end and food stored in burners along the front. Cutlery and napkins at the far side. A separate table was set up with coffee and juice. Her eyes bulged. Did they have all this every day? As much as she wanted to eat, Liza approached Mabel first. She spotted the woman easily: small in stature but big in voice. She wore an apron, barked commands, and generally oversaw everything.

"Clay asked me to report to you. I'm Liza Meeks."

Mabel gave her a quick once-over and said, "Haven't seen you in my line yet. I don't need workers who gone fall over from starvation. Get yourself a plate, and I'll get you set up in the back."

Hmm. Gruff on the outside but probably all sugar and sweets on the inside.

Mabel grabbed Liza by the wrist and partly dragged her from the end of the buffet line to the front. She shoved her in front of another carnie. As the man made to protest, she cut him off. "Shut your high-falutin mouth, Freddie. Don't you see a lady here? I swear some of you carnies ain't got the good sense the Lord gave you."

Mabel shoved a plate into her new charge's hand and said, "Eat up and come to the back. Clay said you good with numbers, and I can use some help with my ordering system. Seem to keep running out of eggs." She walked off muttering something else derogatory about carnies.

Liza could only grin. She didn't look back at Freddie but loaded up her plate with eggs, grits, and fatty bacon that a butcher probably couldn't sell to anybody else.

～

As the sun began to settle over the tops of the trees, Mrs. Shippen huddled at Bacchanal's entrance with a sizable crowd of townsfolk, staring in awe. What had been a spattering of trailers and tents when a few of the locals came out to nose around the previous night now looked like a full-fledged carnival, albeit a small one. The closer she looked, the more it all seemed half-baked.

Still, that buzz of activity had become a controlled hum, the fine working of an oiled machine that had been taken apart and reassembled time and time again. She couldn't downplay the smell of rare delicacies that filled the air: fried dough, french fries . . . and was that cotton candy?

The tiny woman was dressed like a vamp. Long beads draped down the front of a cotton drop-waist dress—a holdover from her self-perceived heyday in the twenties. Gloves covered her hands, and her hat had a black ribbon curled on the side.

The barker called out his ballyhoo: *"Step right up, ladies and gents, cats and vamps. Bear witness to freaks and oddities from the far reaches of the globe. Be thrilled by dangerous beasts from deep in the African jungle. Wanna win something nice for the little lady there, buddy? Try your hand at one of our games of skill or chance! And if you're feeling brave, see if you can last a minute with the strongest Senegalese grappler of all time. And I hope you came on an empty belly, 'cause we got mouthwaterin' southern treats that'll make your granny green with envy. Come see the most exotic, the most spectacular show in all the universe . . . Bacchanal!"*

The crowd was riled up, pushing and shoving to get through the fenced-off entrance framed by a latticework structure, a good eight feet high and equally wide. Mrs. Shippen muttered her indignation at being jostled about so but elbowed her way to a spot right in front.

Thick vines the color of tree bark throbbed and writhed, wove and knit around the frame. Green pods erupted from yellowish flowers and burst to reveal nuts of varying shades, yellow to red to brown. She drew in a sharp breath, then narrowed her eyes. "What kind of flimflam—"

"Come on now. Nab a kola nut off the vine. Nobody gets in without one. That's it, peel and chew, folks." Pause. Indecision. The landlady and likely most of her Baton Rouge neighbors had no idea what a kola nut was. A small child pulled away from his mother and darted forward. A vine curled out to meet him. He plucked a ripe nut and popped it into his mouth.

The effect was immediate. The boy spun back toward the crowd wearing the muddled grin of a much older man who'd had at least a couple of good shots of corn whiskey. As near a guarantee of a good time as was possible. They surged forward.

Customers were ushered in and clustered around an inner courtyard. Torch lights sprang to life, illuminating a rectangular space as they flickered from the strong wind that blew through. White scarves whipped on the breeze. White was for welcome, someone whispered. The crowd pitched and murmured, oddly subdued.

The scarves spun and spun, a whirlwind of white and earth, until the wind died down and the blur dissolved into five forms: three women, each with a scarf in her right hand, and two drummers.

The drummers raised their drumsticks in unison, and when they came down against the drums, a dance began. Fast, measured stomps. The white scarves keeping time with the hypnotic sway of arms and hips. Graceful, acrobatic kicks and leaps so high they defied reason.

With a final beat of the drums, the dance ended as mysteriously as it had begun. Torch lights extinguished, the dancers gone as if they had never been there.

The crowd of people seemed to come back to themselves and were immediately greeted by a sensory overload of big band music piped through a phonograph. Blinking lights called them to the various joints and attractions.

Mrs. Shippen stood transfixed. She trod the area where, moments before, those shameful half-naked dancers and drummers had been. Nothing remained, not a trace. "Foolishness," she spat before she ambled through the carnival midway, her unwavering mission to find fault.

~

Liza's assignment was to be a roamer. Pitch in and help whoever needed it. For her troubles, she would be paid a whole half dollar of her own.

Once she got her act up and running, she might be able to keep every-thing she brought in—minus carnival expenses, of course.

"Hey, Liza," Hope called out. "Would you mind running back to the trailer and snagging my pitch cards outta my trunk?"

"Sure thing," Liza said and then darted off. Already, patrons were streaming through the carnival grounds. Rides swirled, lights flashed, bells rang, games were hawked. The sounds of Baton Rouge at play. The carnival, near as she could tell, was set up in a half circle. Rides filled the center, games and shows the back and sides. The trailers were parked out in what they called the backyard.

A group of performers cut a path through Liza's like an earthbound rainbow of merriment. Dancing women, stilt walkers, men wearing painted masks. The women wore scandalous costumes of beads and slivers of bright silks. Their heads were covered in sky-high crowns of gold. The way they jiggled their nearly naked bodies . . . brazen.

She guessed the figures jitterbugging behind the creepy masks were men. But the stilt dancers sent shivers up her spine. They pranced about with ease, one covered in silver from head to toe. His arms moved like an angel's wings. The other wore red garb, but his face was painted in the black-and-white image of a skull. The massive orange-and-red wig he wore shot out in all directions. The walkers wove around Liza and passed on to harry another pack of carnival patrons.

Liza collected herself and hustled off to Hope's trailer. On the way, she passed those women soldiers. They, too, had a show. They wore the strangest clothes: loincloths, leather covering their breasts. Bandannas wrapped their heads; beads draped at their waists and ankles. They were demonstrating their prowess with spears, throwing at a target set up more than twenty yards away. They hit the bull's-eye time and again and identified marks to come up and give it a try.

Mico chose that moment to leap out of her pocket.

"Mico!" She took off after him. Hope would have to wait. Liza darted through the shadows, dodging customers, and then pulled up short. Mico sat perched in front of the red trailer. It was still set off from the rest of the group, Clay's dark trailer off to the side.

"What is wrong with you?" Liza scooped up her pet and hastened to back away: slow, quiet steps the way her father had taught her. Movement caught her eye.

A lone light flickered in the red trailer's windows. Multiple shadows filled the space. Animated voices and the rhythmic beat of African drums drifted from the open windows.

The drums stopped. She froze, but Mico screeched . . . loudly. As badly as Liza wanted to turn and run, she couldn't. Something held her in place. Not even the terror-stricken scream trapped in her chest could escape. A thick, swirling white smoke lilted out of the window and snaked toward her. The screeching rose.

Scared out of her mind, she couldn't obey the images her pet was sending her—*danger* and *run*—so in desperation she called on a flock of birds flying overhead, sending an image of them flying down toward her and protecting her.

The flock diverted from its celestial path into a fierce dive. They tore around the smoke but failed to penetrate it, bouncing off like Ping-Pong balls. But it was enough. Whatever held her faltered.

Liza ran back the way she'd come but not before her peripheral vision caught sight of a fluttering of colorful skirts. Gone in a backward glance. As she reached the carnival again, she bent over, breath coming in ragged gasps. Her breath stopped altogether when the Ferris wheel, in midspin, went dark.

Everyone seemed to look toward the Ferris wheel at the same time. They moved like a river of bodies, as if toward the edge of a waterfall. As Liza approached, the lights came back on and the wheel started turning again.

Hope was there. "And where are my—"

She didn't get to finish her sentence.

"I tell you, Mrs. Shippen went up on that thing! Flowered dress, about yea high." The farmer held his hand up to his shoulder. It was Albert, the man with the sick calf, talking to Clay. Liza ducked behind Hope. She hadn't forgotten about how she'd fled town days before. With the sheriff's lazy constitution and the extra coins in his pocket from whatever deal he'd struck with Clay, she didn't think he'd bother looking for her any further, but if trouble was brewing, there was no telling what would happen if he got wind of her presence.

"Even took off her hat before she climbed in. What did you do with her?" Albert's eyes had gone wild, and a crowd of angry onlookers gathered behind him.

Mrs. Shippen, lost?

"Sir," Clay said, "I haven't seen anybody matching that description go up on my wheel. Now I tell you, your lady friend is probably over on another ride." The redhead hid his nervousness well, but to Liza's trained eye, it was plain as day.

"You callin' me a liar, mister?" Albert stomped up to Clay's face, spittle flying. "I know she was on there. Waved to her as she went to the top myself!"

"Why don't we talk about this over here."

Clay took the man's arm and tried to lead him away, but all hell broke loose. Albert swung a fist, connecting with the carnival manager's jaw. Clay tackled the man and sent him sprawling. A gang of other locals jumped into the fray, landing blows on Clay's back before Bombardier lifted two by the scruff of their collars, jostled and tossed them around like empty potato sacks, and sent them flying. The women soldiers appeared, too, and elbowed their way into the fray, not to be outdone. They cracked many a head with those short sticks or spears—Liza wasn't sure what they were.

∽

The female—of that much Ahiku was sure—had run off before she could tell who it was. The demon stood outside her trailer, vaguely aware of the commotion happening in another part of the carnival. She flicked her wrist in the direction of the Ferris wheel. One of her spirit friends had shown up, as the spirits were known to do from time to time, and caused a bit of mischief with a certain spiteful landlady.

This Ahiku allowed in exchange for the alliances she'd relied on over the centuries. And for the thus far useless hints on where to find her adversary.

She stalked around, kicking at the dead birds littering the ground. Zinsa ran up, eyes screaming murder. Efe must have been back in the thick of it still. She would never miss an opportunity to hurt or kill if it was necessary. Zinsa scanned the area, determined that her mistress was unharmed, and dropped to one knee.

"Oh, get up." Ahiku waved at her dismissively. She turned back into her trailer.

Had what happened been chance, or design? What, or who, could control a flock of birds this way? A thought nudged at the back of her mind. The new girl had some command of animals, but the bones had spoken—she was harmless. Ahiku didn't know who or what it was, but she would find out.

The fight raged on. A spool of sound unfurled and lengthened into the raspy groan of something ancient and powerful. Slowly, the Ferris wheel started to spin . . . in reverse. The crowd became confused. Eventually, the row, Mrs. Shippen, all was lost, and nobody recalled the reason for the upset in the first place. By the time the Ferris wheel had completed its reverse circuit, everything was forgotten.

CHAPTER NINE

A BEGINNING

The sun had reached its midday peak, a lazy orange ball dripping its formidable heat across the plains. Liza and Autumn sat rocking back and forth in the trailer, feeling every bump and hiccup in the road. Jamey was driving. He'd barely spared Liza a glance when he'd told them to settle in. The carnival's week in Baton Rouge had flown by, and before Liza knew it, the carnies were tearing down the rides and tents, packing everything up in trailers, and she was saying goodbye to the place that she'd stayed the longest but would never think of as home.

"You have any notion of what happened to Mrs. Shippen?" Liza finally worked up the courage to ask Autumn. Since the night of her ex-landlady's disappearance, she hadn't had a minute to spare. There was so much that needed doing. In helping out, she'd gotten to know a few more of the carnies, but not a single one of them had mentioned anything about a missing woman. She'd been reluctant to ask about it, not knowing whether this was another one of Clay's mysteries that wasn't to be discussed. But Autumn seemed more inclined to buck the trend.

"Who?" Autumn sat sewing beads and other embellishments onto her costume.

Liza shifted on her bunk, trying to find a comfortable spot. "She ran the boardinghouse where I lived. Was as mean as they come. Could have sworn something happened to her on opening night, but nobody remembers a thing about it."

"Accidents happen. People go vanishing." Autumn scrounged around in a box for the right piece of ribbon.

People go vanishing. Unbidden, the sounds of African drums and the red trailer came to mind. Every peculiar notion of an explanation of what might have happened that night only left her more unsure. Maybe her mind had been playing tricks on her. "There a lot of accidents in this carnival?"

The needle paused in Autumn's dainty fingers. "You can either go back to scrubbing toilets and toiling away for another mean old witch, or you can see the world and get three squares. Up to you." She gave Liza a glare before she and the needle went on about their work.

A nasty bump in the road sent Autumn's box tumbling to the floor. She banged on the front of the trailer as she stood. "Dammit, Jamey. Watch your driving." She sank to the floor to collect her things. Mico leaped down to help, gathering pearls and stones in his little hands. Liza joined them.

"How long you been . . ."

"A working girl?" Autumn glanced at her sideways.

Liza huffed. "Before you assumed I'd have a problem with you, I was going to ask how long you been with Bacchanal."

"Why, thank you." Autumn smiled down at Mico as he handed her a glittery sequin. She turned to Liza, gave her a *touché* look, and said, "On about a year now. Beats the streets, let me tell you. I got a trailer, food, respect. And those men I perform for need me. I make their day a little easier. What's so wrong about that?"

Though Liza could think of more than a few things that were wrong with that, maybe they were only wrong as far as she would consider something like that for herself. People had looked down on her for scrubbing toilets for Mrs. Shippen. Despite herself, her heart constricted.

Maybe, sensing Liza's own escape, the old woman had taken a good long look at her own life and found it wholly unsatisfactory. She guessed that Mrs. Shippen must have decided to leave it all behind. Shaking herself out of her reverie, she met Autumn's accusing eyes.

"Not a thing," she said. "Not a thing."

~

As the carnival set up on a grassy knoll outside the city of Lake Charles the next morning, Clay knocked on the trailer door. Liza watched curiously as Autumn took a moment to straighten her hair before she opened the door, letting in a stream of hazy white light. Even the dust bunnies that were illuminated seemed to drag, weighed down by the humidity.

"Why, Mr. Kennel, to what do we owe the pleasure of this visit on this cool, breezy Louisiana morn?"

Clay gave Liza a curt nod that she returned. "You got a spot of tea to go along with all them flowery words of yours?"

Autumn flounced down on her bunk opposite Liza. "You and Mabel have conspired to not let a girl get a good cup of tea around here. Always coffee, black coffee. How American."

"Hell," Clay said. "You weren't over there in London but for a hot minute. You're as American as I am."

"And you're uncultivated," Autumn said.

"You ready to get started?" Clay turned all business when he spoke to Liza. "I can walk you over to the animal tent, maybe hash over a few ideas I got."

"Lead the way." Liza scooped up Mico and waved goodbye to Autumn, closing the door behind her as she trotted down the steps. Startlingly clear daylight stretched over the carnival grounds like a delicate second skin, shutting out any sensation of the outside world. The place had something akin to a heartbeat, a rhythmic cadence all its own. An undercurrent of voices, tools clanging, and fleet footsteps.

They strolled deeper into the heart of the carnival tents. "Now you know that pole is too far from center," Clay called to a worker. "Don't have the sense I taught them."

"I was thinking about my act," Liza broke in. "I've got a good sense of the animals, but this stage in our relationship is critical. An ample bonding period is what's essential, and I don't dare rush it."

Clay looked at her as if she had spoken French. "What kind of time you talking about? Listen, I'm paying you."

"I was under the impression that I'd be paying myself. You know, what I earn from my show." Liza couldn't help herself and wished she could bring back the words. Still, for some reason she trusted Clay and felt that he was the type you could speak your mind to plainly.

"Don't get smart, or I'll bounce your butt right back to that swamp sinkhole where I found you."

She couldn't bring herself to say she was sorry. "Just you wait and see what I come up with—after the bonding, of course. The customers will love it."

"Don't get too fancy," Clay said, electing not to press her on what constituted an ample bonding time. "And not too short, but not too long either. We run in several groups a night. Charge a nickel a head. You keep your take, minus expenses, you know: management's cut, electricity, a little something to your pitchman, and other incidentals. If you got a good show, though, you'll make a good buck."

As they reached the animal tent, out stepped the man she'd caught a glimpse of during her earlier visit with Hope. Up close, he had burnished skin, a smile missing a front tooth, and cudgels for hands. "This here's Uly. Picked his ugly butt up all the way down in Panama. He takes care of the animals. Uly, show the little lady here around." With that, Clay stepped aside.

"You the lady that talks to animals?" Uly appraised Liza, all skeptical, narrowed eyes. His accent was one she hadn't heard before; "animals" became "ah-nee-mals."

"More or less." Liza hadn't finished the cup of coffee she'd had with breakfast, but that question was so full of expectation, all at once, that her bladder became uncomfortably full. She squirmed past the man into the tent, where the animals sat in their cages: two large metal contraptions lined up side by side. Straw littered the bottom of each cage but had been spread around the tent too. A trough of fresh water sat in one corner of the tent, but each cage also had a smaller bowl of water. One cage was large enough for a few feet of walking space and contained a shallow pool that looked like an overlarge bucket. The animals eyed her warily, and Mico emerged from her pocket, climbed up her arm, and took his usual spot on her shoulder.

Uly tossed a thumb at the first cage. "This is Ikaki—"

"Yes, the tortoise."

"The expert is not so expert after all. It's a turtle." Uly beamed.

Liza resisted the urge to correct the man for all of a few seconds. "I communicate with animals. How you make the leap that I can identify every species on sight is apparently outside my range of understanding."

Uly stiffened, the smug smile falling from his face. Clay chuckled but managed to keep his features stony—an impressive feat.

Liza tilted her head in disbelief. People would spend money on the silliest things. Even Mico chuckled in his own weird series of chirps. They moved down the line.

"And next here, we have our star. From what I hear, one of the last on earth: the Tasmanian tiger. A high-strung, temperamental little thing, if you ask me."

Liza bent down and stared at the animal. She wondered if it was a fake. But the long snout, the stripes, the tail, the size—it was all right. She'd only read about the legend, but to see one in person . . .

"Sabina," Uly said.

"Huh?" Liza straightened.

"Her name. It's Sabina."

"I need some time alone." Liza dismissed the handler. "That'll be all."

Uly fumed. Probably thinking, *How dare this girl wave me off like I'm a nobody? Who does she think she is?* But when Liza turned to settle her impassive gaze on him, he turned and stormed out. Clay, though, stayed put.

"Well, go on." He made a spinning motion with his hand. "Let's see a little demonstration."

Liza fidgeted under his expectant gaze—hair smoothed, shirt adjusted at the waist, where it all of a sudden chafed.

Clay only stared harder. "You waitin' on a special invite?"

Liza knelt in front of the cages and formed an image, something she could send to them both. An introduction. An offering. Sabina and Ikaki watched her as if in anticipation. Ikaki crept forward while Sabina stayed put, unblinking.

The image in her mind dissolved, unsent. "I'm . . . they're not ready yet."

Liza managed not to bolt from the tent, which would have made her look even more incompetent. "I'll know when the time is right." She turned to the animals. "They'll let me know."

She left Clay where he stood gaping at her and strolled outside, the picture of composure. She wilted as soon as she was out of sight and steeled herself for what she had to do.

All she could find and trap easily was a grasshopper, which was actually fine with her because if things went badly again, the guilt wouldn't consume her so. The casual glance over her shoulder was forced, but anyone watching wouldn't have taken special note of what she was doing. She crossed her fingers and began.

Minutes later, the grasshopper lay on its side, unmoving.

When Liza was a child, she believed that her tears held a power that might bring dead creatures back to life. But it had never worked, and this time was no different.

CHAPTER TEN

ISHE'S STORY

Ishe Okoye was one of the special ones, one of *hers*. Ahiku had recruited him for her carnival personally. He had been little more than a wandering ghost, driven by a heavy, grieving sadness. His firstborn, Achan, was a girl who, the first day she smiled a toothless grin at her father, had won his heart in such a way that even the sun no longer held sway over him.

His daughter had lain dying on a pallet, his wife, Talia, fretting over her, when he'd made the fateful decision to seek out the help of the witch doctor. The healer in his own community had been unable to help their daughter. The illness, marked by fever and, judging from the child's soul-searing shrieks, racking pain, remained unaffected by his herbs and mumbled prayers. Talia had pleaded with Ishe not to go; his father had called him a fool. Told him that if he lost this child, she would be duly mourned, but another would soon take her place. The witch doctor's aid came with a cost too great.

Ishe ignored the warnings and set off to find the one person whom people had told him not to seek. He walked the well-worn path out of his village, blanketed on both sides by tall grasses, followed by the eyes of the animals that lurked there. His target, a mountainous outcropping, lay ahead. It was a path known by everyone but sought by few. He didn't know what he'd need, but he'd taken a lock of his daughter's hair, a piece of her clothing, and the sweat-soaked cloth that he used to mop at her smooth, round little face.

The sun was beginning to crest over the mountain, bathing the savanna in henna and gold. At the base of the mountain, Ishe used his walking stick to balance himself as he climbed. The way was steep but not treacherous. At a rise, a full hour later, he came to the cave, but whether it was natural or unnatural, he did not know. A figure stood at the opening and beckoned him inside.

The man he met looked like a skeleton wrapped in the ashen skin of a human being who had seen too many years. Dressed in a flowing, long robe the color of dried grass, a satchel tied in a rope at his hip. Eyes that were covered in a white film but still somehow able to see. His hair was knotted in gigantic roped tangles that swept down his back and brushed at the earth. The hair looked to weigh more than the man's collection of bones.

As soon as Ishe stepped into the cave mouth, it was as though all light from outside was blocked. He blinked, his eyes struggling to adjust. Candles, some tilted in melting wax, dominated a space that was no more than three arm lengths wide. Thin trickles of water flowed down the sparkling stone walls to form depressions in the otherwise smooth surface of the rock, a trail of acidic tears.

He dared another step, wincing at a crunching sound beneath his feet, and he looked down to discover that the cave floor was littered with bones, human and animal alike. Ishe barely maintained control of his bowels at the sight. The doctor's art was a dark one—a witch, he was called by some, an instrument of the afterlife by others.

The witch doctor laughed at the things Ishe had brought with him. "The spirits don't need these trinkets; save them for that fool in your village. The spirits know all. They are with us every day. You, Ishe Okoye, come seeking relief for your mewling infant. Sit, I will consult with my spirit-god."

"I would give my life for hers," Ishe said.

"You may have to give more than that." The witch doctor pulled a pinch of powder from his pouch and tossed it into the circle of rocks that sat between them, and a small fire erupted. Blue-orange flames sparked high and settled into a low roll. The man began to chant, swaying to and fro. The name "Ahiku" was sprinkled throughout the chant. And from the fire, a dark vapor emerged. One slender tendril wafted up, grew, expanded. A smoky head formed atop a neck; arms stretched out from what was a thin torso. Stumps became legs as the figure drifted away from the fire.

Ishe's eyes bulged, his mouth hung open, and he battled the urge to bolt back down the mountain. A cold sweat trickled down his back. A sick smile spread across the witch doctor's face as his chanting ended.

A woman in traditional Nigerian dress stood before him. A multicolored wrap draped her body, most of her hair hidden beneath a matching *gele*. Her face was perfectly round, her eyes bright above sculpted ebony cheekbones. Ishe admonished himself for noticing that she was a shapely woman—spirit. When she smiled, a dark cloud seemed to smother the candlelight.

The witch doctor lay prostrate at the woman's feet. She spared him a cursory glance and turned to Ishe.

"You know what I am?" The demon's voice was like clear marbles tumbling down a pristine waterfall.

Ishe's insides turned to pounded yam. Could he get up and run? Could he thank the demon spirit for her time and say that he'd changed his mind, that he had climbed the wrong mountain and was looking for another spirit instead?

"Ah, you do." The demon smiled when Ishe couldn't bring himself to answer. "The white people and their strange religion make some of our people forget me, forget all the spirits. This . . . is a mistake. Don't you think?"

Ishe could only blink.

"The underworld tells me you have a sick daughter. She is infected with the spirit of one of your ancestors taken across the ocean. A most angry soul. I can make this spirit go away, if you are willing to provide a gift to another spirit in exchange."

The mention of his daughter both frightened and emboldened Ishe. "Name your price, demon."

The demon woman's eyes flashed.

"A man of courage," she said, gliding forward and forcing Ishe to crane his neck to look up to her. "One of my spirit brothers has succumbed to the call to walk the earth again; his time of rest is over. You must willingly accept this spirit, to live alongside your own. I will call on you and this spirit one day. You must heed this call, or your daughter's life will be forfeit. You will be released from this contract at the time of your death. When that death is, is wholly dependent upon you."

Ishe didn't hesitate. "So be it."

Ahiku drifted close, an incantation in the language of the dead flowing from her lips. A wisp, translucent in the candlelight, quivered into being less than a pace away from him. She held out her hand and blew what looked like dried clay toward the being, and it surged forward and *into* Ishe's body.

It was as if his body had shed a dead outer layer of skin. Every slack muscle, the unhearing right ear, the spot at the crown of his head where his hair thinned—it all tingled with new life. Fresh blood rippled through his veins; his heart beat faster, stronger. He smelled food cooking from what must have been miles away. Adrenaline surged as he pictured himself, a man, running through his land as if hunting unseen prey. An endless hunger drove him on.

Ishe was a desperate father. He had no idea what he had agreed to, nor the nature of the spirit that was settling in with his own. And much later, when the female demon did call on him, a resigned Ishe bade his wife, daughter, and the son who had completed their family goodbye and joined her minstrel show across the ocean.

"There is no natural reason a place should still be this hot at this time of year," Hope said as she and Liza strolled around the bustling midway. "I don't know how you can be used to it."

Liza blew at the cup of coffee in her hands, trying to cool it off. "Who says I am?"

"I don't suppose Pensacola was any better?"

"Why do you northerners take that haughty tone about the south all the time?" Liza asked. She sipped at her coffee, burned her lip, and winced. "I believe Baltimore also knows a summer season."

Hope looked over at her. "What tone? I didn't take no tone. Askin' questions is all. And why do you take that educated tone when somebody gets your hackles up?"

It was Liza's turn to look at Hope. "I do not."

"You sure as cotton do."

"What did you say?" Liza put her hands on her hips.

"I . . . I said . . . Don't you try to twist my words, Eliza Meeks. And yeah, us poor colored folk did get our hands on a book or two up north, but we don't have to go waving it around in folks' face to prove something don't need provin', 'specially"—Hope gestured at their surroundings, dragging a finger through the air—"in this—this goddamned traveling freak show."

Before Liza could form a response, Clay approached, the picture of calm chaos. "Ms. Child." He tipped his hat at Hope. "Animal tamer, I need—"

"You call me by my given name," Liza broke in. "Or I'll figure you ain't talking to me."

Hope grinned, did a mock curtsy, and walked off. Clay turned bright red.

"Go help the game runners get set up," Clay said, not calling her by any name. "Start out with Ishe. He runs the milk-bottle game near the front gate. And I want to see what progress you've made with your animal show tomorrow."

He didn't stay for an answer, and Liza shot daggers at his retreating back.

"I've been here all of five minutes, and he wants progress," Liza muttered. Mico stuck his head out of her pocket to join in with his own chitter. She wove through the crowd, stumbled upon Jamey hauling tent poles for one of the shows. They met eyes for a moment, lingered, then looked away.

She wound her way around the horseshoe-shaped midway to the coveted third spot on the right side of the entrance. The milk-bottle game had a square tent set up with one pole in the middle and smaller posts in each corner. The tent flaps were pulled back with rope. A long table covered in a white cloth sat at the front of the tent. Another table behind the first held milk-bottle pyramids. A man stood in front of the set, turning this way and that, reshaping the bottles in a pattern that Liza couldn't understand. It was the man she'd seen that first day, the one she'd tossed the stuffed animal to.

He turned suddenly. "What you standing there gaping at me for?"

She froze. That pair of wide-set, dark eyes was as deep as a thousand-line poem. Eyes that seemed to size up the whole world between blinks.

She inhaled and exhaled, annoyed at his tone and enchanted by a facial constitution that was downright unfair. "A big difference between gaping and looking. I'd think somebody who worked in a carnival would know that."

Mico had scurried down her arm and now sat on the table eyeing Ishe, turning his head at an inquisitive angle. Ishe looked from the little monkey to its owner. Mico sent Liza an image of a howling dog. *What is he going on about?*

"I'm not one of these sideshow freaks, and best mind your manners," Ishe said.

"Well, I guess I *am* one of the said 'sideshow freaks.'" Liza couldn't stop herself. "Look, let's start over. I'm Liza, and Clay says you need some help."

Ishe stared at her a moment, but Liza never blinked. "Get that thing off my table before he soils it, and come on around back."

Mico wasn't quite sure what the human had said but seemed to sense it was directed at him, and the man was none too flattering. He screeched his outrage, and despite herself, Liza laughed, scooped him up, and dropped him in her pocket.

With that settled, Liza's curiosity took over. "Show me how this game works."

"You see." Ishe held a milk bottle in his large hands. "The pyramid is simple. Two bottles on bottom, one on the top. You need to slide one of the ones on the bottom forward a little bit, like this." He took the bottle in his hand and set it next to the one on the table, but he moved it forward ever so slightly. "And put the last one on top. This way, the mark may knock off one, two if he's real lucky—but no way, almost never, gets all three."

"But that's cheating." Liza looked up at Ishe with no accusation in her eye, only stating a fact, while trying to ignore how beautiful he was.

"So it is." Ishe moved over to set up the next pyramid. "Let me tell you something about the carnival business. There *ain't* no business if the marks win too much. We'd go broke inside a month. You, me, everybody here that need this job in one way or another, we all back on the street, jail . . ." He paused, looking introspective. "Or worse. Every now and again, you let somebody win. But we got to make the profit. That way, everybody happy. Get it?"

Liza was no fool. She herself would be running around doing Mrs. Shippen's bidding right now if not for the carnival. She winced, remembering her landlady's disappearance back in Baton Rouge. "I get it."

Ishe finished setting up another two pyramids and gestured to the last spot at the end of the table. "Now, you do that one."

◇

That night, the carnival opened in Lake Charles. Clay had paid off the local sheriff, and luckily there was no mayor with his hand out this time. Not only had the right to perform for a week been secured, but also a good helping of supplies from the general store.

Though Liza was still supposed to help out and be a runner when needed, she resolved to check in with Ishe. Not that he'd asked for her help outright, but just in case. Later, she wanted to observe Sabina and Ikaki, how the customers treated the animals and, more importantly, how the animals felt about the people coming through. Hopefully she'd pick up something that would help her put together a show that didn't risk their lives.

For such a small town, the turnout was huge. Liza found herself unexpectedly wound up, for in every child's face, her hopes of finding Twiggy were briskly raised and dashed. A swampy-tinged tide of revelers swarmed the midway. Pulsating swing music escorted the impenetrable stream, drawn as if on an invisible string between them and the trail of prancing and preening carnival performers. Castoffs gained and lost at each moneymaking stop along the way: games, rides, aromatic concession stands.

In the animal tent, a white family of three muddled through. The man, sour faced and short, wore a pair of glasses that looked like they were barely able to rest on such a tiny nose. The woman was a few inches taller than him but had the demeanor of a mouse; she wouldn't raise her eyes and said nothing to the boy constantly yanking and pulling at her hand.

"What do we have here?" the man said, even though he'd seen the banner out front proclaiming the "World's Last Remaining Tasmanian Tiger," alongside the African turtle. He turned to Liza and, obviously unsatisfied, looked at Uly, who was standing behind her.

"This some kinda trick?"

"No, sir," Uly said.

"She's a Tasmanian tiger, all the way from Australia," Liza broke in. "Her name is Sabina."

Both men glared at Liza. The woman stared at her feet. Liza'd seen that look before: How dare she, a woman, open her mouth?

"Don't you have some muck to go clean out or something?" the man growled.

Liza threw a thumb over her shoulder. "That's his job."

Uly was about to charge in on Liza when they both noticed the boy was tossing rocks with great precision at Ikaki. Uly was about to give the boy a good wallop when his father launched himself onto the carnie's back. The woman inhaled sharply but stayed rooted in place in front of Sabina's cage.

Liza gasped when Sabina hurled an image at her: Sabina gnawing the hem of the woman's dress. Before Liza could form a countering image, the tiger acted, poking her snout through the bars and clamping down on the woman's dress, careful not to nick her legs. As expected, the wife produced a bloodcurdling scream, and the boy ran over and tried to pull his mother away from Sabina.

Uly and the man forgot their fight. "What the . . . ," the man stammered. "Get it off her, get it off!"

"Liza," Uly said quietly.

The man turned between them and regarded Sabina, who watched Liza intently, growling deeply in her throat.

Liza hesitated. All eyes bored into her as fear wormed through layers and layers of doubt. The man balled up his fists, poised for another fight, while Liza conjured and fumbled one wrong comeback after another like an amateurish juggler. *Wait.* Hadn't Sabina sent the first image?

Liza steadied herself and sent Sabina the message to back off. She bent to nuzzle the tiger's neck, but the animal backed away from her and, despite everything, still refused to send a return image. A puzzle she had yet to piece together. She looked up at the gaping family.

"Freaks." The man spat in the corner and hustled his family away from the tent.

Uly stormed off muttering. And Liza danced around the tent celebrating.

~

Liza wondered whether the foreign sense of calm, the comfort of a new routine, was what somebody would call happiness. As the next-to-last day of the carnival wound down, she contemplated her newfound luck. She'd been with the animals every night, and they'd had no more incidents with customers mistreating them. And she'd settled nicely into her new trailer. Her stomach and Mico welcomed the well-cooked meals Mabel provided. Soon they'd be off to another city, one that she'd actually suggested to Clay.

Liza made sure Uly fed and cared for the animals before she wandered off to see where she could be of assistance. Although she wanted to earn her keep, she was also growing attached to the tiger and turtle. Theirs was a budding rapport formed by companionable silences and expressive gazes that spoke more than words. If she wasn't mistaken, the air about the tent became charged in a positive fashion when she entered. The misgivings she'd felt, the weirdness she suspected lurked beneath the carnival's surface, were all melting away.

Jamey ran toward her, waving his hands, frantic. She turned to see if he was looking at somebody else. "You gotta come quick. Clay . . . we got a problem," Jamey huffed. He grabbed Liza by the wrist and dragged her off.

As they neared Clay, he strode toward them. He was the picture of outward calm as usual, but he couldn't mask the trembling in his voice. Her boss was normally as coolheaded as they came, so seeing him rattled set Liza's teeth on edge. "What's going on?"

"We got us a situation." Clay struggled for the right words. "It's Ishe. He's run off again."

Run off? Liza's panicked glance flowed between Jamey, who could barely look at her, and Clay, who—for the first time since she'd met him—seemed to be tongue tied. This couldn't be good. She waited.

"I know he's probably in town somewhere. We gotta find him before . . ."

Before what? What the hell was going on? "And why are you asking me?" Liza asked. She was a woman, and a Negro one at that. She wouldn't want to risk going into town at night. Come to think of it, Jamey wasn't the best one to go either.

"He turns," Clay said, as if that answered everything.

Liza cocked her head. "And that means what?"

"Dammit," Clay said. "I ain't got the time. Jamey, get a couple of the boys, meet us at the truck—quick now."

Liza was poised to say she wasn't going anywhere until he told her what was going on, but her curiosity clamped down on the words with a vise grip.

Jamey gathered a number of white carnies, and they piled into the back of the truck with netting, billy clubs, and tear gas. Clay and Liza rode in the cab. They rattled down the road, and a pair of headlights approached. "Put your head down," Clay said. "Last thing I need is a race war with the locals."

Liza complied, and in the back of the cab, so did Jamey. The folks in the oncoming car waved as they passed.

They rounded a corner into town, parked the car, and got out.

"Liza, Jamey, Jones, you stay with me," Clay said. "The rest of you, hit the usual spots, and come grab us if you see him."

Clay distributed flashlights, and both teams set out. Liza followed, keeping to the shadows, lurking around corners as they conducted the search.

Finally, a sharp whistle called Clay and Liza over. A carnie was standing pale faced at the end of an alley, pointing. The group huddled together and peered down the alley. Dim moonlight illuminated the outlines of two figures. One lay unmoving on the ground; the other hovered above it.

"Go get the others," Clay whispered to the carnie. "And bring the truck on around." He turned to Liza. "Now don't go pestering me with a bunch of questions. That there is Ishe, and I need you to talk to him, get him to come out of it."

Liz craned her neck. "What are you talking about? What's stopping you from calling him?"

"Woman, what did I say? Come on." They eased down the alleyway. "You better get to talkin'—he can be unpredictable when he's like this. Done lost one too many men trying to bring him in."

Liza didn't understand, but in her mind, an image coalesced. A ripple on a pond, a water lily floating atop. A field of green as far as the eye could see, sunlight glinting off the blades of grass, where she and Ishe sat together on a blanket loaded with the makings of a picnic.

The standing figure stopped, looked up. A wedge of moonlight fell across its face before a cloud blotted it out.

Liza blanched. "What the . . ."

Clay shined the light on the creature. It walked toward them on two legs and had a mane of spotted hair around its face and the snout of a hyena; saliva and blood dripped from its maw. Chunks of human flesh were wedged between the teeth and trickling down the hairy chest. The arms and feet were those of a man-size dog.

The creature sank to its knees as the truck pulled up. "Come on!" Jamey yelled from the back.

"Hush up!" Clay said. He eased around the creature, who had fallen to the ground in silent convulsions. The other shape on the ground turned out to be that of a very dead older man. Clay spun around. "Goddammit, Ishe, hurry up!"

Liza approached the creature, lowered herself to the ground, and tentatively stuck out a hand.

"Wait, you don't know—" Clay called out, but her hand landed on the creature's head. Her insides had turned to liquid, but her heart raced with the undeniable thrill of it all.

Ishe, human again and naked, curled into a ball. He looked at Liza with the satiated but guilty eyes of a hyena.

CHAPTER ELEVEN

THE TIDE RISES, THE TIDE FALLS

It was the balloons that had drawn him in. John-Avery would never own up to it, but it was his childhood self's want of another dang-blasted balloon that had coaxed him through the carnival gates. He'd had one before, sure enough. A blue one, tied to his wrist by a stranger who'd taken pity on the scruffy kid gawking outside another carnival long past.

He'd had one dusty, bare foot on his front step when the other boys had wrestled him to the ground and torn the ribbon that fastened his prize to his wrist. He hadn't cried out to his folks inside as they kicked and beat him, only watched through tears as that blue balloon sailed off into the night sky.

But soon he'd have a baby boy or girl of his own, and such nonsense was behind him. With Ophelia at home, the baby due any time now, the midwife had shooed him away. And though he'd set out for an evening stroll, he'd wound up taking in the last night of the carnival. *Bacchanal.*

He moseyed around, hands shoved deep in his trouser pockets, sly glances at the sights rather than looking at anything straight on, as was his nature. A half-eaten candy apple lay in his path. A fly landed on it, but before it could stake a claim, a trail of ants had swarmed the apple, lickety-split. The fly didn't give up its stake right off, but directly that apple was overrun, and the fly let go of its trophy.

John-Avery made his way on around the bend and paused at the darts game just as a fella he recognized from town won. The man threw his fists in the air and strutted around like a peacock, then placed a doll in a little girl's outstretched hands. *That's it.* He'd win a teddy bear for the baby. But which game? Truth be told, he was the bookish sort. Not particularly skilled at shooting, nor was he what you'd call a strong fella. He lowered his gaze and shuffled toward the exit. *Ding.* The sound came from another game; he frowned at the words **HIGH STRIKER** printed in large block letters on a wooden sign. The man running the game had the biggest arms he ever did see.

And right there on a shelf with all the other prizes was a teddy bear with a snazzy red ribbon tied around its neck, Ophelia's favorite color. He inched forward and watched as, one by one, men more strapping than him failed to ring that bell. The big man grinned as the last losing customer skulked off; he then scanned the crowd and locked eyes with John-Avery. He squirmed and backed away, but the man leaped down from the platform and marched right up to him with a good-natured smile.

"Come," he said. "You, my friend, are next."

John-Avery tried to pull away, but the man had clamped a bear claw of a hand around his arm and didn't wait for an answer before dragging him up on the stage. He was sweating in earnest now. The man handed him the hammer, which he promptly dropped, just hopping out of the way in time for it to not smash his toe. The crowd chuckled and jeered.

"Try again," the big man encouraged.

John-Avery was ready to turn tail and bolt, see if there was a think-ing man's game somewhere, but the teddy bear . . . it, it turned in his direction. His mouth was still hanging open when the big man shoved the hammer in his hands again. But this time, when that fella's hand brushed his, a spark of some sort stung John-Avery. That hammer felt lighter than the blanket he'd just draped in his baby's crib. He swore before his maker he didn't do a thing, but the hammer swung up and came down. *Ding*. The puck nearly blew that bell clean off.

Then the teddy bear was in his hands, warm, like a living thing. It nuzzled into his chest. John-Avery left the carnival. As he neared home, he smiled at the unmistakable sound of a baby's cry and the curious sight of a blue balloon tied to his porch.

~

For most of her life, Liza had been an oddity—*the* oddity. The carnival had changed all that. She was in the midst of a band of folks far stranger than herself. But what she'd seen last night was the strangest of them all. Ishe was as much a man as he was some kind of doglike creature. She'd grown up hearing all sorts of folklore and had read about enough weirdness in her treasured magazines, but never had she seen anything like him. The question was—and she had every intention of finding out the answer—how had he come to be the way he was?

She hadn't seen him since, but repulsed or not, she'd make it a point to seek him out.

She buried herself in an old issue of *Astounding Stories*, which featured a gigantic sea creature with a marked taste for human meat. Mico sat beside her, eyes intent on the page, as if he, too, were enjoying the read. The magazine was yellowed, a few pages torn. It was a luxury she couldn't afford while she lived at the boardinghouse, but she'd kept every one that Mrs. Margaret had bought for her, reading them over and over again.

A shuffle of feet outside the trailer got her attention. She looked up and tilted her head, Mico mirroring her movement.

A hand banged on the side of the trailer; a hushed male voice she didn't recognize drifted up through the window. "Might wanna check on that Tasmanian. Seem old Uly is having a time of it with her."

"Huh?" Liza said, swinging her sturdy legs over the side of the bunk. Uly tried to care for the animals—she couldn't argue that—but he had no real way with them. She snatched the rag from her head, revealing a mass of thick black hair that she secured and tied with a strip of cloth. She placed the serial carefully back into the bottom drawer on top of a stack of others.

"What's all the fuss about?" Autumn called out and turned over, drawing a pillow over her head. Liza ignored her as she pulled on a pair of trousers and slipped her feet into her only pair of shoes. With Mico in tow, she pulled the door closed behind her.

Liza advanced through the series of trailers and lounging carnies, catching snatches of conversation and drifting cigarette smoke as she went. On the way, Hope fell in step beside her, still dressed in her fortune-teller's garb.

"Hear our little star is kicking up a fuss something terrible in there."

Liza barreled into the tent, where the prized Tasmanian tiger sat in the corner baring her sizable teeth. Liza gave Uly the evil eye and then opened her mouth to tear into him, but he spoke first.

"I don't want to hear it, Liza," Uly said. He was all hard faced and bull nosed, panting with a belt wrapped around his fist. "That bastard has bit me for the last time."

Liza moved in front of the cage, putting herself between Uly and the tiger. She was a full head shorter than the animal handler but didn't flinch when she chastised him. "This is the last time I'll tell you not to mess with my animals." She wondered when they'd gone from being the carnival's animals to hers. It was now, at this very moment. She glared at him, turned her back, and bent down in front of the cage. Mico used her hair like jungle vines, swinging around to the back of her neck, eyeing Sabina cautiously.

"Why, I oughta . . ." Uly made to raise his hand against Liza.

"You oughta pipe down," Hope said, coming up behind him, smiling. Already, she and Liza were friends of a sort. Her husband,

Bombardier, held himself up at the corner of the tent. He didn't say anything and didn't have to.

The women soldiers, always looking for a good scuffle, found their way to the tent, like lionesses sniffing out their prey.

"I did not like this new girl the moment Clay brought her to us," Zinsa said, always the instigator.

"I see two witches." Bombardier made a show of craning his neck to look behind the women. He turned back to his wife and hunched, his shoulders massive. "But I do not see their broomsticks." He snapped his fingers. "Ah, now I see. Efe rode in on her horse's back."

"I have no need for witchcraft to handle a clumsy elephant with the brain of a gnat," Efe said.

The trio erupted into a shouting match that drew a small crowd. Hope launched herself between them, arms outstretched, trying unsuccessfully to calm them all down. Bombardier wrapped his hands around her waist, hoisted her up, and set her down behind him as if she weighed the tiniest fraction of her no doubt 150 pounds.

Meanwhile, Liza opened the cage, and the tiger trotted out, licked her hand, and sat beside her. She was still mute, even after the incident with the customer the other night, but at least she remained agreeable enough to Liza's presence.

The bickering stopped in the middle of the insults as all eyes snapped onto the unnerving sight of an uncaged Tasmanian tiger. Liza didn't dare try to touch her again and turned back to Uly. "What did you feed her?"

"Ain't no better or worse than what we eat," Uly huffed. "She get what I get my hands on the easiest. I don't have time to be separating out food for one or the other."

"Clay said she gets fresh meat," Liza said. The Tasmanian had apparently survived at times on carnival food scraps. She hadn't gone hungry, but Clay had made it clear it wasn't exactly her preferred meal. Liza gestured toward the belt still in Uly's hand. "And if you hit her—"

"That animal bit—"

"That's why she bit you," Liza said, cutting him off.

"Did she also tell you what the weather gonna be in the next town?" Uly said.

Liza didn't let on that the tiger hadn't said one word to her. "Don't be jealous, Uly. You got your gifts . . ." She looked around at the muck in the tent. "And I got mine."

Uly's brown eyes turned mean. He stomped out of the tent. Zinsa and Efe, sensing the lost opportunity for a fight, walked off after him, sparing Bombardier one final dirty look.

Again, Liza bent to Sabina, reached out a tentative hand. The animal didn't pull away this time, allowed her to smooth her striped coat. Mico screeched and Sabina growled as the two eyed each other.

"Now, you two cut that out," Liza said. "Let bygones be bygones. Mico, come down from there." The little monkey skittered down her arm and stood in front of Sabina, so small he could fit between the bars of her cage. Sabina, for her part, tried to seem unaffected. Mico stood there, looking between Liza and the tiger.

"I don't have all night," Liza said. "Make up now—go on."

Sabina turned her head and eyed Mico. She lowered her nose for a sniff, and as she did, Mico reached out and swiped her on the nose and then darted back up Liza's arm. Sabina snarled.

"Now, you stop it right now."

Liza directed Sabina back into the cage and closed the door. The tiger lowered her head and retreated to a neutral corner of the cage. "I'm tired, and I'm not dealing with you two tonight."

As she left the tent, Hope fell in beside her. Bombardier followed at a discreet distance. Carnival tents and rides were unassembled, their run in Lake Charles at an end.

"I caught Clay carrying something in a sack from the red trailer," Liza said.

Hope turned to look at her as they walked. The commotion over, the other carnies had retreated to their respective sleeping spots; some were under trailers or wagons, while those who ran a show and pulled in some money had bunks in shared trailers. The night was still—too quiet. Few stars dotted the sky.

"Remember when I said you weren't supposed to ask about what goes on in the red trailer?"

Liza gave her the side-eye. "Don't act like you ain't the least bit curious."

"Did you get a glimpse of what he was carrying?"

"Not a chance," Liza said. "But I'm going to find out."

"Stay out of it," Hope said without much conviction. Liza wondered at her friend's tone. "I'd rather collect my pay and not worry about it."

"Suit yourself."

"I'll see ya in the morning."

CHAPTER TWELVE

The Clues Are Evident

"You'd be in the way." Jamey pushed past the animal tamer. She was angling to go along with him and Clay on the short ride into Houston, where they were headed to ask about setting up for a carnival run. Those times he got to slip away from the carnival and be a man were his. *His.* Clay understood that and gave him space. This girl needed to get it in her head that she couldn't tag along whenever the notion struck her. It would be like having his mother's ghost cutting her eyes over his shoulder the whole time.

"We go in, negotiate the fee, and get out," Clay added. "All I need is for some yokel to take a shine to you, and I got another fight on my hands, or somethin' worse."

It was before dawn, and but for the few stray dogs that inevitably appeared whenever they set up, things were quiet. The trailers were still sprawled out in the serpentine line in which they'd traveled and then arrived on the outskirts of sleepy Houston's Fifth Ward. Jamey was itching to steal away.

"I can take care of myself." The girl trotted forward and jumped in front of them. She was walking backward, so she didn't see the rock in the path, or the mischievous glint in Jamey's eye, before her heel connected with it. She stumbled and toppled over onto her back in a dusty thud.

"Yeah." Jamey chuckled but still could not look her in the eye—something he was sure she noticed and was glad she never made mention of. "That much is clear as a bell." Still, he stuck out a hand and hauled her to her feet.

"Truth is, I want to get a look at the place. Haven't seen it since . . ." She looked away too. "I was with my family. Long time ago."

"You don't hold no water for your kin, do ya?" Jamey asked.

Liza shifted her feet. "I got . . ." She fumbled over whatever she was about to say and picked at a ragged fingernail instead. "I got a little sister."

She took the picture of her family out of her satchel and passed it to Jamey. He studied it a minute before he handed it to Clay.

"Fine," Clay said. Jamey cut his eyes at him, but he didn't spare him a glance. "If you ain't at the truck in ten minutes, I'll reckon you had a change a heart. This is a mostly Negro town anyway, but don't go gettin' yourself into trouble. That ain't what we here for. And don't go flappin' your gums neither. Let me or Jamey do the talkin'."

Jamey huffed. He didn't need this girl nosing around after him. He was looking forward to uncovering what lay at the town's underbelly. "You sure 'bout—"

"And another thing." Clay turned serious, thrusting the photo back at Liza. "Don't go thinking we can take on any brats, even if they are your kin. Ain't even got a show set up yet. And if you don't have one soon, I'll bounce you out on your behind."

Jamey rolled his eyes. Clay was always going on about stray kids, as if stray dogs weren't more likely to attach themselves to the carnival. Especially since Liza had joined them—the dogs had doubled in number, causing all kinds of mischief by the food tent and stinking up the place with their shit. They never crossed over into the carnival, though, and they kept some of the dumber thieves and lowlifes who tried to sneak in away, so the carnies put up with them.

~

In a mirror image of the first time they'd met, Jamey, Clay, and Liza piled into the truck on their way into the small but surprisingly prosperous Fifth Ward. Jamey drove, gripping the steering wheel harder than was strictly called for, squinting against the building sunlight. He managed to chuckle as the little marmoset tumbled off the dashboard twice before settling on Liza's lap, but really he felt about as comfortable as a proper Englishwoman in a cotton field. His body seemed pulled into itself, as small as he could make it, plastered against the door. When they hit a bump in the road, his leg touched Liza's and he pulled it back as if he'd been burned.

Clay looked over at them both. "What you two all wound up about?"

Jamey shot Clay a dirty glance. Clay could be a right asshole sometimes.

Liza answered, "Ask your right hand there. I don't have the faintest idea what his problem is."

Jamey kept on driving. She annoyed him to no end, but he couldn't shake the fact that, given the chance, he'd love to be alone with her. How far would she let him go? They crested a ridge that overlooked Houston, the road smooth as they approached. Haphazardly placed but well-constructed little shotgun houses lay all along the path. They passed a fenced-in graveyard, not more than thirty paces across, with an archway entrance with a large cross on top. The graves were neat, some with fresh flowers.

Some locals were already outside tending small plots of land, sweeping dusty steps. A woman hanging sheets over a clothing line and taking great swats at them paused to wave and called out, "Good morning!"

The trio waved back and bounced along into town. Like most of the places they visited, the Fifth Ward featured a main street with smart-looking buildings: a barbershop, general and clothing stores, restaurants.

A three-story hotel was flanked by an impressive church and a movie theater. And everywhere, the people were Negro. Jamey hadn't noticed another white face besides Clay's. He snickered. The locals had built up a real nice place here, no doubt, but Aunt Queenie had the real money. And the real power: fear.

He rolled down the window and waved over a young boy of about twelve. "Mornin', son, can you tell me where I can find the local police?"

The boy looked past Jamey into the truck and eyed Liza and Clay before he answered. "Down that way a spell, next to Mrs. Beaulah's dress shop." The boy ran off like he had an important appointment to get to.

"Kids these days ain't got a bit of manners." Jamey rolled up the window and drove down the street, where he soon found the local law enforcement office and parked outside.

As they filed out of the truck stretching, Liza peered up and down the street in evident awe.

"Best if you wait here," Clay said. "Jamey and me will handle this. Don't go wandering off."

Liza made a flourish of waving them on. "I'll be right here like a good little filly."

"Come out of your mouth," Clay called over his shoulder. "Not mine."

Jamey and Clay knocked once and entered the police office as a voice welcomed them in. The space was larger than it looked from the outside. Two large, barred windows sat on either side of the doorway, benches to the right and left, where anxious friends and family had likely spent many an hour. A long counter separated the waiting area from the office space, and behind its width, according to the shiny badge on his shirt, stood the officer in charge. He was a big barrel of a man with a raised scar like a misplaced smile curving out from his right eye down to his mouth. The gray hair sprinkled throughout the black marked him a seasoned man, but the smooth charcoal skin made his age hard to pin down.

"Name's Jamey Blotter." Jamey stuck out his hand, any traces of the angst he'd felt when he was around Liza shed. "This here is Mr. Clay Kennel, owner and proprietor of the G. B. Bacchanal Carnival."

The officer shook Jamey's hand first.

"Officer Anderson," the big man said and then gestured for them to pass through the swinging gate at the far end of the counter. Jamey and Clay settled into chairs in front of the man's desk, while he sat, hands clasped together, on the edge, looking down at them. "And you'd like to set up your carnival here in our little spot?"

"That's right," Jamey said. He made it a point not to look at Clay, who sat as unobtrusively as possible, complicit in the little game they played with the law. He took the lead in a white town, Jamey the lead in Negro-run towns. The other piped in only where necessary. "Assuming we can work out a deal that suit you."

Officer Anderson rose and circled behind his desk. He removed a red handkerchief from his back pocket, shook it out with a flick of his wrist, and ran it over a framed yellow newspaper clipping hanging from the wall. In large, bold letters, the headline read: **Famed Officer Harley Anderson of Houston's Prosperous All-Negro Fifth Ward.**

Clay and Jamey exchanged a glance. The officer went on to reposition the frame, which had slanted down a little too far to the right.

Finally, Officer Anderson turned and hooked his thumbs into his belt loops and rocked back and forth on his heels as if considering a matter of national importance. After a time, he settled into his chair, slid his feet up on the desk, and leaned back. "All depends on what you gentlemen got to offer."

"We're a small show," Jamey said, commencing with his sales pitch. "Got more colored acts and workers than any other carnival in these here un-United States. Reckoned this was a show your town would want to see. We're prepared to work out a deal." He stopped short of offering a price first.

"What figure you got in mind?" The officer wouldn't let him off the hook.

"Anybody 'sides you need, uh, to be convinced on the merits of our little show?" Jamey asked. He sensed Clay's approval, but his boss's face remained impassive.

"I don't suppose there is."

Jamey leaned forward, caught himself, and eased back in the chair. He'd have to name a price, but he didn't want to seem too eager. "Would ten dollars cover the necessary licenses and such?"

"Twelve dollars sounds better to my ears, son." The officer couldn't mask the excitement on his own face. "Kick in a little something from the back end, and if your carnival folk would be good enough to spend some of their money here in town, we could waive the inspection fee."

It was time to close the deal. Jamey, proud of his negotiation, relaxed. His part was over.

"You run a hard bargain," Clay said and then rose, counting out the bills.

"And one more thing," Anderson added, pointing a finger at each man. "I know you got women of ill repute run with these kinda shows. But we got a decent town here. No full nudity and no after-the-show specials. We understand one another?"

"Yes, sir," Jamey and Clay said in unison.

"Shall we drink to it?" The officer reached into a desk drawer and pulled out a bottle of whiskey and three shot glasses.

Jamey shared a few shots and then excused himself. He had other business to see to.

He walked into a corner store to get some tobacco and took in the offerings crammed into the tight space.

"You looking or buying?" Liza asked, standing too close. Jamey silently cursed himself when he moved back a step.

"Can a man take some time to decide?" Jamey turned and ambled down an aisle. She was right behind him, probably laughing.

"Wait a minute," she said. She paused at some colorful baskets hanging on the wall. She marched up to the shop owner with a basket. "Where did you get this basket?"

"A good day to you, too, ma'am." The man hiked up his chin and his pants at the same time. The belt around his waist was already pulled tight to the last hole.

Liza exhaled, loud and all bothered-like. "Excuse my manners. A good morning to you, sir."

"What you doing traveling with him and that white man I saw earlier? I don't see no ring on your finger."

Jamey winced. Old people didn't know how to mind their own business.

Liza huffed. "I work with them, at the carnival, sir."

"Humph," the old shopkeeper said. "Young girl by yourself traveling with a carnival? That ain't no life for you. Where are your peoples? You done run off and now wanna go back home?"

Liza rubbed her forehead; Jamey tensed. "Other way around. They left me."

"And you got some sort of score to settle, that it?"

Now Jamey was getting riled. The man had no right to ask all these questions. The girl, though, was cool as they come. "Nothing like that."

The old man narrowed his eyes and, after a moment's contemplation, finally started stacking up his supplies again.

"Was a woman, quiet thing, passed through here with a man. She was your spittin' image, though."

Liza perked up. "Are they still here?"

Something in Jamey stirred. If those were her people . . . she might be inclined to go off and join them. And it hit him: he didn't want her to.

"Said they passed through," the man said, to Jamey's relief. "Traded for some supplies and moved on."

"Did they have a little girl with them?"

"Naw, they was by themselves."

"Thanks."

Jamey felt strangely unsettled as the girl with the sharp tongue he'd come to appreciate seemed to slump into herself, her sparkle gone. He gently steered her out of the shop after hastily paying for his tobacco.

When the sun hit her face, she got some of that spirited manner back. "My selfish parents abandoned me so they could traipse off and have one less mouth to feed."

Jamey didn't know what to say to that. His family had their own troubles. He led her back to the truck. Clay was waiting for them, and they piled into the truck. Not another word passed between them as they rode back to the carnival.

∼

Jamey headed back into town with a warning from Clay not to be too late. After Jamey's mama died, he'd spent time up in Harlem with his aunt Queenie off and on. Summers, holidays, a birthday every now and again.

It was more than enough time to get a taste for the good life. She was a woman with power . . . and money. He came to appreciate the things she sent him and the way folks bowed down whenever she opened her mouth.

It was with her henchmen that he'd taken his first drink and learned the game of craps. The carnival had taken him away from all that, mostly. But every once in a good while, he was drawn back.

The Fifth Ward was exactly the kind of place to get lost in. He'd gotten away long enough to have a few drinks and was three hands down in a game of poker when Clay came to drag him away. He wanted to argue but didn't. He pushed away from the table and the cards, downed the last of his drink. On the way back to the carnival, his mind wandered; he anticipated seeing the soft contours of Liza's face and remembered the warmth of the whore's bottom on his thigh while he played a winning hand.

CHAPTER THIRTEEN

Two Sides of the Coin

In Houston's Fifth Ward, the Depression had been no more than a looming, ugly storm cloud. It had gathered up steam and then billowed and buffeted. But when it came time to unleash its destruction, it tossed only a spattering of angry drops over the city and moved on, leaving most of the residents untouched.

Negro-owned businesses along Lyons Avenue largely survived, fueled in part by the opening of the Houston Ship Channel and the Southern Pacific Railroad, where many of the middle-class Negro folks worked. They served to cushion against the worst of the Depression.

A good many of the locals could be said to be prosperous. And, as Clay witnessed, fairly free with their money, both at the carnival and in town. Other than your typical scuffle or two, nobody had caused trouble. Even Officer Anderson had made an obligatory appearance, checking a safety clasp here, questioning the workings of a game there. Clay tolerated the airs, knowing full well that the man's real mission was to try and count up how much he might have coming on the back end.

What Clay could barely tolerate was that his trailer always had to be within spitting distance of Geneva's, Zinsa and Efe standing at their posts as if the British guard were moments from attacking with a full military complement.

With the coming of dusk, the carnival was ready for another night in the Fifth Ward. The first time they'd put up banners and posters in the town, some night riders had come and torn them down. But they'd put some up again and spread a few warnings, and this time the posters stood.

The barker called out his ballyhoo, enticing the building crowd with the fun that awaited them on the other side of the entrance. The midway horseshoe was all set up, the most select games on the immediate right. With few exceptions, the marks flowed in that direction first, and the games never failed to loosen their grip on their coins.

Reprieve. Clay allowed himself a self-satisfied exhalation.

~

"Zinsa, Efe!" Ahiku called from within the trailer.

They took one look around, as if to ensure anyone lying in wait couldn't attack them without warning. Zinsa followed Efe inside, where they each dropped to one knee.

"I suppose telling you not to do that anymore wouldn't change it, would it?" Ahiku sat sprawled in a lounger beneath the window to the left of the door. She would sit there, beneath the open window, the pale-yellow curtain fluttering on a cool night, a faraway look in her eyes, as if contemplating the nature of her long life.

Efe offered, "A soldier is but a tool, trained by habit, practice. To take that away would change the nature of what we are, of why you brought us here to you. Is that what you want?"

"Far be it for me to change your nature," Ahiku said. Her hair was uncovered, the radio on the small stand next to her chair tuned in to an Orson Welles show. There were things of this world that she did enjoy. The afterlife offered none of them, so living between both worlds was something she would not give up.

Ahiku cupped her hands together in front of her mouth and whispered something inaudible. "Take this." She handed Zinsa a small bone so highly polished it looked like ivory. "The Fifth Ward smells like the perfect place for my enemy to hide, do you not agree? So many of Africa's children are here." The women concurred. "This will tell you if she is here. Go."

The soldiers turned to leave, and Ahiku said, "My carnies are in need, and it seems the good Officer Anderson is the greedy type, pressing our Mr. Kennel for extra money, so that leaves it to us to teach him a few lessons. Go into town and secure supplies, expertly and discreetly."

They exchanged a glance laced with barely suppressed conflict.

"What you ask is beneath us," Efe protested.

"We are not thieves," Zinsa added.

Ahiku's eyes flashed a murderous glint; she was sick of their foot-dragging whenever she asked them to carry out a simple raid. She laughed. "You fool yourselves. Pillaging for war spoils is much the same, no?"

The pair had become hers near the end of the Second Franco-Dahomean War. Their unit had suffered a resounding defeat, their last. Hunted because they had chosen to fight and not stand aside, they had gone into hiding and called on the spirits for help. Ahiku cared little about such mundane matters of tradition and had an unflappable admiration for the women soldiers. She readily answered.

"Do you want us to stick to stores or homes?" Efe asked, but she wouldn't look at Ahiku.

"Not the businesses, besides one for staples. These people can't shop anyplace else, and those stores will be their future. Take what you must from anyplace else, deliver food to Mabel, and give everything else to Clay to distribute as he sees fit. Workers in the G. B. Bacchanal Carnival will never go without."

The women tensed. "We will not be here for protection . . . ," Zinsa began.

"I will be taking a trip to the other side," Ahiku said. "Things are arguably more dangerous there. But unless you would like to change the nature of our relationship, I'll rely on my own devices for defense in my realm."

Zinsa and Efe touched fists to palms and made a quick exit. They would get someone to drive them into town, hit as many spots as they could, load up the truck, and return like African Santas, bearing a bounty of food, fabrics, and treats.

As most of the townsfolk would be at the carnival, this provided perfect cover. They would start first with the general store. It always surprised them how shop owners sometimes left their doors unprotected. And in the rare instances when they didn't, entering was as simple as breaking a window or knocking off the often unstable door handles.

They would grab staples first: meal, flour, sugar, butter. Next they'd get treats like candy, drinks, and chips. If whiskey was available, though they hated it, they would snatch that too. Sometimes they broke into houses to get clothes. The shops had little on display, usually opting to sew and tailor to suit. Homes provided good clothes, shoes, and, often, comforts of home: new pillows, blankets, sheets.

As Ahiku had said, all in the name of supporting the army. The people they protected had changed, the carnival workers not of their homeland, but still they were their charges. With an occasional reminder, they would see what they did as a necessary part of the job and take it seriously.

Clay had given Ahiku a description of the boy, one whom he'd lured under the guise of helping out around the carnival. No matter the town, there was always an ample supply of abandoned kids. Parents would not forgo the acts that yielded such discards. No, it had become morally more acceptable to leave the children to their own devices. To perhaps copulate that night to soothe their anguished hearts, to create another child, that the cycle may continue.

Such were the complexities or, rather, the unfathomable nature of humans. Though Ahiku had been saddled with an uneasy conscience when she'd first committed her soul to the demon, it was quickly eased by the fact that her irresponsible parents had brought their deaths and hers upon themselves.

The witchcraft rumors that swirled around her own mother had begun well before she decided to birth a child in the midst of the talk. Ahiku had yet to see her tenth name day before the village elders came for her reckless parents, leaving her outcast. Grief stole her innocence but gifted her a plan. Slinking back into the compound under the cover of night was easy enough, setting fire to the chief's hut more fretful. She hadn't run away but had sat nearby, flames licking at her back. When they came for her, she'd stood and walked, slowly at first, then set off at a trot into the flames and the viperous arms of a demonic dignitary.

Her gift from the afterlife was invisibility. Like angels, demons walked the earth unseen, unless they chose to reveal themselves. Given to the dramatic, she was indeed an Orson Welles fan, so rather than the mundane act of opening the door and simply walking down the stairs, Ahiku dissolved into black smoke and propelled herself through the open window. Outside, she materialized into her human form.

It was a form she'd taken from a woman in New Orleans, one of the few times she'd had to consume an adult soul—a wholly dissatisfactory endeavor. Adults left a horrible taste in her mouth, slithering around in her mind and stomach, fighting and clinging to life long after it was over. This was before the carnival, before Clay and her cover story, with her, in afterlife terms, still a newly dead demon, trying to find her way after Queenie—the illustrious Madame Stephanie St. Clair—had unleashed her on American soil.

She had wandered the streets of the French Quarter, blindly hunting. Needing to feed, she'd snatched at a child, but its mother had fought tooth and claw. Ahiku had vanquished the woman in front of her shrieking child and had so liked the look of her that she'd continued to use the form, and the woman's name, ever since.

But someone powerful *had* been there as well and had spirited the child away as Ahiku unleashed her nascent power at her retreating form. Pursuit proved fruitless, though she was certain (or hoped) she'd injured or maimed the rescuer. The meddlesome Oya was probably behind the escape. The smell had lingered, and Ahiku had followed its trail ever since.

The boy, Clay had told her, would be wearing a red cap, and she found him easily. He was wide eyed, excited, and looking forward to the ice cream and five-cent piece he'd been promised. Though his family lived on the street, and the money wouldn't get them a place to live, it sure would help get them something to eat.

When Ahiku, under the guise of a pretty lady as colorful as a clown, approached, he was all too eager to help her with her special project. He followed her easily, trust as complete as a full circuit of the moon around the earth. He was held motionless in the chair that Ahiku reserved for her most special guests, watching unblinking as she turned, changed, disappeared. Settled onto him.

Ahiku had promised him ice cream, and she supposed that his last thought was whether the ice cream would have been chocolate or vanilla.

CHAPTER FOURTEEN

THE HOUSE OF WAX

Officer Anderson was one of the last remaining patrons strolling around on the final night. He felt sorry that the show was leaving; not all the good shows stopped in their little town. More likely, it was the fleabags—the shows with rigged games, cheap food, and hoaxes for acts. He didn't let some of them even set up.

Of course, no sooner had he allowed this show to set up than a string of thefts had followed. He nodded to himself; he would haul the carnival owner in for a chat. A hint of foot-tapping drums brushed against his ears, and he suddenly wasn't quite so sure. Was he mistaken? Hadn't the robberies been the month before? He let the matter drop and strolled onward.

He nibbled on a candy apple. Anna, his wife, would have his hide if she caught him. Sweets always upset his stomach, but that hadn't stopped him from sneaking them from time to time, or from stockpiling them in his desk drawers at the office.

The officer considered the game of strength where you had to ring the bell with the hammer. A big man stood there, flexing for a few folks. He passed but then stopped in front of the house of wax to peer at the banners lining the tent. They advertised real-life-looking statues and busts of everybody from movie stars to Indian warriors and famous outlaws.

"There's still time!" the pitchman called out. "Step right up, sir. Take your time—there's no rush. See all there is to see. If you don't have any stories to tell your grandchildren, you will."

The officer looked around, thinking he should get on home. Anna would be waiting for him. But it was his duty to make sure everybody got home safe, and maybe if he killed some time in the museum, things would be wrapping up by the time he came out.

"Law-and-order discount," the pitchman coaxed. "Only a nickel, 'specially seeing as how this is our last night and all."

Anderson grinned, flipped the pitchman a nickel, and moved the front tent flap aside.

The inside was dimly lit, a naked, lone bulb hanging from the ceiling and oil lamps strategically placed to highlight certain figures. As the officer moved through the space, cordoned off like a maze, its walls lined with what looked like sheets of black velvet, he came to the first exhibit: a full-size statue of an Indian man. The statue stood a full head shorter than himself, his massive mane of a headdress giving him the look of a peacock. His dead eyes gazed at an unknown point. Officer Anderson wondered what the sculptor was trying to capture with that look. The statue was bare chested and wore a fine pair of animal-skin pants. Splashes of paint covered the cheeks and chest. The warrior stood holding a spear. The sign beneath the exhibit read: TECUMSEH.

As he moved past a few other exhibits of characters he didn't recognize or care about, the maze curved, and from the corner of his eye, a shadow.

"Somebody in here?" The officer furrowed his brow. When nobody answered, he turned back to the next wax figure. He pegged this one right off. It was the lady who'd gotten lost flying that plane somewhere she shouldn't have been anyway. "Uh-ME-lee-uh Air-haart," he said, sounding out the name aloud from the tag on the right side of the wall. It said that she was the first woman to fly across the Atlantic by herself.

"Never get me on one a them fool things," he mumbled aloud and then moved on.

The maze shuffled him along farther: a bust of Jesse Owens, the track star who'd shamed them Germans real good. Full-size figures of Max Schmeling and Joe Louis—facing each other, boxing gloves at the ready.

The officer then came to a wax statue that was so real he had to blink once or twice to believe his eyes. It was the woman from that movie poster, *Gone with the Wind*. The white lady and the maid—Hattie McDaniel was her name. Officer Anderson tilted his head, peered this way and that at the statue. The skin, even the hair, looked so lifelike. The woman even smelled of a fresh-baked pound cake.

"What the . . ." He moved closer. It looked, sounded as if the maid had actually, well, *inhaled*.

Despite the warnings posted all over the display to not touch them, Officer Anderson cautiously reached out his hand to touch the statue. Again, the shadow. He jerked around and called out again; nobody answered. "I'm letting my mind get the best of me in here."

He turned back to the figures and brushed his fingertips, ever so lightly at first, across Hattie's supple cheek. Warm. *What in God's name?* He poked an index finger, and the skin dimpled and sprang back. Anderson's heart pounded in his chest, and a mischievous grin split his face in two. His hand traveled down her face and neck, flattened against her collarbone, and settled on her right breast.

Emboldened, the officer lifted his other hand and gave her impressive bosom a solid squeeze, caressing. He couldn't believe how real she felt. For a moment, a split hair of a moment that he would forever be ashamed of, he considered undoing the blouse, taking a closer look, perhaps planting his lips on what he envisioned as a set of bold, dark nipples.

An image of his beautiful wife passed before his eyes. And yes, Anna was *still* beautiful. Smooth caramel skin, not a sign of a wrinkle, which she attributed to the steady, ardent use of Vaseline. A sturdy-built woman like Ms. McDaniel—he didn't like them skinny. They'd had three children and were grandparents now. They had a good life, more than their parents, slaves, could have hoped for.

A wave of guilt passed over him. He covered his eyes with his hands and backed away. He wanted to go home now. As he turned, he could have sworn the eyes on that Hattie McDaniel statue narrowed, seething at his retreating back. The officer wove through the maze, expecting to find the end at every turn. But the maze had him perfectly trapped, every turn leading to another set of too-lifelike statues.

He'd begun to sweat. He plunged behind a statue and tore at the black velvet wall, expecting to lift it up and escape back to his life. But the wall wouldn't give at first, and when it finally did, he exhaled an exasperated yelp, stepped under the curtain, and found himself back in another wing of the wax museum.

"Hey!" he screamed. "Which way is outta here? Get me out!"

The officer raced through the maze, passing statues he swore he'd passed before. Even Tecumseh, who sat where the exit had been, only the exit was no longer there.

He wound his way through, desperate sweat soaking his back and crotch, pouring down his face. He drew and raised his gun as he came into an opening and found a group of the statues standing before him. Arrayed behind Hattie McDaniel were "Bugsy" Siegel, Amelia Earhart, Tecumseh, and more. They advanced, and the officer hollered curses and fired his weapon into the flock of waxed death moving toward him.

Anderson emptied his pistol, unable to affect the horde coming at him. He turned to run, only to come face-to-face with more figures.

They converged on him. He fought valiantly, tearing off an arm here, scratching out an eye there. Wax body parts pooled around him as he lay on his back on the ground, still fighting. But he grew tired; he was no longer a young man. His shrieks died out eventually, like the wail of a dying beast, carried on the wind.

When the scuffle and air cleared, the G. B. Bacchanal Wax Museum stood in complete order. Tecumseh near the entrance. Amelia, the boxers, the movie stars all perfect, still. Beside Hattie McDaniel and Greta Garbo, a new bust stood on a high podium. A light bulb shone above it.

The head of Officer Harley Anderson sat flawlessly preserved, even wearing his favorite hat. His brown skin looked real, his beard, trimmed that morning, would be forever in place. The gray speckles gleamed in the light. The eyes that looked out from his face contained a desperately aware look for those who cared to see it. Beneath his bust, a new plaque, freshly minted, hung.

It read: HARLEY J. ANDERSON, FIRST NEGRO AMERICAN OFFICER OF HOUSTON'S PROSPEROUS ALL-NEGRO FIFTH WARD, HOUSTON, TEXAS.

CHAPTER FIFTEEN

PROSPECTING

Clay rode along in the truck with the windows down, hot wind whipping his red hair all around his head like a band of ruptured veins. The heat had dissipated from a rolling boil to a low simmer as the sun sank below the horizon. He was on a scouting mission to check out another performer Geneva had set her sights on. She had an eerie knack for sniffing out talent. Well, not too eerie, he amended; she *was* a damn demon, after all. But if all went well, he'd have a passenger on the trip back.

Only he should have reached his destination long ago. He peered out the front window, searching for a landmark of some kind. The road was well paved, but he hadn't seen a streetlight for at least a mile, and there wasn't a single sign to suggest he was headed in the right direction. All he had was an outdated map and faded memories.

After a few more nondescript miles, mercy came in the form of a gas-station diner. Clay told the attendant to fill up the truck and tossed a few coins into his outstretched hand. A sturdy, clean-faced young man who looked about as out of place in the run-down station as one of them Italian opera singers in a southern carnival.

"It would be my pleasure, dear sir," the boy said. Clay did a double take and walked the few steps to the dilapidated diner. The only word he could find to describe the smell inside was "old," from the grizzled man slumped behind a long, empty counter to the grease that must have been reused since the day the place opened. It was like the diner had been built in the last century, and nobody had bothered to open a window and let a little fresh air in.

There was one lone patron, mumbling to himself in the last of the four booths lined up against the cloudy windows.

Clay extended a hand to the man behind the counter. "Evenin'. Does this road lead to Cleveland, Texas?"

"Today's special is the meatloaf." The old man gave Clay a limp handshake. "Come with a side of taters and beans."

Clay imagined himself pulled over on the side of the dark road, puking his guts out. His stomach might fare better snatching a live coon from the side of the road and roasting that up. But it didn't take a genius to see that he wasn't going to get so much as the next day's weather forecast without paying one way or another.

"Give the meal to my buddy over there." Clay gestured toward the mumbling man, now rocking back and forth in the booth. "And I'll take a bottle of Coke if you got it."

The old man smiled, revealing a surprising set of good pearly whites, minus one front tooth.

~

Clay had escaped the diner with a full tank of gas, the Coke he now sipped on, and what he hoped were good directions. *Being lost ain't all bad.* Few were the moments he had to himself. Truth was, he savored the quiet.

After traveling another several miles without so much as a hint of life, Clay banged his hand on the dash and decided to circle back the way he'd come. Looked like a dirt road ahead. He pulled in to turn around.

As he swung down the path, an orange light glimmered. He pulled forward, hoping there would be somebody who could point him in the right direction. The road was little more than a dirt trail. Clay suspected a shack of some sort at the end. Trees, tall grass, and brush lined the trail, cutting off his sight in both directions. Luckily, the truck handled the dirt path easily. He rounded a bend, and the light grew brighter.

A bonfire sat at the center of a clearing. A group of men, robed in white from head to toe, stood jeering and jostling a Negro man. The man was naked as the day he was born. He took wide swings at his tormentors and, for each attempt to connect, was rewarded with a slash of a knife, a kick, a punch.

Belly turning, Clay counted five robed men, armed to the hilt. He warred with himself for what seemed like forever and finally put the truck in reverse, but he cursed and put it back in park. His stomach was in pieces. The man was on the ground, with the foot of one of the robed cowards on his neck. The others had his hands and ankles pinned to the ground.

The sound of Clay slamming the door to the truck caught their attention. He squared his shoulders and trudged toward the group on leaden legs.

"Lost, friend?" One of the Klansmen came forward. From his bearing and more elaborate robe, Clay judged him the leader.

"Yep." Clay trembled with anger and only hoped they couldn't see it. "For the life of me, can't find my way to Cleveland."

"That's where we live," the man said. "'Scuse my manners—I'd shake your hand but got this coon's blood all over me. You on the right road, even if it don't look that way. Keep on down the way you come, maybe five or six miles."

Clay thanked them and let his eyes drop to where the poor soul lay bloodied and beaten on the ground.

"You want a little piece of this action?" another Klansman said with a chuckle. "Still enough left of 'im to get in a good lick or two."

"Just as soon be on my way," Clay said.

"What's your business in Cleveland?"

Clay's declination to participate in the festivities had earned him a few suspicious glares.

"Clay Kennel." Clay turned on his sales pitch and felt his stomach settle. He had a plan for them. "Owner and proprietor of the G. B. Bacchanal Carnival."

Their eyes lit up. Suddenly they'd turned from racist killers to a bunch of eager ten-year-old boys.

"We'll be settin' up in Waco next. Might be a bit too far off for you . . ."

"Nothin' but a day trip," the leader piped in. "Earn me some points with the wife and my boy."

"You have kids, families?" Clay was in his element now.

"Sure enough."

"Well, if you up to the trip, check us out in about a week's time." He reached into his pocket and procured a free pass from his wallet. "You'll be my guests. We got all sorts of rides and attractions. Bet you'll love the wax museum. And that boy of yours will get a special tour."

Clay felt bad about that last bit he'd added. A boy didn't necessarily turn out like his father. Too late, he'd talked up another meal for Geneva.

"I'll be on my way, gentlemen." He retreated back to the car. He had no chance of saving that man's life, but he'd done what he could to avenge him—if the Klansmen came to the carnival, that was.

He climbed into the cab and clutched the steering wheel until his nails dug painfully into his palms. There was a time when he would have joined in. And he promised himself he'd never forget it. He wished he'd come to the conclusion that their cause was chicken-hearted nonsense on his own, but that honor had fallen to the man he'd saved from a lynching years prior. When it came time to kill, he couldn't do it to the fellow, who'd wished him a good day every time he'd passed him on the street.

He started up the truck and then turned to back out of the trail. From his rearview mirror, he saw the Klansmen raise the dying man to a tree to finish the job.

Clay was numb. Sure, he could've dived in, maybe even wrestled a shotgun away and taken out one of them bastards. But there were too many, and what was the sense in him dying too? He closed up the whole affair into a tightly bound box as far away from his conscious mind as he could send it. He was getting pretty good at that.

The sun crested the next morning, a bright ball of pink-orange heat, as he rolled into the town of Cleveland. The place had sprung up as a junction for the Gulf, Colorado and Santa Fe Railway. Posters announcing **P. T. BARNUM'S CIRCUS, THE GREATEST SHOW ON EARTH** were plastered everywhere. Clay hated it when people confused a circus with a carnival; he'd had to explain it more times than he cared to remember. He parked in front of a restaurant and sat down to have a much-needed breakfast.

"Got anyplace a man could get a bed for a couple hours?" he asked the proprietor as he paid his bill.

The owner added the cash to the register, counted out some coins, and plopped them in Clay's outstretched hand. "Does the man in question want some company?"

Clay shook his head. "Need a few hours of sleep is all."

The man looked disappointed. "Old Bob's place will do ya," he said. "Go on down the street to the schoolhouse and hang a right, few doors down. Can't miss it."

Clay thanked the man.

"Tell him I sent ya!" the owner called out behind him.

After a welcome rest, Clay emerged. The circus wouldn't open until later in the day, so his plan was to work his way around the joint like he was inquiring about work, then find the "Human Pincushion," give him an offer he couldn't refuse, and be back on the road before the sun was halfway across the sky.

The big top was assembled, the rounded red-striped tent raised as soundly as if it'd been done under his watchful eye. Performers streamed inside: clowns, trapeze artists, even a fella who, based on the flashy getup, had to be the ringmaster. Unlike the carnival, their show was one big spectacle, a steady stream of performances all under the same roof. Workers hefted shinier tools, hauled unblemished wood, tended canvases that didn't need patching. And everyone moved with a practiced efficiency. Despite his best attempts, Clay could find no fault in the outfit. A well-tooled machine if he ever saw one.

The man proved easy to find. He sat on the ground outside a trailer, stretching and contorting his body into forms no human body had a right to make. Clay watched as he removed a few pins from a small box, folded his legs up like pretzels, and plunged them needles right into his face: three of them right between the eyes.

When Clay strolled up, the man untwisted himself and stood. He wore only a pair of cutoff shorts. He was tall and lanky, with not one ounce of muscle seeming to stick anywhere to his body. Clay stuck out his hand.

"Clay Kennel," he said. The man's grip was firm. "Owner and proprietor of the G. B. Bacchanal Carnival. Pleased to make your acquaintance."

The man's dark bushy eyebrows, knit together in one ragged line, rose high on his sizable forehead. "Malachi Dumas," he said, removing the needles. "The Human Pincushion is my performing name, but I suppose you already know that."

Clay looked around, to make sure nobody was paying them any particular attention. "Getting right to the point," he said. "I like that. Well, then you know why I'm here. Bacchanal is prepared to make you an offer to join our great show. The best food, accommodations—"

"All things I have here with Mr. Barnum's circus." Malachi clasped his arms behind his back. "Why should I leave?"

"Here, you're a cog in the wheel," Clay countered. "How many acts in this outfit? One, two hundred to compete with? Our show is small, a family atmosphere. There you could be the star. You keep everything you take in, minus expenses—you know, electric cut-in and the like. All your other necessities will be provided."

"I'm not just a performer," Malachi said. "I'm a man of letters. Does that bother you, coming from a Negro?"

"That's what makes our show unique." Clay permitted himself a half a smile. "Shall I say, we are a bit more . . . colorful than most shows. Think you'll find yourself right at home."

"And I'm a vegetarian," Malachi added. "I have specific dietary requirements."

"You'll love Mabel," Clay said. "Best cook there is, and she'll throw together whatever you want."

"I get to keep everything I bring in?"

"Minus expenses. You heard me right the first time."

"I'm a man of few possessions, most of them books," Malachi said. "It will only take a moment."

Clay rubbed his hands together, another job done. "Let's slip outta here unnoticed." He didn't tell his new recruit that if Geneva found him somehow lacking, he'd have to come begging his way back into the circus manager's good graces on his own dime.

Malachi had not been recruited by P. T. Barnum himself—Barnum was long dead when he joined. He had been performing in fairs and festivals in Washington, DC, funding his education, one course at a time, and earning a fairly good wage. He was living a mostly chaste life, but he had no wife yet. Past your normal college age but still a young man, and he wanted to have his life and income set before taking on a wife and child. Though his mother had bugged him about when he would produce her grandchildren daily.

Life had been good. He had a small room that he paid for himself. Sufficient food. All obtained using the talent for pain endurance that had made him a laughingstock as a child. His former classmates now earned their livings breaking their backs. He worked outdoors beneath the tiring sun, but at least he was his own man.

The lure of working in the big city was a great one. The idea that he was attending classes filled him and his parents with pride. But conditions on the farm and the plight of his younger brothers weighed heavily on him. He had agreed to go with the circus men at once. He would be able to send a sizable amount of money home to his parents, fulfilling his duty as a son. He'd return to his schooling once his brothers were old enough to work. His mother assured him she would search for a suitable wife, and he would return home to marry when he was done, in what he estimated to be about five years.

That had been seven years ago. The woman his parents had chosen for him had moved on, creating a bit of a scandal. But Malachi had not yet had his fill of performing. His education, long forgotten. And truth be told, he didn't have much interest in women either.

He could do feats no other could. He had the ability to stick pins into his skin, to lay on a bed of nails and experience not one bit of pain. It was a practice he'd simply read about in a book. What people didn't understand was that if you inserted the needles properly, there was little sensation associated with it. The Egyptians talked about the twelve vessels of the body; the Chinese called this ancient art *zhenjiu*. Combined with the Kemetic meditation practice he'd picked up in another book, it all brought about an overall sense of well-being that permeated Malachi and those who came near him.

The manager at the Barnum circus had called him the human relaxation drug.

~

On the way back to the carnival, Clay ascertained much of his new act's history and even learned a few tricks about Barnum's circus. He filled Malachi in on how things worked at the carnival. Once those pleasantries were done with, the two fell into an amiable silence.

The silence lasted until the smaller but equally impressive outline of the carnival came into view. Malachi, who looked to have been daydreaming, perked up. Once out of the truck, he fell into an odd series of stretches. Clay looked on, first skeptical, but then he yawned and gave his own neck a good cracking. Jamey walked up to greet the pair.

"What cha got here?" Jamey said. He was wearing a pair of jeans and a plain white T-shirt. His hair was freshly cut, and it looked like he'd even shaved.

"This here's Malachi," Clay said.

Malachi grabbed his bag from the truck and bowed slightly. "Malachi Dumas. Pleased to make your acquaintance."

Jamey gave Malachi a look that said he had no idea what an "acquaintance" was but figured it must have been something special. "Jamey." He seemed confused as to whether to offer his hand or imitate the bow. "Right hand to our man here, Mr. Kennel, used to be a pretty fine baseball player, and follower of the Lord."

That earned an easy chuckle from Malachi.

"And before you start talking about your hobbies, favorite foods, and next of kin," Clay said, "got some business to attend to."

Clay led Malachi through the series of trailers and wagons toward the most important one. They had reached Geneva's trailer, and Clay pulled up. Zinsa and Efe stood as still as statues. "Wait here," he said.

"But I . . . ," Malachi began, spreading his hands. "I don't understand."

"Wait right here," Clay said. "This will only take a minute."

"The gopher has returned," Zinsa said, the smile evident in her voice if not on her face. She didn't turn her eyes away from Malachi either.

"And the soldiers without a cause stand at the ready," Clay said, brushing past the pair.

He emerged minutes later. "You're in," the carnival manager said. "Let's find you some accommodations."

Malachi inclined his head toward Zinsa and Efe, which they met with blank stares.

G. B. Bacchanal would always be a small outfit, and this suited Clay fine. In fact, he preferred it that way. The Barnum outfit was too big. Taking on too many people, you couldn't get to know them, and that led to problems, especially with Geneva's particular tastes.

Still, the carnival was growing, adding acts that would put them on the map. Clay was immensely proud of this, and he knew it showed as he guided Malachi through the grounds. He stomped and silenced the voice that reminded him that there was something actually evil about the proprietor. All bigwigs were evil; it was all a matter of degree. If you had to work for one of them, you might as well choose a place where you could be somebody.

There was no such thing as downtime in a carnival. Even when they were traveling or between shows, they had endless repairs, show practice, and a million other things to do. Clay remembered one more thing that needed his attention and called to a chubby teen who was already running purposefully on some mission, his knobby knees ashy in his short pants and his shirt plastered to his chest, thanks to a full sweat he'd worked up.

"Go tell Jamey to meet me over at the Ferris wheel. Gotta take a look at that blasted thing again."

"Yes, sir, Mr. Kennel, sir," the youngster said. He saluted and ran off.

"Manners in a young man is an honorable thing," Malachi offered.

"That it is," Clay said. "Here we are."

~

They had come to a nondescript trailer, similar to all the others, save their first stop, the one with the women standing outside. A group of carnies knelt arguing and tinkering over the front-right wheel. The clapboards were worn by the sun and elements. The back door was closed. Clay knocked.

"Eloko, open up. Got a new roommate for ya." The carnival manager had explained that Eloko was the last act to have a trailer to himself and that he'd brightened at the prospect of having a new companion to share his space with.

They'd been waiting at the door long enough for Clay to begin pacing and mumbling to himself about malcontents, but Malachi didn't share his impatience. He guessed instead that this Eloko was taking extra care to ready the place for his new trailer mate's arrival.

Soon enough, Eloko opened the door, and when he did, he eyed Clay, then Malachi. Malachi took in his grass-covered frame, golden eyes, and claws and was certain that when most people laid eyes on Eloko for the first time, they either gasped with fright or looked down upon him with pity. Malachi did neither.

"The name's Malachi. Onstage, it's the Human Pincushion. I would forever be in your debt if you would allow me to share a space with you."

Eloko blinked, his snout quivering. He looked at Clay and motioned for Malachi to follow him into the trailer.

Malachi tested the bunk, settled his things in the corner. "Better than what I had back at the rooming house," he said with a smile. The place had the smell of the outdoors. A dark-green color covered the walls, making it extremely difficult to see his new trailer mate. He suspected this was by design. There was much to this fellow, who needed to blend in, to hide, even in his own dwelling.

"You are a performer?" Eloko asked the question he'd already answered.

117

Malachi grinned. "I am. But first, if you would do me the honor, I would like to hear your story."

They talked into the night.

⁓

Ahiku had stood by the window, watching Clay walk off with the new act. Again, the duality struck her. She took pride in the carnival, considered them all her responsibility, her legacy, if there was such a thing. Yet she could not lose sight of her real quest. She had to find the remaining powerful ones who could take it all away from her.

The spirits had been no help in narrowing down the field for her. They had said only that they would be special persons, what the Americans called "freaks." She'd concocted the plan for the carnival based on that notion. And it had worked well in the beginning. But either she'd done too good a job, and there was only one left, the most powerful. Or they'd figured out her game.

Another chance to end this tiring search had come and gone. Hopefully he would at least be a good performer. She also wondered if she would continue the carnival after she found her foe. She reaped some amusement from the mischief she and the other spirits caused with the occasional carnival patron. But if she could feed without worry, then maybe they would be of no further use. And what would happen to her precious carnies, to her—could she even think of him this way?—friend, Clay? Some of her workers would return to their homelands—that much was certain. But others would be lost without her.

Sighing, she walked to the front of the trailer and popped her head out the door. Her soldiers were ever present. "I do not wish to be disturbed."

Zinsa and Efe touched fists to chests, and Ahiku closed the door and retreated behind the dark curtain at the rear of her trailer. Back to the world of the demon spirits.

CHAPTER SIXTEEN

STRANGE FRUIT

For this occasion, with the wife and kids in tow, he left the white robe and pointed hood at home. Instead he wore his favored navy, wide-legged trousers and white shirt. The wife had scoffed when he added the bow tie, but she'd planted a kiss on his cheek all the same.

His little girl slipped her hand in his as they strolled around the carnival grounds. He winced at the chafing in his palm where, a week back, he'd nobly earned the rope burns from a righteous killing.

"I see you made it." It took him a moment to place the stranger. Then he recalled the way he'd looked like the devil himself when he'd stepped out of the truck that night at the Negro lynching. That bright-red hair had caught the glint of the fire in a way that was off-putting.

"Clay Kennel, owner of this here carnival." The patron of the evening's entertainment introduced himself with a little bow that made his boy giggle.

"Much obliged for the invite, Mr. Kennel," the man said.

"Couldn't think of anybody more deservin'. You folks enjoy yourselves, then."

Inhospitable not to offer us a personal tour of the place, the man inwardly scoffed. *But you can't expect much in the way of manners from his kind. Any decent sort of man would find steady work and settle down with a family. Probably why he's hired so many darkies too—no upstanding white man would settle for this kind of life for too long.*

He left his family in a longish line for a ride with enough money to see them through a few games to boot and then went in search of the beautiful woman from the poster plastered on the outside wall. The one his wife had caught him gawking at.

He swore he'd circled the place twice. Now he stood scratching his head, looking out at the empty field behind the last tent, when the lights flickered and flared. Yes, it made sense that they'd move the burlesque show off a ways.

The tent was a grimy white and otherwise unadorned. Man-size shadows jostled around inside. Hoots and hollers and sultry music drew him forward like the righteous to the pearly gates. A slow smile spread across his face. He didn't break into a run, but his pace did quicken.

At last, he yanked back the tent flap, stepped inside.

He blinked at a sudden fog. Shadows dissolved. The man screamed.

In the standing room–only space, every seat, every corner was filled with an abomination more horrific than the next. On the stage, a horned monster held court. In a sickening parody, the twisted form jerked its body through suggestive movements—hip thrust, shimmy, a behind slap.

The man turned to the entrance, but each time he ripped back the flap, another appeared. Translucent hands fell on him, searing his skin. The devil flew from the stage, grabbed him by the throat, planted a fiery kiss on his cheek, and pulled him into the underworld.

There, the man awoke to the flames. A rope tugged at his neck. He couldn't see what his feet were propped up on, but when a demon—of that he was certain—stepped away from a jeering crowd and kicked it out from beneath him, he swung from an unseen tree. He mumbled a blubbering prayer as his life thankfully ended.

Until he awoke again.

The rope and stool in place. The devil and his minions howled as, once again, he hung limp from the rope.

The man lost count of how many times this happened. A millennium later, he would still be counting.

~

Liza stood outside her trailer gabbing with Hope like old friends. It was one of her favorite pastimes; she'd never had a girlfriend before. Women understood other women in a way that a man couldn't, or refused to. She'd been able to relay how she'd foolishly gotten herself so excited about finding her mother's baskets in the Fifth Ward and her disappointment when she discovered Twiggy wasn't with their parents. Hope had listened and understood, sharing her own family woes, and Liza already felt better.

Jamey, meanwhile, inhabited a space a few feet away, trying hard to act like he wasn't watching her. The poor boy probably had no idea how distressed he looked. Sweat already stained his armpits, and he took to flapping about, probably in an attempt to dry himself off. Liza smirked, and Hope followed her gaze and soon took in Jamey's suffering.

"If you got something to say, may as well come on over here and be done with it," Hope said. "We don't bite."

Jamey shoved his hands in his pockets and then yanked them out again. He pulled off his baseball cap, then huffed, put it back on, and walked stiffly toward the women.

Unbidden, Liza's hand straightened her long dress, smoothed at her hair. Hope rolled her eyes at her.

"Ladies." Jamey took off his hat and inclined his head toward them. "Uh, Miss Liza, Clay wanted me to ask you to come take a look at one of the chickens. Having some trouble passing eggs. Maybe you might be able to help out some."

"I guess that's my cue to go and find my husband." Hope smiled and strolled off without another word. Liza was stripped bare without her.

Jamey fidgeted with his hat, and Liza let him. Eventually, he calmed himself. "You coming, or you gonna stand there ogling at me?"

Liza allowed a hint of a smile. He was shy—that she liked. But she'd also seen him directing folks around the carnival, working side by side with Clay. He wasn't a pushover. She liked that even more. The tip of his right ear tilted down, giving him the look of a sweet puppy dog. And from what she could tell, he wasn't actually part dog, like someone else. The ice chip that she'd lodged in her heart when she'd had to say goodbye to her family melted a little. "Lead the way."

Glancing down at her from the corner of his eye, Jamey said, "So how you gettin' on?"

In her mind, Liza said, *What are you worried about it for?* Instead, with effort, she got her mouth to say, "Well enough."

The sweat came back with a vengeance, and it seemed that Jamey struggled for something else to talk about. His armpits soaked, his back a swatch of black on his blue shirt. Liza imagined the sweat even dribbled down his backside. She stifled a laugh and let him off the hook. "You seem to like it here."

Jamey exhaled. "I do. Clay treats me fair. Earn a good wage and everything. Man couldn't ask for more."

It's hard to change one's nature, and Liza wasn't even working on it, so it was no surprise, at least to her, when she said, "And what about whoever sits in the red wagon?"

"Ain't nobody in the red trailer," he said. "Clay runs this show. That's all I worry about."

After that he clammed up, and Liza abandoned that line of questioning. They made it to the chicken coop, where Mabel stood stewing and complaining. Jamey shuffled off without a backward glance, and Liza felt bad, but by then Mabel had hold of her arm.

"Hasn't laid any eggs in days," Mabel said. "She waddles around, slow-like. Suspect she might be gettin' on in age, maybe her egg-layin' days is over. Don't know for sure, but Clay said you could talk to her."

The last was a statement, not a question, so Liza swallowed and settled her gaze on the chicken.

It started running around the coop. Liza didn't want to shoot off her message to the wrong bird, so she ran after it, feathers and muck kicking up. Laughter rang out as others gathered to watch the ruckus. Finally, she caught the chicken and turned to sneer at the onlookers while she caught her breath. Busybodies. She swallowed the tongue-lashing they had coming; she had more important things to do.

Intent, Mrs. Margaret used to say, is half the battle. Liza's intent was to send the chicken an image of itself settled down and passing eggs like chickens do, but instead an image of a fine plate of scrambled eggs slipped across the connection. The chicken squawked. It shuddered in her hands and went limp.

Mabel gasped and cursed. "I told you to talk to it, not send it to its maker. Well, least I can salvage it for a good stew." She snatched the dead chicken from Liza and stalked off. The onlookers watched Liza warily, mumbled among themselves, and dispersed.

She looked up to find Jamey back, staring at her with his mouth open. He looked away but not before his eyes had betrayed him. She got that look from everybody sooner or later. It pronounced her a monster.

She sought solace behind the cook tent. The earth was still, the sun hazy. Grasses stood tall and green, a few brown tufts mixed in. She sat staring out at the peaceful surroundings until, after a time, Hope came and sat beside her and slipped her hand in hers.

～

"You've been avoiding me."

Liza had been trying to get a few minutes alone with Ishe ever since the incident in Lake Charles. The alley, Ishe as a hyena, the man he'd attacked lying in a pool of blood. She hadn't mentioned it to Autumn or Hope. Clay wouldn't even want to hear it. The man could be so obtuse when he wanted. And Ishe was like a ghost, materializing and disappearing right before her eyes. When she did catch sight of him, he'd find a way to get away. But not this time. Here was a human whom she could communicate with as she did with animals. She wasn't about to let that go.

He had been testing out adding a penny to his milk-bottle pyramids. His back had been turned, and Liza startled him. He paused, the penny hovering over the lip of a bottle. She almost expected him to spin like a top and zoom off over the horizon. Instead, he said, "You give yourself too much credit."

Liza hauled herself up on the bench in front of the trailer and crossed her legs. Moving from her shoulder, Mico used her hair as a makeshift swing, grasping hold of a braid and swinging out widely, tumbling in the air and landing in front of Ishe. The little monkey sent her an image of the hyena in the savanna and, almost as an afterthought, an image of herself all reddened and blistered. She ignored it.

"Do I?" Liza planted her chin on her fist and stared at Ishe, who tried to ignore her and go on with his work. "You trying to find another way to fix the game?"

Ishe seemed relieved to talk about something other than himself. "A good gamesman is always looking for the advantage. Trick is balance. Another trick is not resting on your old tricks." He chanced a glimpse at Liza, and she couldn't hide the fact that she was sizing him up, measuring like a tailor fitting him for a new suit.

"Your parents never told you it wasn't ladylike to stare at folks?"

Liza almost chuckled. "Lady" didn't even crack the top ten of the names people had slung at her before. "They didn't keep me around long enough to get to that one, I suppose."

"You ain't the only one left home a little early." Ishe set up the milk bottles again, dropped the penny in the one to the left, and continued adjusting and readjusting the bottles. "Been on my own longer than most myself."

"How . . . how does it feel?" Liza tried another line of questioning. "I mean, does it hurt?"

Ishe stopped his arranging and turned to Liza. "You don't know when to quit, do ya?"

"That man in Lake Charles—I think he died."

Glaring down at Liza, Ishe said, "Hear tell you done a fair amount of killing of your own."

Liza bristled, tried to straighten her back. "I don't kill *people*."

"And if you think that make you any different than me, you dumber than you look."

At that, Mico screeched. Even if he couldn't understand the words, he picked up on the heated exchange easy enough. Ishe hissed an inhuman sound, and Mico clamped his mouth shut and darted to safety behind Liza.

It was silent as Liza took in the barb and turned it around in her mind like a puzzle. No matter how many ways she tried to make a different answer come up, she couldn't. The half man, half hyena had a point.

Unable to contain her curiosity, she let an image slip from her mind to his like a fish flapping out of her hands. The image was a simple one: a large male lion, standing atop a mountain, surrounded by his pride. A pack of hyenas in their sights.

Ishe doubled over at an injury that she couldn't see or fathom. She scrambled off the bench. "What is it? What's wrong?"

Eyeing her dubiously, he said, "Did you put that image in my head?"

Liza blinked. She'd sent it but meant it only as a barb, a way to aggravate. When she didn't answer, Ishe, who had composed himself but still clutched at his head, asked again, "Well, did you?"

"I only meant to upset you," she said. "I didn't know it could hurt you."

He pondered this before he took a seat next to her. "Tell me what you sent."

"A lion with a pride staring down a pack of hyenas. I swear it. Nothing more."

Shaking his head, Ishe said, "That lion attacked me. I don't know how it did, but it did. What the hell kinda curse you saddled with?"

Liza sank back to the bench. Was this what happened? It didn't make any sense. She'd always assumed that the images she sent were received exactly the way she'd sent them—the animals couldn't tell her otherwise.

"From the look on your face, I'm guessing you didn't know that. And I'm guessing you've got no idea how to use it."

He'd figured out her secret. She stammered a response. "I, uh . . ." She gulped.

He leaned forward. "As far as I'm concerned, it's nobody's business but your own."

Acceptance. It began as a fluttering in her chest that spread its warmth throughout her limbs. As she looked into his earnest eyes, it was as if the knot of anxiety she bore like an incurable disease suddenly had been cured.

"But maybe I could help."

Liza blinked back the unexpected tears. "Half the time the animals I try to communicate with end up dead. Sometimes when I get too excited and send too many images at once, a jumble, it seems to overwhelm them."

"It's pretty obvious what makes me different than the other animals, don't cha think?" Ishe said as he leaned forward.

"You're half-human—"

"I'm one hundred percent human," he corrected. "Got an evil passenger—a soul that shares my body."

He was splitting hairs, in her opinion.

Ishe stood and began pacing. "Got a couple of what they call theories that might shed some light on your predicament. Need to test 'em out." He eyed Mico and gestured with his head. "And what makes this little rat immune?"

Mico looked worriedly between them both as if something had changed but he didn't know what. Likely the jealous stirrings of a new and unwelcome alliance forming. He chittered nervously.

"Guess we'll have to figure that out," Liza said. As excited as she was by the prospect of working with Ishe, she couldn't help wondering if she might one day end up like the man they'd left for dead in a Lake Charles alley. But despite what lived inside him, he had a calm, strong manner. He didn't judge her. And he wasn't unpleasant to look at, either, even if he was part dog.

At last, she'd found someone to fill the gap in her practice that her father had left.

CHAPTER SEVENTEEN

ELOKO'S SONG

Ishe and the new girl were in an open field not far from where the carnival had camped after a long day of dusty travel when Eloko noticed them. Liza sat on the ground, a small animal of some kind, a raccoon or a possum, lying sprawled between them, legs stiff as a shot of corn whiskey. Ishe stood with the look of a man long past the point where his patience was spent.

Eloko moseyed up to them. "I don't believe Mabel is in need of roadkill for dinner, so I suppose you two are up to something else."

Ishe looked down at him and scowled. His mouth worked, but then he turned back to Liza, threw up his hands, and stormed off.

Liza got up. "Pigheaded, impatient quitter!" she called. Ishe kept walking. When she turned back, Eloko stretched his snout into a grotesque grin. The new girl—she smelled delectable—took two steps in the opposite direction before his words stopped her.

"Used to running away, are you?" Eloko asked. He sat on the ground and leaned casually on a grassy elbow that someone had told him had the look of a bent log covered in moss. His eyes traversed the length of her body, a deep hunger stirring within him. A satisfying layer of meat coated her bones. She gawked back at him.

"Yes," he drawled, crossing one leg over the other. "Take it all in. This once, I will allow you to leer like an uncivilized roadie."

Eloko endured the appraisal. Like most, she probably struggled with his age, his grass-coated skin, his origins. Boring, unimportant matters. Finally, she gingerly lifted the dead possum and took it a few feet away, where she laid it gently on the ground. *Hmm, what's this now?* he mused. *Genuine remorse?* Exhausting. A useless emotion that did nothing to change one's circumstances. Stripped of the comforting veil of Zaire's lush, verdant forests, he'd done the only sensible thing he could and purged any sense of regret for doing what his nature demanded.

Taking a seat on the ground as far away as she reasonably could from him, she snatched a blade of grass from the earth and twirled it around her finger. Judging from her furtive glance, the irony was not lost on either of them.

Tilting her head up, squinting at the sunlight, she asked, "What are you?"

Eloko stiffened at the affront but then softened. At least she was direct, didn't waste time like most people. "A creature not much different from you. I walk, talk, shit. It's a wonder that I can even read and write."

"You know what I mean," Liza said. "You sure don't look like anybody else I ever seen."

Inclining his head, he agreed. "A point I can't argue. An exchange, then. I'll show you mine if you show me yours."

The girl frowned but didn't run off, so he continued. "You can't control your power. That mongrel tail-wagger was trying to help you, but still, you killed that possum."

Liza shifted, and Eloko imagined the ground on which she sat had suddenly become uncomfortable.

"I can control it," she said after some time. "Some. I mean, it doesn't happen all the time." Then she changed the subject. "And back to you."

He lifted his snout and sniffed. A pleasant aroma carried to him on a delicate breeze. A trace of lavender—not the real oil, a cheap substitute—and . . .

"You had some of Mabel's apple pie with dinner?" His snout quivered, and he scooted an inch closer.

"Huh?" She furrowed her brow and eased back.

"I hail from the great nation of Zaire." Eloko refocused. "We are a unique people. The hair, the skin, a condition for which there is no name." What he didn't voice was the burden of the heart and of the mind he carried, much like she did. "And you have strong African blood running through your veins."

The girl twitched but held her ground. "All my mother said is that our people are Nubian descendants."

Exquisite. "You have a war within you," Eloko offered. "Your African and conjuring sides have not come to terms."

"That was technically two questions," Liza said. "How did you come to the carnival?"

"Since the tenuous beginnings of our friendship hinge on counting," he said with a wave of his hand, then let the practiced lie roll off his tongue, "our Mr. Kennel made me a fair offer. I had nothing left to keep me home, and I welcomed the idea of an American adventure." He looked away, contemplating another time.

In Eloko's former life, his people had been hunted to extinction. He let his golden eyes close. The music . . . ahh, the magical notes. His right hand lifted into the air, playing along with the song. His long snout distended; his jaws spread wide to reveal two lines of lizard teeth. The body of a partially consumed human woman, her leg, midthigh, hanging from his mouth.

Geneva Broussard, who had gone by a different name then—Ahiku, the demon spirit, the name Eloko was still allowed to call her—had offered him an escape. One he shouldn't have taken.

For centuries, the dwarves had lived like little green wraiths, darting in and out of the forest, their perfectly camouflaged bodies making them nearly impossible to spot until it was too late. Hunting humans was a child's game. The song lured them in. The humans provided a tasty meal that satiated his people, the minions of the God of Death, for weeks before they needed the next kill. No African rat provided such a delicacy.

His people's pleas to their god had gone unheard. Eloko wondered if they had somehow angered him. Without their god's protection, the humans began picking them off. One by one, they fell. The Yoruba demon had appeared to him to warn him that humans were approaching. She could whisk him away, but she, like all demons, had not offered her hand out of any goodwill. He had consumed the last of the human flesh, discarding the woman's sandal, suckling on the last toe.

Then he had become a carnival freak, tasked with observing the other freaks for anomalies, little more than a spy to do her bidding. It was not the most honorable job, but the pay and food—such as it was—made up for it.

Liza's irritated coughs had gone unnoticed with Eloko so wrapped up in his reverie. Finally, she blurted out, "I'm still here. Why do you talk, uh, speak the way you do if you come from Zaire?"

Eloko's eyes snapped open. They flashed pure gold, and Liza's sharp inhale brought back his doglike smirk. He rolled over on his stomach, planting his chin in the cup of his palms. In the process, he'd closed the gap between them. If Liza's legs hadn't been folded in front of her, he may have landed right in her lap.

"Whoever schooled you ignored your African history—a pity." He crossed his feet at the ankles and lifted them up and down, shedding sprinkles of grassy skin. For a moment, he imagined he looked like a playful child. "The French also took a liking to our dark continent after they shipped your ancestors off. They burrowed in like snakes. We got shackled with their language; they got the land. Their bad taste in food, however, has luckily escaped us."

The look in her eye told him she didn't like him. No matter. Eloko's emotions were plain enough and changed as quickly as a cranky infant's. This game, though—that he lived for.

131

Eloko inhaled deeply. "Your monthly visitor," he began. "Your time of the month is a day, no, two days away."

"Not something you should be pointing out to a lady." She scrunched up her face and clambered to her feet. She headed back to her trailer without a backward glance.

"Do not put your trust in that mutt!" he called out. "Surly animal." He watched her go. Had Ahiku truly checked this one out? There was something about her that set him on edge, tantalized him, but if the demon had approved of her being here, then who was he to question it?

Eloko had made a promise to Ahiku. And if she was aware that he had broken that promise a few times over the years, she had never said so. But then he had never infringed on her precious carnies before. Would one indiscretion catch the attention of a demon who spent more time in the world of the dead than the living?

He didn't know if he wanted to find out, but already, he was consumed by Liza. He pondered what intricate, scrumptious tastiness might lie within the flesh of one with such a power.

CHAPTER EIGHTEEN

CURIOSITY KILLED THE CAT

Even the smallest, most unremarkable cities in Louisiana had a certain vibe, a history and soul that were baked into the moist soil. But the sleepy town of Waco, Texas, was devoid of such a nature, and things moved at a pace akin to a lame snail's. After a long trek to the west of Houston, the carnival had crawled up to a lot outside town. Clay stretched out the kinks in his back and exhaled a tired breath. They were still months off before they'd hit Tulsa and the big trifecta: the biggest score of the season, a weeklong break afterward, and a chance to see his son. Everybody looked forward to Tulsa, but seeing his boy made it that much more special for him. Waco wasn't exactly what you'd call a bustling town, dusty and slow, more like; it was all he could do to not pack it all up and head out sooner.

Two hours after opening around noon, the traffic wave, consisting of a sorry trickle of cheap, unwilling marks, had all but dried up. Candied apples sat untouched, the cotton candy machine unused. Even the normally animated barker sat idle in a rickety-looking chair with his hat over his face, taking an early-afternoon snooze.

Clay stood at the entrance with his hand shielding his eyes, as if searching the abandoned horizon might make a crowd appear. He finally spit in the dirt at his feet and spun around. The banner that read **G. B. BACCHANAL—THE GREATEST CARNIVAL ON EARTH** drooped from the entrance tent.

"I said secure that damned banner!" he boomed at nobody in particular and then walked through the flaps. He made his way around the curve of the midway, correcting this, reordering that, and generally shouting out unnecessary orders.

Finally, he made his way to the cookhouse. Mabel had long since cleaned up and put away everything from the morning meal, but when Clay settled on a bench, she walked over to him.

"I expect I could find an egg, maybe some bacon in the back if you want." She had a bit of flour on her face and a perpetual spoon or some other cooking instrument in her hand. She smelled of cake batter.

Clay picked at the worn, bleached wood. "Naw. Food ain't what I need."

"Suit yourself," Mabel said and then went back to whatever she was preparing for supper.

Picking the right spots for the carnival was supposed to be Clay's specialty. But once or twice every season, he'd make a blunder like this one and stumble on a city that had no interest in the type of entertainment they had to offer. Geneva would scold him—in her way. Sometimes it seemed she cared less about the money and more about keeping the carnies happy. Idle carnies were not happy, and idle carnies found their way into trouble. He'd have to keep an eye out, make sure things didn't get out of hand. He set off to find Jamey; they'd need to keep a tight watch.

~

Even Benny Goodman's band blaring through the speakers did little to lift the spirits of a bored carnie. Liza put down the latest issue of the *Argosy Weekly*, left Mico feasting on a bushel of grapes she wasn't sure how Mabel had found, and went in search of Hope.

Passing Bombardier's station, she waved to the big man as he hoisted a barbell that looked like it held an airplane engine on either end over his head. "They'll come!" she called out. "You wait and see."

"I will gather up some of the boys." He flashed his brilliant smile. "Lead a team to go out and beat them about the head and body till they can no longer resist. Drag them in clutching great handfuls of money."

Liza chuckled. "I'll take your questionable suggestions to Clay. Who knows? It's such a ghost town around here—he might agree to it. I'm going off to find Hope. See ya later."

As Liza turned to go, she bumped into Efe.

"Excuse—" Efe began but stopped midsentence when Zinsa glared at her.

Then Zinsa turned her ire on Liza. "I would think that one with your skill would not be the clumsy type."

Bombardier spoke up before Liza could say anything back. "Why don't you make like an ostrich and hide your ugly face in the dirt."

Liza held up a hand as if the gesture could shush everyone up. Didn't anybody ever tell Zinsa that if she didn't have anything nice to say, then, well, she should shut up?

"There is no one left for you to fight, so you stand outside that trailer half the time, and the other half you walk around here flinging that acid tongue at everybody in your path. Women soldiers!" He threw up his hands. "You do not even know what you are."

"Whoa," Liza said, trying to interrupt.

"At least we were in the fight against the French," Efe piped in. "Where were the men of Senegal? Hmm? Off beating your women or playing with each other in the sand! Oh, I forgot, you call that wrestling. I say it is an excuse to grope at each other."

"You watch your tongue, woman." Bombardier moved closer, menace on his face.

Liza looked back and forth between them. The normally buoyant, happy Bombardier had a bigger problem with the women soldiers than everyone else, and she wondered at its source. It seemed to go beyond just reacting to their prickly nature.

"Or you will do what?" Zinsa asked. She shrugged off Efe's attempt to pull her away.

"And a good afternoon, folks." Malachi walked up to the group twirling a sharp, lengthy nail between his nimble fingers. He wore a pleasant smile that Liza noted was genuine. "I don't believe we've all met." He took a step closer, and his legs suddenly turned to jelly. His fall was braced by outstretched hands, the nail still wedged between his fore and middle fingers. He cried out as he careened toward the tip, the nail piercing his right shoulder.

"Are you all right?" Liza said as they all crowded around, helping him to his feet. He smiled and slowly pulled the nail from his shoulder. Not a trickle of blood escaped.

"They call me," he said with an elaborate bow, "the Human Pincushion."

Bombardier's shoulders relaxed. Zinsa and Efe actually chuckled. The tension escaped into the ether like air escaping an overly taut balloon. Liza, as usual, was curious. After curt introductions were made, Bombardier, Zinsa, and Efe departed. Malachi fell in step beside Liza.

"How did you do that?" Liza said.

"Do?" Malachi twirled the nail again.

"Guess it doesn't matter how you did it, only that you did. Almost got lost in a flurry of fists back there." What Liza didn't say was how she had considered calling on any animal in the wild she could to help her and Bombardier, if it had come to that. She'd seen those Dahomey women with their spears and had no doubt about the fact that they could and would kill. Hope had filled her in on where they'd come from. Liza didn't think there had ever been women soldiers before, let alone in Africa. It filled her with pride, even if she didn't exactly like either of them.

"And what, may I ask, is your act?"

Liza shifted, uncomfortable. She didn't have an act yet. The last time she'd practiced with Ishe, after yet another disaster with a possum, she'd managed to keep the rabbit she was working with alive, but nothing beyond that. Her power still didn't obey her.

Malachi, as if sensing her unease, switched the conversation. "My show isn't set up yet either."

She listened in wonder as he explained his ability to withstand pins and needles. She couldn't wait to see it. Clay was ordering in supplies for his act, and he should be ready to go soon.

"That fire head just showed up at P. T. Barnum and talked me into coming back with him. I left almost everything there."

"When Clay brought you to the carnival," she said, biting her lip, "did you go to the red trailer?"

"I did," Malachi said. He walked with his arms clasped behind his back, and it seemed as if he glided, his feet barely disturbing the earth. "Pretty strange experience, as all I did was stand there. Yet that must have been enough for whoever was making the evaluation."

"You didn't see anybody either?" Liza pressed.

"You looking for answers of some kind?" His smile had been replaced by a look of pure serenity.

"You're not the least bit curious about who is in that trailer? I mean, what does he do, peek out the window and decide if he likes the look of an act or not without even talking to anybody?" Liza felt an urge to tell Malachi about the strange energy she felt every time she came near the trailer. The compulsion to investigate that Hope was constantly telling her to forget about. That no one seemed to want to talk about. Even Ishe had told her to leave it alone. "What is the big secret?"

"Knowledge of all things is sometimes more of a burden than the liberation you thought you were looking for."

Liza had to think about that one for a moment. They had come to Hope's trailer. "Well, it was nice to meet you and all," she said. "Good luck with your act."

Malachi inclined his head slightly. "And to you."

                          ~

Hope lounged behind an elaborate wooden table inside her comfortably appointed trailer, the air perfumed with sandalwood incense or whatever questionable imitation the Dahomey women found for her. The inside was lit only by the light limping in from a couple of windows. Secrets uttered during a reading were better suited to a certain murkiness. Not that she'd had any customers.

Tarot cards sat stacked to her left, and her pitch cards, some she had already signed, were in front of her. These she sold for a nickel.

The door to her trailer was open, and Liza peeked her head in. "I see you got about as many customers as everybody else."

Hope waved the girl in and gestured to the chair in front of her. "The sooner we blow this flytrap, the better." With a mother in need of pricey cough medicine and a son back home in need of, well, everything, every stop mattered.

"Is this the worst spot the carnival has ever stopped in?" Liza sat in the chair and fiddled with some of Hope's pitch cards. The girl could never sit still. But Hope enjoyed her company anyway. Kind of like having a little sister.

"We've seen worse. I'll give Clay that much—usually he picks good spots for us. And with nothing else going on, people are usually dying to see a carnival. I'd give anything to go into town, see what it's like."

Liza looked down.

"What?" Hope asked.

"Why doesn't Bombardier like Zinsa and Efe?"

Hope lay down her pencil and resettled herself in her chair. Her husband's constant beef with those women exasperated her. "Who does like them? They don't exactly try to endear themselves to anybody."

"But there's something else there, I know it."

Why did the girl have to keep nagging about things she didn't understand? "Does all that reading make you ask so many questions?"

When Liza didn't answer, Hope exhaled. "He's an African man, okay? He's got ideas on what a woman should and shouldn't do, and fighting a war alongside men isn't one of them."

"He shouldn't worry about what they do." Liza had the good sense to avert her gaze and say that last bit under her breath.

"That's my husband you're talking about, you know?" Hope folded her arms. Liza was right, and Hope knew it. Why did she have such a tough time admitting it?

"I like Bombardier," Liza said as she sat back in the chair. "That don't make him right about everything. Things are changing for women. I bet Negro women will get the right to vote one day."

Had she ever possessed this type of wide-eyed optimism? This child really was naive. "Never gonna happen," she said. "Not here, not anywhere else. And especially not for us."

They fell into an easy silence, and Hope went back to signing her cards. Liza strolled around the rest of the trailer. The girl was all restless energy; Hope could feel the power burning inside her. She didn't like it.

Her trailer was relatively small, but Hope had managed to fit in another bench along the right wall, a waiting space for her customers. Posters of actors and singers filled the walls. A lone votive candle burned next to a picture of her son, on a shelf she was proud that Bombardier had made for her.

Liza came back and picked up the tarot cards. "What does all this mean?"

"You want a reading?" Hope stopped signing again. Her heart stilled, unsure if she even wanted to read for this girl whose fate almost screamed out of her pores. Somehow Hope knew her own fate was tied up in it. And although she enjoyed reading the cards and telling others her visions, she didn't fancy ever doing it for herself.

"No." Liza set the cards down and fidgeted in the chair, suddenly looking uncomfortable. "Asking a question is all."

What could it hurt? Bombardier would laugh at her, call her a silly woman. "Come on, hand 'em to me." Her friend complied but with little enthusiasm—a true nonbeliever.

She shuffled the cards, asked Liza to pick out five, and lay them on the table in front of her. Hope flipped over the first one, the Empress. Harmless—the nurturing feminine. "This one here means you'll have a long and healthy life." That she'd made up to make her friend relax a bit, but Liza affected the look of one whose interest lay elsewhere, glancing out the window, picking at her fingernails.

"The next one is also pretty standard. Hierophant. You have a talent, one you haven't fully developed yet, but you will. Learn everything you can." Hope breathed a little easier. With a flick of the next card, the Lovers, she pronounced, "And there is a man in your life. But you are resisting him. He's a good man, though. But it looks like you also have a choice to make." She grinned and batted at Liza's arm. "Wonder who that is? That boy Jamey you always trying to act like you don't see or the other one?"

"I'm not even responding to that," Liza said. "I'm going to go, see if somebody else needs some help."

"You'll sit right there till I finish your reading." Hope flicked over the next two cards at once and knit her brows into a frown, shifted gears into panic, and turned the corner at horror before skidding to a halt with a futile attempt at composure.

"What?" Liza said. "What is it? What do those cards say?"

"Nothing." Hope grabbed the cards and shuffled them back into the stack. "Go on now, I'll see you later."

Liza stood over her, not moving.

"I don't know," Hope finally said. "Look, it doesn't make any sense."

Liza opened her mouth but thankfully held her tongue and left.

Hope studied the cards. *Death.* It didn't mean death in the literal sense, like some other readers tried to frighten people with, but the death of something else, an ending. Coupled with the next card—the Wheel of Fortune—it meant Liza was in for a major transformation, one that would affect them all. In a bad way. Hope stared after her friend, her stomach fluttering like it held a thousand butterflies.

CHAPTER NINETEEN

So Long, Waco

Liza lounged half-asleep in her trailer, the morning sunshine slicing through the windows. As usual, Autumn lay with her eye mask on, one arm flung luxuriously overhead, the thin blanket bunched tightly in her right hand.

Liza was restless. Mico slept as he always did, in the uppermost corner of her bunk, nearest to the wooden wall. The little monkey had the sleeping habits of a cat, curling up for a snooze whenever the urge hit him. He lay, snoring and clasping one of Autumn's beads possessively. She'd given it to him as a gift, since he so admired all the shiny stuff on her costumes.

Liza had read about many places. At times, those writers Mrs. Margaret had introduced her to made her fantasize that she had sipped coffee at a café in Paris, strolled along the cobblestone paths in England, and run through the outback in Australia. But Liza was not a worldly woman; that was different from being well read. She spent her life in lazy places like Pensacola and Baton Rouge. Colorful places, with even more colorful people, but nothing of note ever happened there. She'd figured they were probably the most boring places on earth.

But Waco claimed that prize. It was one of the few places where Mama was able to find the specific pine needles she needed outside South Carolina, so Liza recalled the family passing through more than once. Twiggy was just a toddler then, and Liza had spent most of the time delighting in entertaining the giggling child to fend off boredom. The town was little more than a few squat, sun-worn stucco and adobe structures that looked as though a city builder had gathered them all in enormous hands, rattled them about like marbled dice, and tossed them out along the ground. There were no signs or banners to indicate what was where.

Which meant the carnival was quieter than she'd ever seen. Liza sat up. Most wouldn't be up for several hours, and she could spend some time with her animals without anybody hovering over her shoulder. It was a rare opportunity.

She rose, grabbed her few toiletries, and exited the trailer, careful to quietly shut the door behind her. She was disappointed to see she wasn't the only one with the same idea. A few carnies were already up and about. She supposed no matter what happened at night, each day started with the hope of profit.

After making a quick business of the showers, she pulled on a cotton skirt, poked her arms through the crisp but faded white button-up shirt, and tied up her boots. Outside it was still calmer than she'd ever seen it, which meant her animal tent would at least be empty.

"Wait up!" a voice called.

Liza tried not to groan as a fresh-faced Jamey came toward her. Like the first time they'd met, she couldn't help but admire his walk, his sleepy brown eyes, the curve of his shoulders. But another memory nudged its way forward, his face stained with all the shades of judgment when she'd killed the chicken. She liked this boy, but he'd been avoiding her ever since then. Why was he bothering her now?

"You smell mighty nice this morning," Jamey said before a look of horror crossed his face. "I mean, you always smell nice. But today you smell, well . . ."

Liza laughed. Apparently he liked her, too, even though he'd seen what her power could do. A warmth filled her, not like the heat she felt around Ishe, but something softer, easier to control.

He looked behind her, around her, on the ground. Finally, with effort, he met her eyes. "Want some company wherever you off to?"

Liza shuffled awkwardly. The door that was beginning to crack open slammed shut. No way she could practice her show around him. He might be able to overlook a dead chicken, but if something happened to the carnival's animals while he was watching . . .

"No," she said. "Thank you." He looked so disappointed her heart lifted, and she added, "But I'll be back soon—I guess Mabel will have the cook tent flag up, and we both gotta eat, right?"

Jamey's face lit up like a jar of fireflies. "That sounds about right. Well, then. Enjoy your time with your act. I know Clay's looking forward to what you're going to come up with. I am too." He tipped his hat to her and made it a point to turn and leave before she did.

Liza's mask of calmness rolled off like a broken wheel. She'd practiced with Ishe so often, but that was different. Her livelihood depended on not messing this up. If she hurt these animals, Clay would toss her out of the carnival faster than a rumor from Mrs. Shippen's flapping gums. How would she know how far to take it? She couldn't do it.

Instead of the animal tent, she headed for the exit.

The carnival had set up not too far away from the town. Liza strolled along the route, frustrated with herself. A stray dog galloped down the dusty road, a child close on its heels pelting it with rocks. She turned to make her way back to the carnival.

Perhaps the dog had grown tired of being tormented by the child, or maybe it hoped that a better life awaited it wherever Liza might lead. Its reasons were its own, but the stray trailed her at a respectable distance. Twice she'd stopped, hearing something behind her. And twice, it had frozen into place, its foreleg lifted, as if, like a cactus, it could blend into the surroundings unnoticed.

She knelt down and called to it, first with her mouth, then her mind. The smoldering ripple that began in her stomach gushed up through her body, coalescing in her mind. The immaterial likeness of herself with other dogs she'd met during her travels drifted across the ethereal link between her and the stray. *Practice,* Ishe had said. *You need to practice. And if you lose a few in the process, better than losing Sabina or Ikaki.*

Grudgingly, Liza had agreed, though she could never look so callously on an animal's death as Ishe could. She supposed it was the predator side of him.

Along their link, the stray channeled a happier time of itself on a farm with a strapping white man. But its owner was shot, the farmhouse pillaged, the dog beaten and stolen. Then it had been abandoned—the same as she'd been.

She sent the dog another image, one she didn't like to replay. It was of the last time she'd seen her family. Of Twiggy wailing, of herself holding her own tears until she was in the car and riding away. She hadn't looked back.

The dog whined in response, and with control she cut off the connection. She rose and allowed herself a momentary satisfied smile. Her time practicing had paid off. The dog followed her back to the carnival and fell in with the other strays that attached themselves to the show like leeches. It sent her a happy parting image with a wag of its tail, vowing its loyalty to the human who had showed it kindness.

Her confidence buoyed by images the dog had sent her of it playing and wrestling with the other strays outside the carnival, Liza pushed herself to enter the animal tent. Uly was nowhere to be seen. The turtle swam lazily in circles, and the Tasmanian tiger lay sprawled in a square of sunlight. Neither acknowledged her presence. A small shadow passed through, and Mico leaped onto her shoulder, chittering, annoyed that Liza had been gone too long. She calmed the marmoset with a few scratches and sent him to guard the entrance and warn her if anyone approached.

She moved to the first cage, the turtle's, and sat down cross-legged. Liza considered what turtles would like to eat. An image bloomed in her mind: the two of them together, sitting near the edge of a quiet river, her holding out a leaf. When the image was solid, she slid it from her mind, a tendril tethered to her like a kite, sending it floating on nothingness toward the animal . . . Ikaki.

The image floated, floated, hung in the air. As if lowering a child into a crib, she settled the image over Ikaki and waited. It made no notice that it had received the image, still swimming peacefully in circles, its dark-green back glistening, its head tilted up slightly above the water.

Minutes passed with Liza observing, Ishe's words in her head: *Be patient. Don't demand; ask the animal what it wants.*

The turtle continued its leisurely swim for a while longer, then crawled over the lip of the pool. It walked so slowly it seemed to float to the front of the cage, where it waited.

An image came back, and Liza exhaled a breath she'd been holding. A small clear river hidden by tall grass in a vast open land. The warmth of the sun on its shell. Human noises remained distant. She was there feeding him a palm frond. Then in the image, Ikaki changed. The turtle stood on its hind legs and did a sort of pirouette, leaping into the sky. It danced, whirled, and took a giant leap before dissolving.

Liza blinked. What was happening? She steadied her pulse, and a dark-green sprite appeared in the place where the turtle had disappeared. It spun above the earth, hovering over the river, pirouetting, spinning, and twirling, in the form of a fairy of indeterminate sex. It took her a long time to interpret the image, but when she did, she nearly keeled over.

Ikaki was a water spirit.

The spirit then formed an image of being pulled, called forth by an unknown force. When Ikaki emerged from the river as a turtle, a woman waited on the riverbank. She was tall, draped in colorful garb from head to toe, striking. The next image—Ikaki in a box, traveling a great ocean before landing with the carnival. They yearned for home but felt bound, compelled to stay with the carnival. They couldn't or wouldn't explain to Liza why, but she felt their profound sadness and loneliness. Who was that woman who'd captured the turtle? And how far had Ikaki traveled to join the show? Across an ocean at least.

Along with a handful of geography books, there had been a globe in Mrs. Margaret's library. She'd demanded Liza remember the capitals of all the countries that made up the continent of Africa. The geography books were illustrated, and although some of the images ran together in her memory, others she recalled like the back of her hand. So when Ikaki sent an image of themself in their native land, it looked like Nigeria.

And if she didn't understand that, she was downright perplexed when Ikaki conveyed a fondness for Liza because of her grandmother—in Nigeria. A woman she'd never met and whom her own mother had avoided talking about. Her grandmother, it seemed, had a way with magical creatures. And the part of Liza that felt like an empty house just crying out for a well-worn sofa, a freshly painted fence, a toddler's unsteady first steps to make it whole, that part of her ached for the comfort of a Nigerian grandmother's strong embrace.

In the end, what Ikaki wanted was simple. They only wished that somebody had asked them before. They were a water spirit, after all, and since they couldn't be free, then at least they wanted to dance.

Stunned, Liza sat back. A Nigerian water spirit. Trapped in a cage in a traveling carnival. How was that possible? Not wanting to convey her foreboding, she severed the connection. Ikaki seemed fine, resuming their place in the back of the cage.

What kind of carnival was this? Her thoughts returned to the red trailer. What was Clay hiding? How had he managed to trap an African spirit in an American carnival?

Scooting over to the other cage, Liza peered in at Sabina. Was she also a spirit? She'd never even seen a creature like this, had assumed that Tasmanian tigers were a legend. Sabina gazed at her with thoughtful eyes, then came to the front of the cage and sniffed. Her tail stood at attention.

The image Liza conjured was of herself with the tiger, sitting amiably as the only human surrounded by other tigers. She neither harried nor pursued but let them sniff and investigate her and Mico. The animal almost nodded, or at least it looked that way to her. She lifted her head in the air as if seriously contemplating the correct response.

Liza's legs stiffened, and she even drifted off once or twice. Sounds of the carnival readying itself for a new day filtered into the tent. The tiger regarded her in silent judgment, any response for now unspoken. Finally, when Liza felt her temper beginning to rise, she decided to stop while she was ahead. Even if Sabina wasn't ready to connect, she could at least do something with Ikaki. The smells, the fluttering flag, and the gathering of people outside told her that breakfast was ready anyway.

She stood up. Mico chittered, sending his own never-ending hunger images to her. She sent a goodbye to both the turtle and the tiger, her heart lifting when Ikaki sent her a response, a graceful bow over sparkling water.

Tables and benches were filled, a beehive of performers on one side and workers on the other, the steady hum of their conversations filling the air. Liza gathered a plate and settled right in the center of the tent. In a minute, Jamey settled across from her. Hope and Bombardier had been coming to sit with her as well but veered away, snickering and blowing kisses her way as they settled at another table directly in her line of sight.

Chewing became hard. The excitement she had felt over discovering Ikaki's true nature and willingness to dance for her show was muted by other uncomfortable feelings. Liza wiped at her mouth aimlessly, hoping that grease or something else hadn't lodged itself on her face. She moved her food around on her plate.

"Best not let Mabel see you playin' round with her food," Jamey said. "Good way to get yourself on her bad side."

As if reading their minds, the older woman, who took her roles as both cook and hostess seriously, came up behind Liza. "You sick or something?" Mabel asked, lifting her chin, studying her face.

Liza pulled away. "No, ma'am."

"Then why is that food chilling on your plate 'stead of in your stomach?" She looked over at Jamey. "You worried about this here boy? That it?"

If she had been able to turn into a bird and fly away, Liza would have.

"Jamey, get up. Can't you see the child is too shy to have you staring at her while she eat? Go on over there and bother somebody else."

Jamey sat with his eyes wide and his mouth open. Unfortunately, he hadn't finished chewing the bacon he'd bitten into.

"And close up your mouth 'fore a fly get in there and snatch that piece a bacon off ya tongue."

Liza giggled and covered her mouth. Jamey got up to leave. "Stay," she whispered.

"Well, if he does stay, you both better finish ya food. Don't got nothin' to waste around here." Mabel finished her command with a slap to Jamey's back and waddled off to see if her other customers were slacking.

Though they managed to say little more than pleasantries to each other, they finished their meal together. When they were done, Jamey grabbed Liza's plate. He told her he'd call on her later, and she allowed herself to look forward to it.

~

Uly was irked to no end when Clay announced that the carnival would be moving on at first light. They'd begun taking down all the displays, all the tents, packing up. Waco proved not to be the money magnet they'd hoped for. Near the end of the day, Uly led a few of the carnies off to the town proper in search of a drink and maybe some company.

What passed for the saloon was a square adobe house. It was dark inside, had a bar lining the right wall and tables arrayed around the rest of the small space. There was a room, little more than a closet out back, where "special customers" could be entertained by someone of the female persuasion.

Gathered at a table, the carnies ordered one round of drinks, then another. The rest of the crowd was made up of a mixture of Mexican, white, and other men of mixed or indeterminate race. When he'd first passed through the country, he'd marveled that he and the Mexicans could speak the same language but have such a time understanding one another. All eyes on the carnies, and not in the friendliest manner neither.

Well into their third round of drinks, a beautiful woman emerged from the back room. The man with her went to the bar and left a few coins on the counter before exiting. The woman wore a low-cut red dress that gathered at her small waist, her breasts nearly falling out of the bodice. Jet-black hair was bluntly cut at her chin. Dark makeup decorated her eyes; red painted her lips.

She sauntered over and began flirting with the men. After a heated exchange, Uly decided to go first. But in record time, he was finished. He was gearing himself up for another try when the woman left the room. He stormed out behind her, eyes blazing. "I ain't done yet."

The woman planted a fist on her ample hip. "Could have fooled me, señor." And the rest of the bar patrons, including the carnies, laughed.

"You had your turn, Uly." Another carnie got up and grabbed the woman by the arm. They were walking toward the back when Uly pushed him from behind. The carnie fell into a table of other men, one of whom cracked him over the head with a bottle.

The table of carnies cursed and surged forward like a band of agitated honeybees. They fell onto the other men with stings of fists and feet. A lone gunshot rang out in the air. A plume of dust fell from the ceiling, and the bartender looked up with a concerned frown, likely concerned more for his establishment than the men inside.

"That'll be enough," a tall man with abnormally pale skin and wire-framed glasses perched on the tip of his nose said. He looked more a librarian than a sheriff, but the shiny five-pointed-star badge labeled "McLennan County Sheriff" marked him otherwise. He lowered the shotgun at the carnies. "If you boys will follow me." He pointed out the door with the gun. "Send word," he said to the bartender on his way out.

~

"God dang it." Clay paced back and forth. "Shoulda listened to my first mind. Bad idea to stay on here." He kicked at a crate, a strand of slick, fiery-red hair whipping across his forehead. "Shake a leg, people. Soon as I get back, we're blowing this town. Jamey, get the truck."

"What's going on?" Liza and Hope asked Jamey before he could hurry off.

"Some of the boys done got themselves into some trouble," Jamey said, not stopping. "Sheriff sent word."

Liza turned to Hope. "In for a show?"

Hope was already moving. "We shouldn't."

"We should."

They watched as Clay hopped into the truck and he and Jamey sped off. A group of other carnie workers followed on foot. Idly, Liza wondered why they even took the truck, they were so close to town. The women brought up the rear, the carnival's stray dogs trailing them. The stray Liza had picked up earlier had become leader of the pack. Liza sensed their eagerness; they wanted to please her. She allowed the connection to open. Mirthful . . . no, jubilant. Of all the words she'd learned under Mrs. Margaret's tutelage, those best described how she felt about this kind of progress. She had control of the pack.

The stragglers were a few minutes behind and caught only snatches of the conversation as they watched from a corner of a building.

"I already paid you your fee," Clay was saying under the dim glow of the streetlamps. "What you're asking now is plain robbery. I haven't even made a dime off this city. And you promised me the folks in this town would come out for the show. Why, I'm the one ought to be asking for a refund."

The bookish-looking sheriff was no longer alone. Clustered around him, a hodgepodge of deputies all sported shiny, official-looking stars on matching vests. Guns must have been in short order, because they were armed only with sticks and cudgels. Others stood glaring, as if their ugly looks alone could beat back the growing throng of carnies.

Liza and Hope looked on in anxious silence and sank back deeper into the shadows. Their presence would not be welcomed by either side.

"You will pay the fine," the sheriff said calmly. "Or your men will remain guests of our town until such time that you can acquire the fee. Of course, there will be additional charges, as meals are not included."

Clay looked as if his red hair might blow off his head. "All right, then," he said through clenched teeth, waving the carnies back. "Let me see what I can do about coming up with your fee."

The group rounded the corner from where Liza and Hope had watched everything. Clay spared them only a censuring look before he ordered everybody back to the carnival so they could prepare to leave, save himself, Bombardier, and Jamey. He asked one of the carnies to go and get Zinsa and Efe.

Liza and Hope slunk back farther across the street, where they had a good view, but they didn't want to leave when things were getting interesting. Although neither were fans of the women soldiers, a quiet thrill filled Liza's belly at the thought that even though a crowd of men was filling the streets, Clay had chosen two women as the ultimate threat.

In short order, Zinsa and Efe came, eyes flashing with the anticipation of a chance to beat up the locals. They stood with Clay just outside the lighted street, three heads bent together, two dark, one red. Liza could see how tightly coiled they were and marveled at their control. She determined she would emulate it.

As the deputies dispersed and the sheriff retreated inside the jail, they made their move. The band of carnies tiptoed to the door and blasted through. The one deputy inside yelped as Bombardier bore down on him. He sidestepped the big man and jetted through the door, where Zinsa and Efe caught him and batted him around like a child's toy.

Clay shoved the sheriff's gun aside and knocked the glasses off his perfect nose. The dogs started yapping, but Liza held them back, trying not to laugh when the sheriff righted his glasses back on his face and said, "Perhaps a compromise can be reached?"

The emancipated carnies emerged from the jail, along with Clay and the rest. They hightailed it around the corner, Hope and Liza already in the lead.

They were no sooner among the trailers than the sounds of trouble filtered through the night. The deputies had followed them. Zinsa and Efe snarled and then prowled back into the night. The group followed the female warriors. Liza could feel the bloodlust hanging in the air from the rest of the carnies, and she knew, despite Clay's hissed orders to stand down, that this would not end well.

An image formed in her mind, clear in its violent purpose. She sent the image to the dogs, pushed it along as if on a slow-moving cloud.

At the last second, she wove in images of Zinsa and Efe as part of the pack, not to be messed with.

Howls filled the air along with screams, snapping, biting, tearing at limbs. The deputies were no more than civilian men, and when two female warriors and a pack of demon dogs descended on them, they quickly fell apart. The torches that they had carried bobbed and sputtered as they scattered, dogs nipping at their heels.

Liza panicked. She wanted the pack to stop, but she had lost control.

Ishe stormed up to her. "Stop it!" he boomed. "They'll kill one of them, and we don't need the trouble."

"I can't, it'll kill them all if I try like this," she panted.

"Breathe," Ishe said. "Clear your mind, slow now."

Liza inhaled and exhaled a long breath. When the image from Ishe came, she squeaked in surprise but allowed it. The two of them stood together as alpha hyenas on the savanna. A cool breeze ruffled their fur as their pack yipped and played around them. They were in control; the pack would listen to her.

Her heart rate steadied, even as the frenzied sounds from the real world got louder. She sent an image of her leading the dogs away from the attack, mixed with her approval and happy tail-wagging.

Soon the sounds faded, and as the strays came streaming back, Liza and the others made their way down the road in time to see the thugs scrambling to their feet, one man shuffling off dragging a maimed leg behind him. Zinsa and Efe stalked after them to warn off any stragglers.

The crowd of carnies turned as one to look at Ishe and Liza. The looks of horror were replaced by smiles and looks of admiration.

About as comfortable with the attention as whores in the church choir, Liza and Ishe exchanged a heart-fluttering glance flush with mutual admiration and walked off in separate directions.

CHAPTER TWENTY

At Home among the Freaks

It crept up on her like the first inklings of a cold. A sniffle, a tingle in the back of her throat. From Baton Rouge to Lake Charles, Houston to Waco, and miles of travel in between filled with helping the other acts while practicing for her own, the carnival had become something Liza had never before fully experienced. It had become home.

But like a cold, home had always been a temporary thing. Here for a week, maybe a day or two more, then gone. Liza let the gentle warmth generated by the idea of a sort of permanence wash over her. Only Twiggy's absence marred the feeling. She chided herself. She mustn't get too comfortable; she would stay until she'd saved enough to set out on her own and find her sister. She set aside the book she had been reading, stood, and stretched.

Autumn looked up from her copy of *Vogue* magazine and watched as Liza paced the narrow path between their bunks. After folding down the corner of a page to mark her place, she slid the magazine aside and announced, "Sit."

Liza blinked and looked over at her.

"You're driving me and poor Mico crazy. Something's eating you, and you may as well spit it out." Autumn rearranged her silk gown, the one she always wore inside, and crossed her long, lean legs in front of her.

Dropping to her bunk, Liza diverted, her usual response to any inquiry that made her uncomfortable. "There's nothing wrong; can't I think on things sometimes?"

"My mama told me that all that thinking don't do a lady much good." Autumn looked down at her pale toes and must have noticed a chip in the red nail polish, because she rummaged through her box and found a bottle of nail lacquer and set to work on the offending toe.

Liza's mother didn't talk much, but when she did have something to say, it was profound. "And my mama told me anytime somebody asks you not to think, run the other way."

Autumn couldn't help but chuckle. "Well, what is it that's got you wearing the floorboards thin?"

For some reason, Liza looked down, expecting to see the wood wearing thin beneath her feet. She caught herself, scooted back against the wall, and stared at her own unpainted, misshapen toes. She'd never bothered with such adornments before but wondered if Jamey would like that. Or Ishe. Quickly, she shoved the thought aside. She lowered her eyes and exhaled. "I'm wondering how long I can stay on here."

"You got somewhere else you need to be?" Autumn leaned over and blew at her toes.

"Well . . . ," Liza began, then decided she didn't need to tell Autumn about Twiggy. "I mean, what if something goes wrong? What if Clay decides he don't like the act I put together?"

"Some say Bacchanal been around, under some name or another, for a hundred years. Winding back and forth across the country till the Tulsa blowout and returning again the following year."

Liza didn't know if she believed that, but it flew off Autumn's tongue as easily as a sunflower seed shell with all the salt sucked off, so maybe it was true.

"You think that red trailer has been there the whole time too?"

Autumn's hand froze, brush hovering over the bottle. "The carnival is a part of America. Won't never go no place. And as long as you do your job and quit worrying about things that don't concern you, no reason you can't stay on as long as you like."

Another door slammed. Nobody wanted to talk about the mysterious red trailer. It was as if they all were keeping the secret and were determined not to let her in on it. She hated that feeling, had known it growing up, held on the fringe of belonging. It was like looking at everything through glass ten inches thick. It was the same feeling she'd had with her mother, before she'd been shoved aside and abandoned. That red trailer represented something that could end the comfort she'd found at the carnival. Liza was certain of that. "Where are your people from?"

"Sounds like it's time for both of us to get back to our reading." Autumn reached for her treasured copy of *Vogue*.

A hard woman to know. Autumn didn't need to say the same about her; it was true. Some secrets were better left in the past, where the damage wasn't so fresh. Liza propped up her pillow, picked up her book, and leaned back, but her eyes couldn't focus on the words. Memories she carried around like layers of slack, useless skin resurfaced. Things she wouldn't want to share with Autumn either.

For long stretches her family would spend time in towns that weren't all too welcoming of strangers. Even when they were with these people, they were separate. Some hated the fact that her father never joined in their drinking or carousing. That her mother didn't hold any sway for gossip. They traded, and the family largely made their own way.

Invariably, in one of these towns, a question for which she had no answer arose time and again: *Where do you live?* Live? Why, they lived everywhere and no place at all. Only, the more her younger self thought about it, the more she saw definite advantages to settling. A real home. Friends. Waking up early every morning and walking a country mile to a little schoolhouse, where she'd elbow herself to the front row if she had to. Her parents simply hadn't grasped what this could mean for her.

One night, sitting around a fire outside (again) a town whose name she couldn't recall, Liza suggested that their family settle there. That they buy a house like other families did and that she promptly be enrolled in school.

Her mother was not a demonstrative woman, not given to outward signs of emotion. She was incapable. But if the expression that came over her mother's face was terrifying, it was nothing compared to the tongue-lashing she unleashed. Liza shrank, backed away under the onslaught. She could remember cowering behind her father's leg. As swiftly as he doled out punishment when she did something wrong, he would not fail to protect her when the tables were turned. This was not one of those times.

He'd only laid a hand on her shoulder and said, "The soul would have no rainbow if the eye had no tears." Unexplained anger spent, her mother's gaze did soften, but later their family packed up to leave. She never asked the other question that had been crowding her thoughts. Why were there no aunts and uncles? No grandparents or cousins? No other family.

Liza swept the memory from her mind, but like the dust that accumulated around the window frame above her bed, it would eventually return. She put the book down; smiled at Autumn, whom she was beginning to understand in her own way; scooped up Mico and placed him on her shoulder; and left the trailer in search of mind-clearing air.

"Hey, Eliza!" a carnie Liza barely recognized called out. She waved, muttered her own greetings, and meandered through the maze of trailers and vehicles. They were camped out somewhere northeast of Waco. People either walked about talking and chatting or sat on crates or fold-up chairs outside their trailers. Some worked on the endless list of repairs that were a part of the carnival life.

Zinsa and Efe, ever the soldiers, walked by with measured steps. Zinsa sneered at her, while Efe seemed to take her in and size her up in one blink, somehow finding her lacking. Liza let her gaze fall over the women as they approached and willed herself not to blink. The game of stares ended with neither of the women giving way. But after they moved on, she couldn't stop herself from turning to look behind her; she'd seen how they sneaked up on Bombardier. The women were also appraising her, but they walked on.

"Miss Meeks." Malachi waved her over to the trailer he shared with Eloko. The door to the trailer was open, and he sat on the top step. He had been reading a thick book, and another sat beside him. The sound of those pages flipping was beautiful, bringing back memories of her time with Mrs. Margaret. "I hope this day finds you and your friend well." He gestured to where Mico sat on her right shoulder.

Eloko appeared in the doorway. He yawned, his mouth a forest with trees of sharp, jagged teeth. Liza contained her shudder. Try as she might, she could not come to terms with his creepy ways. She was used to his unusual appearance, but it bothered her the way he looked at her like she was something delicious to eat.

"Did you not hear?" he asked, his eyes wide with mock concern.

Liza narrowed her eyes. "Hear what?"

Eloko brushed at his grass-covered arm, shedding a few blades. "Maybe it was nothing. I may have misunderstood."

"Misunderstood what?" Liza asked as she and Malachi looked at each other.

"Seems Uly is having trouble with your Australian feline again." Eloko blinked innocently. "I could be wrong, but you might want to check it out."

Liza didn't know if she believed the little man, but she wasn't going to risk it. She was going to visit her animals anyway. "Thanks," she said. And to Malachi she motioned to the books and said, "Maybe you'll read some for me, later?"

Malachi's smile returned. "I would be happy to."

≈

Of course nothing was wrong with Sabina. But Ikaki sent her an image as soon as she came in. It was the image of themself beneath the sun, floating in the river.

"Uly," Liza called. "Ikaki wants a little sun today."

Uly set down the newspaper he had been reading. "I don't know if I will ever get used to this," he said.

She stuck her hand through the bars of Sabina's cage as Uly and Ikaki made their way outside. She rubbed Sabina under the chin the tiger elegantly lifted. She understood her—of that much, Liza was certain. She had become more comfortable with her too. Maybe today . . .

She conjured the same image of them sitting together and then sent it. This time, the response was so quick that Liza nearly fell over.

What Sabina sent startled her. A woman, the same woman from Ikaki's vision. The terror of being trapped, unable to move. Sabina being transported and landing at the carnival.

Liza supposed that, given the choice, most animals would rather be free than in a circus or carnival, but there was something more going on here. Something to do with that woman.

The next images the tiger sent, powerful, painful, made her heart ache. Sabina with a litter of pups, men taking them away despite her snarls and snaps and protests. Full teats, unused, dried. Images of other members of her species, alive, then dead or taken. Maybe some of them were Sabina's kin. The profound sadness was balanced by a stark pride. Sabina, with her head lifted—the last of her kind. She would represent the Tasmanian tiger species with pride in the carnival and not have to endure the human hunters.

In another image, Sabina portrayed herself standing over a supplicant dog with its legs up in the air, her forepaws digging into the flesh of the dog's soft middle. The message was clear. Sabina was no dog and would not do dog tricks. She was above such things.

Sabina's last image was of herself walking beside Liza. There was also a rather disparaging scene of a dog walking behind its owner on a chain, conveying all the disgust the Tasmanian tiger could muster. She wouldn't abide a leash.

Liza told her the rules: no biting, no running off too far, no snarling at the carnies (unnecessarily, anyway). Sabina sent back her response, of Liza walking round and round in a tiny, endless circle, her way of saying the human was repeating herself.

They set off to find Ishe, Liza nearly bursting with pride.

As she and Sabina wandered through the grounds, people gave them a wide berth.

"You should put her on a leash," Clay admonished her when he spotted the pair.

"She won't wear a leash. She told me."

The carnival manager shook his head. But even if he didn't believe her, Uly had the scars to prove that messing with Sabina was a bad idea.

"Besides, I'm practicing for the act. It's almost ready."

"About time," he muttered, but he appeared mollified.

Ishe was sitting outside his trailer carving when Liza approached. Too late, she wondered if a half hyena and a Tasmanian tiger would be at odds, but to her surprise, Sabina curled up at Ishe's feet as if she'd known the man her entire life. Liza settled herself onto the lush grass.

Ishe looked at Liza, then Sabina. "She spoke to you, didn't she?"

Liza beamed. "Finally. Now I can put my show together."

"One step at a time," Ishe cautioned, but he half grinned his approval and went back to carving.

"A hyena?" Liza asked, shocked. "You're carving a hyena?"

"You think you the only one tryin' to make sense of something about your nature you don't quite catch yet?"

"And you think the carving may help?"

Ishe held out the figure in the palm of his hand, turning it around, checking out his work. "Can't say I know. Can't even say this is what I expected when I started."

Liza watched Ishe from the corner of her eye and worked up the nerve to ask the question she'd been wanting to since that night in the alley. "How did you come to be the way you are?" she eased out.

Ishe kept on carving, but she could see his chest heave with a heavy intake of breath. When he met her eyes, the pain was as raw as any she'd ever seen. He leaned forward, forearms on his knees. "Partnership of man and beast is sometimes an invention of the devil."

Liza frowned. "I don't like riddles."

"Me neither."

There wouldn't be any further discussion on the matter—that much was clear. Liza leaned back, palms outstretched on the ground behind her, and accepted what Ishe could offer. It was enough. She contented herself watching him work, Sabina curled at his feet, and judging by the way he occasionally stopped to show her his progress, he was pleased to have her as his audience. Letting the peaceful day wash over her, she removed her amulet from the pouch and tumbled the discs inside between her fingers.

He set the carving down. "What you always fiddling with there?" He gestured at the amulet. Sabina lifted her head, did an owl-worthy neck swivel between them as if assessing the change in mood, but finding everything in order, yawned loudly and lay down again.

Liza grew protective, went to put the amulet back in her pouch. "Something my mother gave me . . . before. Before I left."

Ishe held out his hand, waved his fingers in a come-on-let-me-see motion.

Liza huffed and placed the amulet in his outstretched hand. Ishe studied the discs for a moment and looked back at her. "You don't know what you got here?"

"I told you, some old necklace." She shifted on the ground.

Ishe came to his feet and, with him, Sabina. "Didn't your mama teach you nothin' about your people?"

Liza stood, dumbfounded and the tiniest bit annoyed. Ishe had been born in Africa; she hadn't. Who was he to judge her if she didn't know everything about the place? "I didn't stay with them long enough, I guess."

"We got our own animal spirits like these at home." He paused, then said, "Nigeria."

This was the first time Ishe had mentioned something about his life before the carnival, and though Liza wanted to probe, to find out more about him, she was too caught up in the new discovery. Nigeria, same as Ikaki. It all seemed to lead back there.

"What do the carvings mean?"

Ishe gave her back the amulet, and she secured it away. "I don't know how yet, but this must be a key, and you gonna have to figure out how to put it in the lock and open the door."

CHAPTER TWENTY-ONE

THE MYSTICAL BEASTMISTRESS

There were two sides to every coin, and in Liza's experience, the same could be said of most towns she'd visited. San Antonio, Texas, was no exception. East San Antonio was reserved for the Negro population and was home to the famous Sutton family. They were big-time firsts in an era that wasn't too friendly to pioneers of a certain hue. Owned everything from a funeral home to the farm where Liza's family had stopped to buy vegetables once.

It was fitting, then, that this was where she'd debut her animal show.

Despite Clay's repeated attempts to get a glimpse of the show Liza was putting together, she'd told him that he would see it right along with everybody else. Problem was, animals were fickle—everybody knew that. She hoped that today, her opening night, wouldn't be one of those times. She was looking forward to running her own show and the bump in pay that went along with it.

"You owe me one." Wendell was one of the most skilled carpenters Liza had ever seen, so she'd asked him for a little help building a set for her act. "Go on—take a peek." He beamed.

Liza lifted the cloth and grinned. "Perfect. And I promise, I'll pay you out of what I make from my show tonight."

"I don't know what you got planned, but can't wait to see it. Wouldn't hurt if you slapped a coat of paint or something on it," Wendell added. "You know, jazz it up some."

"I'll do that," Liza said, but she wondered if she'd make any money at all if she had to go and beg and borrow for paint too.

She'd barely finished the thought before her trailer mate, Autumn, strolled in. "Figured this is where I'd find you," she said and then turned to the builder. "Hey, Wendell."

If Wendell were a white man, he'd have been blushing like a rose in full bloom. He looked as if he was going to bow but pulled up short. "Autumn. Um, Ms. Autumn. Uh, you look . . . well, you look nice today."

"As nice as I do with my clothes off?" Autumn teased. Liza put her hand to her mouth to stifle the laugh that tickled the back of her throat.

Wendell opened his mouth but tripped repeatedly over his own tongue, spewing a string of unintelligible words before making a hasty exit from the tent. Autumn and Liza broke out laughing.

"You shouldn't tease him like that," Liza said once she'd composed herself. "I think he likes you."

Autumn pulled the shawl over her shoulders. Liza couldn't figure out for the life of her how the woman could be cold. "Like the rest of these carnies, he's in love with the woman they sneak in to see up on that stage. That lady isn't any more real than the broads they gawk at in their girlie magazines. Sad thing is, the poor idiots don't even know it."

Liza pondered this for a moment. Autumn surprised her sometimes, and she wondered again why she did what she did. "Maybe they're happier that way," she said finally. "You know, sometimes real life isn't so much fun."

"Whatever gets you through the day," Autumn replied, then gestured at the animals. "Anyway, you tore out of the trailer so fast . . ."

It was Autumn's turn to be uncomfortable. She tugged and pinched at Liza's new uniform, a gift from Clay. A garish pair of ballooning red pants cinched tightly at the waist and ankle, paired with a blouse of finely woven white muslin with embroidered gold-and-red fringe surrounding the wrists, some beaded embellishments Autumn had sewn on. Silken booties with a neat bow and a sharp gold vest completed the outfit.

"I wanted to wish you good luck with your show."

"Thank you," Liza said. "I appreciate it."

With that, Autumn sashayed out of the tent.

~

Liza gaped at the new banner that had joined the others on the makeshift carnival wall: a hand-drawn picture of herself, flanked by her animals, Ikaki on the right and Sabina on the left.

Clay had scheduled Liza for only one show tonight. Said he had to see how she would do before he would gamble on any more. Liza couldn't blame him; had she any coins to spare, she'd likewise place her bets elsewhere. She'd built each piece of the act steadily, if slowly, with what Sabina and Ikaki had agreed to do. The question remained of whether they would do as asked on her command. If they refused to perform, then her place with the carnival, her new home, would be no more. She hadn't even saved enough for a ticket back to Baton Rouge. The whole thing sapped her appetite and rattled her nerves so much her head throbbed.

She felt Jamey's presence, her senses attuned to the earth, just as her father had taught her. He touched her elbow as he stepped up next to her.

"Gonna be a good night," he said. "I can feel it."

"You really think so?" Liza asked, unconvinced.

"I know it." Jamey met and held her eyes. "You look mighty fine in that getup."

They were admiring the banner when his fingers sought out hers. Gently, he pulled her to him and took her other hand. He met her eyes, and she fought not to look away from the intensity of his gaze. He leaned down; she raised up on the tips of her toes. And there, on the wings of the most important day of her life, their lips met, flooding her body with all kinds of pleasant sensations she'd never felt before. She carried the grin all the way to the animal tent.

◦

By nightfall, the carnival atmosphere was in full swing. On her way to her performance tent, Liza skirted scantily clad women with their beaded garb and towering headdresses. They pulsed through the crowd with frenetic dance moves. The stilt walkers waded through on their stilts along with the others. Games, bells, and the thump of African drums filled the air.

Once inside her tent, Liza paced nervously while the pitchman wooed the crowd. "Come one, come all. See the enchanting, the beautiful, the Mystical Beastmistress!"

The animals' cages had been moved behind a curtain at the rear. The set was impressive: an ornately carved wooden frame met a slightly raised platform, leaving the audience to think they were looking through a picture window. Inside, a large pool sat enclosed by a tiny picket fence with a set of five steps placed diagonally across from it. Low benches filled the remainder of the space, and already they were full, with more waiting outside.

Liza emerged from behind the curtain with a flourish. Ikaki trailed slowly behind, making their way over to the pool, and Sabina stood beside Liza, snout lifted to the air, tail stiffly out behind her. Liza's hair was parted down the middle, plaited into braids, then wrapped atop her head. Mico sat on her shoulder, peering alternately at the crowd and the animals. Sabina bared her teeth and growled at the audience, earning a few gasps. One person even ran out.

From the corner of her eye, Liza noticed Clay settled in as unobtrusively as possible near the tent entrance.

"Ladies and gentlemen." Liza's voice cracked as she stepped forward, flashing a smile she'd worked on all afternoon. "Welcome to my show. I'm Liza, the Mystical Beastmistress. Meet my friends Mico, Sabina, and Ikaki." A small bit of applause filled the space. The crowd was not won over yet.

"Our Sabina here is what you call a Tasmanian tiger, and she is the last of her kind. Come to us all the way from Australia. Ikaki is a turtle, but don't be fooled. They're not any ordinary turtle but a *dancing* one." At that the crowd whooped and hollered. "And this little guy"—she pointed to Mico—"he found me, and, well, I don't know where he came from, and he wants you to know that he's here as our eager assistant. He's a pygmy marmoset. They are the smallest monkeys on the planet, hailing all the way from South America. Now, on with the show."

Liza moved first to Ikaki. "Ikaki would like to ask for a volunteer from the audience, a child, please." Several hands shot up, and Liza picked a bright-faced little girl from the front who had a gap in her teeth so like Twiggy's that Liza's heart squeezed. "Looks like we have our volunteer." Mico scurried down to provide an escort. The crowd clapped.

"What's your name, little lady?" Liza asked.

"Beaulah!" the girl said loudly.

"Okay, Beaulah, Ikaki would like to ask you to do a dance, a simple one that they will imitate."

"Nuh-uh!" the girl said, and when Liza grinned, she whipped out a simple two-step dance.

Ikaki, who had been stationed by Liza's feet, looked up at her with obvious disinterest, sent her an image of themself swimming, and promptly waddled over to the pool. The turtle hoisted themself in with a splash and swam as if this were the most natural thing in the world to do at that moment. Liza's insides crumbled, her armpits soaked with sweat.

The crowd collectively leaned forward, anticipating. Then they laughed.

Liza's smile disintegrated. She pleaded, sending Ikaki images of the dance, of their agreement. Ikaki swam a few more laps in what Liza figured was a perfect display of being downright ornery and then emerged, water glistening on their back.

Ikaki took their time positioning in front of the crowd, then raised up and imitated the little girl's dance perfectly. The child beamed and giggled, the crowd roared, and Clay stood at the back gaping, his hands now at his sides.

"Thank you, Beaulah," Liza said. "Anybody else? Ikaki says they're good for at least three more dances."

Volunteers surged forward, and even when Ikaki couldn't imitate the dances exactly, they improvised, caught up in the action, inventing their own moves and getting the crowd going. Abruptly, though, Ikaki grew tired of the games and waddled back to the pool. It was time for Sabina.

"Now we have our girl Sabina," Liza said.

Sabina first shocked the crowd by raising up and walking a few steps on her hind legs. Then, at Liza's command, she moved over to the steps and hopped up each one. At the top step she peered out at the onlookers, and in a show of her incredible sense of smell, she deftly sent Liza an image of all three people in the audience who'd had whiskey before the show. Liza informed the crowd of the tiger's picks and commanded two men and one woman to stand. When she spelled out the trio's choice of after-supper spirits, the crowd guffawed. Sabina then leaped off and landed in front of the crowd, who broke out in cheers.

Mico then emerged from the corner, pushing a large round ball and earning delighted giggles from the children. Liza said, "Did you know that a Tasmanian tiger can open its jaws a full twelve inches?"

With that Liza tossed the ball up in the air, and Sabina leaped to meet it. Her jaws snapped open at a seemingly unbelievable angle, revealing a series of sharp, jagged teeth. She caught the ball in her mouth and landed elegantly back on the ground. She dropped the ball at Liza's feet and pushed it toward her with her snout. The ball rolled, completely intact, over to Liza, who put her foot on top of it and threw her arms out in a flourish. The crowd came to its feet, clapping and cheering.

"Steps!" Liza called out, and Sabina trotted back to the top stair. "Open." Sabina opened her mouth, and Liza leaned forward, turned to make sure she faced the crowd, and slid her head between the gaping jaws.

"Sweet Jesus!" someone from the crowd called out.

"Okay, now I need three more volunteers!" Liza announced. Clay had moved even closer by now.

Liza had one volunteer line up on his hands and knees, with the next two standing in line by order of height. After a bit of cajoling, she got the last man to place an apple between his teeth. She then waved a hand, and Sabina took a running start, leaped over the kneeling man, then rose on her hind legs and hopped over the first woman. For the finale, Sabina bounded into the air, snatched the apple from the man's mouth, and landed lightly on her feet.

Despite the look of composure on Liza's face, her stomach was doing somersaults inside. She plastered the smile back on her face and took a bow.

After the show ended and everyone had filed out, Clay stepped forward. "I'd say that was a fair first show."

"It was a darn good first show," Liza countered.

"Got another gasser on my hands, I see." Clay couldn't manage a smile, but the look of satisfaction was unmistakable. "The animals up for another show?"

"I believe they are." Liza grinned.

Clay slapped his thigh. The burgeoning smile faded, replaced by the normal, grim set of his mouth and a touch of melancholy. He turned then and left the tent.

CHAPTER TWENTY-TWO

SOWING THE SEEDS OF TROUBLE

The G. B. Bacchanal Carnival crept into the city of Amarillo, Texas, under the cover of a baleful indigo night sky. Prickly tumbleweeds rumbled across the sunbaked terrain, and the catcalls of crickets and rodents and their predators sailed on the wind like a primeval orchestra. Lightning cut through thick gray clouds bunched up like bushels of oversize grapes.

Nobody was much interested in sleep with the excited buzz of being in a new city. Folks tossed dice, threw back beers, and swapped stories.

Bacchanal didn't seek to compete with the likes of P. T. Barnum's circus but had carved out a niche all their own in the smaller towns and those places off the wider circuit. In places where law enforcement wasn't always so boastful in their work, a little coin was all that was needed for the special types of dispensations Bacchanal required. And for the occasional disappearances that seemed to occur whenever the carnival was in town.

Clay negotiated a fair deal with the local law. As he saw the small but bustling city during the day, he was more hopeful that Waco could become a distant, if unpleasant, memory. They'd set up for two weeks— a little longer than he wanted, but if customers kept coming, then it would be worth it.

Because of the bad roads they'd traveled, many of the trailers needed repairs. The crew was handy, though, and Jamey would make sure everything got done; still, Clay walked around barking orders.

"All right, you lazy bums. Shake a leg. We got a show to put on tonight." He marched around rallying his troops. "And you, Denny, if I see you slackin' off one more time, I'll bounce you outta here right on your hide." Denny was good at two things: electrical work and drinking himself under a table—not the best mix of skills.

Clay continued on his way and ran into Malachi. "Wendell making sure you got everything you need?" he said.

Malachi put a finger to his chin. "I think I have most everything except—"

But he didn't get to finish his sentence, as Efe appeared at Clay's side.

"A word," she said in her light voice. Geneva had told him that, often in battle, men had mistaken Efe's lithe body and the sweetness of her face and voice. Clay had never made such a mistake. Malachi, being himself, ignored the menacing look in her eye.

"The Human Pincushion," he said to introduce himself. "Malachi—"

Efe curled her lip and moved away a few paces. She left Malachi standing with one confused hand in the air and beckoned Clay to follow.

"The mistress is back," she whispered when Clay joined her. "She would like to see you."

Clay kept his face steely; he'd figured this would be coming. Silently they wove through the carnival, and soon the red trailer loomed ahead. It sat there, seemingly innocuous. Soft, muted light cascaded from the windows, giving the place an eerie glow that sent an unbidden shiver up Clay's spine.

"If it is not the big man." Zinsa was standing on the right side of the stairs leading up to the trailer door. "We will see after the mistress is done with you."

"Every day that passes," Clay said, walking past her and then knocking on the door, "you grow more loathsome. Mighty lucky that Geneva took pity on you. Hear tell, no man would have you."

Zinsa's eyes shot murderous spears, sticks, and rocks at Clay. "And no woman, man, or lonely goat would have *you*."

Clay took the short flight of stairs two at a time. He steadied his breathing, rapped once on the door, then opened and closed it behind him.

In all these years, Clay had never seen Geneva in any clothes other than those she wore now. Her customary headband wrapped skillfully around her head, long black braids peeking out. The bracelets covered both arms, and her skirt was of colorful rags. Instead of her normal lounging spot on the plush chaise lounge, she stood near the rear of the trailer, fussing over the black curtain.

Her hands wove something in the air, but Clay couldn't make out what it was. With a soft blow of breath, she sent the glowing thing between her palms forward. It inched toward him, growing bigger until it was the size of a human head.

Clay gasped, and the veins in his forehead and neck bulged with his pointless struggle to escape. The glowing green ball was a writhing mass of worms, twisting and turning on each other. They had enormous mouths that they used to bite and tear at their own heads and tails. Geneva poised the abomination precious inches from his face. The worms turned to Clay, snapping at his sweat-covered face.

Clay stood frozen for what felt like an eternity, certain that the mass would settle on his face and destroy it, but with a gesture from Geneva's elegant hand, the mass of worms disappeared and the invisible hold on him dissolved. One of the fading snake-worms sprang out and nipped the tip of Clay's nose. He called on every muscle in his body and will to hold him up.

His clothes must have looked as if he'd pulled them on after a run through a river. He swiped his forearm over his face. "Some employers would dock a man's pay a day or two for a screwup," he managed to say, but he couldn't prevent his voice from cracking.

Geneva smiled and sauntered over to the lounge, where she lay down like an Egyptian queen. "When I saved you, most employers wouldn't have you. Even your wife looked upon you with shame, not with the love of a woman."

She knew where to hit him, this one. Clay swallowed hard, his bravado deflated. "It was one bad stop," he said, trying to find something to do with his hands. "Nobody gonna go hungry."

"Because I will not let that happen," Geneva said. "The least you could have done was to bring me a child. You ignore my needs *and* those of the carnies."

"I didn't think you were due—"

"And I hear that electrician you hired is a lazy drunk."

Clay's previously liquefied backbone was finding its way back to solid form. "Unless you tell me different, all worker personnel decisions are under my purview. If it's all the same to you, I'll handle it my way."

Geneva turned her head in dismissal. "Send Zinsa and Efe to get whatever we lack the money for."

Clay lifted his chin and turned to leave.

Geneva called, "And Clay, I hope this date turns out to be a prosperous one. After Tulsa, I'll have a new route for us to explore, so we need to be solidly in the black before then."

He stopped, then exited the trailer short of a run, but he caught himself quickly.

"We're good on food," he said to the women outside. "But the carnies need some toys. Their magazines are old; maybe some hard candies." He paused, considering. "Think they could use some new linens, too, a few European soaps for the ladies."

Clay stormed off without a backward glance. He didn't know how Geneva told them to go about getting the things that they did, and he didn't care. It was one less thing he had to worry about. He didn't even stay to trade barbs with Zinsa.

He waited till he was out of their line of sight, commanding the taut muscles in his legs to carry him with an aura of calm authority he no longer felt. When he was far enough away, he tore off into the surrounding fields, plowing through knee-high grass until he found a clearing. Settling on a rock, Clay slipped out the simple silver cross he kept tucked away from prying eyes and kissed it.

He lit a match. His right arm was still tender from the last time, so he rolled up his left sleeve, bit down on a strap of leather, and let the flame do its work.

～

Eloko kept to the shadows on his way to see Ahiku. Along the way, he spied Jamey and Liza standing outside her trailer and watched as they shared a kiss.

It seemed an awkward thing, a mingling of lips, saliva, and inexperience. They'd hurried off from the rest of the carnies after supper like a couple of schoolkids; such had become their pattern. Eloko contemplated them as if their clumsy coupling were a new sideshow oddity.

"You lost something?"

Eloko bristled and nonchalantly turned to face Autumn. Had he been so wrapped up in Liza that his senses had gone numb? People didn't creep up on *him*; it was the other way around. "Besides all the time I've lost wondering why such a chaste lady such as yourself chooses to show her body to strange men?"

Autumn flushed a deep red that matched the polka dots on her blouse. "Don't go taxing what little brain you must have worrying about me." She pushed past him and slammed the trailer door behind her, startling Jamey and Liza, who quickly composed themselves. Liza joined Autumn inside.

Slipping back into the dusky gloom, Eloko pressed on. Zinsa and Efe at first stiffened, then relaxed, when he suddenly appeared, he so well blended into the surroundings.

"You keep sneaking up on us . . . ," Efe began.

". . . and you may find yourself gutted like a fish," Zinsa finished.

"You ladies try too hard," Eloko said. "You should settle into your role; you don't have to appear on the verge of a murderous rampage at every moment. A more subtle approach is sometimes called for. In case you had not noticed, the war is over."

"Maybe for you," Efe said with a far-off look in her eye. "Never for us."

Eloko understood, for he, too, had lost every last one of his people. Zinsa and Efe were the last of their kind, warriors with no war left to fight and no spoils to revel in, no home to return to.

"Our good Mr. Kennel exited. I assume Ahiku has come back to the world of the living?" he said.

"I will ask if she will see you." Efe disappeared behind the door and quickly returned. "You may enter."

Eloko took in the African masks, swaying a bit to the drum music emanating from a source he couldn't identify. He inhaled deeply through his pulsing snout, for the place even smelled of home. The demon lounged on her blessed chair like a leopard. Beautiful, majestic, but were one to peel back the spotted coat, the claws and fangs of the afterlife would be clear. He walked to her and knelt.

Ahiku rested a palm on his head, petting him like an animal. He hated the gesture so much, and his closed lids did little to contain the flash of red behind them.

She chuckled and lifted her hand. "Our friend Mr. Kennel trembles when he sees me. He tries to hide it, but I smell the fear on him like a lion's musk. But you . . ." She sat up. "You war with your anger and, what is that, admiration?"

"A monk cannot go about without his robes."

"And a dwarf cannot forever suppress his hunger for human flesh."

Eloko turned his back and moved to the window farthest away from her. He was an open book to the demon. He wondered how she could justify denying him when she had never forsaken her own urges. Demons were given to odd, unpredictable behaviors, none of which could be categorized as logical or fair.

"Forgive me, mother of demons, for I have sinned."

"My taste is for souls, yours for human flesh." Ahiku came up behind Eloko, reached a hand out to stroke his grassy mane.

"That is not why I'm here." Eloko would not apologize unless she demanded it. He had eaten only a few humans since he'd come to America. It took great effort to retrain one's tastes to cooked animal flesh and green things. She ought to give him more credit. "It is about the girl."

"The one you ate back in Florida?" Ahiku looked genuinely curious.

Eloko folded his arms and spun around. "No, no." He stopped short of stamping his foot. "The one your good Mr. Kennel picked up in Baton Rouge, the one who speaks to beasts."

She narrowed her eyes. "What about her?"

"You felt nothing when you checked her out?" Eloko asked.

"The taint of Oya's touch was not upon her," the demon said. "She has not always done the right thing, has impure thoughts, even wishes badly on her parents for leaving her. But she is not the one I seek."

Eloko rubbed at his grassy chin. "But there is something about her. And she and that Nigerian bush dog have begun spending a lot of time together."

"Ah." Ahiku tilted her head. "The man who has remained faithful to a wife he will never see again has finally given in. Such a strong soul, that one. I had taken him for one of those who would not bend."

"Not in that way," Eloko countered. *He will not have her.* "He is helping her somehow. You know she can kill as easily as she can cajole the beasts."

"Well, then it will be your job to watch her. You can see the wrongness even in good people. I cannot. That is why I have added you to my little collection." Ahiku walked back to the dark curtain. "I must return to the underworld for a time. I don't expect you'll find much other than some harmless coupling, but you can give me a report upon my return."

As Eloko turned to leave, she called out, "And to show that I, too, have a heart, you may eat that loafing electrician—Denny."

Eloko waltzed away from the trailer with a renewed spring in his step. He wondered whether, if he were to find something amiss with Liza, Ahiku would let him eat her as well. Saliva dripped from the corners of his mouth in twin slimy strings. Eloko two-stepped his way to find Denny.

CHAPTER TWENTY-THREE

AUTUMN IN THE SUMMER OF 1939

Autumn had lit up like primed and ready wood tinder when sullen Zinsa and Efe appeared at their trailer toting the latest issues of *Vogue* and *Life* magazines for her. They then dug deep in their sack and tossed out copies of *Argosy Weekly*, *Black Mask*, and *Astounding Stories* for Liza. They added a bar of lavender soap and new toothbrushes. Autumn had been glued to her magazines ever since.

"You better get your nose out of that magazine." She glanced up and found her roommate standing at their door, all ready for another night of her animal show. As the days marched on, Amarillo's townsfolk had been coming out in droves.

"I'm coming." Autumn tucked the magazines atop the wooden shelves that Ishe had installed above their bunks. Both were now filled with stacks of magazines and Liza's new copy of *A Tale of Two Cities*. Ishe had been hanging around quite a bit since Liza had moved in. So had Jamey, come to think of it. Autumn smiled—that girl was working it with the best of them.

"Gotta pull on my stockings." Autumn was draped in a skin-hugging, sheer material that sparkled with intricate beadwork. Her shoes were of the baby doll variety, with a keen strap across the top of the foot and a good two-inch heel. She'd had Liza try them on once, and the girl'd nearly turned an ankle, then barked on about how Autumn could possibly dance in them.

She pulled on the silk robe, and both ladies gave each other the once-over, twirling in the small space before they left.

"May your tip cup be overflowing," Liza called out.

"And yours," Autumn returned. Her tent was set up near the rear of the midway, and she walked slowly, thinking about all the beautiful models and celebrities in her magazines. At another time, so long ago that she couldn't remember where the idea had first caught fire, she had believed she could be one of them.

It was her mama. The way she told it, five minutes into Autumn's first tottering steps, she'd danced her first jig. Her mama had proclaimed Autumn a wunderkind right then and there. Told her that one day she'd be like all the stars in the big movies. Mama had acted in small community theater—such as it was in Chicago—before she'd married Autumn's daddy. She'd dressed her only child impeccably, like a little mirror image of herself. Autumn learned to walk like a lady before she could count to one hundred. Could recite a poem before she learned the alphabet. All that grooming was supposed to set her on a path to the pages of those magazines she read so much.

But tuberculosis had stolen her mother. Like one brutal swipe of an eraser across a chalkboard, the illness had wiped away her present and her future.

"I'm sorry," her daddy had said with his hat in his hand as they stood on the porch of his mother's house in rural Alabama. "I ain't never been no good with little girls." Daddy had taken her hand and coaxed her into the dim, close, ramshackle house that smelled of stale bread and blight. He had deposited their suitcases in a back room, plopped down onto the worn sofa, and picked up a bottle of whiskey. It was a rare, special occasion when she would see him without a bottle again.

Somehow, he managed to hold a job, even met a real nice lady once. But his drinking buddies convinced him that any woman would put too much of a damper on their fun. The lady was gone. And when one of her daddy's drinking buddies groped her, she and Grandma put such a whupping on the drunkard (Grandma was surprisingly nimble with a rolling pin), the drinking buddies were soon all gone too.

When the G. B. Bacchanal Carnival came to town, ten years of broken dreams and backwoods squalor propelled Autumn toward it. She'd walked into the audition with Clay with a straight back, her head held high. She danced a number she'd learned with her mother, a tamed version of something she'd read Josephine Baker had made famous. Clay had welcomed her in but asked if she could dance a little differently.

Like everybody who joined the G. B. Bacchanal Carnival, Autumn recalled her first and only trip to the red trailer. With Zinsa and Efe appraising her, the experience was about the same as standing before her grandmother that first time. The touch of something unseen fluttered across her skin.

Now she pictured herself in the magazines she treasured, dreaming of the life that should have been hers but accepting the one that was. She had been firm with Clay. She wasn't all too keen on the type of dancing he needed her for, but if she could make the show classy, make it her own, she'd do it. She didn't have to make it as raunchy as some of the magazine clips he'd shown her. And she would never turn any tricks afterward. Clay respected her and her decision. He'd since found other girls to do that.

Slipping through the back entrance of her tent, Autumn noticed the large crowd of men gathering and, as usual, pushing and shoving each other out front. Wendell was there—her bodyguard. Sometimes men got rowdy, wanting a little bit of the show after the show. He'd club a few of them over the head, and the rest would fall in line.

"Evenin', Miss Autumn," he said.

It pained Autumn to see that puppy-dog look in his eyes. If she ever married, it wouldn't be to another carnie. Some small part of her, growing quieter every day, hoped that perhaps she could still have a career like Greta Garbo did.

"Wendell," she said, and she accepted his hand as she shed her robe and mounted the steps leading up to her stage.

She gestured back down to Wendell, and the curtain slid open and the music began. The crowd whooped and hollered. Autumn danced easily on the balls of her feet, twirling and spinning into a pirouette. Clay had prodded her to add in a few more suggestive moves, and she'd complied grudgingly. When she launched a kick in the air, spun around, and then dropped into a split, a man in the audience surged toward the front of the stage.

"I'll pay ya good money if you show me that move out back," he slurred.

Wendell came to her rescue, dragging the man away, and she continued the dance. She would do two more shows before the night was over. But the take was beyond even her hopes. She gave Wendell a sizable tip that he tried to give back to her.

As she donned her robe, she decided to find Liza. But a man, draped in enough shadow to conceal his face, blocked her path. Autumn looked to her left and right and was about to scream when the man moved into the light, removing his hat. Autumn's wild eyes softened with recognition. Her heart pounded like she'd run a marathon, her breath ragged.

"Daddy." It came out barely a whisper.

Her father held a rose in trembling hands. "You put on a real nice show. Classy, same as your mama."

Autumn took the rose but couldn't conjure up any words to give in return. Her father ran a rough finger along her cheek, slipped his hat back on, and disappeared into the thinning crowd. She sniffed the rose and allowed a thin smile to spread across her face. It didn't matter how he'd found her, only that he had. And in time, when she was ready, she, too, would seek him out again. She wore the smile all the way to the animal tent.

Liza was closing the latch on Ikaki's cage, while Uly was refreshing the hay in Sabina's.

"Good night?" Autumn asked, settling onto a bench.

The beast girl was surprised to see her—she'd put bets on it. For all the time they spent together in their trailer, Autumn knew she never talked much, and she would clam up whenever Liza pried too much. She just didn't like spilling her guts much. Women chattered about her behind her back enough; she felt no need to talk about it face to face.

"Darned good night," Liza answered as she came to sit on the bench. "Where'd you get that?" She pointed to the rose.

"A customer," Autumn said, tucking the rose into her hair, behind a pink ear. She still couldn't believe her daddy had found her.

"There's different ways of being a star. Only some of them, a small bit, are in the movies. How many pitch cards you sell tonight?"

"Ain't counted them all up yet," Autumn said, but she beamed. She supposed Liza was right: she was a bit of a star. "I only had a couple left on my table when Wendell left, though."

"And how many cities you been to?" Liza continued. "Nearly two years with Bacchanal? I seen you get two or three print runs since I joined. Yeah," she said, rising. "I'd say you got about as many fans as those famous people in the wax museum."

Autumn batted her arm and let out a girlish giggle. "Not that many."

"Let's get outta here," Liza said. "Need some fresh air."

~

The cook tent was closed, but it was a warm night and many of the carnies had gathered around the picnic tables still set up in the large open tent. People had also dragged chairs around a few of the tables. Autumn and Liza drifted to the picnic table that Hope, Bombardier, and Ishe shared. Clay, Jamey, Wendell, and many others were at the next table. Malachi and Eloko had chairs in the center of it all.

Even Zinsa and Efe stood at the fringe, looking uncomfortable.

A carnie named Mosley was leading a story about the dumbest mark he'd ever seen.

". . . so I tell the big lummox," he said with a chuckle, "that Bombardier is as weak as a church mouse. The secret to his strength is this here hooch." He held up the bottle they'd taken to selling at the concession stand. "'It'll grow hair on your chest and increase your strength and virility by a factor of ten,' he'd said. Told him, after takin' a swig, that a lady, our very own Miss Autumn here, had pinned Bombardier like a shirt on a clothesline. And that if he, too, drank two bottles, he could whip the big man in a wrestling match."

Autumn blushed.

"For only an extra nickel, too, I betcha!" somebody from the crowd called out.

"Make that a dime," Mosley corrected. "And I got two ace notes for our special tonic." The crowd roared.

"And I am watching this snake oil salesman the whole time," Bombardier chimed in with a big grin. "And I'm thinking to myself, if he does not get this mark to pay up after painting *me* the picture of a chicken-livered cream puff, I will drag *him* into the ring and teach him some manners."

"Anyway," Mosley continued as if a little rattled by the idea, "the mark downs two bottles like that." He snapped his fingers. "Then he steps up into the little ring with our buddy here." Mosley stood behind Bombardier and clasped his shoulders. "Our man Bombardier tussles with the guy for a while, even lets him take him down a couple a times."

"I saw the whole thing," another carnie added. "The guy was getting hisself all worked up. Flexing his fat, flabby arms—you had to be there."

"Let 'em tell it, now!" another carnie called out.

Mosley looked slightly annoyed by the diversion but didn't miss a step in his storytelling. "The mark is standing over Bombardier, acting like he's out of it on the ground. He lifts his foot like he's intending to bring it down on our man's chest. All the while playing to the crowd."

"And what did he go and do that for?" another carnie who couldn't contain himself asked.

"Bombardier grabs that foot midair," Mosley boasted, "and flips our good mark outta the ring. He landed headfirst in a heap." Mosley waved his hands now, animated. "That ain't all! The mark—he, he lets out the loudest fart I ever did hear!"

The carnies went wild. People doubled over laughing, waving their hats, even the normally brooding Eloko.

"You're making it up," somebody said.

"I swear before my maker," Mosley said, making a cross over his heart. "Even sold outta the hooch!"

"And I was not done with him," Bombardier said, taking over. "I had to make this man suffer—the crowd demands such things. But the smell! Every time I touched the man, he erupted like a firecracker."

A carnie laughed and spit out a chunk of the apple he was chewing. Unfortunately, it landed on Zinsa's foot. She plucked the short knife from its sheath at her waist and held it to the man's throat before he could utter the apology on his quivering, wet lips. Her nostrils flared. Everyone tensed, holding their breath. Even Clay froze in midstep. Zinsa lowered the knife, snatched the apple, and sliced it in half. One half she tossed to the man; the other half she took a big bite out of. The crowd exploded in snorts and squeals of laughter.

The stories of how they'd taken the locals in with this trick or that carried on into the wee hours of the morning. Autumn suspected some were true, some embellished, but it didn't matter. The times the carnies got to spend in fellowship weren't often, and even Clay stayed to take it all in. Zinsa and Efe did not take seats, but they had moved in closer, their stoic faces creasing with smiles like everyone else's.

Bacchanal was back on a winning streak.

"All right, you lazy louts," Clay announced finally as he stood. "We break camp by midday. Get a couple hours' sleep if you can; then we pack it up and move out. By the way, anybody seen Denny? Got some bad wiring that needs fixing."

Eloko lowered his eyes and scampered away. When nobody answered, Clay said, "Good riddance—probably done run off. He was a half ass anyway."

Autumn rose and made her way back to her trailer, each step buffeted by the flutter of emotion she'd felt at seeing her father again after all these years. She imagined a new start for them, an honest-to-God father-daughter relationship thundering to life like a fledgling star.

CHAPTER TWENTY-FOUR

SOMETHING LOST, SOMETHING GAINED

"Nomad," "vagabond," "gypsy." When Liza was growing up, all these scornful terms were slapped onto her family. The words had clung to them like heavy, condemning extra appendages, a summary judgment of the way they had chosen to live their lives.

Her family were wanderers, clamoring to spread a little of themselves along the way. She'd never questioned her family's choices again. And though that life had come with its own costs, it suited her.

Mama was the most closemouthed person she had ever met. Even now, Liza struggled to remember the pitch and timbre of her voice, at once soft but husky. She was more broken and resigned than meek. It was as if whatever part of her cared one bit for her life or those of her children had retreated to some unknown and little-accessed corner of her brain. Her behavior incensed Liza to no end.

Twiggy was the opposite of them both. Her little face would scrunch up in concentration, straining to make sense of what her sister was talking about. She would let out a stream of nonsensical babbling noises, blinking and huffing at Liza like she was an idiot when it seemed she didn't understand. She was so eager to be a part of the conversation. She'd learned to talk early, but the child had no sense of the word "tact," couldn't even mouth the word with coaching. And before long, her mouth had gotten her into trouble. One day, on the unsteady legs of a four-year-old, she'd marched up to one of the Gullah elders and told him that he acted simple when he drank and wanted to know why he bothered.

Nights were tough for Liza's family. Most of the shacks they called home didn't have indoor plumbing, let alone separate bedrooms. The kids usually huddled together on one side of the room, their parents on the other. If they were lucky, a hastily drawn towel or sheet provided a flimsy scrap of privacy. But not seeing and not hearing were two totally different things.

One night, irked by the muffled sounds of their parents' late-night coupling, Twiggy had squirmed right out of Liza's arms, dodged her attempt to grab her back, snatched down the curtain, and said, "What y'all doing over here? I can't sleep with all this noise. You hurt, Mama?"

On the day when Twiggy had been born and placed into Liza's outstretched hands, Liza fell in love. She had fallen infinitely more in love every day after. Her heart had curled up and grown over with mold the day they'd been separated. The only thing that seemed to be coaxing it back to life was the family she'd found with the carnival. Where had her parents taken Twiggy? Would the child even recognize her after all this time? And if she did find her someday, what did she plan to do, take her with her in the carnival? There was no way Clay would allow that. Not with his "no kids" policy. Hope had confirmed as much when Liza had asked why Hope's son didn't visit. Liza could understand why kids couldn't come on the road with them, but they couldn't even visit? Didn't make sense. And what about families? What if a kid was conceived while on the road?

Jamey.

"What about him?" Autumn asked.

"Huh?"

"You whispered 'Jamey.'" Autumn turned serious. "Look, I know you like him, and he seems like a decent-enough guy, but carnival romances." She whistled. "Bad idea. I mean, what kind of life would you have here?"

"A life like Hope and Bombardier," Liza answered, and then folded her arms in front of her like a shield. "But who says I want to marry him or anything? And who asked you, anyway?"

The dancer rose. "You're the one whispering his name and going all googly eyed. Do whatever you want. I couldn't care less." She exited the trailer in a huff. Liza flung her pillow at the door as Autumn slammed it shut.

~

The carnival had been traveling north, eventually crossing the state line dividing the never-ending state of Texas from Oklahoma. The sky had taken on an ashen cast and ushered in a fine dust that clogged throats, settled into engines, and irritated eyes. Clay was set to go out scouting later in the day.

Liza left the trailer after she was sure Autumn was gone. Mico's head stuck out from her pants pocket. She made her way to Hope and Bombardier's trailer to see if they were up and about. Liza didn't want to admit it, but Autumn's words were playing over and over again in her head. Hope's son didn't even live with her—she hadn't seen him for a year, at that. The carnival sometimes wound its way up north, but not every year. Hope sent money home and peppered in telegrams with the rare phone call, but the truth was, Hope and Bombardier's son would know them only peripherally.

After losing Twiggy, Liza wasn't sure she wanted kids anyway. Would Jamey? And why was she even thinking about all this? All they had between them were a few kisses, some hesitant groping, and a fading awkwardness, and already she was thinking about what their life would be like together. No, she'd make the call right then and there. She would not get too involved.

"Looking mighty fine today," Jamey said as he came up behind her. His smile, the drooping right ear; all Liza's resolve melted.

189

She patted at her hair, wondered if she'd removed all the dust. "Thank you." He wore his usual overalls with a crisp white shirt, buttoned all the way to the top. He didn't have on his cap, so his hair glistened with the pomade he sometimes used to slick it back. She didn't have the heart to tell him she didn't like the way it smelled.

"Where ya headed?" he asked. These days he'd actually worked up the nerve to look her square in the eye.

Liza watched him. "Do you like kids?" Why on earth would she say that? She wanted to slap herself. Instead, she chomped down hard on her tongue.

Jamey blinked, and Liza could read him like a book in the look he gave her—*First she acts like she could do with or without me; now she's asking about kids?* "Never thought about it," he admitted. "But I suppose every man ought to have a son—"

"And I suppose a daughter would be, what, chopped liver?" Liza snapped. The argument they'd had on their first meeting flooded back.

Jamey looked flustered. "Now, that's not what I meant at all—"

But Liza had turned away from him and stormed off, sparing one spiteful glance over her shoulder in time to see Jamey pick up a rock and throw it hard at the wooden sideboard of a nearby trailer.

"Hey!" somebody called from inside.

"Hey!" Clay snapped his fingers in front of Liza's face, bringing her out of her angry reverie. "If you don't have nothing better to do than stare off and chew on your lip, do me a favor and find Malachi. Tell him the rest of his supplies are in."

Liza was about to protest, but Clay had already moved on to handle the next emergency. The man lived in perpetual motion; she suspected he woke up in sweats from all the running he must do in his sleep. People who tried to stay too busy were only running from something they didn't want to catch up to them. *I wonder what Clay is running from.* She rolled her eyes and set off to find Malachi.

He was right where Clay could have found him himself—outside his trailer, doing a series of stretches, movements she'd never recover from if she tried. Bent over at the waist, he stood slowly, as if he were stretching each bone in his back.

"You have finally agreed to join me in my morning exercises." He grinned, and as usual when she looked upon a face so serene, all her troubles slipped away. His gaze was calm yet intent. "Something's bothering you," he said, then gestured for her to join him. "Sit."

"I shouldn't," Liza protested. "Clay wanted me to tell you the things for your show have come."

Malachi swatted the information away like a pesky fly. "In a minute," he said again. "Sit."

Liza complied like a sullen child hopeful that there might be a treat at the end of the sermon. When Malachi didn't say anything else, only held his head back slightly and let the sun fall full on his face, she huffed—loudly. Well, she wasn't going to say anything; he was the one who'd invited her to sit.

Finally, he said, "You are uncomfortable with quiet?"

"No." Truth was, discomfort squirmed in Liza's gut like week-old gumbo. "I don't like to waste time."

Malachi opened his eyes. "Whatever time you can manage to spend alone with your thoughts is never wasted. Care to tell me what's clouding that face of yours with such consternation?"

Why should I? But something about Malachi wouldn't let her turn her sharp tongue on him. She was surprised when she let the words spill out, explaining the amulet, her problem with sometimes killing the animals, her attempts at learning to control her talent with Ishe.

"You believe that there is no separation between the spirit world and ours? That they are always around us?" Malachi rested his hands on his knees and regarded her without a hint of judgment in his eyes.

Liza tugged on her braid. "My mother spoke of them . . . some."

"Then you must know that they influence us in ways we don't always understand."

The man goes a long way around to making his point. She shrugged. "And what does that mean to me?"

"It means," Malachi said, stretching out the last word, "that I've studied myth and religion from many cultures, and they all have some form of that belief in common. Answers are often right in front of us; you just have to tune your mind to the right station to find them."

With this Liza perked up; she could almost see the path of where he was going. "And you know what the discs mean?"

"No," Malachi said, gesturing with his chin. "What animals are carved on there?"

Liza recounted the elephant, the raven, and the badger.

"Hmm. And of your African lineage, you know nothing?"

She bit her lip in answer.

"Let's try this. You ever heard of ancient Kush?"

Liza may not have read as many books as a man who'd been to college, but she'd read her fair share. "Ethiopia, Egypt, Sudan," she said.

Malachi beamed. "The birthplace of Kemetic meditation. Some say all meditation sprang from that practice."

"Meditation?" That hadn't been in any book she'd come across.

"Rest your hands in your lap and close your eyes," he instructed. "Breathe deeply, count your exhales one to ten, then begin again. Let your mind wander, and if a thought intrudes, push it gently away until the image you want, what you seek, comes to mind."

Before Liza could say that she had no idea what she was looking for, Malachi added, "You'll know when it comes to you."

Skeptical, she tried the exercise, breathing in and out, in and out. The stilt walker—what had that been about? She shoved that aside, only to have it replaced by an image of Jamey, the curve of his lips; she quickly pushed it away and started her counting over again. Mico—had she fed Mico? She pushed that aside as well. What kind of show would folks like? Ishe . . . she didn't want to think about the way she felt around him.

"I can't do this," she said, opening her eyes.

Malachi simply said, "Try again."

Liza gave him a side-eye, which he luckily couldn't see, as his own eyes remained closed. She blew out an agitated breath and let her eyelids flutter closed again. It took some time, but soon, the sounds of the bustling carnival-setup activities around her faded away. The steady stream of mind chatter slowed some. For a brief, blissful moment, her mind was blank.

Unbidden images—not her own—played through her mind on a slow flicker: a raven soaring through the air, black, yellow beak, sleek, lean body. She pushed the raven away, and it floated from her consciousness as if on a cloud. Then the elephant came, followed by the badger. Her heart beat faster in her chest, but she kept her breathing to a constant in and out; she had even stopped counting. She felt totally at peace.

The next image that floated into her mind was of a woman. Gray hair parted down the middle, her eyes round and intent, skin the color of charred wood. The woman's name flooded her mind: Oya.

"It has taken you long to find me. I am your grandmother, goddess of winds and storms, of death and rebirth." The woman's voice rattled around Liza's brain like a pinball before it settled. "I have a vision for you. A prophecy."

A water buffalo thundered along on a wide-open plain. The beast stopped, dissolved into a pile of dust, and swirled upward into a tornado. When the tornado died down, Oya stood at the gates of a cemetery that stretched as far as the eye could see. The landscape changed, revealing centuries of death and destruction.

The badger spirit appeared then and took an ineffectual swipe at Oya. A burst of wind from Oya's mouth sent him away. The raven swooped in, circling Oya's head, and with a clap of her hand was zapped out of the sky with a lightning bolt. The elephant charged at her back, but she spun into a hurricane and tossed him into another place.

"You must make your peace with them. Accept the spirits. We cannot defeat our enemy without them," the voice said. "And accept me." Then Oya smiled at Liza and began to fade away.

"Wait!" Liza screamed aloud. "What enemy? What does all this mean? Who are you?"

"Liza." Malachi was shaking her. "Liza, open your eyes."

She jerked away from Malachi and scrambled to her feet. "What the hell was that?" she shouted. "Are you playing some kind of trick on me?"

Malachi stood and regarded Liza curiously. "You had a vision?" He sighed. "Your path is not an easy one, then. Sometimes the spirits have plans for us that we don't like. But when your path is laid out, you have to walk it. I only hope that you learned something that will help you in what you must face."

Grandmother . . . huh. Ikaki had told her that they liked her because of who her grandmother was. Was this Oya her grandmother? She'd said she was a goddess. Liza deflated. She'd learned more, all right, but this business about her animal spirits and nameless enemies—why drop that on her and then disappear? "I understand more and am more confused than before I started."

"It will become clear."

"And what am I supposed to do until then?"

"Nothing," Malachi said. "Live. The ancestors will call on you when it's the right time."

"Why can't the ancestors stay dead and gone like they're supposed to." Liza made it more a statement than a question. She met Malachi's eyes and hoped her own conveyed some sort of gratitude for him trying to help her, but she stopped short of thanking him. Before she turned to leave, Eloko appeared. The grassy dwarf with his menacing snout winked at her before she hurried off.

∾

Liza's face was twisted in confusion when she passed Zinsa and Efe, who were practicing spear throwing at the expense of stuffed targets. The two women may as well have been Siamese twins for all the times they were ever apart from each other.

"Have you eaten a sour fruit today?" Zinsa said, and she and Efe laughed as Liza kept walking. If only she could whip up a clever retort, something snide about always being glued to some old, empty trailer, but after that vision, her mind was a mess. All she could think about was what Oya had said about accepting the animal spirits, but where on earth was she supposed to find them?

Then she was right in front of the red trailer. Clay's, as usual, sat to the right. Zinsa and Efe were still practicing.

Crouching and watching, Liza told herself to stand and back away slowly. But there she sat like a fly that couldn't be shooed away from a freshly baked pie, even with somebody standing there, flyswatter held high.

Maybe the answers to her particular situation weren't inside that trailer, but something was off, and whatever it was, it wasn't quite right. Liza was sure of it.

With elephants and ravens and badgers churning in her head, she approached at a wobbly crouch. It was as if she watched herself from outside her body: mounting the creaky stairs, a jittery, sweat-slick hand reaching out, the cool steel door handle. *Locked.*

She edged back down the steps and circled around to the open window on the back of the trailer, an empty field of brown and green grass the only witness. Even after she reached her arms to their full length above her head, the open window was still out of reach. She searched around for a crate, a box, or anything to stand on but came up empty.

When she leaped, her fingers only scraped the windowsill. She tried again, using her feet to scramble upward.

She'd peeked inside—a fleeting glimpse of masks, pale-yellow walls, and underneath a lounger, a child's slingshot like the one she and her father had made for Twiggy—when, from a reflection in the window, Liza caught sight of one of the stilt walkers right behind her.

She cried out and tumbled to the ground. Mico chittered wildly and dropped deeper into her pocket as Liza tried not to crush him. The stilt walker closed in: the red-and-black-painted face was of a skeleton, body armor made of bones. A wild red-and-yellow headdress sported an array of tinier skulls.

The walker lifted a long leg and stood over her, peering. Liza's breath and voice tangled and lodged at the back of her throat as the skeletal face detached and oozed downward. As it neared her face, the dark mouth crowded with teeth, the little skulls all became the bloodied, decayed faces of every animal she'd killed. They rippled through. With the face now inches from hers, the inexplicable sound of an elephant's trumpeting rang out. And the stilt walker disappeared.

"Eliza Meeks. What in God's name do you think you're doing?"

Liza froze. Where had the stilt man gone? And she knew darn well she'd heard an elephant.

"Come on, get up!" the voice demanded.

Liza turned to find Hope standing there looking like steam was coming from her ears. Her hands were on her hips and her mouth set in a grimace. "Jamey said you were in some sorta state this morning." She stalked forward and grabbed Liza by the wrist, pulling her away from the trailer. "You diggin' into things you don't know anything about."

Liza pulled her arm away, but she still followed her friend, ruffled like she had been chastised by her own mother. "Something's wrong in that trailer. I can feel it. Don't you want to know what Clay is hiding?"

Hope stopped and turned to face her. "I'm curious, but I got the good sense to keep it in check. We got a good life here, and ain't neither one of us gonna mess it up."

"What is the big deal? Is there some mysterious man in there watching what we say and do?" *Man.* Liza remembered that flash of eye-catching garb she'd shaken off as her imagination. "Or woman. Is there another performer here that I haven't met? A woman that wears a long colorful skirt?"

"Huh? No." Unease slid from the side-eye glance the fortune-teller spared her before she charged ahead. "Way I see it, long as we keep getting paid and fed, ain't none of my concern." Hope started walking again. "And what on earth did you do to Jamey?"

"He's got some strange opinions."

"That makes two of you." Hope had a point, but Liza wasn't about to admit it.

"He run to you to tell on me or something?" Liza was growing angrier.

"No, he didn't," Hope said. "I ran into him looking for you. Wasn't hard to see he was upset about something. Had to drag it out of him."

They had arrived at Hope's trailer and found Bombardier standing outside with Ishe. He shielded his eyes, squinting at the sight of an approaching vehicle. "Looks like we got company."

CHAPTER TWENTY-FIVE

A Stranger in the Night

The car—a fancy shiny new Packard—rolled to a stop. A crowd had gathered around, oohing and aahing at the fine piece of machinery. The driver, a white man, emerged and held the door open for someone in back. A gloved hand snaked out from the car, taking the driver's arm. An elegant Negro woman stepped out.

She wore a black hat with a big sparkling pin on the side. Her dress was a simple, pink, V-neck affair in a fine silk. It cinched at the waist and flowed outward, down to midcalf. Smooth mocha skin made it hard to place her age, but her dress, even the way she walked, screamed that she was somebody formidable, and younger women rarely possessed that sort of swagger.

The driver leaned against the car and thrust his hands into his pockets. His shoulder holster held a sizable gun, and the carnies backed away in a hush.

Clay emerged from his trailer, shirt and pants dusty, and streaks of grease smeared his left cheek. He walked out in front of the carnies, wiped his hand on his pants leg, and extended it.

"Clay Kennel," he said. "Owner and proprietor of the G. B. Bacchanal Carnival."

"May I present . . . ," the driver began.

"Madame Stephanie St. Clair," Clay finished. He kept his expression vague, but the admiration and suspicion in his voice slipped out, unmasked.

"Queenie," the woman answered. She looked at his outstretched hand and, with her eyes, made it clear that there was no way she was placing her silken-gloved hand in his.

Whispers of awe rang out through the crowd like tiny bells.

Jamey, as usual, was not far behind Clay. "And this here is my right hand, Jamey Blotter," he said, introducing the young man. Queenie smiled, her expression soft, steeped in a gentle warmth that wasn't there a second before.

Jamey's eyes grew wide. He mumbled a greeting as he looked anywhere but directly at the woman. What had shaken the boy's manners? Clay turned back to his esteemed guest.

"You come through Louisiana recently?" the woman said, walking forward, assessing the group of carnies but directing her question to Clay.

Clay recollected on what trouble they may have left behind them; sometimes he lost count of the weird trail of mishaps that followed them. Thankfully, people often had more important things to worry about than what strangeness followed the carnival's arrival and departure. Outwardly, he was composed.

"We travel quite a bit, as you might expect." He motioned for the carnies to move out of their way. He then held out his arm to Queenie, inviting her to follow him. "But yes, we were in your home state."

"The news does travel far," she said, walking beside Clay now.

"Everybody knows about you, ma'am," Clay said. Working for Geneva, he'd come to have a respect for Negro women. His perspective was one that most white men wouldn't allow themselves to have. This woman was a criminal, but who wouldn't admire a southern woman running a numbers game up in a big city like Harlem, and even going up against the mobster "Dutch" Schultz? Clay didn't know how it was that she was still alive.

"Half lies," Madame St. Clair said. "About a quarter embellished, the rest. The truth depends on who's doing the telling."

Clay had ordered a carnie to have Mabel bring out something for their guest to eat. He gestured for her to join him at one of the picnic tables. She glided in opposite him and fixed her unsettling gaze on him.

First Geneva, now Queenie herself. I got a thing for powerful women. "What brings you to the carnival?" He didn't think the visit was a social one, and she didn't look the type for the Ferris wheel.

Madame St. Clair appraised Clay for a full minute before answering. "Looking for someone," she said finally.

"And who might that be?" Clay leaned forward.

"Believe you already know." Madame St. Clair raised the cold glass of iced tea that had been deposited at her elbow, took a sip, and set the glass back on the table. It was the most elegant motion Clay had ever seen.

The resemblance was clear to Clay now. The slightly wide-set eyes, the coloring, the less noticeable but still present strong chin. And the odd behavior.

"How's Jamey related to you?" he asked. "And why don't he seem too keen on admitting it?"

"You know he was born and raised in Louisiana," Madame St. Clair said. "My sister's boy. When his mother died, I took care of him . . . in my own way. I couldn't raise any children with the life I led, you see. But I made sure he was taken care of. He stopped accepting my money years ago, and guess I got you to thank for that, Mr. Kennel. Guess you can say that my life up in Harlem has kept me preoccupied. Now, I need my kin near me. Whether he likes the total package or not, we are all we have left."

Clay had read about how her goon "Bumpy" Johnson had hooked up with them Italians. He'd also read that she'd quieted down her business in the last few years, but maybe she needed some new muscle. If she was counting on Jamey for that, she didn't know her nephew at all.

Almost reading his thoughts, Madame St. Clair intoned, "He always got good marks. I don't need another Bumpy—I need somebody with a good head. That understands numbers."

As much as Clay wanted to tell her to scram, he had to let Jamey make the decision himself. "I know where he run off to. I'll send him on over to you."

~

"Madame," two women said in unison, bowing on one knee. "We are honored."

Madame St. Clair looked up from her plate and took in the women's roughshod clothing, the beads, the daggers at their hips. "And you are?"

They stood.

"Zinsa," Zinsa said.

"And I am Efe," Efe added, lifting her chin. "We are the last of the Dahomey women soldiers."

Queenie set down her fork and stood. "The soldiers of West Africa," she said with unmasked admiration. "The honor is all mine, ladies. Join me." She sat back at the table, but when she looked up, Zinsa and Efe stood where they were, looking dumbfounded. She gave them a look, and they all but scrambled to the bench.

"We have read about you," Zinsa said.

"The way you handle all those men," Efe added.

"You would have made an excellent commander in our army," Zinsa added. The women gushed on and on interminably, and Queenie endured it all, answering their questions politely.

"I could use two women such as yourself," she said. "What, if you don't mind me asking, would you two be doing in a carnival?"

Zinsa and Efe at once looked at each other, their expressions sullen. Didn't take much to piece it together—their homeland, their particular set of skills. Yes, her friend Ahiku had snared them somehow. That meant they weren't here entirely of their own will. But they didn't get a chance to answer, for Clay approached with a reluctant-looking Jamey.

"Quit bothering the lady." He shooed away Zinsa and Efe.

"No bother," Madame St. Clair said. "You ladies think about what I said."

Queenie watched Clay try to puzzle out her meaning and left him to it.

～

"You got your mother's eyes," Queenie said. "And mine."

Jamey stood rooted in place. Funny how the times when his aunt had cuddled him, taught him the latest dances, and even sneaked him candy his mama said he couldn't have were dimmed by the one memory he tried the hardest to forget.

He'd run the food his mother sold back and forth to the patrons of her sister's weekly card games. On this night, things were a little slow, so Queenie sat in with the other men in a game of bid whist. Her neatly painted fingernails gleamed against the backs of the cards. The pearls at her neck were out of place with the rough loose trousers she favored. His mama always wore dresses.

His seven-year-old self braced for a fight. That drunk was right on the edge of trouble with all his blubbery flirting, but when he laid his hand on Queenie's wrist . . . his aunt had pulled out a gun and pistol-whipped the man bloody.

"Go on now, sit," Queenie prompted. "You think I got fangs or something?"

"Aunt Queenie," Jamey said finally. "Excuse my manners. I . . . I don't know what you doing here."

"It's time for you to come and be with me."

"I ain't no criminal," Jamey said and then caught himself. "I mean, I got a good job here. I don't want no trouble."

Queenie looked around, even sniffed at the air. "I bet there is more trouble here than you letting on, but you can keep that to yourself. I need your mind. I can give you a good home, a good salary. Cops don't bother me none anymore. I'm an old lady. But I need somebody to handle my business. You are the only kin I have left." Then she looked around. "Unless you got some baby running around someplace. Am I a great-aunt?"

Jamey flushed. "Nothin' like that," he stammered. "No kids here."

"Smart boy," Queenie said, looking around the grounds. "Get the feeling children wouldn't thrive here. Not the way they would in a stable home, I mean."

Liza strolled idly by the cook-tent entrance, trying unsuccessfully to look inconspicuous. *Why she gotta be so nosy?* Queenie followed Jamey's eyes.

"A girl," she huffed. "There are so many beautiful, clean girls in Harlem you will have to hire a guard to keep them away. I'm offering you something real. Do you want to work at a carnival all your life? Think about it. It is nearly 1940. How hard has it been for you to find new spots? You don't even come north much anymore; you know why? It's because they consider the freak show vile, looking at odd folks not as popular as it once was. Carnival may not even be around in a few years. What will you do then?"

Jamey didn't want to admit that, over the last couple of years, it had gotten tougher to secure dates. But Clay always pulled things out. No, G. B. would be fine; folks would always need entertaining. "You want me for my brain; guess somebody else would, too, if it came to that."

"And we are family," Queenie added. "When everybody else leaves you, family is all you have."

"You only coming to get me now 'cause you and Bumpy on the outs?"

"Bumpy works for them people, but he still looks out for me," Queenie said, taking another sip of tea. "I wasn't there when Myra first died. But I'm trying to be now."

Jamey considered the vision of himself as a businessman, in a fine suit up in Harlem, New York. Owning a fine house, not breaking his back anymore. And he wouldn't be second to anybody when his aunt died. But there was Liza. Would she come with him? And after their fight today, would he even want her to?

It was getting dark, and the crowd watching them, including Liza, still lingered. Jamey was surprised to realize that he was glad she was there.

"You gonna have to stay the night," Jamey said. Queenie had probably timed it that way. When you dropped something like this in somebody's lap, a decision wouldn't come easy. She said she was prepared to stay for as long as a week, but then she would need to head back north to check on her business.

"You won't like some of the ways we live out here," he said. "None of the fine things you used to. But we can make you comfortable."

"Me and your mother may have been born on that plantation in Martinique, but Lake Charles was our home, same as you," Queenie said. "I know how to make do. I won't break."

Jamey stood to lead his aunt away. He walked past Liza on his way out. Maybe he was seeing things, but it seemed like her eyes were telling him she wasn't mad no more.

He steered his aunt toward the trailer he shared with Wendell and three others. "I'll get some clean sheets," he said. "The boys will bunk up under the stars tonight. It's no trouble."

Queenie let a grin warm the right side of her mouth. "Nobody will need to give up their bunk tonight." She took his arm in hers and led the way, shushing his protest. But Jamey's alarm heightened when she strode toward the red trailer.

"You can't go in there." He looked at his aunt. "Nobody can. Clay uses that trailer for carnival business."

Queenie smiled. "I'll see you in the morning, James."

Jamey stood with his mouth open, and the last protest died as Zinsa and Efe actually smiled—smiled! They dropped to one knee and lowered their heads as Queenie mounted the steps and entered the enigmatic red trailer.

CHAPTER TWENTY-SIX

WICKED ALLIANCES

Madame St. Clair entered the trailer, and soft, muted lights sprang to life. The light painted the festive yet brooding interior with a warm glow that achieved the goal of providing a demon *or* her honored human guest with the aura of comfort and luxury. The plush chaise lounge, where Madame had first sat several years earlier, still occupied the same space beneath the large wooden-framed window. Somehow, it still looked new. The breeze fluttered the yellow curtains, ballooning them outward.

Her gaze drew her toward the mask she had given the demon woman: pewter-bronzed, embellished with a pattern of maroon-and-gold-sparkled flowers, broad curved brows, a soft golden mouth. The mask was adorned with black feathers at its crown and a silvery tassel dangling on the right side. It was perfectly at home between the masks from the Congo and Zaire. A gift from the New Orleans carnivals of her youth. This small gift had sealed the deal on their first business relationship. It was strange, the things that spirits treasured.

Madame St. Clair lowered herself onto the lounge, reveling in the luxuriousness of the plush velvet beneath her fingertips. Inhaling the scents of the carnival, the bayou, and the homeland that she had never visited, she exhaled the words that would summon Ahiku—Geneva Broussard, she corrected herself—back to the land of the living.

"Mo pe awon dudu emi."

She was the only living human being who knew how to speak those words.

It was a language of the medicine women from francophone Africa, a mixture of genetic ancients that some called evil while others, like her, called the advantage that she needed to survive in a world stacked against her.

Madame didn't need to look behind the curtain; she never had. When it stirred, Geneva was coming. Soon enough, the drapery lifted and a roiling, thunderous black-gray smoke emerged. It hovered like a thunderstorm trying to decide if it wanted to kick out a bit of rain, churning, spinning. Finally, within the empty space, Geneva Broussard—mistress of the afterlife—coalesced.

The women regarded each other carefully. It had been years since they had last seen each other in person, though they had spoken. Queenie had the ability to communicate with the spirit world when the need arose; she need only whisper the words. With Geneva's arrival, the interior of the trailer thrummed to life with the continuous, rhythmic beat of African drums.

"The queen has aged well." Geneva smiled, and Queenie found it genuine.

Queenie stood. "And you, Ahiku, have not aged at all."

That earned a chuckle from Geneva. "A gift of committing I made in my youth," she said. "Sit, sit. I need to settle myself into this body, stretch my legs. How you people live an eternity cooped up in a shell . . ." She waved a hand and stretched, walking back and forth. "Without the relief of the underworld, I don't think I could bear it as long as I do."

"I'll meet my maker soon enough," Queenie said. With the difficult deals she'd made, she supposed she would spend more time with Geneva in death than she had in life.

Geneva rolled her shoulders and cracked her neck. "You have found your nephew in good health and spirit?"

Queenie leaned back and planted her hands behind her, crossing her legs at the ankle. The demons couldn't take her before her time; it was always reassuring to tell herself that half-truth. "He is healthy, happy. He has a good position here—"

"But your herd up north is thinning," Geneva said, interrupting. "You have come to claim your lamb." She turned her back on Queenie and made an intricate weaving with her hands. When she turned back, her face had grown stony. "And what if I am not ready to let him go?"

Queenie kept her face impassive, but this was the moment she had dreaded. She had already committed her soul to damnation in exchange for the powers of persuasion that had kept her largely unscathed in the war for Harlem. The power had insulated her from bullets, deflected knives, and thwarted would-be assassins. The rest—the cunning, the building of the business, the politics—that had all been her doing; the spirit could not take credit for that. And the souls that she and Bumpy had donated to hell's cause—well, that was an extra tossed in to keep Geneva happy. Apparently, this had not been enough.

"Your promises are about the only sure thing left to me in this life. Toy with somebody else—I'm tired." It was a gamble, but that *was* what she did.

The demon's shoulders slumped like those of a sullen child. Her laugh was a horrible sound, like a dying child's cry, the sound of a hyena's brutal cackle. "I chose well, dear queen, on our first meeting. I am rarely wrong."

Despite herself, Queenie relished the compliment. Now, the next difficult topic. "And what about your enemies? Have you found them all?" Her luck would dry up if something happened to her friend. It was a hard truth she took to bed with her each night.

The demon edged closer to Queenie and joined her on the lounge. "One still eludes me. Perhaps she is dead already."

Queenie doubted Geneva believed that, but hope was a precious thing in a sea of uncertainty. She left the matter there.

"There is another reason for my visit." Even though demons could roam, most were territorial sorts, and just like the living, their gossip traveled far and wide. And those who favored Harlem had a story worth sharing. "Hear tell those friends of yours, the others like you, I mean. Word is, they are using your lack of progress to amass support against you. Don't be surprised if one, or all of them, try to make a move against you."

"Those insolents!" Geneva seethed and then grilled Queenie for the scant remaining details she had.

When that business was dispensed with, the old friends settled in like a pair of schoolgirls and traded stories. Only their tales were not of boys and latest fashions, but of grisly murders, artful treachery, and general mayhem in the lands of the living and the dead.

Late into the night, Geneva whispered a few words, and a fresh blanket, a pillow, even a pair of French slippers appeared on the chaise lounge. "I would conjure an indoor shower and latrine"—Geneva's voice carried even as she dissolved and moved away on a whisper of smoke, retreating behind the dark drapery—"but there is a limit to even my powers."

The resplendent sound of her laughter trailed her back to the underworld.

≈

Liza sat outside her trailer, back against the stair railing. Jamey arrived wearing a sullen expression.

"Who is she?" Liza asked, patting the ground next to her.

Jamey obliged and sat down on the soft grass beside her. He drew up his knees and breathed deeply. "She's my aunt—my mother's sister."

Liza gasped. The most famous Negro woman gangster in history—as she'd just learned from the others when she'd asked about the mysterious woman—was his distant, yet watchful, second mother.

"Nobody's family is perfect," she said. What she didn't say was that at least the woman had come to find him; it was like her own family was running from her as fast as they could. "Are you all upset because you think the carnies will judge you for her choices?"

He stole a look at Liza, straightened his legs, and blurted out, "She wants me to come back to Harlem with her. That's why she's here. Folks back in Louisiana, where we picked you up, they told her we had passed through. Didn't take long to track us down."

As soon as the word "Harlem" had tumbled out of Jamey's mouth, Liza turned to gape at him. Her moldy, forgotten heart had begun tentatively to beat again. Then her eyes turned hard.

"Well," Liza said finally. "If you don't mind going in with a known criminal, I guess it would mean a pay raise for you. But be careful of stray bullets. Don't bother to write." She made to get up, but Jamey grabbed her by the wrist—not all that gently.

"We all got a past," he said, more gently pulling Liza back down beside him.

"It's your *aunt*—"

"This ain't 'bout me." Jamey kept right on talking but released his grip and kept his hand on top of hers. Liza looked at it like it was a viper. "Whatever happened in your past, maybe you tell me 'bout it one day. Maybe you don't. Clear to me, though, that whatever brought you to be out there on your own in Louisiana still hurt you. You think anybody get close to you is a minute away from doin' you harm."

Liza stilled her trembling lip. Jamey had seen right through the walls and parapets she'd so carefully constructed around herself. Thankfully, he didn't look at her. She didn't want him to see the unmasked pain on her face.

"Truth is, can't nobody hurt you like the folks you love. I can't promise I won't make you mad or cross at me from time to time. But if you ask me, right here and now, quit dodging around, and ask me to stay, I do promise I won't leave you."

Liza dared not speak right away, or all that would come out would be a pathetic sob. She turned her head away so Jamey couldn't see the welling tears and made her face as blank as possible. When she met his eyes, everything was clear. He was an earnest man, and it had taken a lot for him to say what he had. She put her hand back atop his.

"Don't stay on my account." She spit the words out quickly and stood to leave.

He didn't call after her. As much as she hoped for him to, he didn't. He was not going to make this easy for her. Only a few steps away, she turned to find him still sitting on the ground, not even glancing in her direction. She cursed him with every step she took back, till she again was with him. She sat in front of him this time but settled her eyes on her fingers in her lap.

"I wouldn't be too happy to see you go."

Her words came out in a croak.

Jamey exhaled. "One thing settled." He pulled at his ear. "Another thing to consider, though. How you feel 'bout coming north . . . with me?"

Liza blinked. "I—I've got a home here. I'm putting a show together. I'll make my own money for the first time in my life."

Jamey stood and held out his hand for Liza. He didn't say it, didn't have to, but her little show must have looked like a joke. Queenie offered him a ready-made empire, in a city where a Negro man at least had a chance to make something of himself. Too much to think about.

"I'll talk to Aunt Queenie in the mornin'," was all he said.

Before Bacchanal, Liza's life's work was driven by a spark, the base instinct of self-preservation. It led to the creation and tender care of her self-protective little fortress. But the carnival, her friends, they had shattered it all into a dusty pile of stone. Liza sighed. She felt as if she were stepping outside for the first time in years, able to breathe beyond the walls.

She stood beside Jamey, absorbed in the boring but aptly diverting task of figuring out whether or not the grass was growing beneath her feet as he talked with the high-and-mighty Madame St. Clair. She wore a beautiful baby-blue silk dress with cuffed three-quarter-length sleeves and a scooped high neck. A matching hat sat skillfully tilted on her head.

"I've made sacrifices for you that you don't even know about, and I'm not looking for any special favors for doing so." Queenie cupped Jamey's face in her right palm.

"And I appreciate it," Jamey said.

"I know you and some other folks around here think you know something about my business." She turned her gaze on Liza. "But don't insult me or yourself by thinking that evil only wears one mask. Choosing not to see it, especially when you find yourself right in the muck of it, don't make it any less real."

That last bit made Liza finally raise her eyes. Queenie then turned and settled a gaze on her that made her take an involuntary step back. The look said that she was unwelcome in this conversation, an intruder.

"She may not know it"—Liza didn't doubt for a minute who "she" was—"but I know you want more than this. I'll get you reacquainted with the business and step aside. I'll be there to help guide you, of course, but what's mine will be yours. And we both know that you have appetites such that Harlem can more easily accommodate."

Appetites. Liza's temper flared. *What kind of appetites?*

When Jamey didn't utter the decisive "no" that she was expecting, Liza craned her neck to try to get a look at him. In her sideways glance, indecision, a bona fide war on his face.

"I'll expect your answer by the time y'all wrap up in Tulsa."

Queenie climbed back into the Packard as Liza and Jamey stood shoulder to shoulder again, watching the outline of the car grow smaller until it was no more than a tiny dot. Queenie had given Jamey a kiss on the cheek and a mother's smile. All she could spare Liza was a barely concealed evil eye.

Jamey had promised to visit her, to keep in touch. Liza wondered if her anger at that promise had to do with the woman herself, the kind of life she led, or her own jealousy that no matter how small it was, Jamey had a family and she didn't.

The next day brought a break from the heat. The wind swirled, tossing dislodged banners and debris, perfuming the air with the scent of a not-too-far-off rain shower. Relief and fear and God knew what else bubbled and burped in Liza's stomach as she relayed everything to Bombardier and Hope.

"I am not saying Jamey is a bad man," Bombardier said while doing one-handed push-ups with Hope perched on his back, her arms held out for balance. There wasn't one ounce of strain in his thunderous voice. "But he is barely a man."

Hope huffed and swatted him on the head, and he summarily tilted over and dumped her on the ground. She righted herself and lurched at him, taking a swipe at his stomach. "Don't listen to him, Liza. 'Sides, she's still a girl herself."

Liza sniffed at that—she was a full-grown woman, just like her friend.

Dodging Hope easily, Bombardier caught her in a light chokehold. After a largely insubstantial struggle, she nestled into the familiar curve of his arms.

"Jamey is a sapling. You don't even know yet what his roots will look like when they stretch and settle," Bombardier continued. "What you need is a baobab: strong and tested by the elements."

Liza rolled her eyes and stalked off.

CHAPTER TWENTY-SEVEN

THE SHOW MUST GO ON

The people of Texhoma, Oklahoma, had been slapped and berated by the backhand of good fortune. Economic hardships had settled into the town a decade ago, an incurable ache deep within the bones. It was an internal wound soothed by promises of relief from the government but cleaved and gouged repeatedly open by blunt-force disappointments.

Hardship made itself at home on both sides of the racial line. But both communities rallied, definite but separate, in their attempts to help their neighbors. Food, clothing, and homes: all were shared, even as nerves and resources thinned to the point of fraying. But the carnival, any distraction from their daily lives, lifted spirits. And so it was that they swarmed the carnival, ready to spend what little they had to take some of the sting off their poverty.

With the scents of hot french fries, candy, and treats filling the air, a juggler zigzagged through the crowd, tossing bowling-ball pins in the air and narrowly missing a patron or two. A throng of small children trailed behind him like he was some sort of pied piper.

Liza slipped into the rear tent entrance, mumbled a greeting to Uly, and sank onto an overturned crate. She picked at her fingernails. She stood and paced. The crate called to her again. Then one of her plaits needed rebraiding. Uly looked at her as if to ask what she was waiting for, but she held up a hand to forestall him. Mico chittered his agreement. It was time.

Only, she wanted to do her next show like she wanted to return to Mrs. Shippen's boardinghouse. Which was to say, not at all. Concentration was proving impossible, but the sounds of a restless crowd urged her to stand and drag herself onto the stage with a look on her face that would have won her top prize at a sour candy–eating contest.

"Welcome, everybody. I'm Liza, the Mystical Beastmistress." A tepid applause in return for a lackluster greeting was fair. She'd better pull herself together.

Sabina floated her an image. It was of Liza sprawled out on a cloud while Sabina and Ikaki regarded her from below in an open field, with a mass of people closing in from all corners. The tiger's message: *Kindly remove your head from the clouds and consider joining us back on earth before the crowd turns feral.*

"Get on with it, already!" came a shout from the audience.

Liza straightened her vest and cleared her throat. "I guess it's time for the dance."

That didn't come out right at all. She closed her eyes for a moment and started over. "Our friend Ikaki is what you call an African turtle sprite. And what do turtle sprites like to do? Why, they dance! If I can get a volunteer, I'll show you just how well."

She pointed to a small boy who, despite the hardship evident in his attire—a season or two past an untimely growth spurt—still had a child's glint of wonder in his eye. But as Mico darted over to greet him, a woman decked out like she'd copied the look straight out of one of Autumn's fashion magazines sashayed onto the stage.

"You don't mind if I go first, do ya, hon?" she said without looking at him.

The boy shook his head and lowered himself back onto the bench, his expression more curious than offended.

Mico escorted the woman forward, and the way she slurred her words told Liza she was a little drunk. But what she lacked in walking a straight line, she made up for when the music started. So convoluted were her moves that you would have thought it was Josephine Baker herself strutting around.

Ikaki did their best but soon communicated their concerns. Liza waved off the protest and implored them to continue. And the turtle soldiered on impressively.

"All right, then, why don't we give someone else a try," Liza said. It was way past time for this woman to sit down.

But in some kind of grand finale, the show-off threw a leg up in the air and sank to the floor in an impressive split. No way a turtle, even a magical one, could manage that one. Liza conjured an image, one with Ikaki swimming in their little pool—a way to tell them the show was over—but the turtle sprite was not to be outdone.

They bounded up into the air, thrust their squat legs out, and tried to land in their own version of a split. But they came down hard on their back leg, sent Liza an image of themself all bandaged up, and snapped their body back into their shell. Liza cried out and ran over to them. They sent mollifying images, she apologetic ones.

The woman muttered, "Sorry," and went back to her seat.

After sniffing her animal friend as if to make sure they were all right, Sabina trotted forward. Liza signaled to Uly, and he rushed out and took Ikaki backstage. With effort, Liza and Sabina finished the show. Afterward, Ikaki assured her they were fine.

And at the end of it, even though the animals had done all the work, Liza was still exhausted. But Oya's vision was like a muted beacon, just bright enough to keep sleep at bay. Liza took refuge outside the tent and watched the stars glimmering against the night sky. A section of the canvas flapped in the breeze, the frayed edges, much like her own shredded nerves, in need of mending.

Her show had limped across the finish line—a fluke, or the long-awaited mastery of her gift? That she hadn't hurt Ikaki directly didn't matter. It was her inattention, her lack of focus, that had paved the way. Liza sighed. She had better practice.

The idea had no sooner sprung forth than the elephant swept into her mind and swatted it away with a deft trunk twirl. An obsidian blotch then moved against the even darker sky, a skillful rising and spiraling. The raven. Her skin prickled with the badger's presence, even if she couldn't see him.

Her animal guides narrated a gruesome tale, images of the animals she'd tried to help and lost. As far back as she remembered, and another when she was too young to understand what she'd done. She whimpered with the pain of it. Her greatest shame, her greatest fear, laid bare. Why?

They'd been with her all along; she knew that now. Watching, waiting. Out of ignorance, whether willful or otherwise, she'd ignored them. Ignored the broken fragments of her own story. An ancestry, a heritage, that needed her as much as she needed it. Oya had said she must accept the spirits, but she hadn't the faintest idea how.

As quickly as the horror film started, it stopped, replaced by an image of Liza herself, bound. No practice, no more killing. But it wasn't as if she wanted to hurt them. Couldn't they see that?

A raven caw, then an image of all three with their eyes closed for a beat and then opening slowly. Yes, of course, they understood; they could see. But she must control it now and end her unpracticed blunders.

She endured the pang of the animals fading to the background once more, leaving her with an image of ruin. Bits and pieces of carnival debris. *Bacchanal?* The spirits didn't answer.

CHAPTER TWENTY-EIGHT

THE CHALLENGE

Absently, Liza sat on her bunk, cracking and feeding Mico his treasured sunflower seeds. Her mind reviewed the possibilities of her vision like butter in a churn. As much as she tried to fancy herself a woman whom African spirits found worthy of some grand purpose, she could only see herself as a scared and broken little girl, riding away in a fancy car, hastily dousing herself in the camouflage of bravery and indifference.

The rising sun cast the inside of the trailer in a subtle orange glow. A chilly breeze carried the heady scent of grass and earth through the windows they'd left propped open overnight. Liza shivered and tugged the blanket up beneath her chin. Getting up to shut the window would wake Autumn, who lay across from Liza on her bunk covered in fancy pillows and other finery, the ever-present eye mask covering most of her face. Mico chittered his annoyance, and Liza cracked another seed.

"I'm surprised you haven't given yourself a fit with all that concentrating." Autumn rolled over on her side and lifted a corner of her eye mask. "I can almost *feel* you thinking over there, and you're messing up my sleep."

Mico snatched a seed from the pile and scampered over to make an early-morning gift offering to Autumn. She smiled and removed her mask, taking the seed and popping it in her mouth. She tickled the marmoset beneath his chin, and he beamed his pleasure. Soon enough, he came back to Liza's bunk and sat on her knee.

"Sorry I was thinking too loud," Liza answered. "Some of us have more on our minds than the latest fashions."

Autumn flung off her thin blanket. "No need to insult me because you got family problems. You bite off every hand somebody extends toward you, and see how many fans you make around here." She stretched and put on her robe, then hefted a little basket of scented soaps and oils to head out to the donnicker, slamming the trailer door behind her.

Liza exhaled. She hadn't meant to snap at Autumn. Why was her life so complicated? She contemplated leaving the carnival, but she discarded that nonsense as quickly as it had come to mind. For one, where else was she going to be able to earn a living? And what about Jamey?

After cleaning up, Liza surprised herself by not seeking out Jamey or Hope but instead heading straight for Ishe. The carnival was yawning its way to life, and the sun sat full and round in the sky, shining down on her face, with Mico perched on her shoulder. Smells from the cook tent did little to spur her appetite.

She found Ishe with Bombardier.

"Morning," she said without any enthusiasm. She shoved her hands into her trouser pockets, looking at anything but the two men in front of her.

"My mother used to have a saying," Bombardier said. "A woman is like the skin of a *kabundi*, a tiny wild animal on which two men cannot sit."

Liza finally met his eyes, offered a smile as welcoming as a cup of watered-down coffee. Ishe looked to his friend and mouthed a silent scolding. He turned to Liza and placed his hand on her back, gesturing for them to move away. They walked side by side, away from an ever-watchful Bombardier.

"Brooding don't help none," Ishe said as they walked. "Tried and tried, but never did change nothin' about my circumstances."

"You are one to talk." Liza scrunched up her face. "What do I know about you? What do I know about how you came to be . . ." She struggled to find the words. Ishe didn't even like to hear the word "hyena." Finally, she settled on, "What you are?"

"The 'how' don't matter much, now, do it?" Ishe kicked at a rock and folded his hands behind his back. "That's how it is. Only thing that matter is learning how to live with it."

"I don't know what anything means," Liza huffed and immediately felt five years old.

"What's bothering you?" he asked, his eyes warm.

She exhaled and told Ishe about the vision with Oya. "You would think my *grandmother* would have made herself known a long time ago, back when I didn't have a home or enough to eat, let alone anyone to pass a kind word with. Would have been nice to step in and lend a helping hand when I killed that first animal or the third. Bad sense of timing, if you ask me. And when she did choose to make herself known, she couldn't or wouldn't explain what she wanted in plain English."

"That's your first problem," Ishe said. "You think the spirits are like real people. They don't think like us. Don't got the same motivation."

"If you know—" Liza caught herself, remembering her spat with Autumn. "How come you can't control your spirit?"

Ishe rubbed the back of his neck. Liza knew she was taking him to a place he didn't want to go, but this was about her, not him. Maybe he shouldn't have tried to help her. She looked over at him, admired how the sun fell across his face, lighting up his eyes. What was she doing? Liza turned her gaze back ahead and took in the outline of the town in the distance.

"My spirit is a demon. He's got the control, and he know it well as I do," he explained flatly. "You got a chance, if you want it. I don't. Those discs and seeing Oya all point to one thing: somethin's comin'. Walking round here poutin' like somebody stole your lunch ain't gone change a thing."

Liza didn't know what to say to that, so she kept her mouth shut.

Their uncomfortable silence was broken by Jamey marching up to them.

"Don't start nothin' you can't finish, lil' Clay," Ishe said as he walked past Jamey. Liza cut her eye at Ishe. Jamey hated it when people called him that.

Liza steadied her breath and cleared her mind.

Jamey tapped her on the shoulder, and she blinked up at him. The war was plain on his face. She tried to mask the war that was struggling on her own. Was she developing feelings for Ishe? Liza hated herself for what she must be doing to them both. But when she smiled at Jamey, she was certain the angry tongue-lashing he was going to give her had died away; he returned the smile.

He held her for a time, inhaling the scent of the top of her head. "Gone be time to get ready soon," Jamey finally said and then took her hand, leading her back to the carnival.

Liza's hand was limp as a wet leaf in Jamey's. Fear of the spirits, the unknown magic, the pressure she could sense but not put her finger on, dogged her, between breaths, in her dreams, slinking around after every other thought. Something was threatening their way of life here, but what? She wondered if she would fare better joining Jamey and fighting gangsters up north with his aunt Queenie.

Jamey must have known there was something wrong, but Wendell ran up to him. "Need your help over with the Ferris wheel," he said. "Damn gearshift again."

Jamey turned to Liza. "I gotta go. And I want you to stop hanging out with Ishe so much—you know something about him ain't right."

Liza bristled. If being in a relationship meant she had to take orders from a man—well, she didn't know much, but she would never turn into the distant, go-along-with-everything kind of woman her mother was.

"Ishe's my *friend*," she said. "And that's all."

"Make another one!" he called out as he turned to hurry off to the Ferris wheel.

CHAPTER TWENTY-NINE

CLAY'S HOUSE OF CARDS

With one date in Texhoma, Clay had the G. B. Bacchanal Carnival back on track. Liza'd had her little mix-ups, a couple of missed cues that made it seem like she didn't have full control of the animals, but she'd recovered well enough and had at least finished the show. Malachi's Human Pincushion show was a big hit, and he even tossed in some contortions that had the crowd oohing and aahing all night.

As was often the case, on the last night, a few stragglers remained. One lady in particular roamed around the Pickled Punks tent, gawking at the oddities even after the operator had blinked the lights once to signal closing. Malformed fetuses of everything from birds, to lions, to monkeys sat inside their liquid bottled tombs, staring at her with unblinking eyes. Up and down, up and down she prowled as if she were on the hunt. Her eyes inspected each fetus with the intensity of a mother lion probing its young for signs of lameness.

"Last call, ma'am," Clay called out from the entrance.

"I paid my nickel and I'll be done when I'm good and ready," she snapped. Clay eyed the woman furtively as she ran her fingers over the bottles, returning again to one in particular. The card said it was the fetus of a monkey, but no one could tell for sure. The arms and legs were so humanlike, the bald head and toothless mouth calling to mind a human infant. It floated pale gray in an amber-colored liquid. She tilted her head to and fro. "Why, in the right light, it looks so much like a human child," she muttered.

"You say somethin', ma'am?" Clay poked his head back inside.

"No." She waved him off. "Give me a moment, would you? All your yapping won't get me out any sooner."

"That a fact?" Clay said. He tipped his hat to the woman and backed away.

≈

The woman had not quite recovered from the loss of her own child three years prior. The pain was as raw as the expertly covered bald spot on the back of her head where she'd yanked out strands of her hair.

She lifted her hand to wipe away the tear tracing a path down her cheek but never made it, as she stumbled backward, staring at the bottle in disbelief. Had that thing smiled at her? She chided herself. Her mind was playing tricks on her. Still, when she took a few tentative steps forward, her legs were as wobbly as the stock market.

She gasped, drawing her hands to her mouth. The little monkey fetus made swimming motions with its hands, as if life in a bottle were simply nothing more than an afternoon dip in an Olympic pool.

The woman screamed and knocked the bottle to the ground. When the lifeless object only stared at her with its dead, unblinking eyes, she fled the tent.

≈

"Thanks for your patronage!" Clay called after her with a wicked grin. He walked into the still tent and went down the aisle. The bottle containing the monkey sat right where it was supposed to. He leaned in, tapped the bottle with an index finger, and winked at the fetus. It grinned in response.

Outside, Clay bid Jamey good night with an order to make sure the last of the stragglers were out before he closed things up. The kid was proving more capable every day, and Clay wondered if the boy seeing his aunt hadn't done some good after all.

Clay trudged to the rear of the midway and the sanctuary of his trailer. He contemplated the warnings that littered his road to perdition: a call for a U-turn when he got puffed up with false pride. A sharp curve in the road had tried to turn him away from his sinful pursuit of the almighty dollar. He'd crossed that blighted bridge going a hundred miles an hour and had stood helpless as the grotesque outstretched arms of salvation struggled in vain to pull him back.

The seemingly conjoined trailers: Geneva's and his. Always side by side, looming. Geneva would probably pop her demon head out soon.

His own trailer was wood, weathered to a dark gray. The words **G. B. Bacchanal Carnival** were painted in ornate red lettering on both sides. Like Geneva's, there were two windows, one on either side of the trailer, propped open by a stick. Inside, Clay tossed his hat onto the small writing table to his right, took one last look over at the demon's trailer, and closed the door. He tripped over the stool in front of his writing table again and muttered a curse. There wasn't any other place for the thing, so it stayed where it was.

He flicked on the lone bulb hanging from the ceiling. A metal bunk was pushed into the far-left corner. Unlike what he ensured his carnies had, his bed was covered with a simple white cotton sheet and a rough woolen blanket. The pillow was a case stuffed with hay pilfered from the animal tent. At the foot of the bed sat a black chest that held his few worldly possessions. He reached inside, moved the two neatly folded pairs of pants and shirts aside, and took out the picture of his wife and the knife.

Crosses of every shape, size, and constitution lined the interior walls. The largest was a wooden carving mounted at the rear wall. He struck a match and lit the two votive candles on either side of the cross.

Beneath the wooden cross, a small altar held a mirror, a picture of Jesus, rosary beads, and a Bible. He kissed the picture of his wife and carefully positioned it next to the Bible. Clay removed his shirt and draped it on the bed, revealing a patchwork of scars on his chest. He knelt and prayed, rocking back and forth, tears streaming from his eyes.

His first recollection of the urge had been as a younger man, fighting in the First World War. The boy, who reminded him of Jamey in some ways, looking back, couldn't have been a day over seventeen, but he was right there with the rest of them Harlem Hellfighters, signed up to fight for a country that hated him. Didn't he know that? Didn't they all? What type of simpletons would fight for a country that didn't want them?

He was strongly built, with a bright smile and hands that had never seen the rough quarters of a cotton field. Clay and the other white soldiers hated him for it. Too cocky. His unit had stumbled upon the boy alone in a hollowed-out house, taking a crap. The unit decided then and there to teach the boy a lesson.

They roughed him up some at first, each of them taking their turn to give him a good wallop. Then the beating turned ugly. It was going badly, and when the feeling of the boy's pending doom stirred, Clay recoiled and stifled it. But there, in France, was where he'd first confessed to the Catholic priest. Prayer and marriage were his prescribed cures for murder.

It had worked, inasmuch as when he had joined a Klan group when he got back home to Tulsa, it was only in the name of protecting good white folks, and he never participated in another murder. He would die before he would. Before long, he couldn't ignore the error of his ways and left that band of fools behind too. He and the wife he'd chosen in haste were estranged. Two adults living in the same home but barely speaking, not knowing each other, and almost never having marital relations. Mary had cursed him, threatened to tell his friends that he was off. But he'd stayed to provide for her and their boy.

Then, in a moment as blissful as it was foolish, he'd beaten the daylights out of one of his former Klan brothers for getting too friendly with a young Negro girl. Clay lured him deep into an alley, his intent only to give him a good whupping. But like in France, things went awry and the man lay dead after hitting his head. When the police came, Clay didn't even try to run.

The inside of a jail cell was a fair tumble downward for a former soldier in the US Army. And it would be only a matter of time before gossip in the tiny town had his name on everyone's flapping gums. Clay had pried a wire loose from the steel bunk and dragged a piercing line across his chest. He'd hacked and sliced three letters into his skin by the time the woman appeared, standing on the other side of the bars.

Geneva looked exactly the same as she did now, the same beautiful face, the same clothes that never changed or wore out. Clay had scrambled to the rear of the cell. The malevolence the woman wore made him want to shield his eyes. Nobody else seemed to see her. On that first visit, she'd asked about him, his family. It was like she was a priest or something, but that wasn't possible for a Negro woman.

The next visit, she spoke of Clay's crime. Asked him all sorts of questions about how he felt about it. On the last visit, she told him she wasn't too keen about the fact that he had killed one of her people, said a spirit had whispered it to her. One that would be waiting for him, or his son. The last visit, she offered absolution that came with another steep price that would protect his boy. Clay already suspected he'd gone mad. But not mad enough to not agree to take the hand she extended, the hand that felt like salvation had finally come. She offered him a way out: join her. Said they were kindred spirits.

Long, difficult weeks later, the sheriff appeared and pronounced him free. Clay had stumbled into the bright afternoon, where the woman who had paid his fine—Efe—waited with Geneva. He didn't concern himself with how she'd managed it.

Over the years, Clay had completed the desperate engraving on his chest. The mirror revealed the ragged, inexpert carving of the word "Redemption." The raised and puckered skin had barely healed. Clay unfolded the knife, sank it into the tip of the letter *R*, and carved anew. He bit down on the piece of wood he'd clamped between his teeth. He would not cry out. Skin opened and blood seeped from his chest.

Muttering his apologies, Clay begged God to fix him before he died. He was going to hell, for the murders, and for what he'd done to help the demon. But he did not want to go into the afterlife not having been healed.

When he finished, Clay rose, put away his torture and worship implements. He cleaned his wounds with alcohol and covered them with a loose bandage. He sat on his bunk and fell into a fitful sleep, wrought with nightmares and visions of what horrors awaited him in the afterlife. He wondered if Geneva spun them special for him, if she'd cracked him open and looked inside at every horror.

In the morning, sunlight streaming into the trailer, a bird sang its song at the base of his window. Clay rose, peeling back a corner of his bandage. The wound was another shot of whiskey shy of being healed.

∼

Eloko had to admit: he liked Malachi. From the first day they'd met, the man had simply put him at an ease he'd never felt around humans before. He didn't have the slightest urge to eat him either. They sat this early morning, going over the highlights of Malachi's new show. How excited he was that people had enjoyed it.

"The key," Malachi explained, "is that up to a certain point, right below the skin, you don't feel pain when the needles enter the body. And, of course, it is a matter of mental acuity. Mind over matter."

Eloko's snout parted in a grin. "When you lie on the bed of nails, you simply tell yourself you will not feel the pain, and you do not?"

Malachi waved his hands noncommittally. "More or less. To be fair, the nails are not as sharp as they could be, and these"—he whipped out the small acupuncture needles he'd used in his show—"these will enter the skin, but you feel almost nothing. And positioned the right way, they can actually heal."

Eloko's golden eyes widened. "What sorts of things can they heal?"

"All kinds. The twelve vessels of the body are outlined in this Egyptian medical text called the Ebers Papyrus. I only know a few of them, though."

The two talked more, and Eloko relayed how in his own show, it was enough for people to stare and gawk but that perhaps he should consider expanding. Telling jokes or something of the sort. He would certainly not dance.

"Let's think on it over breakfast," Malachi said, then rose and offered Eloko a bite of an apple he'd removed from his pocket. Eloko declined. "You know, I don't see you eat much, and when you do, it is with little enthusiasm. Mabel has been able to accommodate my diet; maybe she can cook something special for you."

Eloko didn't want to tell Malachi that he doubted that Mabel could accommodate his unusual tastes. "There are certain dishes I miss; it would take some explaining, though," Eloko said and then laughed at his own joke, even though Malachi didn't get it. "I've got to go see Clay first," the dwarf lied. "I can meet you in an hour."

Malachi agreed and bounced outside with a book. Eloko had been crafty, trying to pump information from his friend . . . did he say "friend"? He felt a stab of guilt but quickly unburdened himself; he would do nothing to harm Malachi. He'd learned only that Liza had some sort of vision. It was possible she wasn't the one Ahiku was looking for, but there was certainly something unsettling about her. Eloko only hoped, if she was indeed the danger he thought she was, that after the demon was done with her, he would be able to feast on what was left of her flesh. Yes, that would be a just reward. He salivated and shivered thinking about it.

Ah, he bounced a little lighter on his feet; Ahiku must have read his mind. Zinsa and Efe were standing at their posts at the red trailer, and if they were there, then their mistress had to be inside. The women soldiers' dark skin glistened in the sunlight. As Eloko approached, Zinsa whipped out her short dagger and held it out in front of the dwarf.

"If it is not the eyes and ears." She brandished the weapon in front of Eloko's face.

With one clawed hand, he pushed it aside. "Your mistress has returned?" He ignored Zinsa and directed his question to Efe.

But before she could even answer, a voice from inside the trailer called out. "Send him in."

Efe gestured at the door, and Eloko lilted up the stairs, his snout parted in a gruesome grin. Playfully, he snapped at Zinsa before slipping through the door.

Ahiku lay sprawled on her treasured chaise lounge, her feet crossed at the ankles. She wore the mask this time; slashes of black decorated both cheeks, a creamy tan partway down the center, ending at the tip of her nose. Red filled in the other spaces, including the lips. Eloko didn't fidget while she appraised him. He was certain that she respected him some for that. Ahiku removed the mask and rose to place it back on the wall.

"It is a fine morning that brings you to me so early. You must have something most important to report."

Uninvited, Eloko scooted up into the high stool and crossed his legs, swinging them back and forth. He was bursting with excitement. "I do indeed," he said. "But may we settle the small matter of my reward first?"

Ahiku's smile melted from her face like scalding butter. "Remaining alive and unskinned is your reward, little dwarf."

Eloko's legs stopped swinging. He had gotten ahead of himself. He backtracked. "Of course." He shifted, suddenly uncomfortable under her gaze. "Your enemy—I think I've found her."

Ahiku looked at him, head tilted. "Get on with it." She became angry. "There are many women in the carnival and the town both; do you care to narrow it down for me?"

"The temperamental animal charmer," Eloko explained. "The girl from Baton Rouge you told me to keep an eye on."

"And what makes you think she is the one?" Ahiku sat up, her eyes intent on Eloko.

"She has become friendly with my trailer mate. The Human Pincushion we got from Barnum's outfit. He's not like the rest of them; he's studied much about the continent—"

"About the orisha?"

"No." Eloko was getting flustered. He wanted to tell the story, but she kept interrupting him. "I mean, yes, of a sort. He is into this 'meditation' thing. Apparently, if one sits long enough and, well, thinks, answers of a kind can come to you." He paused, certain the demon would interrupt him. When she didn't, he continued, even more animated. "It was during one of these sessions that the girl had a vision from a spirit."

"African?" Ahiku had come to her feet and stalked over to her spy.

"I'm not sure," Eloko said slowly.

Ahiku spat out a stream of words in a language Eloko didn't understand but that he plainly took for curses of some sort. He was alternately giddy with excitement and wary with unease. He couldn't say he had ever seen Ahiku worried, and that scared him more than her skinning threat.

"But the age is wrong . . . perhaps—"

"I can easily kill her for you."

"No!" Ahiku snapped. "You must not touch her." Eloko flinched, swiped some of his grassy hair out of his eyes. He didn't understand why they shouldn't go on and end it here. He had not tasted any flesh since the electrician. Surely, she could spare him another one.

"I understand," he ventured. "You must have your time to do what you need to with your foe. But . . . but after you are done, do you suppose I could have whatever is left?"

"You are a selfish creature." Ahiku paced. "You think only of your own hunger."

Eloko didn't want to mention that Ahiku did pretty much the same thing. Best to keep his snout shut.

"I check everyone that comes into this carnival," Ahiku said as if she were talking to herself. "How could I have missed her?"

Eloko blinked but remained silent.

Then a slow smile curved at the corner of Ahiku's mouth. She returned to the chaise, switched on the radio on the side table next to her. The sound of the African savanna piped into the room. Not the drums, as was her usual, but the sounds of the creatures, of the wind brushing against dry grass, of the hunt.

"Could she be a daughter, perhaps? If she is, you've given me a way to lure that witch out of hiding. Tell me what you know of this girl," she said, leaning back. "Everything you know, and leave out no small detail. I must be certain."

Eloko resettled himself in the chair and began a not-too-embellished retelling of the little information he had on Liza Meeks, daughter of an aberration—descendants of Africa who had willingly abandoned her.

CHAPTER THIRTY

THE ROAD LESS TRAVELED

For those who were especially attuned to its unique chorus, life on the road was filled with boundless melodic treasures. Liza was one of those people. More than once, she had fallen asleep to the steady, reassuring rotation of tires against a bumpy road or open field, only to be awakened by the serenade of a new bird. Even the sometimes bleak, sometimes beautiful things outside the window made it worthwhile.

She and Autumn had called a truce and were back in each other's good graces for the time being. Mico certainly wasn't the most friendly animal in the world, so the fact that he liked Autumn counted for something. Liza was certain that deep down, beneath the rouge, below the shimmer of her beautiful clothes, a decent lady was hidden.

The trailer had pulled to a stop, and Liza called out to the driver. "Where are we?"

"Seeing our way a little deeper into Oklahoma," Jamey called back. Since they had begun seeing each other in earnest, it was, more often than not, him driving their trailer. He'd said the small gesture drew him closer to her. And she didn't argue it.

"What city?" she asked, coming outside and stretching.

"None yet," Jamey said. "Have a look around you."

Liza turned in a circle and took in a whole horizon full of dust and empty. There was no other way to describe it. "Well, when do we get to the city?"

Instead of answering, Jamey came up to her and planted a kiss on her cheek. "You meeting some other man?"

"Yes," Liza said. "He is about this tall." She held her hand high over her own head. "Has a sad, stern face and wears a worn cap." She had described her father, but so far, she hadn't told Jamey much about her family.

"You let me get to him first," Jamey said, pulling her close. Autumn emerged from the trailer, and Liza pulled away. Autumn still didn't approve of their relationship, but Liza had no idea why she cared.

"Young love," Autumn teased as she strolled past.

Jamey looked off in the distance, fidgeted, and turned serious. He took Liza's hand and dropped to one knee. He slid a ring, a simple golden band, from his pocket.

"What are you doing?" Liza raised her eyebrows so high they may well have sailed right off her impressive forehead. She flapped her hands, casting her gaze around to see if anybody was watching them. "Get up. Get up!"

"I want to be with you." Jamey wore the expression of a man who'd gotten to his own funeral late. He stood. "We together now; why not make it official?"

"I've barely known you six months."

"And that's more than long enough," he countered. "My parents got married after they parents decided on the match. It don't take long to know. Less you got somebody else on your mind."

He probably meant Ishe. Liza sighed but couldn't ignore the flutter in her stomach. "There is nobody else, and you know it. You don't even know anything about me."

"Past don't matter. I know all I need to know."

Clay came up to them then. "Been looking all over for ya, Jamey," he said. "Give sweet britches here a kiss and come with me—we got work to do."

Liza was glad for the distraction. "We'll talk later," she said, turning to head in the opposite direction.

"Count on it," Jamey said and then went off after Clay.

〜

"I believe it is necessary for a woman to be sure of character before she selects a mate," Bombardier said between mouthfuls of bacon and eggs. "Sometimes the most obvious choice is not the best one."

Hope and Liza shot him a look. He might as well have been waving a sign that said ISHE, ISHE IS THE MAN FOR YOU!

"A relationship"—Hope stopped and took a slurp of coffee—"or a marriage is tough—"

"Our marriage, our courtship, was as easy as a Senegalese sea breeze, as exciting as a *laamb* match, as pure as the sand of Dakar's Ngor Island beaches," Bombardier interrupted and laughed heartily. Both women eyed him until he piped down.

"Even for regular folk." Hope nibbled a biscuit. "But in a carnival? And what about kids? You know you can't be raising kids here—it's not allowed—and 'sides, it wouldn't be much of a life anyway."

"Who said anything about kids?" Liza pushed her plate away. "I'm not sure I even want to get married." She had come to Hope and Bombardier, the closest thing she had to an example of how a real marriage was supposed to work—one where both parties spoke and had minds of their own. Still, how sad was it that they, people in a carnival, were her only model.

"Then, my girl," Bombardier said, zooming in on the opening, "you have answered your own question."

Liza huffed and swept her eyes over the cook tent. Mabel and Uly huddled in a corner—were they flirting? A couple of tables over, Malachi sat with Eloko. Her new friend waved and inclined his head at her. She returned the gesture with a weak smile that faded as soon as Eloko turned to see who Malachi had made the gesture to. There was something creepy about the little man: not because of his appearance but because of the way he looked at her and his slinking around, watching everything.

Autumn sat by herself under a shaded portion of the tent, flipping through a magazine and managing to make eating breakfast in an empty field seem like she shared a table with the Queen of England.

Then Liza swept her gaze to the table directly behind theirs. Zinsa and Efe sat eating and chatting. But it wasn't their food that drew Liza's attention; it was the slingshot that Zinsa was fiddling with. Liza had caught only a glimpse of it before, but the slingshot looked like the one she'd seen from outside the red trailer. Efe caught her staring and whispered something to Zinsa, who then turned toward Liza.

The women finished their breakfast and were leaving the cook tent when they paused at Liza's table.

"Did your boyfriend tell you we had to save his hide at that craps game the other night?" Efe said with a smile.

Liza's mouth felt like it was stuffed with cotton. *Jamey gambling, playing craps?*

Bombardier pushed back from the table. "A woman who does not even know her own true God-given nature should learn to keep her mouth shut about other people."

"Oh." Efe laughed. "He did not tell you? You know, there were whores there too. Your man has interesting hobbies."

The hair on the back of Liza's neck prickled. A searing blitz of destructive emotion set every pore on fire. A snarl, an inhuman sound, wound its way through vocal cords that were most decidedly human and tore free from her throat. Liza dived across the table and crashed into Zinsa. Her own teeth bared, she found herself trying to go for the woman's throat. She couldn't stop herself, but she didn't have to; Zinsa was incredibly strong and held her at arm's length.

Liza felt Bombardier struggle to pull her up. When she had finally gained control of herself, the badger hissed in her mind and then receded. Bombardier shoved Liza and Hope backward, but Liza, still imbued with the badger's spirit, swatted the strongman's meaty hand away and came to stand by his side.

The big man smiled, but the look in his eye told everybody he wasn't playing. "You looking for another fight? I'm your man."

The women ignored Bombardier. Zinsa knelt and picked up a rock. She positioned it in the slingshot and shot the rock at Liza's feet. "Watch where you stick your nose, dog trainer."

"I don't need you to fight my fights," Liza said to Bombardier, and she meant it. Though with the badger's presence seeping away, a knot of fear twisting in her gut pulled tauter with every breath. How could something so easily take over her body? A presence that ignored her will and acted completely on its own? It reminded her of—

"Ain't nobody gone be doing any fighting." Ishe ambled up like he was out for a summer stroll. He walked right between everybody and took a seat at the bench. "If you ain't gone finish these here eggs?" He held up the plate, and when nobody said anything, he started eating and then held up an empty cup, as if hoping somebody would come and fill it.

Zinsa and Efe actually looked a bit taken aback. Zinsa laughed. "As you say, night hunter."

The cup struck the table with a clatter. "My name is Ishe."

They all settled back at their tables, another crisis averted. Ishe and Hope and Bombardier chatted, but Liza could focus only on how quickly and easily the badger had . . . had it come to her rescue? Had it instigated the fight? She stared at Ishe's profile. Was she like him now? Was that Oya's "gift"?

She couldn't shake that she'd liked the feeling. Powerful. It was almost as if she'd watched from a corner of her mind while her animal spirit had done its will. *Mama didn't tell me everything. There's more to her, to me. So much more.*

I'll have to learn to control it. If Ishe is right, my life may depend on it.

CHAPTER THIRTY-ONE

RECKONINGS

The woman stood at the parlor entrance, rigid and worn as the lone faded sofa.

Her fists curled with indignation—weapons she sometimes wielded, though she favored a good sharp slap or three. The sinful child sat in front of the radio—her radio—listening to that *Little Orphan Annie* show. Her face upturned and bewitched as if she were receiving the holy word of God instead of that wicked rabble-rousing nonsense. May as well have been the devil himself speaking right there in her own home!

"I'll tan your hide and good this time."

The girl scuttled up and backed into a corner as her mother tore into the room and silenced the radio. At the barely audible click, the girl's expression crumpled. "No, Mama. Please. I sure am sorry."

"Lord willing, you'll learn to mind me." She moved to the fireplace mantel and opened the velvet-covered box that rested there beneath a simple wooden cross and a portrait of Jesus. The switches had been freshly plucked earlier that week, cleaned and saved for such an occasion.

The child bawled in earnest now. Good.

"Cursed is he who dishonors his father or mother."

Swoosh. Satisfaction swelled and burst as she delivered the stinging blows with an efficiency born of devoted practice. Hers was the Lord's work, after all.

After, they shared a dinner of boiled potatoes. The girl squirmed and winced with every bite, and a curious pang of guilt gnawed at the woman. She gave her an extra potato, one of the small ones, from her own plate.

"It's the last night." The girl didn't look her in the eye; that much she'd learned. "You said that you might take me to the carnival."

She had no intention of doing any such thing, but that curious inkling nudged her again. The woman reluctantly agreed, if only to have something to criticize later.

"One hour, less if you ask me for anything."

The handful of stilt walkers who mysteriously appeared were in full force, taking wide steps around the midway. A ragtime band belted out the latest tunes from the speakers.

Liza felt a chill run down her spine as she spotted the skeletal stilt walker from the red trailer. It passed her without a glance.

She averted her eyes and ducked into her animal tent.

"I said I wanted to separate these out, move this row of benches along the right wall," Liza snapped at Uly, who had been bent over, nuzzling Sabina beneath her chin. She tugged at her uniform, which pinched and chafed in all the wrong places.

Uly looked momentarily stunned but soon recovered. "What's with you? You and that lackey you gone all sweet on have a fight or something? You haven't even been around here as much. You spend all your time with *him*. And don't think Sabina and Ikaki don't know it too."

Liza glared, and it crossed her mind to send a pack of wolves to his throat. "First it was me, now you're jealous that Jamey has a brain? That he works with Clay?" She didn't have time for this. She'd been avoiding Jamey since he'd dropped that bomb, but Uly didn't need to be prying.

"That's sad." She grabbed one end of the long bench in front of her stage and started dragging.

Uly moved as if to help her, then stopped himself. He muttered something about "crazy women" and stalked out of the tent. Liza maneuvered the bench into place and then went to tend to the animals, but already the barker was at it out front. And so was the sweet sound of coins falling into the collection box. Sabina and Ikaki eyed her suspiciously. It was true: she'd been avoiding them, too, as the spirits inside her had jostled for attention.

The stands and benches were filling up. A woman caught her eye. No, it wasn't so much her as the little girl with her. That sadness. Theirs must have been about as happy a home as her own was. Liza retreated behind the curtain and tried the breathing techniques Malachi had taught her. The method stilled her nerves, but images of her animal guides—all vying for attention—rushed right in. She clasped her hands to her head and begged them to go away.

Uly, who had grudgingly returned, peeked his head backstage. "What?" He was looking around, as if he expected someone else to be back there.

"Nothing," Liza said. Her face relaxed. "And I'm sorry about earlier."

"Some kinda trouble with Jamey's aunt?" Uly asked without a bit of laughter in his voice. But he did look away. "My ma and . . . well, I got five sisters." He seemed to want to delve deeper into the matter but didn't. "You're on, kid." He disappeared out front.

Liza smoothed her clothes, plastered a smile on her face, and emerged waving to the crowd. She bowed, thanked everyone for coming, and got set to begin the show with Ikaki. She pointed at Uly to cue the music. In the back, he set the needle on the phonograph, and the classical music selection they'd agreed on filtered out and around the tent. She shivered as the mental connectors locked into place. Before she could press on, the inexplicable screech of a raven hacked through the connection like an ax through a sapling. A few mumbled curses later, she refocused and floated an image to Ikaki to begin the dance they had been practicing, the new one to the music they'd requested.

Only, the turtle sat mute with their back turned to her. Ikaki looked out at the crowd, lifting their head out of the shell, inspecting the patrons as if they were the performers instead of the turtle. Liza's smile faltered, and she tried again.

Ikaki turned to her and, at once, pulled their legs and head into their shell. The shell spun round and round a few times and then stopped. The crowd had begun to grow uneasy. Curious glances were exchanged, and a slight grumble circulated from ear to ear.

Under her breath, Liza cursed Ikaki and promised that they wouldn't have their precious bean sprouts for a week. They wouldn't even send an image back to say they were sick or tired or any indication of what was wrong. But when she turned to Sabina, the Tasmanian tiger was quick to show her anger. She suffused Liza's mind with an image of Uly's dejected face after she'd snapped at him. Next, Sabina transmitted a scene of Liza with her back turned on the animals.

Liza fumbled together an image of apology and shot it across their connection—too late. Sabina sank onto the platform and began licking her fur. Neither the tiger nor Ikaki would communicate with her.

"Show's over!" Liza called.

Uly's mouth dropped open, but he sprang into action. He turned off the music and said, "You heard her, this show's done. Come back to the late show."

"I want my money back!" a patron yelled.

"This is a crock!" came another.

Uly went to try and hustle them out of the tent amid other angry cries.

An apple hit Liza in the back of the head, stunning her. Sabina apparently forgot her own irritation with Liza and bared her fangs. The tiger leaped from the stage, tearing out of Liza's grasp to sink her teeth into the leg of the man who had thrown the apple.

People screamed and tore out of the tent. Liza and Uly tried to get Sabina off the man, whose trousers were now soaked with blood. Eventually Clay appeared in the doorway after they had calmed Sabina and put her back in her cage.

"I'm shutting you down for the night," Clay said, helping to carry the man from the tent. It would likely take a hefty sum to quiet him.

"Why, I ought to tie her up to a tree and give her a good whippin'," the man spat at Liza.

She planted her fists on her hips in invitation for him to try it, but Clay intervened. "Now, I won't be having any of that. Let's get you outta here."

He shot a look of annoyance back over his shoulder at Liza as he shuffled the man from the tent.

She sank to a bench, and Uly patted her awkwardly on the shoulder.

~

The man could walk. Clearly if the tiger had wanted to hurt him more, she could have. But that didn't stop him from milking Clay for all he could get. In the end, it cost him ten dollars, and as they'd all spilled outside Hope's trailer, she'd offered the promise of a free card reading the next day.

"You better have a talk with that friend of yours," Clay said, taking a seat beside Hope on the stairs of her trailer. The commotion had scared away most of the customers.

"She's got a lot on her mind," Hope tried to explain. "Cut her a little slack."

"She better have her show on her mind come showtime," Clay answered. "What she worries about outside a that, I don't care."

The two sat in companionable silence for a time until Hope asked, "You ever think about what you would do, you know . . . if we didn't have Bacchanal?"

Clay hoped he'd be dead and gone by the time the carnival ended. He took off his hat, fiddled with the brim. "I don't think much more than a day or two ahead of me," he lied. Eventually, Geneva's strange tastes would catch up to them all. "'Sides, why wouldn't a carnival survive? Folks need entertainment more than food."

He tried to hide the doubt in his eyes. Hope gestured with her head. "Wanna see what the cards say?"

"Naw." Clay stood but still didn't walk off.

"You don't believe in this stuff noways," Hope said, standing and turning to walk up the short set of stairs. "Come on, what could it hurt?"

Clay squeezed his hat in his hands and followed her. Hope settled behind her table and waved him into the seat in front of her. She took up the cards and shuffled them. Spreading them out, she asked him to pick out five. She took his selections and laid them facedown in front of him. She turned them over one by one. The first, a crowned and bearded man sitting on a stone throne and holding a scepter.

"The Emperor," Hope said with a sigh. "Why am I not surprised? A wise and knowledgeable leader. Strict. A creator of order from chaos. And lots of other stuff you probably already know. Hmm," she murmured, turning the next card. "The Hermit." A wizened and robed old man stood grasping a lantern and staff. "You do like to be alone. Introspection. You're looking for meaning for yourself." Hope paused. "And all this."

The next card featured a man balancing two circular objects that looked like gold coins caught together in a long band.

"The Two of Pentacles. Right now you're juggling things well, but change is coming." Turning over the next card, she proclaimed with a smile, "The Knight of Wands. Rides in with his shining armor, straddling a great mare. Shows your courage.

"And last we have . . ." She turned the last card and frowned. Beneath a black sky, a man lay on the ground dead from the ten swords sticking out of his back. She looked at Clay.

"What?"

"The Ten of Swords." Hope blinked. "All that take the sword, it has been said, shall perish with the sword. This card foretells an unexpected disaster. Some power that is going to humble you. Whatever happens, it will be final. But the sun will rise again."

Clay sat staring at her. He gulped. What he had been doing might catch up to him, or maybe it wouldn't. The damned cards didn't give any real answers. "Well, ain't that the same for everybody?"

Hope inclined her head. "This card, together with the last, means you are making a conscious decision."

Clay pushed away from the table. "Yeah, well. Guess we all got choices."

≈

When Clay left, Hope gathered up the cards and wondered about her own choices. The one that grated most: the decision she and Bombardier had made to leave their son in Baltimore.

They'd met at the hotel in the city. She did the backbreaking work of cleaning the rooms, and Bombardier helped to tote the luggage of the rich, the criminal, and the famous.

He had not been a shy man, even then. His tongue wielded his strongly accented French English and Wolof like an invitation to a world in which he was the center, the light, the opening and closing attractions. He'd fallen in easily with the other men, while she—the American—was seen as the strange one. But it was his smile, his deep throaty laughter, that had won her over.

It had taken time to learn to control her gift, and sometimes, when the visions came to her, she'd blurt out questions or make remarks about things she shouldn't have known. All it took sometimes was a touch, or the passing scent of an earthy body odor. In truth, the cards were a cover. When people picked them, their story was usually more or less laid out. Being from Africa, she guessed that Bombardier was a bit more used to the supernatural than some of the northern Negroes who had the same roots but worked overtime to forget them. When the other men warned him about talking to her, he only grinned his great grin, waved them off, and promptly asked after her parents and when he could meet them.

Their courtship was not long. There were no flowers, no series of midnight strolls and stolen kisses . . . well, there was that one night in room 1206. Bombardier had regaled her parents with stories of life in Senegal: his village and move to the city; the art of *laamb*. He even demonstrated some of his wrestling moves with her younger brothers. After that first visit, his appearance at Sunday dinners became regular. Within six months, they'd been married and were living in a little room not far from the hotel.

Their little light, Bombardier Jr., was born the next year, his crib pushed into a corner of their now-overcrowded room. Hope's parents doted on the baby, her mother keeping him while they both worked long hours. But they were happy.

Her father got sick and died practically before they could figure out what the trouble had been. He was a heavy smoker and had been complaining of breathing problems. He sat in the emergency room at Provident Hospital. The doctors and nurses were mostly Negro and did the best they could, but the place was understaffed. A white administrator had finally come out and pronounced her father dead on the floor. Her brother had lunged at the man and landed a few good blows before the police dragged him away.

The little savings they all had went to getting him out of jail, but not before the authorities had beaten him into a mental corner from which he had never emerged. It nearly broke her mother. Hope believed that if not for her new grandson, her mother would have curled up in bed one night and gone on to join her husband in the afterlife.

Not five months later, Hope had been cleaning a room that was in tatters following a night of ill repute from two shady-looking characters and the lady friends she guessed were prostitutes. She had finished cleaning her last room and was on her way to meet Bombardier outside so that they could go home. Through the revolving door, the two men came racing after her, along with the manager.

"I tell ya, the wench stole my money." The red-faced, disheveled man pointed a finger at her.

"That's right," the other one chimed in. "I saw her do it!"

Behind them, one of the prostitutes held up a bright-red satchel, mocking, and fell into a fit of giggles with her friend. Hope wrung her hands. It would do no good to accuse two white women, even if they were prostitutes.

The manager looked torn. Hope had been a good employee of over six years, but she knew he couldn't rightfully accuse his white customers of lying, especially in front of a growing crowd. He stood looking between the groups. A tense hush moved through the crowd as, from within, Bombardier emerged.

The accuser came face-to-chest with the hulking man. His mouth worked, but no words came as his dwindling courage seemed to seep out. But with a nudge in the ribs from his buddy, he gathered himself. "Look here, boy, if you know what's good for you, you'll back on away from here while you still can. She stole, and I'll see her pay for it."

Bombardier pushed Hope back. "My wife is no tief." Hope recalled how cute it was that he still pronounced the word "thief" without the *h*.

The accuser took a swing at Bombardier, having to leap up to do so. Hope screamed. Bombardier grabbed the man's fist and crushed it in his own, the bones cracking as if they were being shoved through a meat grinder.

The man cried out, and Bombardier grabbed him by the collar and crotch and, with an upward press, launched the man into the crowd.

Bodies fell back like trees bending to the wind and snapped forward in a unified motion, depositing the man on the concrete.

By now, his sidekick had jumped on Bombardier's back and Hope had joined the fray, swinging her purse, heavy with coins from her tips. Bombardier bent over at the waist, flipped the man on his back onto the ground, and held him in a vise grip that had him sputtering, coughing, and clawing at the beefy arm wrapped around his neck.

By then, the manager had grabbed Hope and was holding her back. *Let this blow over,* he'd said. Soon, three other enraged white men had joined in the fray, and Bombardier dispatched them: one solid slap to the nose, a swift kick to a liquored-up liver. Other Negro men surged forward from the cluster of people and joined in, and soon the front of the hotel looked like a riot had broken out. Police whistles rang out.

But there was one man, tall with reddish hair combed back but for a single strand dangling down the right side of his face, who slipped through the crowd. Hope had been clutching Bombardier by the arm, ready to take up her purse swing if needed again, when the man produced a card and handed it to her.

"Clay Kennel," he'd said. "If you don't want your husband to spend the rest of his life in prison, I think I got a better use for his talents."

The man's hand had grazed Hope's when he'd given her the card. She'd seen a swirl of darkness around him but the image of a child, a bloom of goodness, in his heart. She'd dragged her husband away, and they'd followed Clay, slipping away from the still-raging battle. They'd had time to gather a few belongings from their room and then piled into the man's truck, headed south to join the G. B. Bacchanal Carnival.

Clay explained that he had been on a long road trip from DC through Virginia, and finally Maryland, on the lookout for new acts for his budding carnival. He knew of a pair of conjoined twins whom he wanted to talk to, but he had missed them by a few weeks. Neighbors told him that they'd been snatched up by P. T. Barnum's outfit. It ticked off yet another loss, and Clay had been thinking he'd have to head back south when luck had placed him at the Baltimore Hotel, where he'd witnessed some of the best fighting he'd ever seen. Perhaps the trip hadn't been a waste after all.

They stopped at a gas station far enough away from the city, and Hope had tearfully called her mother. Before she could even finish her recounting of the story, her mother had told her it would be best if she kept little Bombardier. Hope and Bombardier had avoided each other's eyes but had not argued. Her mother was right. They had planned to stay with the carnival until things blew over up north and then head home. Clay had an act all worked up for Bombardier, and he brimmed over with excitement as he explained how the wrestling and strongman show could work.

When, at Bombardier's urging, she told Clay about her readings, the man had been beside himself with glee. Said the carnival employed some old hack who didn't know nothing about cards. Like that, they both had new jobs, paying triple what they'd made at the hotel. The money they were able to wire home took care of their son's expenses and helped her mother take care of Hope's still-broken brother. The hotel manager, feeling awful about what had happened, had sent the police on a wild-goose chase so as not implicate either Hope or her husband. They agreed to head back in a year, after they had saved up enough to buy a small house.

That had been two years ago, almost to the day.

Bombardier, as was his nature, had settled in easily, making friends. But Hope hadn't found a friend in all that time, until Eliza had appeared. Sure, strange things went on with the carnival, but money, a meal, importance, and acceptance were powerful drugs.

Hope fingered the picture of her son, now four years old. Their child had her husband's wide smile, his kind eyes, but her brooding nature. Behind the smile lurked that faraway look in his eyes, and she wondered if in a few years he, too, would have her gift. She closed her eyes and wished it not to be so. When she opened them, the tears ran freely. She missed him and cursed herself for not going back. But they were safe here, and he was safe there.

Next year, she said unconvincingly. *Next year.*

❧

The godforsaken carnival had been the calamity she'd expected. The woman had swatted away her daughter's outstretched hand as they'd hurried out of the animal tent with everyone else. Clingy little thing, that one. But now she couldn't find her. She didn't call out; that would be untoward, indecent. A woman stood by a trailer. FORTUNE-TELLER, the sign said. She sniffed. Charlatan.

"This way," the charlatan said. "Over here."

It was like the night pressed in as they walked. Where had that girl gotten off to?

The charlatan stopped and turned with a smile. She raised her hand. One of those crystal balls sat in her palm. If she'd lured her out here to try to swindle—

The ball splintered, shattered. She had no time to react. The charlatan flung the crystal shards into the air, where they swirled like glinting little ice picks and showered down over the woman.

She shrieked and hopped around, trying to brush them off. The whole thing was so improper. By the time she'd collected herself, the charlatan had gone and the carnival with her. The crystals rustled at her feet, flooded upward, and bound together again to form a mirror hovering there in the air. The glass sparkled. The frame throbbed and writhed like the darkest skin. Raised veins coursed through.

Instead of her reflection in the mirror, she saw an image of herself, much younger. She was at the county store with her father. When he turned to speak with the shop owner, she fingered the peppermint he'd denied her and slipped it into her sock. The self-satisfied grin on her face dissolved into the next scene.

An old maid at nineteen. The outrage she'd felt that nobody had asked her father for her hand. She and old Mr. Tate behind the church during the fall picnic. The fumbling, mad coupling. She'd felt no shame, only pride at having won the man's affections over those of his too-perfect wife. Their daughter had his dimpled cheeks.

The woman clasped her hands to her mouth and bit back a sob. She couldn't turn away as the last image coalesced. She was older, much older. Beds filled with people in near-catatonic states. A convalescent home, then. Her bed was soiled with her own feces. Eyes sunken, arms bruised from the nurse's torturous pinches.

Tears streamed from her eyes as someone, she couldn't tell who, hovered over her and slapped her slack face again and again. A fracture split the mirror in half, soon followed by others. Blood seeped from the cracks.

The woman sank to the ground in wordless shock. She didn't know how long she'd been there, but she came back to herself at the touch of her daughter's hand on her shoulder. This time, she didn't shrug it off.

CHAPTER THIRTY-TWO

THE TELLING

The last time Liza had experienced stillness was when she still lived under the watchful eye of Mrs. Margaret. It was the quiet of sitting in the library with her legs tucked beneath her in the high-back leather chair with a seat worn dull from overuse.

Liza had liked to swaddle herself among the great bulky tomes and weathered dime novels that lined the bookshelves, keeping a favorite novel resting in her lap. She liked to trace the gilded lettering on the cover, her fingers sliding along the binder. She wasn't reading; she was only being. Enjoying the stillness. Finding a quiet place like that to think in a traveling carnival was impossible.

It didn't help that Eloko seemed to be lurking around every corner. He had taken to standing outside the trailer, failing to look inconspicuous; was often a few steps behind her when she turned around; and always seemed to be within earshot when she sought out Malachi. She wondered, and not for the first time, how the little man with a snout, claws, and grass for skin could so easily hide in plain sight.

The carnival had stopped for the evening, and Liza shared a dinner with Jamey. This consisted mostly of her pushing her potatoes around on her plate and Jamey brooding. He stood finally and snorted at her. "Any other woman would be happy that a man, a *good* man, wants to marry her. But you sit here moping like somebody just stole your last dime. Well, forget the whole thing." She caught him by the arm as he tried to stomp off and then ran the backs of her fingers down his face. He didn't smile, but he didn't pull away.

"Tulsa," he said. "I expect your answer by then."

As much as she hated to, she let him go without another word. Maybe Autumn was right: carnival romances weren't meant to be. Besides, she had other matters to attend to.

Liza sought out Ishe at his trailer. At her knock, Ishe poked his head out and he held the door open.

"Come on in," he said.

Liza took a step, stopped, glanced around. It was bad enough that she spent so much time with Ishe; if she was seen going inside his trailer, alone, Jamey might never speak to her again.

"Come on out—I need the fresh air."

A look of disappointment clouded Ishe's face when he stepped outside, but he quickly masked it with his normal blank stare. "Your shadow out and about?" he asked.

"Passed him on the way." Liza gestured back the direction she'd come with her head. "I don't know what he's up to. I mean, what has Eloko got to do with anything?"

Ishe leaned against his trailer, and the flutter rippled through Liza's stomach again. "What got ahold of you the other day? Why you let them women work you up?"

"It wasn't me at all." Liza joined him against the trailer wall, and their arms touched. "It was . . . it was the badger—I could *feel* it overtake me." She stopped and shivered, running her hands up and down her arms. "I couldn't control it, or myself." She gazed up at him. "Ishe. I need help."

He shook his head. "I ain't got no experience controlling a demon, as you've seen for yourself."

Her shoulders slumped.

He chucked her under the chin. "Who else besides me and you know what goes on with the dead, with spirits, with—"

"Hope!"

∼

Hope was sitting outside the trailer in a wooden fold-up chair, with a pen and paper balanced on her lap. She glanced up and smiled at Ishe and Liza.

"Letter to my baby," she said and then lowered her eyes but couldn't hide the sadness. She lifted her gaze again; she must have caught Liza's unease. "What? What is it?"

"I think we should go in." Liza pointed at Hope's trailer. "What we have to say isn't for everybody to hear."

They followed Hope into the trailer. She flicked on the overhead light and turned up an old oil lamp. The space was dominated by a full-size bed. Pictures of Bombardier Jr. were taped to the wall, alongside grade reports, drawings in a child's hand, and a family photo of Hope and Bombardier with their infant son. Hope sat on the edge of the bed. Liza and Ishe scrunched together on the padded bench by the door.

"One of you gonna tell me what's going on?"

Liza went on to tell Hope the entire story: Oya's message, the vision of the carnival's destruction, the badger, Eloko's spying. Hope was wringing a corner of her dress in her hands by the time Liza was finished. "That first time you read my cards, you said something troubled you, didn't you?" Liza asked.

"I didn't say that." Hope was defensive. "It doesn't work the way you think. Sometimes what I see ain't clear. Don't make sense even to me."

"Read them cards again," Ishe said. "Tell us what you see. We can piece together whether or not it mean something."

Hope stood and paced. Liza looked to Ishe and threw her hands up in frustration, a gesture he returned with a slight shrug.

"Honey, I'm afraid you stirring up something that could all be in your head," Hope said.

Ahh, she's scared for me. Liza walked over and took Hope's hands. "Let's see what the cards say, okay? If it turns out to be nothing, at least I'll know for sure."

Hope relaxed some. "I don't even need them cards. They're only for show, but—sit." She pointed at the bed. "Sit here and try to relax. Breathe in and out . . . that's it. Close your eyes if it helps."

Liza had learned how to meditate from Malachi, so her breathing fell into a slower, steadier rhythm quickly. Hope took Liza's hands and let her own eyes flutter closed. Liza felt Ishe inch forward, probably perched on the edge of the bench. Sweat had already begun to pool at her armpits and back. The first few seconds passed without incident, but when Liza peeked, Hope's eyes were rolling backward, the dark-brown irises lifting like a curtain before a show. Ishe shot to his feet. Hope jerked away from Liza as if a bolt of lightning had seared her hands.

Liza gaped. Ishe had Hope by the shoulders, asking her if she was okay.

Hope brushed Ishe away, her lips thinned into a worried line. "It doesn't make a lot of sense." Liza rubbed her clammy palms on her thighs. "There is a man, an old and wise man. You must go to him."

"But where—"

"Let her finish," Ishe interrupted.

"The way he showed me is west from here, a large boulder with a carving, an image of his people. A mountain in the distance behind this boulder when I look up, and—" Hope turned around. "That way." She pointed. Ishe and Liza followed the direction of her finger: north.

"At this boulder . . ." Liza stood and walked to the way Hope pointed. "I should see a mountain to the left, and that is where I will find this man?"

"That's all he showed me." Hope sank onto the bed. "But I ain't sure you should try to go wandering off following one of my visions. We don't know what it means."

"I have to," Liza said. Even now she could feel the spirits inside her, restless, trying to break through the surface. "Thank you, Hope. I'll go first thing in the morning. I'll catch up with the carnival later in the day."

"How are you going to do that?" Hope said. "I don't know how far it is. You can't walk—what if it's twenty miles from here? You can't drive. And what if Clay decides to move out before you get back?"

"I'll drive her." Ishe stood. "Get some sleep; we set out at dawn. I'll arrange for a car with Clay."

"Wait," Hope called. "Do you want a reading, Ishe?"

Ishe looked at both women, shamefaced and gloomy. "Naw," he said with his hand on the door. "Ain't no need. Set myself on this road, and I don't need you to tell me how it's gonna end."

~

After Ishe and Liza left, Hope paced in the trailer. She had not told them everything. There was a shadow over Bacchanal. She'd felt it since she arrived and had never told even her husband. That shadow was evil, though its evil never seemed to be directed at the carnies, so it was easier for her to put it out of her mind. But now, that shadow flanked Liza.

Whatever Liza's trouble was, it had something to do with Bacchanal. What brought tears to Hope's eyes was the fact that though she was scared for her friend, she was more scared at what would become of her and Bombardier if they no longer had Bacchanal to rely on.

Hope's vision had been of Liza's grandmother destroying the carnival.

CHAPTER THIRTY-THREE

In Search of a Mountaintop

Morning in Oklahoma was unlike any Liza had seen before. The sun appeared filtered, as if it sought shelter behind a mask of dingy gauze. She had awoken to the taste of grit in her mouth, and her eyes burned with it. Even Mico had fallen into a sneezing fit that worried her now, as she dropped him off with Hope and Bombardier for the time she would be away. She'd given him her blanket, the one that he snuggled and got lost in.

It had taken some doing, but Ishe had secured the car for a few hours—no more, Clay warned. Nobody else was up as Liza and Ishe slipped into the cab and stole away. "How far do you think we'll have to drive?" Liza asked Ishe, who hadn't said a word since they'd left. She fiddled with the amulet.

"No way to know."

The two rode in thick silence as the bleak Oklahoma countryside streaked past. Craggy and depleted, nothing moved. The land was largely empty of trees, and the few shrubs that clung to life seemed on the cusp of giving up the struggle. The sparse sunlight blended so well with the surroundings that the land seemed to be coated with a mask of dull beige that made everything run together. Worse, all they could see for miles in front of them was more of the same.

After a time, Liza glanced at Ishe from the corner of her eye. "Why are you helping me?"

"You helped me once," he said.

Thinking back on that night, finding Ishe turned into a hyena, Liza wondered how he lived with such a presence inside him. The badger taking her over in the cook tent was one thing, but Ishe's spirit was infinitely worse. She supposed that was why he kept everything about himself so close. She was glad that he hadn't had another incident.

"I got to say somethin'," Ishe began. He worked his mouth some and took a deep breath. "I see you with that Jamey fella all the time. How's it workin' out?"

Liza looked out the window, contemplating. "It's not."

"I suppose you could be blind enough not to see. Truth is, I'm probably better than most at hidin'." He flicked his gaze over at Liza and turned back to the road. "What I mean to say is that he ain't the only man that think highly of you."

"Ishe—"

"Let me finish." Ishe gripped the steering wheel and, aside from a pained glance over at Liza, kept his gaze fixed on the road. "I had a wife. I still love her, but I won't never see her again. I made a promise to be true to her until the day I died. But then I met you, and all the feelings I fought to bottle up since that first day—well, they keep bubblin' up. Done blown that cap clean off."

Liza blinked. Her whole body tingled. Relief? Yes, and a gleeful delight. She glanced over at Ishe and wanted more than anything to reach out and squeeze his hand, but no matter what sorry state their relationship was in right now, she had stirrings of something akin to love for Jamey. What could she say, though? She certainly felt something for Ishe.

Her silence said everything that her mouth couldn't, with no words needed. Liza was grateful when, up ahead, a tiny speck that grew as they came closer appeared directly in their path.

"What is that?"

Liza squinted, trying to make out the object. When they were nearly upon it, Ishe stopped the car and they scrambled out. The boulder was exactly as Hope had described it. Liza ran her fingers over the figures. A battle scene was carved into the surface: her people in fields and on plantations, weapons raised, brandished.

"Hope said to turn . . ." Ishe pointed.

"That way," he and Liza said at the same time.

And there it was. About a mile away rose a mound of reddish-brown earth so high they had to crane their necks to take it all in.

"That mountain came out of nowhere," Liza said. "It wasn't there when we first pulled up."

"Sure as hell wasn't."

Back in the truck, they hadn't driven a good five minutes before the mountain, which they were certain was much farther away, loomed directly in front of them. Ishe had to slam on the brakes to avoid smashing into it. He threw out his right arm as he did so to stop Liza from crashing into the dashboard. She gave him a weak smile, and they exited the truck, taking in the sight of the lone mountain in the middle of all the nothingness.

To say that the way up was steep was like saying the boat trip across the Atlantic Ocean was a leisurely ferry ride down the bayou. From the base of the mountain, the slope swept upward to a flattened peak. Liza planted her fists on her hips and stood with a furrowed brow and mouth hanging open. "There is no way—"

"Let's get you to your sit-down."

Ishe spied a path and started walking. Liza huffed and sprinted in front of him. She hadn't even seen the path at first, but there it was. Besides the occasional loose rocks, the way was fairly easy. They moved at a good clip, anxious now. But in moments, it seemed they'd circled the mountain once and come back to what looked like exactly where they'd started. Liza stopped and scratched her head. There the truck sat, right where they'd left it.

"Didn't we . . ."

"Start out here . . ."

Then the low rumble of a hearty chuckle filled the air and grew into a booming sound that echoed all around them.

"Come," the voice said.

Before them, the earth shifted as if a great celestial hand were rearranging the pieces of a puzzle. Their gazes were drawn aloft by a squawking, soaring raven. When they looked down again, the trail had turned into a bed of pebbles, a trickle of water flowing peacefully over the rocks. Beside the bed was a wider path, marked with a sprinkling of feathers. They set off, but as Ishe set his foot on the path, he was held fast.

"What's wrong?" Liza asked as she turned back.

Ishe tried to move again, but a sledgehammer of air and dust knocked him to the ground. "Looks like whatever you need to hear is for you alone. Go on," he said, waving her off. "I'm all right."

Liza exhaled, steeled her wobbly legs, and continued up the path. Within minutes she was breathing heavily, her dry mouth hanging open and sucking in air in short, ragged gasps. The way up the mountain grew steeper and more rugged. Twice already, Liza had had to grab ahold of an outcropping of rock to haul herself up. She had a few bloodied stubs of fingernails to prove it.

Though the sky was coated with thick clouds, the sun battered her every step. It glinted off the stones, blinded her eyes, seared her face, and seeped up through the thin soles of her boots. She seemed to have been walking for hours when the air grew cooler; chill bumps pushed up through the sweat. Liza looked down—and remembered the warning never to do that too late. She stumbled and almost toppled over the edge when she took in the tiny speck below that she could only guess was Ishe.

She bent over, resting her hands on her knees, heart pounding in her ears and chest. Thirst and sore feet and the gnawing pang of a missed breakfast suggested she turn back. And she did.

But the same unseen foe that had so easily flattened Ishe turned on her, one mighty swing sending her sprawling—stopping short of the cliff's edge. Going back wasn't an option.

"Where are you!" Liza cried out and then broke down in tearless sobs; even her eyes were too dry.

She cursed as she struggled to her feet, wincing at the fatigue of a thousand-year march. Plodding forward and growing weaker with every step, she had no idea how long she'd been walking. As she collapsed onto her hands and knees, she willed herself forward, inch by inch.

After a seemingly endless trek, she rounded a bend and came onto a plateau, somehow carved right in the side of the mountain. The glaring sun was replaced by a twilight hurtling toward darkness. A barely legible weatherworn sign hung from a post that read **BRADDOCK'S POINT CEMETERY**. Oak trees soared from the sandy ground, dripping Spanish moss. Graves hastily marked with strips of wood filled the space. The few stone markers were embedded with plates. Liza had read about these; they were meant to give the deceased something to eat from in the next world. A slave graveyard, then.

Drums beat a rhythm that Liza had only dreamed about. But there were no drummers, only a wizened old man dressed in a suit of colorful cloth, a crown of intricately woven straw on his head. His skin was lined and creased as a man in his late years, but he came to his feet with the quickness of a man a quarter his age. The smells of roasting meats and breads and other foods of her ancestors wafted by, teasing her empty stomach.

"Sit." He beckoned Liza forward with a wave of his hand.

Liza got to her feet, staggered forward, and sank to the ground.

"Drink this." The man held out his hand, and a bowl appeared.

Liza snatched the bowl, took a big gulp, and coughed half the bitter broth back up. The man inclined his head at the obvious question in her eyes. She drank again, this time emptying the bowl. Her hunger and thirst were surprisingly sated.

"You know what sleeps inside your companion?" the old man asked.

"I do," Liza answered. She felt a presence shimmering off the man that she couldn't describe. It buffeted her on all sides, but instead of wanting to run, she felt like she never wanted to leave his presence. The warmth and protection she felt were like none other she had ever experienced. She almost wept with the joy of it.

"He will never be rid of it," the old man said. "Even his descendants may not be safe."

Liza shrugged it off. She cared for Ishe. She'd reined him in once, and she would do it again and again if he needed her.

"But that is not why you are here. I have waited long to set my own eyes on Ella's daughter."

A sharp criticism was on her tongue, but Liza held it back.

"Yes." The man stood taller. "Oya's daughter, Ella Meeks."

Daughter? Mama had never talked about her family. What kind of mother was Oya? Warm and loving? Or had Mama inherited her inclination toward distance?

Oya barreled into her thoughts then, her mirth a splinter of lightning. *What kind of mother am I?* A copper sword arced through the sky and landed at her feet. *I am storm-bringing warrior and nurturing mother. I am always with you and everyplace else I need to be. Guardian of the realm between life and death. I am loved and feared, protector and transformer. I am eternal and unforgettable. Does that answer your question, granddaughter?*

Thrilled but terrified, Liza whispered that it did, and with a thunderclap, the copper sword was gone.

She turned back to the old man, who gave her a knowing nod. "Why call me all the way out here? Why put me through this?"

"Did your people not suffer on the Middle Passage?"

Well, of course. Do I need a reenactment? This man—

"Spirit," he corrected aloud. "I am no man. I am a spirit. My name is Ago."

"This amulet." She took it out; much of her soreness was gone. Must have been that nasty broth. "You called me here to tell me about them?"

"You must let go of your anger," Ago said. "It will only muddy your thoughts, and to think nimbly, you must have a clear mind."

Liza was about to say she wasn't angry at anybody, but that would have been a lie. And he still hadn't answered her question. Why could the spirits never be direct?

"Have you considered that it is you, the living, who do not listen closely enough?" There was the beginning of a smile at the corner of his mouth. Ago took the amulet and turned it over in gnarled hands, holding each disc up to her.

The edges of Liza's vision blurred. She swayed but managed to stay upright. In a detached stupor, she felt herself lift and float across the ocean and into what she could describe only as a dream world. The forest and trees looked real enough, but the entire scene was draped in a subtle glow. Liza was drawn to a lone elephant at the edge of a pond. From the plumed headband to the brilliantly dyed cowskin wrap and fringe encircling the ankles, only one word came to her mind: "regal." The large ears perked, eyes looking skyward as if waiting for her. She floated and settled down into its waiting body.

Their spirits mingled and merged, and the regalia faded away. Immediately Liza was suffused with the weight of the new form. It was like the animal's bulk had been slung around her shoulders. Skin dry and mud caked as if baked under a never-ending sun. Liza twitched, squirmed, labored under the burden. In answer, Elephant's trunk snaked out, drank in the pond's cool water, and doused it over her head.

You were expecting a queen's welcome? The elephant spoke in a series of deep groans and rumbles that Liza understood nonetheless. *I am the revered queen of queens; you are but a child. Know this, a hunter who sets out nursing a secret grief or grudge will only wound her prey and will not get the kill. Death has the key to open the hoarder's chest.*

A scene unfolded, and Liza observed herself, as if she were a character in a book. A presence that she knew instinctively was death oozed toward her. Horrified, she bolted. Death was a calm river carving a path through the cracked earth behind her. She ran until exhaustion slowed her to a crawl. And there, where she lay panting, a chest appeared out of nowhere. It looked to be made of human bones woven through with dried grass. Behind her, Death persisted, igniting another jolt of fear. Hadn't Elephant said something about opening a hoarder's chest? There was no lock. She yanked at the cover, which opened a sliver before it snapped shut. Liza pulled and tore at the cover until her fingernails were ragged and slick with panicked blood.

Elephant brought her back.

Together she and Elephant trumpeted before the spirit imparted a bit of wisdom.

The spirits desire to leave two things to our children: the first is roots; the other is wings.

Liza felt a pang of regret as her ethereal self left the elephant and drifted upward. A passing raven latched its claws painfully into her shoulders. She pressed into the graceful, agile form. Swirling around, entangling her soul with Raven's. The wind tufted at glossy black wings three feet in length, and a humanlike caw escaped from a longish beak.

There is a hunger in the ancestor realm, do you not feel it?

Liza did feel hungry.

I will not ask as much of you as the other spirits, but I do need a favor.

Spotting a badger feasting on the remains of a dead antelope, Raven soared to the earth, landing on spry feet with a bounce under cover of some bushes. It was as if Liza's insides were turning inside out as Raven opened its beak wide, peeling it back over its head, spitting her out like an unwanted bone.

Lure the badger away.

Liza hesitated; Raven's eyes were shifty.

Trust me. Now, think of something.

Liza thumbed her translucent chin and came up with an idea. She shook the bushes and made guttural bear noises, causing as much of a ruckus as she could. Before long, Badger retreated someplace out of sight.

Raven coaxed Liza forward, gesturing at the carcass on the ground. The bird sank its beak into the animal flesh, then turned to Liza, waiting. She bristled. The battle of wills continued until Liza realized that this, too, was part of the test she must pass.

Liza gagged at the strip of meat that slithered down her throat, bits and pieces of bloody revulsion.

Raven cawed, and before her, the animal carcass dissolved into a pile of ash and bone. And that awful feeling of the flesh in Liza's gut was gone. As Raven alighted, it swooped over and lifted her by the shoulders once more. They found Badger a few wingbeats away and spewed the consumed ash down on it. Badger hissed, and curses followed. Raven chose that moment to loosen its claws, sending Liza on a nosedive back to the earth. And in her head, the strangest sound she'd ever heard— Raven's sly, cunning laughter.

The ash and bone were right where they'd left them. The ashes, though, began to crackle and smolder. Embers fused and solidified . . . the chest. And in the distance, beneath an ocean-colored sky, Death pursued. She set to work on the chest cover as Death surged behind her with devastating conviction. When it was perilously close, Death extended a ghastly hand to latch on to her foot.

Liza was jerked away and landed into Badger; the new body felt small, low to the ground, but powerful. The spirit fought her initially, trying to batter her out of its body, but soon grew curious enough to leave her be.

In a span of a few seconds, though, Liza's wispy form was expelled and landed with a thud. Badger shook off the offending ash that Raven had spewed and stood on hind legs, roaring right before her. It hissed and bared its sharp fangs. *When that trickster lands again, I will pluck the feathers from its body one by one before I sink my teeth into its belly, but you, on the other hand . . .*

Liza backed away slowly, but the spirit sprang into action, nipping and snapping. At first, Liza sought only to shield, to protect herself. She screamed and pleaded for Ago to end this. Badger bit and scratched as she tumbled to the ground and curved into a tight ball. He was relentless, darting in and out, clawing her hands as she clasped them over her head. Badger taunted her. *You were brave enough to conspire with that flying rat to cheat me of my meal; where is your courage now?*

Liza pushed the anger down—Elephant had warned her, hadn't she? Instead, she turned it into a fuel and drew from it as if from a well and rolled to her feet. Badger charged. She sidestepped a claw swipe and caught Badger with a good strong kick to the side. The alternating swipes and kicks continued until abruptly, the spirit halted its pursuit and nodded its approval. Badger sprinted off but spun and regarded her with a last indignant backward glance before it was gone.

Blood dripped from Liza's mangled hand. The blood darkened and curdled, bubbling up to reveal the contours of the bone-and-grass chest. And soon her pursuer returned with it. Death reached out, annihilation at the tip of its finger. She dived for the chest. It sprang open at her touch . . . but she didn't get a chance to see what was inside.

Liza found herself sitting in front of Ago once more. She pulled her knees into her chest and buried her face. No scars or blood remained, but that didn't stop her from thinking she'd just endured a test a million times harder than anything she'd done before. She gradually arranged the pieces of the message: Death was at her heels, and she'd have to unlock something, a mystery of sorts, if she had any hope of surviving.

When she finally looked up, she accepted the amulet from Ago, and they sat in a tense silence while she digested everything she'd seen. Each animal had a gift, a talent that would somehow help her.

"I need to know how to control them."

"You cannot. You are human; they are spirits." Ago gestured with his chin. "Ask your friend how well he controls his demon spirit. What you *will* do, if you are lucky, is coexist peacefully with your animal guides so that you may call upon them in need and be there for them when they must call upon you."

Liza had never imagined that they might need her for something. But then she'd read many books that talked about how the spirits liked to meddle in the lives of the living.

"Until you learn to summon them at will, you will call them to you by repeating a mantra: *Today, I ask that my animal guides reveal themselves to me. I wish to receive the gifts of sight so that they may reveal what I cannot see, guide, and protect me in the coming storm.*

"Repeat it," Ago commanded.

As Liza was thinking that she should have brought a pencil and paper, Ago's words played in her mind as if she were reading from a magazine. Only the image was imprinted there, like a stamp. She closed her eyes and repeated the words.

Faster this time, the animals appeared, all together. She wondered how best to communicate. She had some questions; she'd start there.

She formed a series of images of herself, starting back to the first time she'd communicated with an animal and how she'd unintentionally killed it, of her family suffering the consequences, of her abandonment when they couldn't stand it or her anymore. Badger and Elephant bristled at her crushing sense of guilt. *There,* she urged. *I've shown you what I do; now it's your turn.*

Raven complied first. He sent an image of himself, chirping and flying, bringing magical images along with it. Badger showed herself in a series of fierce battles, with foes large and small. She had won many of her fights but was not ashamed of those she'd lost. Badger flooded her with a series of images displaying some of her most impressive scars and wounds. Finally, Elephant stepped into the forefront. She showed herself outsmarting a pack of lions, leading them to their doom in front of a group of human hunters. She showed how she had interfered once when Liza was ten, causing her to kill that young calf. Elephant sent a picture of herself licking Liza's hand—an apology of sorts. She was verbose if nothing else. She had taken care to show all the ways she had tricked Liza and others throughout her long spiritual life.

Storytelling. Animals, African spirits, people . . . each had stories that needed telling. An audience to listen and do the retelling. In this way, you were never forgotten.

When Liza opened her eyes, she was struck by both the happiness and sadness on Ago's face.

"It gives the spirits great pleasure to interact with our descendants," he said. "You, however, to succeed in your coming mission, must reconcile your African and American spirits. Oya is a wise goddess, and she will now let you go on your way; she has handed your teaching to me."

Then he turned serious. "I cannot tell you when your foe will come, or what it will look like. But it is a powerful spirit, alive for a millennium. You must defeat it."

Liza's stomach roiled. "Do you know if I will win?"

"No."

Her heart lurched into her throat and sank like a tank into her stomach.

"But I can help prepare you. Only when you learn to coexist with your spirits will Oya become fully accessible to you. Repeat the mantra, call to your animal guides. Again."

Time and again, she repeated the mantra, but her host looked unimpressed. Liza stopped and rolled her eyes.

"This is not some poem you are reciting for school," Ago snapped. "You have memorized it, but that is only half of what is required of you. You must *feel* it." He tapped her lightly on the chest, above her heart. "In here."

"I'm trying." Liza winced. That came out like a child whining, but she couldn't help it.

"When one thinks of someone close—a member of your family. That little sister you guard so closely in the center of your heart. You recall the pout of her upper lip, her bright eyes. The touch of her infant skin. You see her first step. Know the sound of her cry, do you not?"

Yes, she did know it. Twiggy.

Ago began to become ever so slightly translucent. "Tulsa is the key. There you will both lose something and find something lost. Go, now."

His face took on a grim, resigned expression as he winked out of existence.

CHAPTER THIRTY-FOUR

CORRALLING THE SPIRITS

Ishe looked at his watch. It had taken far less time to find this place than he'd expected, but a couple of hours had passed and he was getting worried. Not only would Clay be expecting them back soon, but he couldn't help wondering if Liza was hurt. He'd tried to follow her, but the same barrier still held.

He couldn't believe he'd bared his soul—well, as much as he could anyway—and that she had answered him by going mute. Jamey was a boy and he was a man, a damaged man, but still more than Jamey could ever be. Why she couldn't see that riled and vexed him to no end.

Ishe was about to settle himself back inside the increasingly stuffy truck when it hit him. Drums, and singing in a language he hadn't used since he left home. Food smells. The feathery touch of those same singing spirits against his skin as they swirled around him, whispering in his ear. He spun and swatted at nothing.

His skin prickled as a coarse, spotted coat sprouted and rippled over his body. He doubled over in pain and clutched at his stomach, trying to will an end to his shifting internal organs.

"No, not now," he whimpered, but he would not be able to stop it. He looked up at the mountain and back to the truck. As Ishe broke into a run, the last traces of his humanity gave way to the demon who dwelled within him.

~

The way back down the mountain proved far easier than it had been going up. But when Liza reached the truck, she found it empty. She turned and cast her gaze around in all directions. Maybe Ishe had sneaked off to answer Mother Nature's call or something. After a time, she called out, "Ishe!"

The only sound that answered back was that of the mountain rumbling behind her; she turned as it vanished. Liza caught a glimpse of a footprint. She followed along a few steps till the trail revealed a paw print, the tattered remains of a shirt. She decided to take the truck.

Liza wasn't the most skilled driver, so the truck jerked and coughed along until she got an idea and stopped. She climbed out of the truck and wandered a few paces and used the mantra she'd learned to call on Raven. The bird came to her easily this time, and her heart did a little two-step. Unlike how she talked to other animals, her animal guides dwelled within her. When they came, all she had to do was think about what she wanted to communicate. She formed a picture of Ishe and asked the bird to use its sight to locate the man. Raven responded by showing her an image of Ishe walking this same path and then reaching a rocky clearing. She thanked the bird and set off.

Sounds of a struggle came at about the same time when, not far ahead, what looked like Ishe in hyena form loomed. She set off at a run, calling out to him. "Ishe!"

When she reached him, he had killed a stray dog. Taking a closer look, Liza saw it was the dog that had followed her ever since Waco. Had it followed them here? Her eyes widened, and she gulped back the bitter taste of bile. There was still a last sign of life in the dog's eyes, but it was leaving fast. It had been gutted like a fish, innards splayed on the ground. She laid her palm on the dog's head and sent it an image: the dog, coat shiny and clean, its step spry with renewed youth, a meaty bone in its mouth. Them strolling through a field toward a soothing sun dipping beneath the trees. By the time the sun set, the dog, wearing a happy dog grin, had taken his bone and trotted away.

Ishe-turned-hyena stood before her, covered in blood.

Liza fought back the nausea and took a step forward, holding out her hand. "Ishe, it's time to come back. Come back to me, here. Send the hyena away."

She followed her words with the same images she'd sent that had calmed Ishe that first time.

The hyena fastened its eyes on Liza and snarled. She steeled herself and took another step forward.

"Ishe, you can control it. Come on, come back."

The hyena emitted a heinous, deadly cackle and advanced. Little was left of Ishe in the thing that now stalked her and raised up to its full height: clothes clung to its body in rags; hairy, bent legs and arms; tufted ears and wild eyes and a glistening snout; a spotted coat. A six-foot-tall hyena.

Liza stumbled backward, conjuring and throwing as many images as she could. Under the onslaught, the hyena stopped and grabbed its head and growled. The respite was short lived. The hyena dropped into a four-legged run.

Liza spun toward the truck. Ishe closed on her and knocked her to the ground. She rolled over and threw up her arms, trying to fend off the teeth snapping at her face.

A throaty, piercing howl rang out in Liza's head. Though she struggled with him, it wasn't Ishe. *Badger!* Her animal guide appeared in her mind, standing with its head held high atop an African savanna. Liza felt her own body changing and let out a cry of her own. What had Ago said? Badger was wise, fierce . . . and, like Raven, sometimes a shape-shifter.

Her screams died in her ears as her body shifted. Bones cracked and reformed, teeth stretched into fangs, and the hair on her skin grew shaggy, brown, and coarse. Ishe's scent was pungent in her snout. As a badger, she easily got away from the hyena-man. She came to her paws and stood on her hind legs and roared, spittle flying from her mouth. She leaped up and, with a right claw, slashed at Ishe's exposed chest. He turned and ran, and Liza sank down to all fours and gave chase. In her mind, she screamed for Badger to stop, to release her. She didn't want to hurt Ishe.

As he ran, Ishe changed. The coarse, spotted coat fell away, and the limbs stretched and cracked as he returned to human form. Ishe crashed to the ground, and the transformation completed.

Spent, Liza as Badger fell beside him and came back to herself. They lay side by side, panting, bruised, bloodied, and ashamed.

Breathless moments passed before Ishe's hand sought Liza's, and she eagerly entwined her fingers with his. Her slowing heartbeat revved up again. When Ishe pushed himself up on an elbow and peered down into her eyes, it was Liza who surprised herself by pulling him to her.

There, in the middle of nowhere, Liza delighted in the graceful movements of Ishe's body against hers as they wove themselves together in previously unchartered pleasures.

∿

"Where the hell have you two been?"

Liza could tell Clay was trying hard to sound angry at them, but then he must have taken in their condition: blood, ripped clothes, the way neither would meet his eyes.

"Go get yourselves cleaned up," he said and then left them standing where they were.

They had grudgingly dragged themselves back into the truck, not daring to look at each other or utter a word the whole way back to the carnival. And now, they parted much the same way. Liza hauled herself to the donnicker to clean up and then made a beeline for her trailer.

On the way, she rounded a corner and stopped cold. Jamey was talking to one of the cooch dancers—one who did the things Autumn wouldn't. The girl leaned against a trailer, batting her false eyelashes. Jamey tried and, to Liza's mind, failed to look sharp, his forearm on the trailer, his ankles crossed.

Liza's blood boiled. She knew she should march right up and give both of them a good slap, but after what had happened with Ishe, she felt she no longer had the right to care. She lowered her head, fought back a sob, and made herself scarce.

She found her friend milling around, leaning against the outside wall of her work trailer. "What did he tell you?" Hope's face was dour. There were bags beneath her eyes, and her normally glowing skin was dull.

"Only that I have to face the threat that is coming." Liza picked up a stone and threw it as far as she could. "Couldn't even tell me if I was going to win. Maybe I should leave."

"No," Hope said. "We face this together. It won't do you any good to be off somewhere by yourself. Especially when you don't even know what you're looking for. No, you stay here. I can help you. Ishe can help you."

Liza was grateful for her friend. She hadn't wanted to leave, but then she didn't want to endanger her friends either. She resisted the urge to ask Hope to help her track her animal guides; she understood that she must do that much herself. But she did want help with something. "If you get a feeling, a vision that can warn me . . ."

"You know I'll tell you."

CHAPTER THIRTY-FIVE

LAST CHANCES

The G. B. Bacchanal Carnival crept along Route 66 on its way toward Oklahoma City. The skeletons of abandoned trucks and cars littered the roadside, along with stuffed animals missing an eye or leg; tattered, moth-ridden blankets; shattered soda bottles. A farmhouse sat miles back from the main road, leaning ever so slightly. One front window was blown out, the other mysteriously intact, as if the house were winking at the passing caravan.

There was an uneasy hush among the carnies, as if they were passing through a cemetery, paying homage to homes and cars and people long dead. It was sobering.

After Oklahoma City, it would be on to Tulsa. Jamey would be expecting an answer to his proposal, and given what had happened with Ishe, she was waffling on what that answer would be. And Ago had told Liza that she'd find something lost. She'd puzzled over that in her mind a dozen times since, and being a woman with few possessions, all accounted for, only one thing was left. She dared not hope. Her family had spent time there and in nearby Taft—she'd steal away and poke around.

Not many homes were left untouched by economic hardships, but even the poor welcomed a little distraction, something to take their minds off their troubles. Wives preferred something they could do as a family, rather than seeing their husbands go off and spend their pennies on liquor or whores.

The Choctaw Indians had named the land *Okla*, meaning people, and *humma*, their word for red. Oklahoma was the home to the more than thirty tribes that had ended up here following the Trail of Tears. Her family had often traded with the tribes during their travels.

Liza sat with her back against her pillow on her bunk. The last traces of any pain from her trip to the mountain were gone. She flipped through the latest *Argosy Weekly*, barely seeing the words. What would she do if she did find her family? What was it that she wanted from them? Raven had helped her understand that she needed to let go of her judgment, give them time to explain why they'd done what they did. But the answer was already there.

All she needed to do was to stand up on her knees and peer through the trailer window at the carnage outside. Hers was not the first family to have given up a child they could no longer care for. But there was still the question of how they'd made their decision. Maybe it had been easier to single out the one prone to killing the few precious animals they had for food.

As they came closer to the city, the sound of cars increased. Apparently, the exodus hadn't taken everybody to California. The ride became bumpy and uneven, signaling they'd pulled off the main road, headed for the location Clay and Jamey had scouted out for the carnival to stop over days before.

The carnival caravan came to a rolling, languorous halt, and Liza could almost hear the collective exhale from the group. Carnies were essentially outdoor people and couldn't wait to emerge from the dens of their trailers, stretch their legs, and inhale a breath of dusty, but fresher, air.

"Looks like we're here," Autumn said from her own bunk. She'd been so worked up about getting to Tulsa and a meeting with someone who could help her get a shot at a part in an honest-to-goodness moving picture, only one stop away now. She lay with her elbows propped on her colorful assortment of pillows. She wiped a hand over her bunk and looked at it as though it held a foreign material. "I thought they said the dust bowl storms have passed."

Liza could only shake her head. White people had no idea how to coexist with the earth. They ravaged it, used and abused it, and wondered why it sometimes bit them back. "Gonna take more than a year or two for things to get back to normal with the earth," she said, standing and stretching. "But it will heal." After a moment, she added, "If they leave it alone long enough."

Autumn stared at Liza. "You would sooner see things stay the way they were before Columbus showed up? You wouldn't have that science fiction crap you always have your nose buried in. Hell, and you're a woman, doubt you could even work anywhere, let alone earn your own money and travel with a carnival." Autumn donned an unneeded shawl and squeezed past Liza to the door. "No thank you, sister. I'll take progress, lavender soaps, and moving pictures any day."

Liza had a comb in her hand, and she considered throwing it at Autumn's back but thought better of it. She turned and kneeled at the foot of her bunk and lifted the pouch her father had given her and peeked in. There it sat, the picture of her family. She stuffed the pouch beneath the mattress, repeated the mantra that Ago had seared into her brain, and stepped out into the midday Oklahoma haze.

Ahiku hovered outside the entrance to the Skirvin Hotel in downtown Oklahoma City, at the corner of Park and Broadway. Fourteen luxurious brick stories and a triplet of majestic towers that appeared to have miniature parapets atop each.

She wore her normal bewitching attire: rows of bracelets on both arms, colorful patchwork skirt, and head wrap. She delighted in the deliciously wicked knowledge that the people hurrying on their way had no idea what stood in their midst. She scanned the horde of laborers and highbrows and wanderers, blank faced but blindly determined as red ants doing their queen's bidding.

She wandered a few steps, passing a missing-child poster plastered to the wall to her right. The child had been one of hers, the one with the poor farmer parents. Clay had assured her the child's disappearance would be a blessing, a moral kindness to the parents. He had been wrong.

There.

Ahiku chose a smartly dressed man, round spectacles perched high on a neat, full nose, and trawled through him, leaving her taint on his insides. It began as an itch deep within his bowels that he couldn't scratch before spreading like jam on white bread, carrying the uncontrollable itch to every organ, his skin, his eyes. The man walked a few more steps before he stopped, screamed, and tore at his clothes. They lay in a shredded pile on the ground, long after he'd scratched himself raw and was dragged away naked as the day he was born by the police. Ahiku let out a syrupy snicker.

She figured the other demons were already assembled inside the hotel restaurant, wearing the various masks they'd acquired over the centuries. She would enter soon; they needed to wait. Though she relished this gathering, appearing anxious or overeager could put her at further disadvantage.

A girl of probably six or seven strolled by, her hand in that of a striking man. The child was precious, silvery air bouncing off her in waves, and Ahiku felt the familiar stirrings. It would be time to feed soon, but now, she would go inside and attend the yearly rendezvous. With one last, greedy look at the retreating child, Ahiku sailed up the steps, navigated the forest of wood-paneled columns, and entered the dining room. She headed to the table where her demon horde sat, pulled out a chair, and dissolved into the facade of a progressive Negro woman.

276

A prim hat perched on her head; her smart dress was woven of pure silk, shoulder wrap keeping her modest. Gloves covered her elegant hands. The other demon spirits at the table did not stir, but someone at the next table yelped at her sudden appearance.

"Ahiku. Always the show-woman." Neema smiled, an expression of monsters and menace. "To scare someone is such a simple thing. I am surprised you still find such things provide . . . entertainment." Neema wore her stock human cloak: coloring more Northern than Southern Africa, petite, a halo of black hair, and the diminutive features to match. Her round eyes were enhanced by the dark pencil that lined them.

"I run a carnival." Ahiku inspected her silverware as if the possibility of contracting a germ should give her pause. "I am in the business of entertainment. In *my* country, spirits never tire of playing games with the living. It keeps interest in their lives. To deprive them would be plain selfish." She turned to the man sitting to her right. "Herbert could tell you a thing or two about selfishness, *and* my people."

Herbert's skin was nearly as pale as the white linen covering the table. He had bright-blue eyes, thin dry lips, and a parrot's nose. His brown hair was parted on the right, and he wore the simple clothes of his profession, without adornment. "Missionary work is the only thing that brought your dark continent out of the Dark Ages. Though one might argue there is still work to do. Darkness"—he brushed at his arms, snapped his cuffs—"that needs beating back."

"We took the liberty of ordering for you," Francisco said between mouthfuls of eggs. He sat next to Neema on the other side of the table. He flashed Ahiku his smile. Francisco was handsome, with his frizzy black hair and the darkly tanned skin of one who wore the look of a Brazilian football coach like medieval armor. His lean, athletic frame shrouded in snug-fitting casual dress.

A waitress appeared and set a plate before Ahiku. A largish breakfast of eggs, bacon, and pancakes. A cup of tea. Ahiku would have preferred a breakfast of peppered eggs and fried plantain but reminded herself that she was not in her ancestral home. Spirits didn't need to consume food, but when they did, they could still find certain pleasure in it. After a bite of bacon, she tackled the toughest one.

"Neema." She took a sip of tea, held up a finger, added sugar, and set the cup back on its saucer. "How are things in Rabat? Have your students begun to respond to your new teaching methods?"

Neema dabbed at her rouge-painted lips. She blinked, eyelashes so long it seemed a blink or two more would cause a small typhoon. "Yes, my students are doing well, and I have you all to thank for our enduring partnership. And what about you—has Oya paid you a visit lately?"

Ahiku seethed but didn't have time to respond before Herbert took up the attack.

"Spit it out. You haven't made one iota of progress toward finding our adversary, have you?" Herbert planted his elbows on the table and leveled his gaze at Ahiku.

Clay hadn't brought her anyone even close. "My people tell me you took two children from the same village. The same family!" Ahiku tsked. "Surely you are not one to talk of my failings." Ahiku didn't let the smile threatening to bloom come to the surface. It gave her great pleasure to put Herbert in his place. She nibbled on a bit of pancake. Neema and Francisco kept quiet, shoveling food into their mouths. Herbert reddened and suddenly found more interest in his eggs.

The demons let the moment pass. Neema said, "Herbert's sloppy selection process aside, can we get back to the matter at hand?"

Everyone pushed their plates aside. When the waitress approached with a fresh pot of coffee, Ahiku waved her off.

Francisco clapped and rubbed his hands together. "Ahiku, we should be living our special brand of the afterlife with no worry, but because you tangled with Oya's daughter—"

"When we explicitly forbade it," Neema interjected.

Francisco frowned but continued. "Point is, you put us all in her path. We meet here every year, for the last decade, and you still haven't found her. *You* set Oya on the path to your demise. *Our* demise."

"Which"—Herbert had regained his voice—"is precisely the type of thing I'd expect. Laziness."

She would endure these indignities . . . for now. The demons were creatures of habit, after all; the insults would give way to other chatter soon enough. But the anticipated barrage did not come. Instead, the demon horde fell silent, watching her. Queenie had warned her; still, unease prickled on the back of Ahiku's neck.

"Humph . . ." Neema leaned back in her chair and gloated. "We suspected as much. You really do not know, do you?"

Ahiku squirmed under her cohort's self-satisfied glowers. The miserable wretches had planned an ambush. "There is obviously something on your minds. Spit it out and be done with it."

"You are harboring Oya's descendant right beneath your nose." Neema's nostrils flared as if emphasizing her point.

"Wha—" Ahiku sputtered.

"Incompetence," Herbert added. "Can't say I'm surprised."

"Think about it." Francisco tapped his temple. "We know Oya had to have passed down some kind of defense. We've always assumed it was in the blood, but what if it was something physical, an object? Something our opponent removed or lost. While you were off jockeying for position in the underworld, for a second, what was hidden flared like a bonfire."

Ahiku suppressed the urge to rip them all apart. If they were so worried for their own hides, you'd think they would have done something more to help her. "And you did nothing to apprehend her?"

Neema chuckled. "It is *your* mess to clean up. Why risk ourselves? And we knew where, not who. Your season ends after your run in Tulsa; you have until then. Do not delay here, thinking to buy yourself more time. If you are not up to the task, we'll be forced to take other action. What say the rest of you?"

The congregation considered and nodded their agreement.

Curiously, the sky overhead turned instantly more cloud covered. A sharp crackle of thunder boomed, and lightning zigzagged across the sky. There were loud murmurs throughout the restaurant. The waitstaff stopped in midstride, all turning their gazes toward the windows. As quickly as the storm had flared, the hazy sun returned, and the gasps and murmurs died down.

"This weather ain't been right," a patron ventured with an obvious shiver, and everyone got back to their meals.

"It seems that portion of our business is concluded," Ahiku said and then took a sip of lukewarm tea to stop herself from tearing out of the restaurant. She seethed as the other demons went on to discuss matters of importance in the afterlife: spats and sides taken, the never-ending leadership changes. They traded stories about some of the more satisfying souls they'd consumed and relished in their luck at the endless supply.

Much later, when the conversation ebbed, Ahiku stood. "If you all will excuse me, it seems I have a pressing matter to attend to."

"I suppose it's my turn to pay," Herbert said with a scowl, tossing a few bills on the table.

The demons exited the hotel and, one by one, dissolved into baleful wisps of nothingness, gone again back to their respective corners of the world until the next gathering.

"Bon appétit!" Neema's voice trailed after them.

At the corner of Broadway, Ahiku coalesced into her human form. Zinsa and Efe fell in step on either side of her. Bacchanal would head straight for Tulsa without delay, but the demons would pay. They would suffer unspeakable horrors. She would deal with Oya's minion; then she would call on the support she'd been gathering in the underworld and settle a few scores. She trawled the crowded sidewalk, fingertips grazing a shoulder or arm, laying early claim to a few tainted souls she passed, leaving a trail of bodies in her wake.

~

They'd hightailed it out of Oklahoma City and rushed headlong into Tulsa so fast that Liza wondered if Clay had gotten himself into some kind of trouble there. The carnies had spent the better part of the morning setting up. Despite the dour look of things, there was still some oil wealth left in Oklahoma, and not everybody had left. When the dust storms cleared, residents had begun to return. The government introduced new farming techniques that settled the land, but a total revitalization was still a ways off.

She'd been avoiding discussing a certain incident, but Liza decided to go off and find Ishe all the same. She found him having an animated conversation with Bombardier, but as she approached, the men broke off. For once, Bombardier didn't flash his signature smile. Ishe's eyes, when she met them, held an emotion she couldn't read. The man was so good at covering up that she wondered if even *he* knew the real him anymore.

Ishe started walking, and she fell in beside him. The tension between them hung heavy and dark as the velvet draperies of her performance tent. Neither was quite sure how to get back to where they were before.

Finally, Ishe said, "About what I did . . . what happened between us—"

"Forget about it."

"Easier for you than me."

"We have other things to talk about." Liza knew she was being selfish, but she didn't have time to dawdle.

Ishe looked at her, and she sensed him gulp back what was probably a tight knot of emotion. She recognized it because she'd done the same thing more times than she could count. "I'm listenin'."

Liza explained everything that had happened with Ago, the whole story, and what it had revealed to her. Ishe listened intently, stopping to ask questions here and there.

"Learn to call on them spirits," he insisted. "Don't wait. You got to be prepared. We don't know when or where this thing will strike. And let's ask around, see about finding what you lost."

Clay had grumbled about all the work that had yet to be done, but in the end he turned over the keys and waved Liza and Ishe on. They left a trail of dust behind them as the truck rolled to a stop on the outskirts of town. As much as people had tried to dress it up, to Liza it was still a dismal place. One that in time might soon live only in old folks' memories. She recalled her father's voice when they'd passed through before. "This here is the bigger place, but we headin' on to the all-colored town nearby called Taft. Set up by the freedmen from the Creek Nation."

Liza and Ishe left the truck without a word. Walking side by side, they greeted the couple of folks who were up and about. "I'm going to start at the general store," Liza announced. Outside the store was a truck with the words **COLEMAN FARM** crudely painted on the door. A young man was hauling out large sacks.

"Peanuts," he said to them with a smile. They returned the gesture and entered the store to the sound of a little bell attached to the door.

"Mornin', be right with ya," the man behind the wooden counter said and then limped outside to help bring in the peanuts.

"You looking for somethin'?" Ishe asked Liza as she traversed the store.

"Guess I'll know it when I see it." The close square space was crammed with dry and canned goods, flour and sugar, hard candies, and other necessities. It smelled of dust and cigars. But there, back in the corner, hanging from a wooden pole, Liza spied a couple of caps mixed in with three of her mother's baskets. She snatched one off the nail that served as a hook and dashed back to the front counter.

"Where you folks from?" The shopkeeper pulled at the straps of his faded blue overalls and rocked back on his heels. His smile revealed two missing front teeth. He spoke with a kind of wet smacking sound. His gaze fell on Ishe, but it was Liza who spoke first.

"Nice baskets," she said, holding up a particularly colorful one.

The shopkeeper focused fully on Liza for the first time, and his eyes narrowed as they went between her and the basket.

"Never forget a face." He craned his neck forward and indicated his own eyes for emphasis. "First time y'all came through here, told my wife the same thing. You sho 'nuf got your mama's eyes. I'm real sorry 'bout your pa."

Liza's stricken glance over at Ishe carried the weight of a million unshed tears.

"What do you mean?" Liza set the basket on the counter, and Ishe took her right hand in his. She was grateful for the warmth, as her body had gone rigid with cold. The shopkeeper glanced over at Ishe as if asking for permission to continue. Liza read the unasked question. *Why don't you know your own father is dead?*

"I'm right here," Liza said, and it took everything she had not to bang her fists on the counter.

The man rubbed the nape of his neck, took off his straw hat, and wrung it in his hands. "Well, he was sick 'fore they got here." He stopped. "Can I get y'all somethin'? I sure hate to give folks bad news on an empty stomach."

Liza's voice was raw. "Tell me what happened." And darned if the man didn't look to Ishe again before he continued.

"Doc Morgan said it was his heart. Clutched his chest and fell right there in front of the post office. All you kids wasn't with him this time. First time round, that sister of yours kept pawing at my hard candy jar—"

Liza exhaled loudly.

"It was only the little one with him—cute lil' gal. She was an itty-bitty thing when y'all come through here first. He sold me five of them baskets."

Twiggy. Twiggy was with Pa. "Wait, my father sold the baskets? Did Mama wait outside?"

The shopkeeper looked positively stricken. His mouth opened, his gaze flickered outside the front window, and Liza got the sense he wanted to be anyplace other than standing in front of her. "Well, with your ma gone and all—"

Only Ishe's quick thinking kept Liza on her feet. He held her close to him, and she leaned in for the much-needed support. Her parents were dead. She barely registered the fact that she'd spoken the word "how" aloud before the man answered.

"Your pa didn't say, and I had the manners not to ask. You didn't know 'bout your ma neither?"

Was that a tinge of judgment in his gravelly voice? Liza registered Ishe's quick headshake.

"'Spect you'll be looking for your little sister?"

Liza blinked. "Are you saying she's still here?"

"I got to get these peanuts bagged up and ready for sale."

For the first time, Ishe spoke. "Tell her what she need to know, and we'll be on our way."

"At the center, 'course."

The door slamming told Liza that Ishe was behind her. She'd nearly run from the store, her heart thudding painfully. As angry as she was at her parents, the news of their deaths was a blow. But now, hope urged her on to the truck as fast as her feet could take her. Inside the truck, Ishe mentioned that the shopkeeper had given him directions, and besides telling her how sorry he was, he remained blissfully silent as he drove. Liza marveled at how he instinctively gave her exactly what she needed.

She'd find something lost. The impact of Ago's words, like a pail of ice-cold water thrown in her face.

Ishe and Liza sat in the cab of the truck, outside the entrance to the Deaf, Blind & Orphans Institute. The shopkeeper told him it was the only place in the state that cared for colored children and even some adults.

It had not been difficult to find, one dirt road after another, winding away from Main Street. Now that Liza was here, she felt immobile. Could not command her legs to move. Her heart threatened to leap right out of her chest, but she put on a good face for Ishe.

"Are you sure you don't want me to come with you?"

"No. I need to do this myself." She reached over and patted his hand and got out of the truck without meeting his eyes for fear he would see how scared she was.

"I'll be right here," he called after her and reluctantly stayed in the cab.

The institute sat in the middle of nowhere. It reminded her of the spots Clay so expertly picked to set up the carnival: close enough, but far enough away from everything. The land was flat and expansive, the sky overhead clear and endless. One hundred acres of fine land with water nearby. There were three buildings, one for the mute, one for the blind, and one for the orphans. She'd start with the orphan building—a three-story brick affair, well maintained. A sign overhead read **Orphans**. Liza steeled herself and took measured steps forward. It was early still, so nobody was milling around outside.

But she felt eyes following her from the many windows on the front of the building. At the top of the stairs, she took a deep breath and opened the front door. To her right was a door with the word **Headmaster**. Liza knocked and entered at a call from a voice inside.

The room was comfortably arranged. A large window to her left let in a trickle of sunlight. Portraits lined the walls, alongside a painting of a countryside that was so green it had to be anyplace other than Oklahoma. A large desk sat in the center of the room, two wooden chairs in front of it. The man behind the desk stood.

"Arthur Bacon," he said. He was a tall mustached man who managed to look comfortable in his stiff wool jacket and slacks. "Won't you invite your husband inside?" He flicked his head toward the picture window, where he'd obviously watched them pull up.

"He's fine." Liza decided not to correct him. Sometimes, the cloak of marriage was a useful one for a woman.

"Have a seat, please." Mr. Bacon gestured to the chairs in front of the desk and waited for Liza to sit before doing so himself. "What can I do for you?"

Liza clasped her hands together in her lap to still their shaking. "I'm looking for my sister. I believe she's here."

Mr. Bacon opened a desk drawer and removed a large leatherbound ledger. He lay it open on the desk. "Last name?"

"Meeks." Liza couldn't keep herself from trying to read the book upside down.

Mr. Bacon flipped a few pages, stopped, used his index finger to scan. "Meeks," he repeated a few times. The finger stopped and he looked up. "First name Twiggy?"

Liza nearly leaped out of the chair. "Yes, sir, that's her."

"No real first name? We assumed she was being stubborn. That one's got a streak a mile long, you know."

Liza's face split into an uncontrollable grin. That was indeed her baby sister. Mr. Bacon smiled back at her. He read some notes on the page. "Was brought here a little under a year ago. Both parents deceased. A sister, location unknown." He looked up. "That must be you."

"I'm here now," Liza said. "I need to see her and make some arrangements before I can take her with me."

The smile faltered a bit. "She's scheduled for day labor over at the farm today. And truth is, there's a family that seems pretty set on adopting her." Mr. Bacon gazed at Liza's ringless finger. "What did you say your husband did for a living?"

Liza's breath quickened. "I didn't. And what do you mean 'day labor'? She's a child."

The book closed, and Mr. Bacon pushed back from his desk and clasped his hands behind his head. "We're the best facility in the state. We take good care of everybody here, and that's no lie. But we don't run on the goodwill of the citizens. It takes money, and money is hard to come by these days. The kids go out to do simple housework chores—nothing too taxing, mind you. Does them some good."

Liza took in the comfortable surroundings with a new set of eyes. All these nice things, the fine clothes, were all possible because they made the kids go out and work for them. Liza hadn't thought this through. She hadn't expected her parents to be dead and to now be charged with being a parent herself. But she couldn't leave Twiggy alone in this place, and she sure as hell wasn't going to let some other family she didn't know take her. She needed to talk this over with Clay.

"I need a day or two to make arrangements, and I'm taking my sister with me."

Mr. Bacon rose from his chair. "There is a matter of compensation. And frankly," he said, looking at Liza's simple cotton dress and worn leather boots, "the family that wants to adopt her may be able to provide a better life. You have to think of the child, not yourself."

Liza wanted to rip the man's throat out, and from the bubbling in her stomach, she suspected her Badger spirit did too. She stood. "I need to see her."

Mr. Bacon walked to his office door and held it open. "I'm afraid your sister has already left for her day-labor work. If you come back later with your husband, maybe we can discuss the matter of how to make this right for everyone."

Liza went through the front door and didn't utter another word. This time, Mr. Bacon's smile was that of a greedy rodent. She went out the door, waited a second, and circled around back.

There were children playing, a cluster of girls jumping rope, a few boys kicking a can around. And there . . . a small, thin girl standing off to herself. She leaned against the chain-link fence. A doll tucked under one arm, her face buried in a book.

Liza approached slowly. The child stood with her stomach poking out, her hair braided in precise lines. Her green-and-white dress faded but clean. Her little overbite was more pronounced, but she was about the right age.

Liza held her breath.

And then, the child glanced up from her book. Twiggy.

To Liza, the sight of her little sister was like the uncaging of a flock of doves. Her mind flooded with precious memories; her mouth went slack and dry. Liza dropped to her knees. There was caution in Twiggy's eyes, then a recognition that spoke volumes. When Liza held out her arms, Twiggy came to her and folded herself into Liza as if Liza had left her only the day before. Time and distance had done nothing to break their bond.

Neither spoke for a long time.

When they did, it all came out in a flood. Her precious Twiggy was right here. The little girl rattled on. She showed Liza the doll of straw with a button for a face that their father had made for her. Counted all the way to one hundred in Creek, English, and Choctaw. Within minutes, Liza was as exhausted as if she had run all the way to the orphanage from Baton Rouge.

"How did you get here?" Twiggy asked and then followed up: "Why did it take you so long? I was waiting. Yejide said you'd come."

"A friend brought me in his truck. It's right out front. You can probably see it from your room. I'm going to take you away from here; I just need a day or two to get everything ready. Wait, who is Yejide?"

Twiggy huffed. "You know, Miss Yejide, the witch doctor lady. She said Mama told her I was supposed to do something special when I'm all growed up, but Yejide said it was you instead. I'm glad, though. I think Miss Yejide gone now. She said some bad lady was coming. Made me run off to the secret place. I was real scared but Mama and Pa came for me 'fore long."

The vision swooped in on the wings of Raven, the night her parents had given her away and left.

Ella Meeks freezes. The demon's passage is a blistering sting to the gut—Goddess Oya's simultaneous warning like a raven feather brushing against her cheek. She bolts out of the chair and hastens to her satchel.

The amulets inside flicker, the animals carved into the stones glowing.

Her husband, Nathaniel, knows they're in danger without having to ask. They've had this conversation. Many times. His jaw clenches in that stubborn way of his. He leans back and crosses his ankle over his knee as if his wife is worried about nothing more than a passing heat wave.

They lock gazes, warring in a desperate silence, their children oblivious. She breaks away and presses an amulet into each of her children's palms.

"Wear this always," she says, struggling to look each in the eye. Her voice cracks. "Never take it off. Ever. You hear me?"

"What's wrong, Mama?" pleads her elder daughter, Liza.

In answer, an ache-filled squeeze of the hand.

Nathaniel and Ella hustle away from their home, the last in a string of many across the American south. But this time they don't take the children. Liza sent to Mrs. Margaret, Twiggy to the medicine woman. The demon will track Ella—better the family is scattered.

Liza gasped as the vision faded.

The hasty exit. Mama giving them the amulets. She allowed herself to see the pain in their eyes, recall the lingering touches. Her parents hadn't abandoned their children; they'd done what they could to protect them. All the hatred she'd built up splintered and disintegrated as an elephant trumpeted in the distance.

"Mrs. Meeks!" a voice boomed from behind them. Liza turned to see Arthur Bacon and two women striding up behind the sisters.

"I told you to get ready to go," one of the ladies said to Twiggy.

"But my sister is here," Twiggy whined.

"Inside." Mr. Bacon waved his hand. "We must talk to your sister."

Grudgingly, Twiggy filed inside, but not before she asked Liza to hold her doll for her. Liza's heart turned to melted chocolate.

"I'm going to have to ask you to leave," Mr. Bacon said.

Liza was ready to unleash a series of curses at this man and the two women who stood by him like older backwoods versions of Zinsa and Efe. She did take the time to tell them all, as calmly as she could manage, that she would indeed be back.

As if summoned, Twiggy ran out of the back door again, holding a little bag over her shoulder. "I'm going with Liza," she said, as serious as Liza had ever seen anyone.

Liza gulped back tears. As much as she wanted to take her sister away from this place, she couldn't, not until she was sure things were safe. This battle everyone was so certain she'd have to fight could happen at the carnival or someplace they'd yet to visit; either way, she'd be right in the middle of it, and that meant her sister shouldn't be anywhere near her. She plastered a smile on her face and got down on one knee. "Come here."

Twiggy looked at her veritable jailers and came to Liza.

"You can't come with me now," Liza said, stammering over the words. "But I'll come back to see you. I promise. Okay?"

The little girl threw a fit, dropping her things and pounding her little fists at Liza. "No, you won't come back. Like before." Tears streamed down Twiggy's face. One of the women grabbed the little girl's hand and dragged her away as Liza stumbled to her feet.

"I *will* be back!" Liza screamed and, with a last look at Mr. Bacon, turned and left.

Eyes blurred by tears, she made her way back to the truck.

All the venom, curses, and ill will she'd stored up—all came out not in the verbal assault she'd imagined but in loud, racking sobs as she fell into Ishe's outstretched arms.

The anger dissipated some. They would never get back the time they'd lost. All the hours spent questioning why her parents didn't want her. It was a waste and she hated it. They'd done what they did to protect their children.

Despite the fact that Twiggy didn't believe her, Liza would be back. She had to work out things first.

After she'd composed herself, Ishe asked, "You found her?"

"I did," Liza answered.

"And?" Ishe waved his hand in a motion to tell her to get on with the story.

Liza let everything pour out, grateful she didn't succumb to tears again. She'd cried enough for one day, and she wasn't a lady given to wild fits of emotion.

"Can we talk about it later?" She wanted to help her sister, but she had other things to attend to first.

They climbed into the truck, gunned the engine, and headed back to the carnival.

CHAPTER THIRTY-SIX

WHAT WAS LOST IS FOUND AGAIN

"Liza!" A sharp voice tore her from a daydream in which she'd somehow worked out how to rescue her sister from the orphanage while simultaneously besting the enemy Ago had foretold. Clay stood before her with someone small in tow.

Liza's eyes bulged as Clay, dragging a child in front of him, said, "And what exactly is this?"

Twiggy stood there, looking annoyed and abashed. She wore the same faded green-and-white cotton dotted-print dress. The white fringe at the neck and arms had gone the color of the dusky sky. Socks of the same hue and battered lace-up brown shoes covered her feet. Her doll hung limply from her right hand. She gave Liza a big smile.

"My . . . my sister, Twiggy," Liza chirped.

"I know that." Clay was red faced, a strand of his slick hair falling into his eye. "But what is she doing here, hiding out in the back of the truck and wandering around my carnival looking for you? We're setting up here. Ain't no place for kids. What if she got hurt or somethin'?"

Twiggy retreated behind Liza's leg and poked her head around, sticking her tongue out at Clay.

"If she can't work"—he pointed his finger—"she can't stay." With that he turned and stalked off.

Liza's stomach went sour with fear. At that moment, she recalled the slingshot she'd seen in the red trailer, and Zinsa with that same toy—a *child's* toy. It was like a key had been inserted into a lock, but she still couldn't open the door. The red trailer and children? She couldn't put her finger on the connection, but it was there as inexplicably as her sister was standing in front of her.

Twiggy could *not* be here—not now, when there was some battle coming that even Ago didn't know if she would win. Liza's heart thudded and her mouth went dry, and she broke out in a sweat and turned her gaze on her little sister. Twiggy blinked up at her as if running away from the orphanage to join a sister she hadn't seen in years were the most natural thing in the world. Exasperated, Liza hugged her and tried to erase the worry from her face.

"Does Mr. Bacon know you're here?" It was a dumb question, but Liza had to ask.

"He should," Twiggy responded by not answering.

"You shouldn't have followed me."

"Why not?"

"Because." Liza struggled to answer this part. She hadn't wanted to leave her baby sister in the misery she'd found her in. She could take better care of her here. Teach her to read. Make sure she was fed and clothed. She could sleep with her in the bunk. Twiggy could help her out with the show. She'd have a much better life. But.

"Because everybody will worry about you." Liza's mind raced as she looked up at the already-setting sun. She had to get Twiggy out of here, as far away from her as possible. "Because you aren't supposed to up and leave."

"You did." Twiggy stomped her little foot. "Why didn't you come with me to the witch doctor lady? Miss Yejide disappeared, and I was sent to that place after Papa died. They wouldn't tell me anything. They think I'm too little to understand, but I know stuff. I don't like living there. I want to stay with you. You can take care of me. This place looks like more fun."

Liza's heart constricted, and she choked down a sob. She would have to come back for Twiggy later. And what about Ishe? How would he feel about raising a nine-year-old with a sharp tongue and an independent spirit? He might snatch any forthcoming marriage proposal away and run. "I have to take you back."

"I'm not going back," Twiggy said. "I'll follow you again. And if you don't want me to get lost out there looking for you, you might as well keep me."

Liza wondered where on earth Twiggy had gotten this mouth. She'd been away too long. "All right. I won't send you away. I *promise*. But you have to give me some time to figure this all out." She hadn't mentioned anything about Bacchanal to Mr. Bacon at the orphanage, so he shouldn't have any idea of where to search for Twiggy, but maybe she should stay out of sight all the same.

Twiggy stood with her hand on her hip.

Liza's urge to argue evaporated. She grabbed Twiggy by the hand and was struck by the realization that her sister didn't have so much as a paltry satchel like the one Mama had shoved into her hands before she sent her away. No toys or trinkets, not another dress or underpants, only the one-eyed doll.

"You hungry?" Liza asked after she'd stood dumbfounded for a number of minutes.

"Yeah."

They made a beeline for the cook tent. Afterward, Liza settled Twiggy onto her bunk while she tried to rearrange things. The introductions with Mico went well, and when they tried to leave, the little monkey squawked his annoyance. He now rode on Twiggy's shoulder—much giggling and delight ensued.

By the end of the day, Twiggy had been introduced all around and was a big hit with everyone, especially Mabel, who magically produced treat after treat and demanded that Twiggy be left with her so that the child could have another proper meal.

"Too thin." Mabel had looked on her disapprovingly at the cook tent.

Later Malachi wowed Twiggy with the impossible feat of poking himself with a series of pins without so much as a peep. He did, however, have to caution Twiggy when she unceremoniously leaped up, grabbed a needle, and plunged it into her own arm with a yelp before he or Liza could stop her.

"Practice, little one," he'd warned. "It takes years of practice."

Even the characteristically stoic Autumn had fallen under Twiggy's spell. The dancer showed the little girl all the latest fashions in her precious *Vogue* magazine, even demonstrating a pirouette to a totally astonished Twiggy.

"Don't that hurt your foot none?" Twiggy asked.

Ishe suffered through countless sets of the milk-bottle game, ultimately having to rearrange his bottles so that the little girl could win more easily. Finally, he slipped Twiggy a tiny stuffed bear and shooed them both away. Said he had work to do.

But the real enchantment began when Liza took Twiggy to meet Hope and Bombardier. Twiggy was apparently as taken in by Bombardier's broad smile as anyone. When the big man flexed his muscles for her, she did the same for him. He wrapped his hands around hers, hefted the hammer, and brought it down, sending the ring to the top and clanging the bell. He hoisted Twiggy up onto his shoulders and pranced around, gesturing for their small audience. Hope and Liza clapped enthusiastically.

Hope got a chance to do some mothering. She set the child on her lap and set to rebraiding her hair, telling her tales of living in the big city of Baltimore, how her own son lived there with her mother.

Liza paced around, her mind obviously elsewhere.

"Go on," Hope said. "We don't need you hovering around. Go do whatever it is you're fidgeting about. Me and Twiggy will be fine."

With Twiggy's admonishment not to be gone too long, Liza traipsed around lamenting her bad luck. "I can't take her back there," she said aloud to no one in particular. Clay . . . she'd have to figure that out. She doubted the story about the adoption—probably a way to get money out of her. Either way, that didn't matter now; Twiggy would be safer where she could keep an eye on her. Liza was not prone to praying, but she did beg her animal guides to help her, to not let anything happen to Twiggy and that they help her crush the threat that was racing toward her. Hope . . . Hope and Bombardier would look after Twiggy if things went badly for her. Liza welcomed the resolve that flowed through her.

Liza stared out into the forested area that buffeted the long line of trailers. The sky still had the gray-and-white cast that made it seem more like winter than the middle of summer. The taste of grit in her mouth had been washed away with a cup of water, but the dust still coated her hair. She had repeated the mantra that Ago had taught her. He'd said she should do it every day until she learned to call her spirits at will.

A longing—a calling of sorts—moved her forward into the trees. The sounds of critters skittering out of her way mingled with the crush of leaves and grass beneath her feet. She cursed—she could walk more silently than this.

A bird squawked. Liza tracked the piercing caw to a tree about ten paces in front of her, where a raven sat on a low branch. Her heartbeat quickened. She moved forward slowly and stopped when she was at the base of the tree. Craning her neck upward, she found the raven looking back down at her. It was so close that she could have reached up and touched it. The raven was a shiny black from head to talon. It blinked at her and twisted his head, as if Liza were a human curiosity.

As Malachi had taught her, she folded herself into a seated position on the ground and inhaled and exhaled cleansing breaths. An image of

Ishe pushed to the forefront of her mind. She wondered if someday, when she gained more control of the animals, she could free him of his demon spirit, but she gently let the thought slide away. A few breaths later, her heartbeat had returned to normal, perhaps even a little slowed. The raven appeared in her mind. Perched on a barren tree in the middle of a desert, he squawked, loud and piercing. He was larger than she expected: not quite an eagle but bigger than an ordinary raven.

He opened his beak again, and a bubbling cloud of images emerged from his mouth. Mama held a baby, and Liza guessed instinctively that she was watching her younger self. Mama looked afraid but determined. She slipped an amulet around Liza's chubby neck and hid it beneath folds of blankets. Another woman, tall, fierce, dangerous. Colorful skirts and bracelets. Long braids. Mama gripped Liza tightly in one hand and held out the other. The woman scowled and vanished. She'd glimpsed a woman wearing colorful skirts at the carnival; could it have been the same person?

Next, Liza, with a new baby her mother had just shoved into her arms. That was a happy time for their family, the children brightening whatever spare conditions they found themselves living in. But as the years passed, with Liza still unable to control her gift, Ella began shrinking in on herself. Ella was silent and stoic as Liza's father rattled off a list of the child's inadequacies with her gift. Another scene of the first time that Liza, still too young to decipher the heavy silences in her family, had rushed up to her father to give him a hug, of him stiffening before yielding to an embrace. The last vision of her, riding off in the car with Mrs. Margaret, the curses she had uttered, the ball of hatred that had been building up, coming into full bloom.

Liza tried to fight off the images, even tried to sever the connection with her animal guide, but the raven persisted, playing them over and over, forcing Liza to face her inner conflicts. She loved and hated her family. There it was. She had never allowed herself to think it aloud before. Tears streamed down her face from her still-closed eyes.

The next vision she received was of herself with Ishe, that night in the alley when he'd changed, and the next time, at his trailer, where she'd learned that the man and his demon were not necessarily one and the same. Her animal guide was trying to tell her that there was another side to her parents, one that she might not yet understand. *Understand.*

I can't say that I am not hurt, even a little angry, Liza thought. *But if I had the chance to meet my parents again, and I'm certain now that I've wanted to all along, I would allow them the chance to share with me what made them do the things they did. I would listen.*

Liza came to her feet, brushing off leaves and dirt. The raven on the tree stretched and flapped his wings. He shifted, expanded, threatening to totter off the branch, then turned, taking on every color of the rainbow. It was beautiful. The bird then shrank, twisted, and flattened into a piece of gold. The gold lilted, as if a dandelion on the wind, and rocked back and forth till it landed in Liza's outstretched hand. It then became a lone, long, and regal black raven feather.

CHAPTER THIRTY-SEVEN

FRIENDS AND FOES

For the second time in her life, Liza had people she could count on. There had been her parents, once. They'd given her life—fed and clothed her, after all, even if that hadn't lasted. There'd been few laughs, the affection infrequent but sincere. She remembered those moments, replayed them in her mind and anguished over them because she knew that had she found her parents again, she could have loved them the same.

Hope and Bombardier had become makeshift parents as well as best friends. Autumn, the big sister she never had, was aloof but direct. Though it had become clear to her that she and Jamey weren't meant for each other, she was certain he was also in her camp. Ishe had helped her understand so much about who she was. Ishe—of course she had to deal with what had happened between them.

Eloko had been unsettling from their first meeting. An adversary. Of that she was certain.

The only real unknown was Clay. On which side of the fence did he sit? Besides Zinsa and Efe, he was the only person she'd seen going in or hanging around the red trailer. That nightmarish incident there with the stilt walker still gave her goose bumps, and she *had* seen Clay slinking around, dragging something suspicious out of the trailer too. That meant, until he proved otherwise, he was definitely in the "against" camp. Liza exhaled a gloomy breath.

Malachi was the only one who seemed unbiased, who gave her the sense of clarity she needed to help sort the mess her life was becoming. But she had Twiggy to think of now; if there was a strike to be made, she was determined to deliver the first blow. She made a beeline for his trailer, breathing a sigh of relief that Eloko wasn't there.

"That face of yours," Malachi said with a smile. "It tells a tale of great conflict."

"Walk with me?" Liza asked, and Malachi fell in beside her, her shoulders thrown back, her bearing more determined. Time was in short supply.

Liza would not burden him with her many tales of woe—her parents' death, an orphanage that might be looking for her sister, or that horrible sense of foreboding she now carried—she only wanted a little of the eternal peace that always surrounded him to rub off on her. She liked that, with him, silence spoke more clearly than a mountain of words. And that silence would allow her to think. She needed a plan.

Their feet crunched lightly on the alternately blighted and green earth as they walked aimlessly, both of them taking in the vast emptiness of the flat country.

"What do you think of Clay?" Liza asked. She figured the carnival front man was either an accomplice or an unwitting tool.

"The question is, What do *you* think of Clay?"

Liza kicked at a stone. "I don't know. I mean, I wonder what he's protecting in that red trailer."

"I can't say I wasn't uneasy that first day when he took me there. Nothing I can stick a pin to, I am afraid."

"You wonder about him too?" Liza asked, trying to grasp at anything that might confirm her suspicions.

"When we are no longer able to change a situation, we are challenged to change ourselves," Malachi said, and when Liza turned her perplexed face to his, he translated: "We have no control over who or what is in that trailer; we can only control how we think about it."

With that last thought, Malachi excused himself, and Liza then caught a glimpse of Jamey. She turned toward him, raising her hand in a hopeful wave. He glared and strode off in the other direction.

Liza felt the rejection like a baseball bat to the midsection. *The close of a chapter.*

No, she owed him more than that. Liza called out to Jamey and rushed after him. He stopped but didn't turn around until she laid a hand on his back.

Liza fumbled over a million ways to begin, though none would soften the blow. "I'm sorry," she said.

"Am I supposed to guess that's your way of turning me down?" Jamey wouldn't look at her. He began pacing.

"There's something coming." Liza tried another tactic. "I've had a vision. I have to learn to communicate with my animal guides—"

"Your animal guides?" Jamey looked at her like she was speaking another language.

"Look, it's complicated. But I have to face something terrible, and, well, it's just too dangerous for you to be around me."

"Not too dangerous for Ishe, though?"

Liza could only shake her head.

"Before we saved your ass from a life sentence in Baton Rouge, you wasn't nothin' but a servant girl. Your parents didn't want you. Nobody did but me. But what do you do? You spit on the hand I offered like I'm a piece of trash. Ungrateful is what you are. If it wasn't for me, you'd still have your head stuck in a toilet cleaning vomit."

"You're probably right. And I'll never forget what you did for me."

Jamey stopped pacing and came to face her. He was so close their shoes touched. "But you don't love me."

Liza considered her answer; she *did* love Jamey, just not the same way he wanted. "I do—"

"Not like a wife loves a husband, huh? Not the way you feel about that mutt?"

Liza met his gaze and found she couldn't utter the words. She didn't have to.

"Tramp," Jamey spat and then stormed off.

His words, that disappointment in his eyes, cut Liza to pieces. She wished she'd had the right words to explain. But what could she say? *Something is coming to kill me, and I don't want you to get hurt? I have feelings for Ishe? A kinship that I now know I can't deny? I'm, um, sorry to have to hurt you . . . but in Ishe's arms, I felt . . .*

She grasped her elbows and ran her hands up and down her arms, picturing the scene as she would have liked it to unfold instead of on the dusty road where it had. Her meeting Ishe at his trailer, where she'd bolted the door behind them.

She imagined his smooth brown skin beneath her palms. Could imagine losing themselves in a deep kiss. She might be bold, but she was still modest, so she would ask Ishe to turn around as she undressed and slid beneath the covers. After all, they weren't married yet. Liza's eyes fluttered closed as she imagined Ishe's hands exploring her body: gentle, sweet kisses following their path until they came together.

The sound of Elephant's trumpeting echoed in her ears. "Focus," her guide was saying. And that moment birthed a decision that rose in her like a crimson dawn into a new spring day. Ago and Oya had laid out the path; she need only walk it. Life was a series of moves, a lopsided pattern of offense and defense. There remained no doubt in her mind: she would take the offensive.

CHAPTER THIRTY-EIGHT

AHIKU THE OBSERVER

Zinsa and Efe made a circuit around the carnival. What no one else could see was that they flanked a tall, pretty, colorfully clad woman who, despite her carefully constructed outward appearance, was a creature of the underworld.

After the meeting with her cohorts at the Skirvin, Ahiku was feeling the pressure. Before their revelation, the thought that Liza was her adversary was a mere feasibility. She hadn't wanted to believe that she'd been wrong. But perhaps Eloko's ardent suspicions were right. She'd sensed nothing at their first meeting, but anyone who could best her in battle would have defenses about her, so she would check out the girl herself.

They found Liza in the animal tent. It was the first time Ahiku had visited since she'd joined the carnival, given she'd had no reason to previously. The girl was actually rolling around on the floor with the Tasmanian tiger like it was a tamed puppy. Music blared, something more modern than was Ahiku's taste. And that simpleton Ikaki danced and pranced like a trained monkey!

Was this to be her opponent? A thickly built animal trainer, little more than a child. What tools had Liza to defeat her? Ahiku almost laughed at the prospect. This was who had Eloko so worried? But she cautioned herself not to become overconfident. The demons were quite certain. There might be something she could not easily see. Could that busybody Oya have a hand in this?

Ikaki and Sabina paused and eyed her without the slightest bit of shame.

Suddenly, the girl looked up, straight in her direction. She looked through her. Ahiku blinked once, twice.

"What are *they* doing here?" the girl said as she came to her feet and brushed herself off.

"Beats me," Uly said, following her gaze toward the soldiers.

The girl narrowed her eyes and tilted her head. It was as if she sensed something in the space between Zinsa and Efe. Ahiku bristled. *Can she see me?* Her women soldiers exchanged dumbfounded looks.

"What do you want?" Liza walked toward them.

"I'm going to finish her right now!" Ahiku took one step forward.

A raven soared into the tent.

It swooped at the women with its beak spread wide. Along with the cry that escaped its mouth, it spewed a stream of ashes.

Ahiku had no sooner brought up her hand to repel the ashes than the cursed soot slipped through her fingers and defenses and settled onto her skin. She howled her rage and did something she had not done since she'd been a human toddler—she stumbled. The ashes burned and singed. Her guards took her by either arm and made a beeline for the red trailer, but not before she registered the muddled shock on Liza's face. She'd seen her!

As Ahiku passed the wrestler's tent in a daze—she still wished she'd found that one herself—his wife, the fortune-teller, bounced the most precious of children on her lap. Such a scrumptious aura. *Later.*

As she retreated behind her trailer door, an idea blossomed in her head. "Send me the dwarf," she said to her guards.

The threat was at the carnival. How could she have been so blind? Liza pondered what had happened as the first dull evidence of daylight emerged. Raven had directed those ashes right at the spot where Liza had sensed the presence. And what those women soldiers were firmly planted on the side of . . . was that the enemy? Only one guess where the thing had gone. Liza had tried to pursue but had mysteriously lost them. It was as if the grounds had morphed into a maze, and each time she'd felt herself nearing the red trailer, the path had turned back in on itself.

She shifted on the bunk, trying not to wake Twiggy, even though she herself hadn't had a moment's rest. Every sound, every creak, had her jerking up, calling on her animal guides to the point where they had disappeared, annoyed.

The sleeping arrangements were cramped but surprisingly comfortable. Mico slept at the head of the pillow, with Twiggy curled into Liza like she had since she was a baby. It felt like the most natural thing in the world, but Liza struggled to picture the long term.

The knowledge that her parents were dead had shifted to a dull ache at the back of her head. Trying to stop the tears that sprang to her eyes from falling was like trying to use a thimble to plug an oil geyser, but for the sake of her sister, she managed.

With the first rays of light streaming through the window, framing a small rectangle on the opposite wall, Liza looked down at her little sister. Her mouth was slightly open, a line of drool hanging from the corner, her leg thrown over Liza's midsection. The eye mask Autumn had loaned her—telling Twiggy it would prevent her from getting wrinkles later on—was off, Mico having created a pillow out of it.

Did Liza even have the right to think about a future? She certainly did not. And it was cruel to give Twiggy hope. The possibility of taking her back to the orphanage had resurfaced, earning the ire of her sister and Ishe—she hadn't heard a kind word from either since she'd brought it up. She'd also contemplated taking them both and leaving this place. But deep down, that stirring in her gut all but screamed it: she could not.

Liza shook Twiggy awake, and the first thing the girl said was, "I'm hungry."

After much protest, Liza and Twiggy showered and cleaned up. They had a hearty breakfast, where Liza was saddened to see her sister stuffing sausage and whatever else she could into her pockets—the same as she herself had done when she'd joined the carnival. After, they met Ishe at his trailer. Twiggy pouted, and only with a threat did she give Ishe a sulky, "Morning, Mr. Ishe."

Ishe was silent and so was Twiggy, the anger plain on her face. Did neither of them understand how much it hurt to have even considered leaving Twiggy again? How much she had to deal with? *They* were the selfish ones, not her.

"I'm not taking her back." Liza's announcement put her back in both their good graces. Ishe disappeared inside his trailer and returned with a carving of a rabbit that was so near to the real thing she had to take a closer look. Twiggy peeled herself away from Liza's hip, grabbed the new toy, and thanked Ishe only after Liza had given her a stern look.

"You have to put her out of your mind and stay ready for what's coming." Ishe had guided Liza a few paces away but gestured at Twiggy with a flick of his head.

"Don't you think I know that?" Liza sighed. "I don't know whether to get her as far away from me as possible or never let her out of my sight. The thought that something could happen to her, or that she could lose me, for that matter, just after we've found each other again . . . is just—" She couldn't finish her thought.

"I don't have the answers any more than you do. All you can do in the meantime is practice and prepare yourself."

"That's exactly what I intend to do." Liza fingered her amulet. "Should I leave? Draw this thing away from Bacchanal?"

Ishe scratched at his cheek and then shook his head. "It's tied to Bacchanal—everything you told me so far points to that. No, best you stay here, where you have some help."

It was obvious that Twiggy didn't pick up on the undercurrent of their conversation but had plainly guessed that Ishe was on her side. Liza looked down at Twiggy to find her smiling at Ishe. He returned her smile with a wink and excused himself; there was always a never-ending list of things to be done for a carnival on the move.

Grabbing Twiggy's hand, Liza trudged back toward her trailer.

What if something happened to *her*? What if she didn't make it? What would happen to Twiggy then?

Almost as if in answer, Twiggy veered off and made a beeline for Hope and Bombardier's trailer. Liza tried unsuccessfully to blot out the images of her parents dead—dying—and followed.

There was little that could be done now. The carnival was preparing for the first date in Tulsa. She left Twiggy with Hope and Bombardier and rushed off to the quiet space behind the cook tent, usually the last place to be packed up.

Head on a swivel, she scanned for onlookers. She was alone. She settled in and prepared herself, her eyelids lowered, her lips parted and closed. Ago's words echoed in her mind.

Until you learn to summon them at will, you will call them to you by repeating a mantra.

The time for crutches and novice tricks was behind her. She swallowed hesitation, rubbed her palms together to stop her hands from shaking. A thought coalesced. The introduction, the first time she'd communed with the three spirits. How she'd made the arduous spiritual journey across the ocean to lay herself bare, humbled before them. The trials she'd endured and survived.

And like a strong wind from a limitless sky, they came to her all at once. The terrain changed: the cook tent gone, Bacchanal a thing of another place. The sun sat low on the horizon, illuminating vague outlines of creatures large and small, roaming and grazing. A soft breeze carrying the scent of home caressed her skin.

Raven squawked and landed on a tree branch overhead. A rustling of brush, tall grass parted, and Badger emerged. The ground shook as Elephant ambled forward, trunk held high.

Like roots growing in reverse, a current of warmth surged up from underfoot, through the soles of her boots, and then filled her stomach with such force that she thought she might burst open. But the warmth exploded outward to the top of her head and the tips of her fingers. Her heart beat in time with a rhythmic thump of a faraway drum. She imagined that the sweetness of her next inhalation was like that of a newborn taking a first breath.

An image coalesced, formed of their united thought. They were at the carnival, assembled in front of the red trailer, shrouded in mist and shadow. *This* was where the threat was concealed. This was where together, they would defeat the enemy. But how could she find it?

Badger responded first, an image of herself clawing that trailer to pieces. Elephant interjected, her trunk holding Badger back. "Wait," she was telling her, earning an impatient hiss from the other spirit. Raven, the trickster, showed them the chest from her trial on the mountain, only the lid was open. The message: something other than what they saw awaited them inside.

Liza replied with a thought of her own. Eloko. The dwarf was complicit. Yes, the spirits agreed, deal with him first and lure the enemy out of hiding at the same time.

"Liza!" Clay's voice yanked her back. "We gotta jump! The tents and rides are down. Shake a leg."

It was time to go. The fight would wait another day. But her confidence was building. She'd called to the spirits, and the spirits had answered.

CHAPTER THIRTY-NINE

ELOKO EARNS HIS KEEP

Tulsa. The famed last stop on Bacchanal's serpentine trail. *The big score.* Liza wished she could drum up the excitement she'd felt on the first night she'd started her animal show, but now at the start of each day, darkness seemed to hold back more of the dawn. The more she hunted for the red trailer, the more it eluded her.

Oklahoma had taken the brunt of the economic and environmental hardships, and still Tulsa remained a stable, growing city. Carnival posters had been plastered all over town, and from what some of the carnies said, the locals were ripe to be taken. But she had other plans.

"I guess I picked up a bug on the road." Liza coughed and dabbed a handkerchief at her nose. "I'm afraid I'll have to cancel my show."

Clay squinted, planted his fists on his hips, and cocked his head at her as if she'd spoken in a foreign tongue. "You pick the biggest stop to take ill? The posters are all up—folks will be expecting a show."

"And they'll have plenty shows to see." Liza feigned a sneeze. "Just not mine."

"This stunt is going to cost us both."

Clay stormed off with her promise that she might be up for one show, maybe if she felt better later. She swung by her trailer to pick up her little sister and get her safely tucked away.

She and Twiggy wound through the midway, walking hand in hand. The child was none too happy about missing Liza's animal show, and only the promise of a treat prevented a tantrum that she had no time for. Twiggy had stared in wonder at the concession stand, gawking at everything before she settled on pink-and-blue cotton candy. She looked up at Liza in pure bliss as the sugary confection melted on her tongue. Her giggle was that of only a child who could still be awed by something so simple. Of course, with barely enough food to eat when they were with their parents, a sweet treat was something they'd rarely experienced. And from the expression on her face, sweets weren't much on the menu while she lived with the witch doctor either.

Pitchmen hawked their wares; music thrummed from the speakers mounted near every pole. Dancers and performers entertained the crowd in small groups. And the games—the games were a hit. Liza guided Twiggy to the water shot, where patrons sat on stools and aimed their water guns at a laughing clown. There was an obvious shill in the pack, a carnie Liza had exchanged few words with, but he seemed nice enough, if rough around the edges. As was the common practice, he'd been installed to help convince the marks to step up, drop their coins, and play. Judging by the crowd, he was more than doing his job.

They moved on, Liza maneuvering them to just the right spot, close enough to be seen by her target without making a show of it. Twiggy yanked her hand and pointed.

"Look, look!"

Liza narrowed her eyes at the object of Twiggy's fascination—Eloko. The dwarf had a massive crowd before him. He stalked back and forth across the raised stage, fully in character. If people were not drawn in by the sight of a small, grass-covered, golden-eyed cross between a human and a . . . she didn't know what, it was the way he wove a tale. Grudgingly, Liza admitted he was a master.

They stood at the edge of the crowd. Eloko spotted her and winked. Fine, that part was done. Liza tapped her foot, crossed her arms, and generally tried to avoid looking at the little man. Twiggy, however, was entranced. Eloko continued with his tale.

". . . and the warrior, he was a great warrior indeed. He hefted his spear, the one hewn from the mountains of the savanna, forged beneath the earth, handed down from chief to chief since the beginning of time. The warrior stood with his legs slightly parted and held out his right arm, the long spear held tightly in his fist." Eloko stopped, positioned himself to demonstrate, and raised his hands, using a long stick in place of the spear. "The warrior stalked his enemy across a vast distance. To others he was but a speck on the horizon, but the warrior found him easily, amid a hundred thousand other soldiers. He reared back and sent the spear sailing, as if on invisible wings, through the air, and pierced his opponent's right eye . . ."

"Lies!" Liza yelled. "It's all lies."

Uncomfortable murmurs rose around her. Eloko's eyes flashed, and that disgusting snout quivered. "Perhaps I could expand on my first-hand knowledge for the lady at another time?"

"You know where to find me."

"Indeed I do." Eloko resumed his story, albeit to a slightly smaller crowd.

"Come on." Liza couldn't take any more and dragged away a pro-testing Twiggy.

"I wanted to hear the rest of the story," Twiggy said with a pout.

"If you want to keep the rest of that cotton candy, you won't say another word about it."

The child considered this and kept any further protests quiet.

Back in the red trailer, Ahiku was holed up, attending to the tumult the ashes had inflicted. The vast ocean of souls within her stirred, bucking for release. It had sapped nearly every bit of her power to stay them and keep the girl from finding her at the same time. The child whom Clay had snatched for her was hastily devoured, a reckless necessity. The new soul would heal her, given time, but time was an indulgence she no longer possessed. The demon horde's deadline notwithstanding, the animal tamer had made this personal. Hiding in plain sight for the sole purpose of embarrassing her. Come underworld or high water, the girl would pay. A quickening agent was in order.

Behind the thick velvet curtain, she mixed a noxious brew in a skillfully carved earthen bowl hewn from the underworld. The enchantment trickled out through her gritted teeth. Ahiku lifted the bowl to her lips. After she drank, she placed the bowl back on a shelf. She set her legs wide, braced herself against the wall. When Ahiku opened her mouth, she trumpeted a rapid series of nightmarish shrieks.

～

As they moved back toward Hope and Bombardier's trailer, where her sister would stay until this was all over, Liza felt the hair all over her body stand on end. Goose bumps followed. She stopped at once and then turned around and around.

Twiggy, and every child nearby, tilted their heads, casting their curious gazes up, around. Liza gripped her sister's hand, each cell in her body screaming a warning.

Elephant came to her and sent an image of a woman. Liza recognized the same woman who had stood between Zinsa and Efe that night at the animal tent. This woman rivaled Hope in fortune-teller gear, all colorful rags and jeweled hoops. Elephant's next image was of the woman wearing a mask, a red-and-black thing reminiscent of the season of festivals. The woman was not who she appeared to be.

Was this who she had to face? A woman only she could see? She and . . .

She turned to Twiggy and knelt down.

"Did you hear that? The scream, I mean?"

"Is that one of the shows?" Twiggy asked. "I don't know if I want to see that one. But maybe I can; if I get scared, I can cover my eyes like Mama taught me."

Liza's stomach sank. She stopped a little girl skipping ahead of her parents. "Did you hear a . . . a scream?"

"I knew it! My papa said he didn't hear it, so I couldn't see that show. Thinks I'm a fraidy-cat." The girl's parents caught up and drew her away.

"Hey," Liza said to a little boy clutching a candy apple. "That scream—"

"Was that a phonograph? Never seen one a them before."

Liza ignored the boy and the growing lump in her chest. "Ma'am, sir!" she called to a couple with two children. "Did you hear a scream a moment ago?"

The couple sized up Liza with curious looks and shook their heads no, but their wide-eyed kids muttered in unison, "We did."

An enemy whom only she and, for some reason, children, could see or hear? Liza tugged at the leather cord around her neck and thumbed her amulet. She and the spirits had talked about this; Eloko was the link. One way or another, he'd lead her to that trailer.

"You have to get back to your show?" Twiggy asked, snapping her out of her contemplation. "'Cause if you don't, I want to go see Mrs. Hope."

Liza made the decision then: Twiggy would stay with her friends, tucked into the little pallet at the foot of their bed, with Uly posted outside the door. Liza would let Ishe know about her latest discovery and then set her sights on a certain dwarf.

~

Carnies rarely slept at the end of a night. Everyone was too wound up. Once the last of the locals had left, she sought out Hope, and as she half expected, Ishe was there with Bombardier. Twiggy had climbed into their trailer and was already fast asleep.

Liza guided Hope and Ishe to a spot in the shadows. "I think I know who it is, who *she* is."

Hope and Ishe exchanged a glance. Something passed across the fortune-teller's face. Liza let it pass.

"What did you see?" Hope and Ishe tripped over each other asking the same question.

"A woman." Liza recounted in detail the woman she'd seen, what her animal guides had shown her. And that look from Hope again.

"What is it?" Liza asked Hope. "Did the cards tell you something?"

Hope pressed the heels of her palms to her eyes. "This is all too, too strange."

"If both the raven and elephant pointed out this woman . . . ," Ishe said. He seemed to avoid her eyes. Was he afraid? Ishe? "She gotta be the one."

"But . . ." Liza gestured with her hands. "What am I supposed to do when I do find her?"

"Kill her," Ishe said without blinking an eye. "We know that's what this been leading up to, and ain't no reason to call it any way than what it is. When the time is right, your guides will tell you."

Would it be like when she accidentally killed animals? Liza wondered. "But this is a woman, a human being."

Hope finally spoke. "No. From what you described, she may have been human once, but that sure ain't what she is now."

Liza bid her friend good night with a heavy heart.

She'd wandered a while when Ishe had fallen in step beside her and glanced at her with unmasked admiration.

She caught the look and recalled the time in the truck when he had revealed his feelings for her. Had she been that blind to have not seen it all along? Liza looked at his face, and sure enough, there it was, plain as the day was long. Ishe did almost as good a job at masking his emotions as she did, but now that her eyes were open, it was hard not to see.

"Taking a life ain't going to be easy," Ishe continued. "Used to think that not knowing the details would help with the guilt, ya know? But not knowing, wondering what I did and how I did it. That part will eat you up, if you let it."

Liza felt Ishe's pain as a living thing, something that walked behind him like a shadow. She did not want to kill this woman, though even for all her past and potential future victims, Liza couldn't say she was exactly sorry that she had to. She hoped that after she finished with this woman, her killing would be done and over. Now that her animal guides were more under her control, she figured she might be able to control her communication with other animals. But Ishe, as long as he lived, the hyena spirit would have control of him.

"In case I don't make it, I want to try to heal you now. I think my Raven spirit can help me."

Ishe didn't acknowledge her but stopped walking and turned to face her.

Liza studied Ishe's face. He stood as still as a statue, didn't fidget, didn't bite his lip, but he could barely face her. "What is it?"

Ishe sighed. "No excuse for what I'm about to say."

Liza's heart raced, spurred by whatever awfulness was about to spill from Ishe's lips.

"The demon. We got us a history."

He went on to tell Liza the story of his wife and daughter, the deal and sacrifice he'd made.

"You knew all along?" She snatched away from the hand he laid on her arm. "You act like my friend. Lay all this stuff on me about how much you care, and . . . you let me give myself to you? And have the nerve to slink around acting like you want to help me but didn't think for a minute to warn me?"

"I didn't guess everything at first," Ishe stammered. "And when I did . . . my daughter."

"You should have told me the truth, and maybe we could have worked out a way to fight this demon together."

"That's what I been doing."

Liza threw up her hands. "I—I can't." She turned and stormed off as Ishe, rooted in place, watched her go.

~

The moon sat high in the sky but was overcome by clouds such that only a pale, filtered glow illuminated the earth. The smell of all the food and treats made and consumed that night mingled in with the dust and filled the air. Dusty grime coated her skin, shook from her clothes with every step. The shuffle of feet sounded off to her left, somewhere at a distance. Liza halted midstep, listened intently.

She walked a few steps more and stopped. *Maybe this is it.* Never mind Eloko; was it time she faced the woman she had seen earlier? A wave of fear constricted her stomach, but she shook it off. She wouldn't waste any more time looking over her shoulder, wondering when and where she would be attacked. She wished she could have done this with Ishe by her side, but she shook the temptation away.

Liza turned in the direction of the noise, commanding her legs to move. She walked lightly, the way her father had taught her. *The element of surprise,* he'd said. *You would be well suited to learn its benefits.* Crouching, taking determined steps, she slunk through the shadows still within sight of the perceived safety of the trailers and other carnies. Her heartbeat quickened, sweat and the day's grime plastering her clothes to her skin.

"Ah," Eloko cooed. "The smell of dinner." He held his snout in the air, as if gulping in Liza's scent like a lion lapping at the edge of the river on a summer's day in the savanna.

"What?" Liza spun, and as the clouds moved, revealing a bit more of the moon, she caught a full glimpse of the dwarf. "Did I upset you back there?" She looked around, and besides Eloko, there wasn't anybody else around. The dwarf had outsmarted her, almost.

Eloko began moving slowly to his right, in a wide arc. "She said I should weaken you," he said with a leer at Liza. "But she'll thank me. I will gain much favor for ridding her of her foe. The demons will sing songs of praise in my name."

She. Eloko, with all his skulking around, watching, waiting. She'd guessed right. He knew her enemy. Was working for the woman.

She began moving away from Eloko in an opposite arc.

"I should have known. You're no more than an errand boy. The last of the great errand boys of Zaire." She spoke to keep Eloko occupied while she channeled all her energy into calling her guides. Without thinking, she repeated the mantra Ago had taught her.

"*Today, I ask that my animal guides reveal themselves to me. I wish to receive the gifts of sight so that they may reveal what I must see, guide, and protect me in the coming storm.*"

Eloko growled, revealing a set of grizzled, horrific teeth. His eyes flashed his annoyance. He moved his hand behind his back. "If you think I am nothing more than an errand boy, why don't you slap me around and send me back to Ahiku, with my hair disheveled and pride hurt?"

Ahiku. The enemy's name. "And for all you found out about me . . ." Liza took a bold step closer. "It won't help you."

"But there is much that our mutual friend did not tell you." From somewhere beneath the layers of grassy skin, Eloko produced a long, curved knife. The steel glinted in the moonlight. Behind Eloko, Liza spotted Jamey sneaking up from his left. Darn fool might get them both killed.

"We were a great people," Eloko continued, waving the knife in front of Liza. "A people tasked with a noble calling. A kind of population control. One suited for our most particular tastes."

Snarling, snapping at the air, Badger came to Liza, her beady eyes fierce. She eyed the knife. Between the blade and Eloko's claws, Liza figured she would emerge from this either dead or so bloodied that she would surely die in the long walk back to the carnival trailers. She only hoped Jamey wouldn't get caught in the middle.

"Population control?" Keep him talking while she figured out how to attack.

"Our taste," Eloko droned on, darting forward and taking a tentative slash at Liza, who easily backed away, "is for human flesh. And I have been waiting long enough to fill my belly with you. I will eat you. No matter what Ahiku says, I will savor the taste of your cursed blood. I will gnaw on your bones after I've consumed all the thick meat coating them. I will bottle your blood and sip on it from time to time. A way to remember you after I have shat you out."

Liza shuddered. She supposed those claws and fangs were not for livestock after all.

"Besides Jamey, and that hyena demon that moons over you, I don't suspect anyone will miss you. Aah, but little Twiggy. Know how Ahiku has survived so long? She consumes the souls of children. Particularly the feisty ones like dear Twiggy. Ahiku may gain ten more lifetimes from her soul alone."

The last piece of the puzzle fell into place. Children. The reason Clay always got so riled up about having them around, why Hope's son was in Baltimore and not with her, why the sounds of children playing and laughing were reserved for only when the carnival was open to the public. If that demon thought she was going to get her hands on Twiggy . . . she shuddered to think of how many children had died, walking helplessly around the carnival, only to be picked off like wild game. Liza feinted right.

Eloko streaked forward, dodged left, and swiped the blade sideways, barely missing Liza's stomach, as Badger sent her an emphatic "move left" image a split second before. But Eloko compensated quickly and, with Liza's back turned, caught her with the claws of his other hand.

Eloko's claws grazed her skin, stuck in all the beadwork Autumn had insisted she put on the fringe of her performance jacket. Liza said a silent thank-you to her trailer mate. He yanked and pulled to free his hand, raising the knife again.

Raven surged forward, a magician's deception. The knife in Eloko's hand turned to a black, slithering snake that arched its body up and bit the dwarf on the snout. Eloko tossed the snake as far as he could, still struggling to free his hand. The knife returned to its proper form and clinked against a too-distant rock.

He crouched low and darted in, raking Liza across the ankle, sending her crashing to the ground. Before she could blink, he'd scrambled behind her and pulled her head back with one hand and had the other poised to pierce her throat. Liza's right forearm pressed against his, struggling to push back his claws. The dwarf was deceptively strong. The lights, the carnies—help was so close.

A body slammed into Eloko with a thud. He was thrown from her and she was free, but Jamey—

Liza looked up in time to see a rock in Eloko's hand come down hard against Jamey's skull.

"No!" she cried out, and Eloko turned to her, raised the rock, and snaked out his tongue, tasting Jamey's blood on the rock. Liza's gag died with a scream as she shifted into the illusion of a howling, snarling badger and launched herself at Eloko.

The dwarf's sparkling eyes bulged, and he let out a surprised shriek as they fell into a heap of claws, teeth, and badger attitude. Eloko was a fierce fighter, landing bites and scratches of his own, but Badger was faster and more cunning. Badger leaped and bit Eloko on his face, tearing out shards of grassy hair. She darted around and took a nip out of Eloko's leg, dodging another close call with those claws.

Badger moved so fast that Liza became dizzy, lost in the transformation. Eloko collapsed under the assault, took a few more ineffectual swipes. As life ebbed from the dwarf, his tongue flicked out over his snout and teeth.

"At least I got to taste her blood," he muttered and then lay completely still.

On the ground, inches away, Liza returned to herself. She bore the deep gouges and lighter scratches of the battle she was so relieved to have won that tears of joy mixed in with the pain and fell freely from her eyes. She winced as she tried to get up. Raven soothed her, commanding her to lie still. She would have to let the healer do his job.

And in that moment, the air around her shuddered. Eloko was tied to the demon, and in his passing, his spirit could open a new path to the red trailer.

She closed her eyes to the sound of Elephant and her herd, trumpeting a cry of victory.

In the red trailer, Ahiku's eyes snapped open. She ripped off the wet towel she'd draped over her face. What woke her was the swift, screaming passage of Eloko's spirit. What had the little fool done! Had she not told him to only wound the girl? She had to kill Oya's instrument herself, or another would appear in her place. She called out to Zinsa and Efe to go and look for the girl, to make sure she was safe. They ran off.

Ahiku retreated behind the dark curtain, back into the spirit world, her spell protecting the red trailer forgotten. There, Eloko's spirit was being bandied about like a football. As fast as the teams flipped him about, ripping out his flesh and grassy hair, it grew back, only for him to be tortured some more.

She surged forward and grabbed Eloko's spirit by its neck. He looked at her with horrified eyes. "Please, Ahiku. She's alive. I was only trying to help you."

"Shut up!" she screamed. "If she dies before I kill her, you will suffer unspeakable horrors, every minute of every day, for eternity."

Ahiku tossed Eloko's soul into the waiting hands of a litany of African souls that he had consumed during his illustrious lifetime.

CHAPTER FORTY

THE LIGHT OF DAY

The next day began with a sun so bright, so pure, that one could barely believe the deadly fight that had taken place within sight the night before. Escalating winds sent bits of cotton candy, napkins and posters, and other debris tumbling around the midway. A crowd massed, mulling over the stiff but not yet stinking body of Eloko—former star performer of the G. B. Bacchanal Carnival. Liza fought to appear calm as Clay stood with his fists planted at his sides, a slick string of hair falling over the left eye of his upturned face. The day was shrouded by a brooding, angry haze. Dust particles hung on the air like wheat-colored, earthly stars.

"Eloko's dead?" Uly voiced the obvious, earning himself a narrow-eyed glare from Clay.

Zinsa and Efe—most certainly dispatched by this Ahiku woman . . . demon—had probably expected to drag Liza back half-dead last night; instead they'd found Eloko and unceremoniously dumped him on the ground where he still lay.

"He was ripped apart is what happened." Clay kicked at a rock. "And I want to know how."

Some of the onlookers stole surreptitious glances in Ishe's direction. But usually, when he turned, it was no secret. They'd all had a hand in dragging him back to the carnival a time or two in the past.

Ishe rubbed his chin. "Can't take credit for this one."

Malachi sat on his haunches next to Eloko and took the dwarf's clawed hand in his. He lowered his head, arranged Eloko's hands on his destroyed chest in as peaceful a manner as he could, stood, and blended back into the crowd.

"A misunderstood soul," he said barely above a whisper.

Eloko *had* mattered, to Malachi if nobody else. It wasn't guilt that stirred in Liza's belly but a sympathy. A loss was a loss, and she'd seen her fair share of it to know it wasn't something she'd wish on the man.

Liza and Jamey stood side by side, their lips sealed in a grim line of solidarity. After Raven had healed Liza, returning her to something of a normal physical state, Liza had tended to Jamey, her hands and energy guided by Raven's healing magic. Jamey was no worse for wear, sporting only a small lump and a scar near his hairline that he hid by pulling his cap down.

She was stunned that Jamey had come to her aid. After their last conversation, she'd just assumed he'd never want to lift a finger for her again, let alone put his life on the line. The words he'd flung at her . . . awful words. But a person's anger is often no more than anguish dressed up in a crusty old overcoat. Jamey had been unable to mask his pain, and that saddened her most. Lies rolled off the tongue like gentle coos to a baby. The truth, though, fought its way out like something feral. But doing the right thing and withstanding the consequences gave her a strength she didn't know she had.

"Nobody saw nothin'?" Clay looked from face to blank face. Truth be told, Liza doubted that, besides Malachi, anybody could call up any strong emotion for the dwarf. Eloko wasn't what one would call likable. But he was a good earner; Clay would need another strong act to replace him.

Goose bumps of fear crawled up Liza's arms—Eloko had been one of Ahiku's. She'd never asked about the nature of Clay's relationship to Eloko or how he'd brought him to Bacchanal, because it wasn't her business. It was now.

"Wonder if it could have been somebody local?" Jamey found his voice and moved an authoritative step forward, Clay's steady right hand again. "I mean, we know this sure as hell ain't the work of a carnie."

Liza's eye twitched a little when he added that last bit. A furtive glance around the crowd revealed two scrutinizing gazes locked on her: Zinsa's and Efe's. But instead of their customary scowls, their expressions were something akin to respect. They knew. *Of course they knew.*

Clay considered things for a long moment. "Much as I hate to see somebody get away with this, can't take the risk of having any bored cops sniffing around here where their nose don't have to sway. This here is an internal matter. We're gonna have to bury him."

Bombardier stepped forward and picked up Eloko, cradling him like a child. Clay sent a couple of carnies for shovels, and the rest searched for a suitable burial spot a safe distance from the carnival. There, Liza watched from the shadows as Eloko was buried with only Malachi, Bombardier, two diggers, and Clay in attendance.

The carnival manager removed his hat, said a few terse words, and with a last toss of dirt, Eloko was consigned back to dust. Clay also set others to work, removing Eloko's posters and banners. By opening time, there would be no evidence that Eloko, the dwarf from Zaire, had ever been a member of the G. B. Bacchanal Carnival.

It was the spider that crawled up her leg during Eloko's burial that helped her find the trailer. The lure: an image promising a bounty of insects. The master of webs and mazes, bearer of keen eyesight, navigated what remained of Ahiku's tangled shroud and relayed the fresh path made by Eloko's spirit back to Liza. She stopped by Hope's trailer to say goodbye to her sister and Mico. Twiggy was occupied playing with a ball. She ran and wrapped Liza's legs with a hug. Liza picked her up and held her, conscious of how perfect Twiggy's hands felt clasped around her neck. Their parents gone as soon as Liza had found them. When she set her down, Twiggy looked at her curiously, as if she grasped the depths of her sister's distress, but the child remained easily distracted by a game of catch.

Liza let Mico and Twiggy play together, and she pulled Hope aside. "If something should happen to me—" She looked at Twiggy and choked back tears.

"You didn't even have to ask. And we'll be here waiting when you get back."

"Twiggy!" Liza called.

Twiggy kicked the ball to Liza and ran over.

"How would you like to hang out with Aunt Hope and Uncle Bombardier again today?"

"Where you going?"

"I'm not going anywhere, but I have work to do, so they're going to watch you, okay?"

Twiggy pursed her lips, considering. She looked back and forth between the adults, and the smile on her face faded. "What's the matter?"

A little girl shouldn't have had to witness the things that Twiggy had. She bore scars and wouldn't be placated easily. Liza feigned a chuckle. "Nothing, now that you're here." She planted a kiss on her sister's head and told her she'd see her a little later, praying that she would.

CHAPTER FORTY-ONE

BOMBARDIER COMES TO TERMS

Bombardier was running back to the trailer and smiled when he saw his wife was already there, waiting at the top of the steps. He'd stopped by Hope's work trailer to pick up her and Twiggy, but he had been glad to find that she'd already closed up shop; the storm looked like it could hit at any minute.

Hope had been in a state for the last couple of weeks. Distracted, worried. She was hiding something, and Bombardier had been unable to drag it out of her. He stood on the first step and wrapped her in an embrace before they went inside. Standing in the corner, he focused his clear eyes on his wife. "I have had enough of this," he said in a whisper. "You will tell me what is going on." He held up a hand as she began to concoct another story. "And do not tell me it is nothing. Some may look at me, take my smile, my good nature, and label me a dumb or simple man. I am neither."

Hope cradled his face. "A mistake I have never made."

"Do not let this be the first time." He removed her hands and crossed his arms. "Sit. You have been moping for weeks. Now you will tell me what is going on."

"I'm—"

"Shh." Bombardier flicked his head toward the bed where Twiggy normally slept.

"I'm worried about Eliza." Hope lowered her voice and played with her fingers.

Bombardier shrugged in a *get on with it* motion.

"And . . ." Hope looked away. "I miss our son."

"There," he said. "That one was not the truth; try again."

Hope looked like she wanted to burst. She exhaled, fidgeted, stood, flopped back down. "There is an evil here—at Bacchanal. That evil . . . I believe it takes children. I don't know what happens to them after that. Liza may stop it. But if she does"—Hope froze at the unreadable expression on her husband's face—"I don't even understand how, but I think Bacchanal could end. We won't have jobs. We'll be back in Baltimore cleaning rooms and hauling bags."

Bombardier furrowed his brow. Hope cowered at the look of pure hatred in his eyes. "The red trailer?"

Hope shrank back.

"And you said nothing?"

"What could I do?" she protested and then curled in on herself, crying. "You know I don't see things that clearly. All of this could be my own imagination."

"If it was, you wouldn't have held on to it so long." Bombardier pounded a fist in his hand. He pushed through the trailer door, nearly taking it off its hinges. He stopped in his tracks, afraid that he'd wakened the little girl. And then it came to him. He felt a knot of emotion he had not experienced since he'd had to bid farewell to his own child. He spun around and lurched over to the bed. Twiggy wasn't there. "Where is she?"

Hope fidgeted but lifted her head, taking on a high-and-mighty air. "Zinsa and Efe are taking her to Clay."

Bombardier's face twisted in disbelief. He stomped to within inches of her face. "You *gave* her to them? They work for *whatever* is in that trailer, and you handed over Twiggy?"

"I did it for us!" Hope shrank back. "Is Twiggy more important than our own son? If we don't work, he doesn't eat."

Bombardier ran a hand over his head. "I can't believe you did this. I'm going to find her, and when I get back . . ."

He stormed out of the trailer and stalked the deserted carnival grounds like an agitated lion. Gusts of wind stirred up the earth and anything that lay there: half-eaten food, weeds, and other debris. Trailer windows and doors clamped shut against the racket. Occupants huddled inside.

Bombardier shielded his eyes and trudged forward. Finally, through the swirling mess, he came to stand before the women soldiers in front of a row of shuttered games tents. Their intent plain: keep him away from the red trailer. Zinsa wore a short dagger at her hip, and Efe grasped one of the long spears they used in their show.

"Where is the child?" he asked. All traces of the jovial man with the wide, good-natured grin crushed beneath the weight of his wife's betrayal.

"Go back to your fortune-teller while you still can," Zinsa said. Efe raised the spear overhead, twirled it in a series of poses, and held it aloft, waiting.

Bombardier understood he'd have to get through these women to get to Twiggy. "I will not be lied to by women, nor will I be intimidated by them." He clapped at his forearms rhythmically, one after the other, and crouched. "You want to live like men, I promise you will die like men."

With a growl, Bombardier reached over and ripped a tent pole out of the ground. It normally took a couple of carnies, a few shovels, and a lot more time to do so. He swung it down hard on Efe's wrist as the women closed on him. The distinct crunch of breaking bones loosened her grip on the long spear, but she still held on with her right hand. Bombardier snaked behind Zinsa—the stronger of the two—locked a beefy forearm beneath her neck, and lashed out with his foot, knocking Efe backward and sending the spear into the air.

Zinsa brought her dagger down on his forearm. He gritted his teeth at the deep cut, squatted, and lifted Zinsa in a classic *laamb* move, falling backward and tossing her overhead. Her dagger clattered to the ground. As Bombardier rolled to his feet, Efe hefted the spear with one arm, landing rapid blows all over his body before breaking the spear in two against his back. He stood in time to catch the dagger that Zinsa had recovered and then loosed in his left shoulder. He yanked it free as if it were little more than a toothpick.

Still holding the dagger, Bombardier thrust it into Zinsa's chest. She clutched at the wound, cried out, and stumbled backward. Blood soaked through her shirt instantly. He slammed his fist into Efe's face, but not before she buried half of her spear in his left thigh.

Zinsa was on the ground bleeding but still reached out and grabbed Bombardier's ankle, distracting him long enough for Efe to leap up and slam her elbow to the side of his head in a crushing blow. He managed to stomp Zinsa's throat, and for the first time, not through jest or folly, not to lure in a mark, but from the bleeding wounds on his body and the accumulation of blows, exertion etched plainly on his face, he fell to one knee.

Everyone froze, and the trio inhaled sharply. Bombardier's fixed gaze conveyed his respect.

Zinsa lay back, unmoving on the ground, and Efe fell beside her. She ignored her own shattered wrist and, lifting Zinsa's limp head, probed her wounds and wailed.

Bombardier yanked the spear from his leg, releasing a high arcing spurt of blood. The big man struggled to his feet and lumbered a few steps forward, battered by wind and fatigue. He moved in what he hoped was the direction of the red trailer, blood covering his leg and soaking the ground in his wake. He looked back at the Dahomey women soldiers, and for all the barbs they'd exchanged, all the snarls and snipes, he felt no pride at what he had done. They had fought well. He turned away. Dust and dirt blurred his vision, and his legs felt as heavy as felled logs, but through sheer will, he plodded on.

Short of his destination, he fell.

CHAPTER FORTY-TWO

A RECKONING

The red trailer sat on an incline, reigning over the rest of the trailers like a beast of prey. As Liza marched in the trailer's direction, the early-evening haze grew shades darker. She cast her gaze up at the sky, took in the roiling dark clouds, seemingly bubbling over like a stew. *Fitting.* Ishe strolled up beside her, and she met his eyes. The pain there was staggering, but as much as she tried to muster words of forgiveness, they eluded her. Liza was overcome with a mixture of guilt and relief. She hadn't known if she would have the courage to face Ahiku without him.

She lowered her head and then gasped for breath as a hostile wind picked up, sending the murk scurrying across the sky ahead of an enormous black dust cloud. She had imagined this moment and knew instinctively that this life, that Bacchanal, was about to die. Her steps were unsteady, but she lumbered forward. About ten feet away, the door flew open, and the woman, the demon, alighted gracefully from the red trailer. She was beautiful. Her thick, dark hair fanned out to the sides and back on the wind, her smile sparkling, eyes of ancient evil. It was as if Ahiku swallowed Ishe whole with the look she gave him.

"You would die for her." Ahiku stalked toward them. "How admirable."

Liza fought to stand her ground as the wind battered them all. Their clothes rippling in the wind, dust burning her eyes. Behind the demon, on the far horizon, Liza could see the wall of black gloom rumbling toward them. Her stomach clenched, and more than anything, she wanted to turn and bolt. She allowed her eyes to close briefly; she inhaled deeply and fought back the cough that wanted to escape her dust-coated throat. This time, she didn't need the mantra. Her animals glided effortlessly into her mind as if on a raven's wings, howling, spitting, clawing.

With them, she felt as impenetrable as an elephant's herd. When she opened her eyes, she wielded a predatory smile.

Beside Liza, Ishe had apparently made up his own mind about how he wanted things to go, because he shoved her away and sprinted toward Ahiku. The demon spoke a few words that Liza couldn't understand, and Ishe stopped in his tracks. He turned back to Liza and mouthed the words "I'm sorry" before letting out a bloodcurdling scream and falling to the ground in convulsions. He was turning.

Liza shifted her attention back to Ahiku. "I don't know what you are and I don't much care, but you"—Liza waved her hand—"this . . . is about to be over."

"I beg to differ," Ahiku said, any traces of humor gone now. "And when I am done with you, I will have your precious Twiggy. Such a brave little spirit."

Clay emerged from the trailer, and behind him, hand clasped in his, was Twiggy. The child looked perplexed, and when she tried to go to Liza, Clay held her back.

Liza nearly fainted. Her insides turned to liquid panic.

"You won't lay a hand on her!" she screamed. "And you." She shot Clay a steely-eyed glare. "How could you?"

Elephant sent Liza an image that horrified her. It was of something inhuman. Both gnarled and sinewy. Part animal, part . . . something else. As soon as Liza embraced the image, Ahiku's human shell cracked into a million acidic pieces, carried away on miniature tornadoes up into the swirling wind. What was left was a vaguely human figure, still the shape of a woman but a thousand years old, with reddish-brown skin the color of dried blood. Dark amber slits where her eyes should have been. When the figure opened her mouth to shriek her outrage, Liza took an involuntary step backward.

Ishe had turned completely, a mindless hyena once more, and now came to his feet. He darted straight for Clay. But in one swift motion, Clay lifted a revolver, and in that brief, unspeakable moment, everything else fell away. Liza's hand stretched out; she was deaf to her own horrified screams. Clay fired one shot that blew a hole in Ishe's chest. He spun and stumbled back in Liza's direction before he collapsed to the ground and began turning back to his human form.

Liza ran to Ishe and knelt beside him. She touched his face, wishing with everything in her being that the devastation in his chest could be healed. That the life she'd envisioned with him weren't slipping through her fingers.

"I'm . . . I'm sorry," he said with a mouth full of blood.

"I forgive you," Liza said. "You're free now." She moved away from Ishe's body as his life ebbed away.

Ahiku waved a hand and sent Liza hurtling with an ice-cold dagger of blinding pain, but Badger sprang into her mind, and she landed deftly on all fours.

Clay stood over Ishe and dropped the smoking revolver from his hand. Mouth open, no words. Eyes blinking as if he could unsee. Twiggy screamed and stretched out her tiny hands toward Ishe as he lay dying on the ground. Clay's whole body stiffened with the affront of what he'd done. Clenching his fists, he screamed, "No more!" He shoved Twiggy away from him, and she took off for Liza as Clay swooped up the revolver. He took one shot at Ahiku before she clamped his head between her hands. A flame erupted from his belly and seared him from the inside out. Clay's charred remains ascended into the storm and disintegrated.

Liza's eyes bulged in horror as Twiggy struggled toward her. The girl's little arms tried to shield the bustling wind and dust from her face.

"Twiggy!" Liza shouted.

Ahiku turned toward the child and grinned, a chilling sight. She waved her hands, and Twiggy began moving toward her.

It became difficult to see, the wind picking up even more. The dark cloud that had seemed miles away was nearly upon them. Down the hill, carnies screamed and ran back and forth, seeking shelter, some being carried upward into the storm.

You must accept them. It was as if Oya's edict had ridden in on the wind and besieged every nerve ending in her body. She was positively bursting with the joy of it. She was of two places. American, born and raised, but her story hadn't begun here. She was also African, descended from a powerful lineage, a goddess, her grandmother. *This* was who she was.

Liza screamed as Raven conspired to transform her into the only thing that would give a demon spirit pause—a more powerful spirit. *Oya.* She felt nearly consumed with a blazing, searing warmth that tingled and burned her skin. It was like she'd put on a pair of eyeglasses that had changed the world. Every hair on her body went stiff with the shock of it. The wind slowed. She blinked at the microscopically tiny dust particles slowly churning before her. Whispers. Children's voices, too many voices, cried out to her. Liza welcomed the spirit of the African warrior woman into her body. She took a tentative step forward, and it felt like she sailed on a ray of sunlight.

"You!" Ahiku screamed. She tried weaving waving her hands in another intricate pattern and thrusting it forward. Liza, as Oya, simply waved a hand and moved it aside. A tree was unearthed with the power she'd flung its way. Twiggy stopped moving toward the demon and stared, blinking wildly, looking small and vulnerable against the dust.

"She who invokes a storm on her own people cannot prevent her house from destruction." Liza spoke in her grandmother's husky baritone. "Release the children and slither on back to the underworld where you belong."

"Come, Oya," Ahiku sneered and then urged Liza over with a finger. "Do come on over here and make me."

"Oh, I'd hoped you wouldn't make this easy," Liza crooned.

Oya urged Liza to move, to strike, and she readily obliged. She felt the unfamiliar tug of a leather sheath that hadn't been there before slung across her body. She sought out the source of the weight resting between her shoulder blades, and her hand landed on a hilt that felt sculpted just for her. The sound of metal pierced the air as she slid the sword from its sheath.

The copper-colored blade shone as if lit by a million unseen candles. It had the heft of iron.

Ahiku traced a claw through the air and conjured an even more horrific version of the skeletal stilt walker that had cornered Liza that one terrifying morning, its bony body exposed, save the red-and-black carnival mask covering its face. The headdress of skulls still covered its head. It tossed a massive blade from hand to hand—that was new.

The stilt walker ran forward, its cadaverous feet churning up the earth. Liza bolted toward it.

She raised the copper blade just as the skeleton swung its own weapon down toward her head. Liza attempted to pull back, readying for another swing, but the stilt walker clasped its other hand over hers.

Searing pain flared where its skeletal fingers touched her skin.

But Oya was with her.

Instead of pressing forward, she backtracked, pulling her opponent toward her and taking it off balance. She wrested out of its grip, and though her hand was blackened, she barely registered the pain.

The skeleton recovered quickly. It came at her again. She parried and swung the blade, taking off one bony arm just below the shoulder. The skeleton had raised the blade with its other hand, and Liza met it. As they struggled against each other, those cursed tiny skulls detached from the headdress and whipped out on her flank.

She clawed at the face and tore off the mask, revealing a grisly skull with a full mouth of blood-darkened teeth. While she had a grip on the creature's sword-wielding right hand, the tiny skulls worried at her left, snipping and biting. They had taken out several sizable chunks of her flesh before she freed herself.

The copper blade glowed and sang, as if sensing an opening. This time, when she swung, she sawed through the stilt walker's waist, and it collapsed in a heap of charred bones.

"They were right about you. Your village elders," Liza said, channeling Oya. "They knew you were a creature of the underworld from the beginning. You did not willingly march into the flames; they chose you. And if you'd stayed there where you belonged, no one would have mourned your ending, but true evil knows no shame. You had to claw your way back into the land of the living. And you were willing to sacrifice children to extend your miserable existence."

"Where were *you* when their bellies were empty? Their parents drunk and beating them senseless?" Ahiku said. "Your moral sentimentality is as boring as it is hypocritical. You are no better than I. You have more offspring than you can keep up with and more than one husband, to boot. A leopard will never be pronounced innocent if the judge is a goat. And to my keen eye, dear Oya, you do have the look of a goat."

Liza was incensed. She sailed through the wind, vaguely aware that a shard of her power had cocooned her little sister in a bubble of safety.

Ahiku conjured again, this time opening a chasm in the earth. Hellion hands and wails emerged, grasping at Liza, but she cut through them with ease.

She reached Ahiku and, with Oya, set upon the demon with a vengeance. At the anxious sound of an untold number of little heartbeats, Oya's rage soared.

Liza struck out at Ahiku again and again, amassing a spattering of cuts on the demon's body, but Ahiku proved a commendable opponent.

The demon came down hard with a crushing blow to Liza's forearm, dislodging the copper sword. It clattered to the ground.

But Liza didn't need it. She wrapped her hands around the demon's throat. Ahiku locked on to her, sinking her claws into her flesh.

They grappled endlessly, neither gaining ground. Where Liza was ripped open, Oya healed. Then Liza gave in to the storm bucking to erupt inside her. She unleashed it.

It tore and ripped at Ahiku's body, exposing her chest . . . she had to open it! Oya's power coursing through her, Liza plunged her hands into the demon's chest and, with Badger's strength, cracked open her rib cage, exposing a barely human heart that reeked of rot. Oya streamed from Liza's body in a golden mist that spun into Ahiku and emerged with the souls of all the screaming children she had consumed. Liza was thrown backward and looked on in sickly satisfying horror as the children's souls set upon Ahiku the way she had once set upon them. When they were done feasting, Oya led them away on the wind, and there was nothing left of the demon but a few colorful rags.

Liza ran toward Twiggy, who stood with her arms out. As she reached her little sister and scooped her up and into her arms, the massive dark cloud of the last dust storm to hit Oklahoma swooped down on the G. B. Bacchanal Carnival.

EPILOGUE

A raven flew through the air and alighted on the branch of a blighted tree. Sunlight warmed like a soft golden blanket. The city of Tulsa, Oklahoma, was coming awake in the distance. On the light breeze, a banner announcing a carnival floated to and fro. A wheel rolled along as if it were still carrying the weight of a trailer and then fell on its side.

Where a red trailer had once stood, only scorched earth remained, the fringe already dotted with fresh sprouts of weeds. The rest, flattened grass and trodden ground, a clutch of popcorn kernels.

Farther out into the countryside, on a boulder that a passerby might miss, a girl and her little sister sat panting and spent, huddled together at the feet of their mother, a weary pygmy marmoset, and an ancient African man who, during his lifetime, had gone by the name Ago.

~

Liza sat in a rocking chair holding her granddaughter, Mia. She'd told her the story of a nearly all-Negro carnival during the 1930s. The animals, the people, the colorful characters. Through the wide picture window, a palm tree danced on the Jamaican breeze. And birds sang their songs.

Liza had a room in the May Pen countryside house her daughter, Kala, shared with her family. Twiggy lived in the big city—Kingston—under the watchful eye of their mother, Ella. The shopkeeper had gotten it all wrong, or maybe Papa had lied to protect her. But Ella had been very much alive, and Oya guided them back together after so many years apart. Though Ella was still given to spells of silence, she delighted in her family.

"There wasn't never no black carnival in America." Kala swept into the room, wearing the same grim expression as her father, Ishe. "Don't go filling her head with all those old tales and superstitions of yours, Mama. The old religion's turned to dust."

Liza's room was tastefully decorated with items from their past: A black-and-white picture of her and Hope (it had taken years to forgive her, though if she survived the storm, they never spoke again); an African mask; a picture of a gigantic black strongman; a replica of a carnival poster. Two yellowing newspaper clippings, one featuring a then-budding starlet, Autumn, and the other news of Jamey's indictment on racketeering charges. He'd come out on the winning end, but she'd kept the clipping only because it helped her remember him. And there was a book, authored by none other than Malachi Dumas, founder of the African American School of Kemetic Meditation. Alongside these, on a shelf, an amulet. On the discs, a majestic picture of an elephant, a badger, and a raven.

Liza smiled and kissed her grandchild on the forehead. She called Raven. She snapped her fingers, and the gold coin she held in her palm turned into a long black raven's feather. Mia grinned and snatched the feather.

Liza's gaze drifted back to the picture window. "Who knows what's real and what isn't in the mind of an old woman?"

AUTHOR'S NOTE

THE ENIGMATIC LIFE OF MADAME STEPHANIE ST. CLAIR

December 24, 1897. Most sources agree on the when; the where, though, remains a topic of vigorous debate. What we do know is that Madame Stephanie St. Clair was born to a single mother, Félicienne, in either Martinique or Guadeloupe, West Indies. Both were colonized by the French.

Félicienne, it seems, had a dream for her only daughter. An education, a pathway to a different life. And for a time, Stephanie excelled at school, but when her mother became ill, Stephanie was forced to abandon that dream and go to work for a rich family as a maid. After suffering untold abuses at the hands of the family's son, she took the money she'd saved and fled.

Where she landed is another matter of dispute. One account points to Marseilles, France, where though she spoke and wrote fluent French, her first language, Stephanie was unable to find work; she subsequently immigrated to America. This version of events goes on to suggest that she used the lengthy sea voyage aboard the SS *Guiana* to learn English.

A second narrative paints a different picture. One of Stephanie landing in New York, then traveling north to Canada, where she worked as a domestic servant before returning to the city.

Path notwithstanding, Stephanie eventually settled into Harlem's growing African American community. She embarked upon a series of unfortunate relationships that ended in violence in some form or another, but they introduced her to Harlem's underbelly and advanced her career in the process.

Her first boyfriend she stabbed in the eye when he tried to prostitute her; the second died of a crushed skull when she pushed him so hard that he fell, hitting his head against a table. Some stories suggest that Stephanie became the leader of a local gang, the Forty Thieves, who made their living on theft and extortion rackets.

The tide turned for Stephanie when, in April 1917, a $10,000 investment in the local lottery paid dividends. She soon employed her top lieutenant, "Bumpy" Johnson, and paid the police bribes.

With Madame's success and keen fashion sense, she earned the moniker "Queenie" in Manhattan, while Harlem's residents took to calling her "Madame St. Clair."

Queenie employed many Harlem residents in "policy" making— a combination of gambling, lottery, and investments. Around this time, she also became active in the pursuit of civil rights for African Americans. Her tool: writing newspaper columns and articles advising Harlem's citizens of their rights, advocating for the vote, and calling out police brutality and corruption.

Her outspokenness earned her an eight-month stint in prison on what was believed to be a trumped-up charge. The first of two such tours.

The end of Prohibition in 1933 meant that Jewish and Italian crime families were in desperate need of new revenue sources. They turned their attention to the previously uninteresting numbers racket in Harlem. Enter "Dutch" Schultz. Queenie and Bumpy were never known to back down, and this time would be no different.

They went on the offensive, bombing Dutch's storefronts. The war between them carried on, yielding casualties on both sides. Eventually, though, Stephanie ceded some control to the Italians. Schultz was shot, reportedly by order of "Lucky" Luciano. Among other things, people described Queenie as arrogant, sophisticated, and educated. So none were surprised when she sent a telegram to Dutch's hospital bedside that read, "As ye sow, so shall ye reap." Her parting shot made headlines across the country.

But all the violence had taken its toll. Queenie handed over much of the policy-making business to Bumpy. After leaving the numbers game, she turned her attention back to activism. In a move that would prove a bad decision, she met and married Sufi Abdul Hamid, born Eugene Brown. Much has been written about Hamid's questionable past, and readers can do their own research on this matter. But after Hamid and another woman attempted to steal Queenie's money so they could start their own business together, things quickly went downhill.

The marriage ended, and though the details are murky, Hamid was shot in 1938. Queenie was charged and convicted of attempted murder, but she denied it. In another infamous quip, she said, "If I had wanted him dead, he would be dead."

After her release from prison—some say three years later, while others say a decade—Queenie continued writing and advocating for civil rights. By this time, Bumpy had also left the numbers game and had come to live with his friend, taking up reading and writing poetry.

Queenie died quietly and still quite wealthy in Central Islip, New York, in 1969, just shy of her seventy-third birthday. Bumpy had died a year previously from a heart attack he'd suffered in a Harlem restaurant.

Queenie had no children that we know of. There was no host of cousins, nor aunts, nor uncles. So much of her life remains a mystery, and I believe that's just the way Madame St. Clair would have wanted it.

ACKNOWLEDGMENTS

I was not born with a fountain pen in hand. I didn't begin crafting stories at the tender age when other children were skipping rope or playing stickball. Neither did I pursue writing in college. No, I came to writing late—what some might consider really late. And that suits me just fine.

I can say without a shadow of a doubt that writing a book is simultaneously the most challenging and the most rewarding thing I've ever done. And I thank you, Eric, for driving me to the keyboard. You suggested, urged, and at one point, I think, demanded that I write. Few people can truly see you; I'm glad you took the time to see what was really in my heart.

And to my parents, Hosea and Ressie. It took me too long to recognize their individual and joint sacrifices. Things they did so that I could grow up in the kind of nourishing environment that allowed me to believe that I could do anything. They taught me the meaning of hard work, discipline, and tough love. In more ways than one, I wouldn't be here without them.

To my siblings, my family (shout-out to the Henry, Galloway, and Strange clans), and my friends, and to every one of you who at some point or another put up with me, showed me a kindness, and supported and loved me.

I'm forever indebted to my agent, Mary C. Moore, for her willingness to be agent, editor, and cheerleader. You are a rarity these days, someone who looks for potential, not the quick home run. To my editors Adrienne Procaccini and Camille Rankine: I thank you for helping me make this book better than I ever hoped for. For understanding my vision and for believing in my work.

To everyone at 47North who helped bring *Bacchanal* to the world: thank you for all you do and for going on this ride with me.

Lastly, to my mentors, my beta readers, and to you, my fans: fist bumps, hugs, and thanks.

ABOUT THE AUTHOR

Veronica G. Henry was born in Brooklyn, New York, and has been a bit of a rolling stone ever since. Her work has appeared in various online publications. She is a graduate of the Viable Paradise Workshop and a member of SFWA.

Veronica is proud to be of Sierra Leonean ancestry and counts her trip home as the most important of her life. She now writes from North Carolina, where she eschews rollerballs for fountain pens and fine paper. Other untreated addictions include chocolate and cupcakes. For more information, visit www.veronicahenry.net.